WAX WORKS
A novel

Julia Simpson-Urrutia

Grassroots Writers Guild
www.grassrootswritersguild.wordpress.com

Many thanks to Yousef Talal Eshmawi and David Urrutia for the graphic artwork on the cover. Another round of thanks to Omar Eshmawi for mathematical adjustments! This book is a work of fiction. Names, characters, places, and incidents are either the product of the author's imagination or are used fictitiously. Any resemblance to actual events or locales or persons, living or dead, is coincidental.

ISBN-13: 978-0-9981775-1-9
ISBN-10: 0-9981775-1-2
1.   Finishing schools—Fiction 2. Swiss Boarding Schools—Fiction. 3. Paranormal Investigation—Fiction.

Dedication

To Yousef, Omar, and David, for their love and help. To Suzanne, who befriended me after her hunger strike.
À toutes les filles de Château Mont Choisi à Lausanne,
Et, bien sûr, à toutes les petites fleurs de Mme Junod au Château de Vennes.

"Le Démon fait des trous secrets à ces abîmes,
Par où fuiraient mille ans de sueurs et d'efforts,
Quand même elle saurait ranimer ses victimes,
Et pour les pressurer ressusciter leurs corps."

"The Demon makes secret holes in this abyss,
Whence would escape a thousand years of sweat and strain,
Even if she could revive her victims,
Could restore their bodies, to squeeze them dry once more."

--Charles Baudelaire, "Le Tonneau de la Haine," *Les Fleurs Du Mal.*
From "Hatred's Cask" in *The Flowers of Evil* by Charles Baudelaire
English translation by William Aggeler (Fresno, CA: Academy Library Guild, 1954).

Contents

Chapter 1
A New Dawn

1.

The headmistress of Château Mont Rose, known for the better part of a century as Mademoiselle Wertheimer, fingered the mismatched buttons running up her high-necked dress.

Near her, Asha's sobs grew muffled.

A slate-gray sky did little to brighten the leaded glass panes in the narrow tower room or alleviate the chill. The room was a cold, sullen tomb. Mlle Wertheimer knew that for the girl, however, all reactions to her surroundings had nearly ceased.

The headmistress took several steps closer to the wall the young woman had stupidly leaned back against.

"Do you recognize any of these buttons?"

The eye muscles showed the barest response. A quiver.

"You're not a button collector or you would have cared about these two." The old woman tapped first one, then a second, steel-cut button on her dress. Her crooked finger rested on the depiction of a storm cloud with a lightning bolt. The lightning bolt grew bright red. Looking at it, Mlle Wertheimer smiled.

Her finger dropped to rest on a larger button displaying a rooster's head. No bigger than the top of a matchstick, the tiny head jerked out of the button, turned to peer up at the headmistress. The beak opened, emitted a squeak.

"Too spoiled to use a needle and thread?" Mlle Wertheimer's voice was rough. "You let these buttons fall off. I've had your trinkets for years. They helped bring you back."

A groan slid out of the girl's vocal cords, like wind running through chinks in a broken wall.

Mlle Wertheimer tapped the third button, at the base of her neck. "This is a hand-painted Meijii Satsuma button from Japan. Aren't the flowers beautiful? A wasteful girl from Japan lost buttons too."

The audience was barely human. Mlle Wertheimer cocked her head, eyes squinting at the wall. It was senseless to keep babbling.

She went back to her post at the window in time to see a taxi stop. A burly man got out, slammed the door, passed through the château's gate. He wore a fur-trimmed Swiss army hat, ear flaps snapped up. A rolling piece of luggage made him ridiculous. Mlle Wertheimer sniffed. Not the kind of guest she would have chosen. A pity she was not in charge of choosing clients, as when Château Mont Rose had been a boarding school.

No sooner did the thought cross her mind than the piano jerked forward on its wheels, shoved her against the wall. She threw a hand against the window panes, leaving a smudge.

"I'm sorry!"

The piano rolled back to its previous position. The headmistress's deep-set eyes darted down at the smashed hip that, yes, slowly crept back out. She corrected her thought: She did not preside over Château Mont Rose. The estate presided over itself. It had taken her back, kept her alive.

A tiny sigh, no louder than the tick of a fly grooming itself, detached from the wall.

"Stupid girl!" Mlle Wertheimer spat out. There was no teenage retort, no dramatic young adult sigh, an improvement on the old days.

The headmistress felt better.

If only the late Jeanne Bonami, former owner of the school, could have known the true underlying power of the place, could have lived to see it.

Château Mont Rose was reinventing itself.

It had reinvented Mlle Wertheimer.

2.

"How long has it been, Julien?" asked the woman handcuffed to the bed frame. Shapely legs spilled out upon the mattress like two rivers of warm honey begging for navigation. Her raised arms hitched up the satiny red shirt, offering a peek at the black lace-trimmed port of call.

Detective Inspector Julien Cloquet kept his eyes on the sheets he folded. His fingertips tingled with the memory of Katia's silky warm flesh. Since coming back into the room, he had been struggling against the light patchouli and musk fragrance fogging his concentration.

Now he stretched out his arm, turned his wrist, and frowned. The wrist was bare. He pulled out his phone, pushed a button, and illuminated the display. "You've been handcuffed thirty minutes."

"No, darling. I meant since you invited a woman for a tryst."

"That is not what I invited you for." He slipped the phone back in his pocket.

Katia looked at him, hard. "You know why I agreed to come."

"Money?"

"Don't pretend. No matter what you think—there has been no man in my life for a very long time."

"Really."

Somehow he had remade the bed with her chained up. Katia had thought it a game, refusing to be unlocked until he gave in. But he hadn't given in, did not seem the slightest bit interested. What was he trying to prove?

Cloquet placed the bagged linens on top of the few things in his suitcase. Before he gave the sheets to the police lab, he was going to look at them at home, in broad daylight.

Tossing her head, Katia pulled up one leg so the knee was bent. She crossed the other leg over, offered a more provocative view. The manicured toes on the airborne foot played with the edge of his suitcase. "I have missed you." Her voice was plaintive.

"Please stop that."

"Don't you vant to have a little fun?" Katia's voice reminded Cloquet of an oboe, throaty and full, made dramatic by a Russian accent, which she overplayed in bursts. Her ruby-glossed lips pouted.

"That wasn't the agreement. It was simply to spend the night here." He gathered the toiletries from the desk by the window and arranged them inside his suitcase.

"Agreement, ha," she scoffed. "I agree . . . that you are a handsome man."

Katia had a lot of men to compare him with, and good reason to learn how to compliment all of them. The striking brunette ran a ring of upscale prostitutes from a series of posh flats. Prostitution was legal in Switzerland, but the unending influx of illegal female immigrants bent on the same trade in recent years had put a huge damper on the amount any of them could earn. Competition was staggering.

Cloquet did not want to leave until he found his used Rolex Tudor self-winding wristwatch. He had purchased it after declining a new Rolex from a watch manufacturer years earlier. Detectives couldn't take gifts if they wanted to keep their jobs, so he had splurged on himself. A gift for self-righteousness?

The watch wasn't in the bathroom. He had gone through his routine check for countertops, rims, and floors.

"You are a strange man, Julien," complained Katia. "Why you vant me to come stay with you, in a hotel, to just sleep? You have a house in Lausanne, don't you?"

"A flat."

"I thought you were running away from your wife. Why did you decide to spend a night at this hotel?"

"Two nights." He straightened, gaze panning the room. A tall tree swayed outside the window, branches budding. Where the hell was the watch?

She knit her brow. "You stayed here two nights? You brought me on the second one, but you didn't want to *do* anything. You just vant me sleep. Maybe you have another woman the first night, she made you tired."

"No, Katia. I was alone." He threw her a reproving glance, then softened. She had been a good sport. "I'm usually the one firing questions. You cross-examine very well, considering you're locked up."

She brightened. "I remember the first time I met you. We became friends, didn't we?"

Sort of, he thought. She had her uses. There weren't too many complaints coming in about Katia's girls. They met powerful men through screened connections. Cloquet knew many of their names, but he had no intention of joining the ranks. He no longer qualified, for one thing.

"I thought you needed someone," Katia said, as bewitching with her legs flat as when they had been crossed.

Perhaps it was the resignation in her voice that got to him. "I used to have a wife," Cloquet shared, "but the marriage fell apart. Years ago. Around the time I first met you, in fact."

"So why you lock me up if you don't vant. . . ."

"The handcuffs were your idea, Katia."

She tilted her head against one arm, soft and resigned, a prisoner hanging from the bedposts. "I could have sent one of the girls, Julien. I came for friendship." A curl of hair fell over one eye and she blew it away.

Cloquet almost said he would not dream of taking advantage of her, yet that would be a lie. There was more than one way to take advantage of a person, even if one paid for the privilege in cash. He zipped the bag closed.

She changed tacks: "I hope your daughter is not troubled by bad men anymore. Michèle is her name? See, I remember. Such a pretty young woman."

Cloquet's face hardened. "No. She is not troubled by bad men." He fished for the handcuff key in his pocket, moved towards the bedpost. "I'll unfasten you now if you promise not to go around knocking on bedroom doors."

"Don't unlock. You might change your mind." Katia arched an eyebrow. "Sometimes a man doesn't say what he wants."

"*Ah, bon*? I want to make a phone call." Cloquet pulled a black leather glove onto one hand before touching the doorknob. He moved into the hallway, closing the door.

Morning sunlight lit up dust particles suspended in the stairwell, floating slow motion like debris in a fish tank. He could see grime buildup in crevices of the nearest wax statue's hands and around its mouth.

"*Allô?*"

"Did you stay with the Greek girl all yesterday?"

"Good morning to you, too, Uncle Julien. I stayed as long as was necessary."

"I asked you to *maintain* surveillance." Detective Cloquet's voice struck gravel. His nephew sounded, by contrast, cheerful.

"I trailed her down to Ouchy on foot. She stopped at a *raclette* restaurant."

"For dinner?"

"Lunch."

"No place serves *raclette* that early." Even as Cloquet said it, he remembered the extent of Helena Stamoulos's wealth. Money opened doors and pulled out cheese-melting heaters. "Was someone with her?"

"Just me, on the other side of the room."

Cloquet looked over the balustrade. He moved away from his own bedroom door and lowered his voice. "I hope you didn't do anything to make her notice you."

"I wore a cap, kept it pulled down. She went back to her hotel after her meal and took a shower. That's when I let myself into her room to put a tracker on her phone. Add that to the tracking device on the rented vehicle—"

"She didn't see you?"

"Of course not."

"What about Rachel Gordon? What have you arranged?"

"I'm tracking her phone too."

Cloquet distrusted so much reliance on following mobile devices. "Tracking phones won't keep these girls safe."

"It's easier than cloning myself."

"If you could start a conversation and persuade the American girl, Mademoiselle Rachel Gordon, to stay in a different hotel, that would be more to the point."

"Can you speak up? Uncle Julien, really, there is no hard evidence to prove—"

"*Interpol* sees a problem," Cloquet interrupted. "Lauren Briant arrives in a few hours. You must have *some* idea of how to be charming to young women. Your mother claims you do. Talk them out of staying at this mausoleum."

"Mausoleum" was not really the word he meant to use, but it fit. "Sweep one of them off her feet."

"That's not as easy as—"

"*À tout à l'heure.*" Cloquet ended the call and re-entered the bedroom. "Katia, we're going. Where did you leave your pants?" He unlocked the handcuffs.

She reclaimed her bare arms, rubbing each wrist and looking around. "Did you pack them in your valise?" she asked.

"Of course not."

"Did you push them under the bed?"

"I think I would have seen them two seconds ago when I was looking under there," Cloquet said. Together they looked through the sheets and blankets.

Katia touched his cheek with her fingertips. "What did you do with them?"

He pulled his head away. "I didn't do anything with your pants. They seem to be gone, like my wristwatch."

"Pants are more important than watches when it is cold," Katia lifted her quilted jacket from the foot of the bed. She slid her arm in each sleeve and buttoned up the front.

Cloquet thought she must have taken the pants off outside the room, showing off in front of a hotel client. Or she had stripped in front of the concierge during the time Cloquet had thought her asleep. Prostitutes marketed, just like other professionals.

If Katia wanted to leave her stretchy pants behind as an advertisement, he hoped she had made sure there was a business card in one of the pockets, if they could have pockets.

Seated on the bed, she briskly brushed her legs, then pulled the blanket over them. "You keep me warm?"

"With money, *chérie*. One hundred and fifty francs is my limit today." He zipped the bag closed, extracted two bills from his wallet and held them out.

Katia pointed to the dresser. "Put it over there."

"Are you offended?"

Katia's brow creased. "In Russia, to put money into someone's hand passes bad energy. I feel darkness. Something you are not telling me."

She slid her feet into black ankle boots, rich brown locks swinging around her head as she pushed first one, then the other, heel down. "I accept your fee for the time I gave you, Julien. I have to make a living just like everyone else. But I tell you, I came here because you are special." She stood up and looked him squarely in the eye. "You didn't say how your daughter is."

Katia had an unsettling kind streak for which Cloquet both respected and resented her.

Without answering, he opened the bedroom door. "*Allez*. You can put my jacket on your legs in the car."

He was glad the concierge, Jean Duvanel, was not around to gawk at Katia's long, gorgeous bare legs. He went down first, dropped the key by the sign-in book and heard a shriek followed by resounding bumps.

In her high black ankle boots, Katia had lost her footing. Cloquet saw the end of the freefall: revealed black lace panties, satin-covered buttons flying off the jacket, banging elbows and knees tumbling down carpeted stairs. Katia's body halted at the feet of the waxen Swiss General Dufour.

She lay still.

He raced up the staircase to her, putting his hand out to steady the rocking statue. "*Bon Dieu!* Are you alright?" He ran his fingers over the soles of her boots. "How did wax get on your shoes?"

She moaned, "I think I twisted my ankle."

Cloquet put a hand under her armpit, pulled her closest arm around his neck. "Hold on." He left his bag to be fetched after he got her outside. She couldn't walk on her own. To his relief, the taxi waited by the front steps.

Katia put her palm against the car roof to stop her progress into the car. "Wait, please." She tilted her pretty head up, creasing her brow to peer at the windows.

"We have to get you to a doctor," Cloquet said. "Because your ankle may be sprained or worse."

"Julien, I knew this place as a girl. I was scared of the headmistress. Old bat." Her eyes up close, in the morning light, were not so much brown as copper flecked with gold.

"When I remember her, I try to be nicer to my girls. They are just trying to survive, you know?"

Unwelcome thoughts scurried for hiding in Cloquet's mind, like bugs from under a flipped rock. "What do you mean?" he asked. He failed to brace himself for what came next.

"When I was sixteen, I was a student here, at Château Mont Rose. More than twenty-five years ago. There *are* Russian girls who have studied in Swiss boarding schools." She laughed at the look on his face. "Not as many as Arab or Americans, but there are a few of us. I did not expect to fall on hard times."

The female cab driver called out, "Your time is on the clock, buddy."

"What was her name, the headmistress?" She had to be bluffing.

"You don't believe me?"

He didn't *want* to believe her.

"Her name was Mademoiselle Wertheimer."

Wordlessly, he helped Katia slide into the seat, attentive that she did not hurt her head on the doorframe.

"I'll be back."

Cloquet hastened to retrieve his bag from the unstaffed concierge desk. The statue on the staircase seemed to watch him. That was always the way with statues, wasn't it?

Cloquet slid into the backseat next to Katia, offering his jacket. She pulled it over her knees.

The skin prickles he felt were not from the cold. When one did not know what to say, it was best not to talk.

At the second street light, Katia pleaded, "Tell me about the lovely girl I saved from villains. Your daughter, Michèle. You are not angry with her?"

It was a well-bred question from a person to whom Cloquet owed a debt of gratitude for helping Michele several years earlier when a silly graduation party lured the group into the red-light district. What happened since then wasn't Katia's fault.

"My daughter died over a year ago," he confessed. "A car accident."

Katia winced. "Ah, no!" She laid a hand upon his closest, one human being comforting another.

He allowed the contact for two seconds before pulling his own hand away. There was no room in his life for acceptance of pity. Not if he had so little to offer in return.

Chapter 2

Boarding School Rule #1

Lauren climbed, slightly perspiring despite a biting wind, up a steep Lausanne hill. Her fingers gripped the handle of a wheeled suitcase. She regretted not taking the metro.

The spontaneous impulse to walk to a favorite remembered café on the off chance she might find Rachel there now struck her as ludicrous. Rachel had not been at the station to pick her up because Lauren had missed her train. With her phone unable to pick up a Wi-Fi signal, there was no way Lauren could send Rachel a message. It was alright, she told herself. They would see each other soon enough.

She looked at the traffic and raised her arm. Watching the occupied cabs pass by, she regretted her phone not working. She could have called an Uber or something like it. Each passing car stirred the air, pressing her skirt against her legs, blowing her hair. A free cab pulled up at the curb, window down.

"*Où, mademoiselle?*"

A wiry young man with a curling, brown mustache sat behind the wheel. He was handsome and friendly looking in a businesslike way. Tattoos, loud music or perceived body odor would have had her waving him on. Sometimes one couldn't tell about personal hygiene, of course, until getting into a car, when it was too late.

"*Bonjour.* Do you know Château Mont Rose?"

"*Bonjour, bien sûr.*"

"How much?"

The price he named was higher than expected, but her feet begged for rest. The reflection from store windows of herself pulling a suitcase uphill was not one she wished to encounter again today.

"*D'accord.*" She got in while he stowed her suitcase in the trunk.

She settled in her seat and was relieved his cab smelled of balsam and sandalwood. A considerate driver. Nice looking, too.

He smiled at her via the rearview mirror.

At the first light, he said, "If you forgive my directness, mademoiselle, places like Château Mont Rose are not comfortable. Bad plumbing, lumpy mattresses, and bed bugs. I have heard complaints. You could be in central Lausanne, close to cinemas and restaurants."

Why did a driver care what hotel she stayed at? She raised her eyebrows but did not answer.

The light changed, the taxi accelerated, and the driver's face smiled from the posted identity card. "Paul Junod" sounded like a Swiss name. Ah yes, the Swiss could be opinionated. She pulled the non-functioning phone out of her bag and pretended to read an interesting text message, which of course was not there. Let him think someone knew where she was.

He glanced at her in the rearview mirror, waiting for her response.

"I want to go to Château Mont Rose, the inn."

"Château Mont Rose calls itself a museum, mademoiselle. A hotel *and* a museum, which is curious. Don't you find it curious?"

"I don't find it *anything* except the place I want to go."

"As you wish."

The taxi accelerated and its driver shut his mouth. Reassured, Lauren slipped off her shoes, relieved to wiggle her toes. She stole a glance at his face and found him returning the look. Then a horn blared. He swerved hard and braked.

Lauren pulled herself upright and brushed the long blonde bangs away from her eyes. "What are you *doing?*"

"*Pardon*, mademoiselle." Paul Junod looked flustered. "Some people drive like no one else is on the road."

"I should have taken the métro," she said, half to herself.

"The métro is closed for repairs in La Rosiaz. The bus line also."

Velo riders—people on motorized bikes—shared the road. The taxi proceeded without further incident, despite the traffic. The sky was bright blue with dappled clouds.

"You speak French so well," he said. "Would you mind if I practice English with you?"

Oh sure, that made sense.

"Where you are from?"

"America."

"Which state?"

"California."

They discussed modes of travel in the city, and he told her about a phone app that could help her around Lausanne. "I can find it for you if you let me see your phone when we stop," he offered.

Lauren could feel her face flush and she looked out the window. She didn't want to show him her phone wasn't working. That would make her look stupid. A pizzeria caught her eye. As teens, she and Rachel had eaten pizza all over town. It was the only meal they could afford in those days. Now too, probably. She didn't recognize this pizza parlor.

"That is a charming place," said Paul Junod. "The owners are friends of mine. Would you like to go there?"

"Possibly," she murmured, lost in thought.

"Fantastic! My name is Paul. Do you like mopeds?"

"I've never ridden one." Neither, she thought, had Rachel, who must certainly be waiting at the hotel.

"This car belongs to the company, you see. I will pick you up on my moped. You may want to wear jeans."

"What?"

"You have not told me your name."

Lauren frowned. What had they been talking about, exactly?

Château Mont Rose's sign appeared, set in a stone archway overgrown by vines. The taxi rolled onto the driveway cobblestones. There was no one in sight, unlike the day she had first arrived at the school when dozens of girls had stared.

The only eyes she saw now were those of a doorman, peering out from between lace curtains.

"Why is that man watching us?" The doorman didn't smile or move.

"Whenever I bring clients to hotels," said Paul, cutting the engine, "there are people moving around. This place feels too quiet."

"I am meeting a friend here and all I asked is why that man is watching us, not whether you like noise."

Paul did not show offense. "Do you want me to wait while you see if all is well?"

He *did* have kind eyes, a vibrant brown. A butterfly unsettled her tummy. He was right. Château Mont Rose did not appear inviting in the way of bustling modern hotels. It was remote, aloof. There were no humans to be seen, save the unmoving face in the window. Not a single vehicle save the taxi.

"I would appreciate your waiting." She sprang out of the car before he could offer to open her door.

A small metal sign above the château's main entrance said *Musée*.

"May I leave my luggage for a few moments?"

"I have turned off the meter. Take your time." Paul produced a book and slid down on the front seat.

The doorman watched her ascend without a change of expression. His face struck a chord. One of the old school staff?

She pushed on the door. It creaked open and a bell tinkled.

The man did not say, "Bonjour."

Lauren cleared her throat. The old fellow maintained his position with the persistence of a bloodhound, refusing to turn or acknowledge her presence.

"Are you the concierge, please, Monsieur?"

Silence.

"I have a bag in the cab outside."

A thought came—what a fool she was! The man must be watching the taxi driver. Paul Junod, if that was really his name, was likely a well-known con artist who flirted with lone females and stole their luggage. She had heard of situations like that. Lauren ran back out onto the front steps.

Paul looked up, book in hand.

"Um—Never mind!"

"Please call me 'Paul.'"

"I thought I forgot something."

"I am here if you need me." His smile seemed genuine. "I will bring your bag in if you decide to stay."

Lauren stepped up to the window. The doorman's condescending face was still there, his eyes peering past her as if he knew the world's secrets. She rapped on the window at the level of his chin. He was ignoring her on purpose. She rapped at his nose. He did not blink.

"Monsieur, you are very rude not to answer me earlier, and now you are. . . ."

A plaque at the bottom of the window offered a name.

"You are Carl Gustav Jung, famed Swiss psychoanalyst," she read aloud. "Onetime collaborator of Freud." Lifting her gaze to the erudite wax countenance, Lauren marveled at its realism. Her cheeks burned.

Without turning to see if Paul had noticed her talking to a statue and her now-hot blush, Lauren re-entered the building, took a deep breath, and looked around. Recessed in the inky shadows were six life-size wax figures. Low-wattage bulbs spumed a dim froth of light above their heads. Brass plaques offered hard-to-read names. But of course. *Musée* meant museum. The château was now a hotel *and* a museum.

Her foot found the first step of the stairs. There would be time to study these wax people later. She had to check in with the concierge. It would be nice to talk to a real human being. Relieved, Lauren saw a person waiting to meet her at the turn of the staircase. She climbed quickly.

"Bonjour, Madame. What an interesting place you have! I was a student here when Château Mont Rose was a school."

The middle-aged lady regarded her customer with a cocked eyebrow and smile. It was likely she had overheard the one-sided conversation with the wax figure downstairs.

Lauren reached out her hand, touched the woman's stiff fingers, then plucked her own back.

"Ewww" A plaque on the wall indicated Madame Tussaud, famous Swiss wax figure maker, attired in modern clothes. Lauren shook her head, grumbled, "Can't they afford better lighting?"

Cheeks flushed a second time, Lauren stomped upwards, no longer caring what anyone thought. Enough with the jokes. She groaned at what she saw next.

There at the head of the stairs sat an unmoving female figure behind the concierge desk. On the desk lay an open hotel registry book. A pen attached by a chain to a solid wood block on the desk waited in readiness.

The form appeared to be a fortune teller. "She" was frozen in a haunting look of divination, Tarot cards spread in front of her. Every one of her petrified bony yellow fingers was adorned with a large, jeweled ring. Perfect for Halloween.

"What a campy setup!" Lauren hoped someone real would hear her. She raised her voice: "Karl Gustav Jung looks real, and so does Madame Tussaud, but I'm sorry, this one is *really* bad. Yellow skin, a wig falling apart, and eyes too sunken to—"

The glazed eyes rolled. Lauren stumbled backward with a cry. She grabbed at the staircase handrail.

"*Bonjour, mademoiselle,*" said a rasping voice.

The voice belonged to a demon of the past named Mademoiselle Wertheimer. Despite the "Mademoiselle" title, the woman had been as old as the hills from the first day they met. Now she looked waxier than the figures around her.

"You must speak only in French," said the old woman.

Lauren's jaw dropped. A boarding school rule? It couldn't be.

"*Mais qui êtes-vous?*"

"Lauren Briant. My reservation is under Rachel Gordon's name. We're sharing a room." Lauren studied the woman. She had to be an impostor. Surely Mlle Wertheimer was dead.

The look-alike finger-pecked on a computer keyboard. A screen with a list of names came up on the monitor while a faint odor of long-expired cologne rose from her clothes. Lauren tried not to breathe it in. The Mlle Wertheimer duplicate reminded her of a much-battered doll. Seconds ticked by on a large grandfather clock. Lauren thought of Paul Junod, waiting outside.

"Madame---er—Mademoi—Madame," Lauren said, not knowing what to call so elderly a woman." Students had been forced to call the headmistress "*Mademoiselle*" in the old days, if this was truly she. She pointed and said, "I see Rachel Gordon's name, at the top of the screen."

"*Et ben, oui.*" The old woman's right hand fumbled in a drawer. She pulled out a skeleton key. It bore the number 14—the age Lauren and Rachel had been when they first met here.

"You are in Mademoiselle Gordon's old room."

It *was* her!

There was no way on earth Lauren could express happiness at seeing the old woman.

"Is Rachel Gordon here?"

Mlle Wertheimer settled her withered frame against the back of her seat.

"Has Rachel Gordon checked in?"

The woman pulled a card from the top of the deck and laid it, with wobbly wrist, upon another card. These were just plain cards in a game of Solitaire, not Tarot cards. A hearing aid lay upon the desk. She had removed it from her ear.

"Forget it." Lauren turned to descend to the taxi and get her suitcase.

"Your friend . . . is upstairs, waiting."

That news improved Lauren's mood in an instant. There was no need to be afraid of the once inflexible ruler of the establishment. How frail she looked! Ignoring the elderly woman, Lauren ascended to Rachel's old room, two steps at a time.

A waxen military commander, whom a plaque announced as Guillaume Henri Dufour, did his best to block her way at the turn in the stairs. She ducked under his outstretched arm. The haphazard placing of these wax figures would make it hard to get her suitcase up the two flights unless there was a newly installed elevator. Rachel or Paul Junod might have to help her.

The second floor had been converted into a hall of philosophers. A Jean-Jacques Rousseau statue stood across from the turbaned orientalist traveler and writer Burckhardt, a 19th century native of Lausanne. Doing sentry duty at the end of the dark corridor illuminated by a single 40-watt bulb was a representation of Grock, world-famous Swiss German clown from the turn of the 20th century. The clown stood right by Rachel's old bedroom door. Lauren presumed him a philosopher because, well, life was a joke, *n'est-ce pas*?

She fit the key into the lock of number 14, feeling memories tumble around her. The hinges whined. Her gaze fell on a female form reclining on a cream-colored duvet, cigarette in her frozen fingers. The sight was enough to take Lauren's breath away. The female's short brown locks were cut to flatter the jawline and taper down the neck. The wide-open, staring eyes were aimed straight at Lauren.

This was no Swiss philosopher.

This was Rachel.

Chapter 3

Meetings and Greetings

Rachel smashed out the cigarette and sprang into the air with the cry, "Lauren!"

They talked both at once, their words creating a small vortex.

Finally catching her breath, Lauren said, "Rachel, my bag—everything—it's all downstairs. Hold on, I'll be back in a flash."

She rushed out the door and plunged into Paul, standing in the gloom. The two toppled over the suitcase he had carried up. Thumps echoed.

She lay sprawled, on top of him, and felt his heart beating.

"Are you okay?" he asked.

His arm was around her waist. He had taken the fall trying to protect her.

"Oh my God!" Lauren got up, smoothed her shirt. "I am so sorry." He wouldn't notice her blushing here in the shadows. The scent of a lovely men's cologne tingled in her nostrils.

Paul was on his feet too, righting the suitcase. "I wish the Swiss military service had skirmishes like that!"

She giggled.

"Your hotel is very odd. A dead general is on the stairs."

"Who's dead?" Rachel appeared at the bedroom door. Light from the room brightened the hallway. Grock the wax clown hunkered in the corner with a circus grin.

"Paul, I would like to introduce my friend, Rachel Gordon."

"*Enchanté.*" Paul extended his hand, but Rachel kept her arms crossed.

"Who is this person?" asked Rachel without emotion.

"Paul brought me here."

"And you know him from . . . ?" Frost crept into her voice.

Paul's smile remained, but his eyes grew wary.

Lauren felt a stab of panic. Rachel's mother hen tendencies had not gone away. Her controlling habit had caused arguments between them in boarding school.

"Rachel, please. Paul drives a cab."

"I am an engineering student who must drive a taxi until he graduates." Paul touched his hand to his chest. "Circumstances. It is much more interesting for me to tell you that my cousin, who is visiting Lausanne just now, is a very good dancer. He would be *delighted* to meet you. Do you like to dance?"

Rachel refused to be charmed. "If it's ballet." She disappeared into the room with a few tossed words: "Let him call you!"

Lauren's heart sank. She did not want to fight with the friend she had just been so happy to reunite with, especially not after working hard to save up money for air fare. Ignoring Rachel's gaze, Lauren found a notepad from inside the room on which she jotted down the phone number of the inn along with her own name. Paul waited in the hallway.

She went back out to give him the slip of paper along with a few bills.

He took the slip but pushed the money away. "All I want, really, is your name and a *yes*," he said in a low voice.

"I wrote my contact information down for you. My phone isn't working yet, so I gave you the hotel number. I guess you could get that off the Internet on your own." She smiled. "My full name is Lauren Briant."

"Lauren." Paul took her hand in his, lifted it to his lips, and placed a kiss upon her fingers. The gesture chased words out of her head.

"When you did not come back out, I worried you had been murdered."

Lauren felt her heart skip a beat. Had he heard the history of Château Mont Rose?

"Rachel and I lost track of time."

"Mmmm. Your inn is very dark. Be careful when you walk around. Shall we say, 7 p.m. tomorrow night? I will come to fetch you."

"I guess so," said Lauren, making up her mind. "See you then." She watched his retreating form. The longer she stood alone in the hallway, the more aware she felt of the unmoving wax figures lining the hallway.

But something *was* moving. Lauren had the irrational sensation that the eyes of the clown statue in the corner, next to their bedroom door, were upon her, that he noticed her. More irrationally, she imagined some movement in his face. Was it the effect of a thin sheet of light slipping through the cracked bedroom door?

In the periphery of her vision, the clown's mouth seemed to twitch and begin to open.

She turned her head and stared at him. He stared back.

Then her feet propelled her to shoot past him, and she slammed the bedroom door shut.

"What's wrong with you?" said Rachel with a jerk of her head. "Did that guy scare you? So why did you stay out—"

"Rachel, shhhhhh." Lauren walked on shaking limbs to the window. The tail lights of a car disappeared up the hill. Her heart beat in her ears.

The darkening vista was one she had looked at often in the first months of boarding school, sometimes with tears of homesickness running down her cheeks. It was a view lushly treed, dotted with Swiss villas.

"Paul didn't scare me. I was standing alone outside the door, next to that horrible wax clown . . . ."

"And you got the creeps!" finished Rachel, clapping her hands together like a child at an amusement park. "Perfect! That's what I told them!" She leaped up from her place on her bed, danced to a drawer, and pulled out a pair of jeans and a shirt, dropping her peignoir to the ground. Years of ballet classes had left Rachel stripped of modesty about nudity. Some things never changed.

"Who is 'them'?" demanded Lauren.

"My employers. Remember I said I am here on business? That is how I could invite you to stay with me in this suite. You don't have to pay a red cent. I was just about to explain everything when you and the taxi driver started playing leapfrog in the hallway."

"We weren't playing. I knocked him over."

Rachel shook her head and rolled her eyes. Lauren wondered how she was going to be able to ask Rachel not to be bossy when she was also in her debt.

"You Californians are far too trusting. Forget about him."

"Rachel, please. . . ."

"Can you just listen for a moment? I've been dying to tell you my full position title. I'm the director in charge of location and personnel for 'Ghost Seekers in Europe.' I'm going to travel a lot, all expenses paid. The producers want two or three haunted castles near Lake Geneva to start out with. This is like coming home for me, and how could I enjoy this without you? I've got the Château de Chillon lined up for tomorrow. The second filming location this week is going to be here, at our old school. If the bosses are happy, we'll keep on going from there."

"Huh?" Lauren was not sure what to make of the absolute change in plans. "I thought we were on vacation!"

"We are, Lauren. Sort of. But better, because we'll be paid. And in Switzerland!"

Rachel had spent every summer of her childhood in Switzerland, even if she always said the first weeks of boarding school were the worst part of her life. It was her New York physician father who felt the country had adopted him. Lauren met Rachel's dad and stepmother over a long weekend holiday. She and Rachel had taken the train up to Les Diablerets, a resort in the Bernese Alps, for the occasion.

"Haunted castles? You can't guarantee ghosts."

"Every famous castle is haunted."

"You don't say. Who is the ghost at the Château de Chillon?"

"Lord Byron."

Lauren fidgeted with the window lever. What Rachel was saying was absurd, and she had to know that.

"Rachel, has Lord Byron consented? All he ever did was *visit* the Château de Chillon—and write a poem about its famous prisoner. I would have thought Lord Byron's ghost would be haunting his native country, England, or Greece, where he died. I've never heard of a ghost haunting a place that was visited on vacation and departed from in good health. Hawaii must be full of ghosts!"

"It's about audience expectations," said Rachel in a relaxed voice. "People expect castles to be haunted. They will recognize Lord Byron much more easily than Bonnivard or whoever really is haunting the Château de Chillon."

"At least you remembered Bonnivard, the prisoner of the Château de Chillon."

Rachel hooked her arm through Lauren's. "I admit I never studied literature. But I know that poor old Bonnivard didn't make it into the commercial *Who's Who of History*. Byron did. Some people have actually heard of him. That's the way my bosses look at it. I know you take literature seriously; I respect that. Why else would I have recommended you so strongly for employment?"

The idea of being on a paranormal team was not without appeal to Lauren. "How does this ghost-hunting work?" she asked. "You said 'bosses,' plural."

"One is a man. He's attractive, but not my type. Nor yours."

"These bosses think it's okay to make things up?"

"You could change that," said Rachel. "It all depends on your influence as a writer."

"My influence as a writer?"

"Isn't that what you do?"

"It's what I *like* to do."

"Before you start harping about truth to the people you meet tomorrow, I want you to know what I believe in, what is vitally important to me."

"Okay."

"For starters, I *do* believe in the spirit world." Rachel's voice dropped in pitch but grew in resonance: "I believe in God, spirits, and negative energy. And, my dear friend, I believe in a career. Somebody has to make ghosts cost-effective, which includes helping them out any way possible. In business school, we learned to study competitors as much as market trends, to figure out what competitors have forgotten. So far, most people in the ghost-chasing business have been filming orbs and recording barely understandable voices or telling celebrity ghost stories. We have to capture the popular imagination better than other shows do. Our idea is to feature one famous ghost in each program, in a marvelous and creepy setting."

"'Our idea'?"

"Technically, the show and the ideas belong to my employers—maybe even your employers, if they like you. Aside from the two bosses, there's a Swiss guy and his partner who are going to be the tech experts. We'll meet them tomorrow."

"Château Mont Rose certainly *is* creepy enough to fit into a ghost-hunting TV show," said Lauren. A thought struck her. "Hold everything. Rachel, did your crew *rig* that stunt I just fell for?"

"Me? Rig something?" Rachel wore the same impish look on her face as when suggesting, years earlier, they forge their parents' signatures in order to leave the school grounds for a holiday weekend.

"I should have known!" Lauren exhaled in relief.

"You'll make a great ghost hunter."

"Writer."

"Ghost-hunting writer," amended Rachel. "I've got your best interests at heart. In that spirit, I suggest you stay away from the taxi driver."

Lauren bit her tongue to not say that the scariest part of returning to Lausanne was returning to Rachel's bossiness. It was too close to the truth. Instead, she asked: "Which ghost will we be hunting at Château Mont Rose?"

"I thought you would have guessed! Our dead teacher, naturally."

Chapter 4

A Russian-Senegalese Alliance

Cloquet drove Katia back to her apartment building after a drawn-out stop at a medical facility. The entire morning was gone. He was surprised all she had was a sprained ankle. He offered to take her for groceries, but she declined.

"I have everything I need," she said. "I could make you breakfast." She tossed him a smile as he held the door of her flat open. "Do you like crepes?"

A wire-haired terrier bounced off a couch with a short yap.

"In Russian, they are called blin—Asta!"

Cloquet attempted to field the dog, which ended up with its front paws on Katia's legs, now covered in new stretch tights picked up at a store. "Down! Where did the dog come from?"

"I've had him a little while. Yesterday he was at the dog spa with one of my girls. So clean and pretty! Do you recognize the name, 'Asta'?"

"Should I?"

"It is a detective's dog's name. *The Thin Man.* Do you watch old movies?"

"Sometimes."

"American actors. William Powell and Myrna Loy."

"I thought Russians didn't like Hollywood."

Katia sank onto the couch, and Asta jumped up on her lap. "That's silly," she said. Cloquet leaned her crutches against the back of the furniture.

She caught his eye. "I wanted a smart detective's terrier like the one in the movies. You and Asta must be friends."

"Nothing wrong with pets." He patted the dog's head.

Katia thought he seemed glum. How could she have known Michèle was dead? Katia had carefully avoided reopening that wound at the medical facility. Yet she longed to quell his ache. Russian food could fill in spaces of discontent, at least temporarily.

"Julien, have you ever had bliny? They are delicious Russian crepes."

He shook his head.

Perhaps he wanted something heavier or spicier?

"I also have sausages. So easy to cook."

His hand was on the doorknob. She pointed to her cheek in the hopes of receiving at least a friendly kiss.

"I am not hungry, Katia. Stay off that foot. *À plus tard.*" The door clicked closed and his footsteps sounded in the hallway. The smile disappeared from her face.

Katia pulled out her phone.

"*Allo.* Jawara? Thank you for bringing Asta. Can you come downstairs?"

Three minutes later, Katia heard a key turn. A young Senegalese woman dressed in a light gray and yellow striped knit tunic over gray tights opened the door. Katia's eyes misted with tears.

"Jawara, you look lovely."

The lithe dark beauty, gold rings sparkling in her woven hair braids, brought a scent of Chanel in with her as she kissed Katia on each cheek.

"What is wrong?" asked Jawara, almond eyes widening in concern.

"I fell. Shhh, Asta." The terrier stopped yapping but his tail flapped like a flag in a high wind.

"You are in pain? You have crutches."

"I sprained my ankle." A tear coursed down Katia's cheek, followed by several more. She took a breath.

"I will get ice." Jawara bounded off the couch and into Katia's little kitchen. Asta ran after her, then changed his mind and jumped back up on the couch with the mistress.

"It's okay, darling," called Katia. "My feelings are more bruised than my ankle." She nuzzled her terrier, waiting for Jawara, who came back with ice. The Senegalese woman was young enough to be if not Katia's daughter, perhaps her niece. There were a good dozen years between them.

Thirty or so minutes later, they were at the kitchen table, crepes piled upon a blue and white plate set between them. Washed, topped and halved strawberries sat in a blue and white bowl next to an open sour cream container. Powdered sugar was in a much smaller but non-matching blue and white bowl. Katia loved blue and white in her kitchen.

"You first, Jawara."

Silver Melchior spoons and forks from Russia had been set. Katia admired the filigreed handles glinting in the streaming sunlight. Jawara served herself three crepes. She turned the stem around for Katia to grasp. The cutlery brought back memories of childhood, before Katia's father's bankruptcy and the split from her mother.

The cooking pan sat in a sink full of hot water and soap bubbles. The room felt warmed by the coffee and crepes made swiftly with baking soda. Katia's grandmother might not have approved of using baking soda instead of yeast, but she was long since buried. She had taught Katia that food helped quell any ache.

"What were you doing at that place?" asked Jawara before taking her first bite of hot crepes, sour cream, strawberries and powdered sugar. "I mean, besides—" she cut her words with a wink.

"He was looking for something—police work." Sitting in the sunlit kitchen, Katia felt hope resurge. She would never admit Julien had not wanted intimacy; she insinuated there had not been enough time. Asta lay on his tummy at Katia's feet and licked the un-bandaged ankle.

"A ring of thieves?"

"He didn't tell me anything, but he searched all night. Then he lost his watch and I lost my tights. There's something weird over there." Katia rolled her crepe carefully around the sour cream and two strawberry halves, sprinkled it with the powdered sugar, and took a bite.

Asta whimpered.

"Not yet, Ashtuka."

"You were so happy to hear from him."

"We are friends," broke in Katia. "Just friends. I thought—we had romantic potential. But of course, I am glad to help him in a case." He never actually said she was helping him.

"Maybe he wanted to appear married?" said Jawara. "It will be hard for you to help him with a twisted ankle." She made a wry face. "How long do you have to hop around?"

"I really don't know. Perhaps a few days or a week. We will see."

"What did you have in mind for me?"

"You can find out from Émile what is going on. Julien wouldn't be digging around at Château Mont Rose if it were not police business." Katia had her phone next to her and was typing into it. She stopped to sip coffee. "As I thought, the school closed eight years ago."

"What did you find?"

"An old news item about the school closing its doors. Let me see when it reopened as a hotel."

"I might eat all your strawberries while you are searching."

"No, you won't, you're too considerate."

Jawara laughed. "If you say so. I don't think Émile likes your man very much. They are rivals."

Katia was reading and her eyebrows raised.

"Even if Émile Moser doesn't like Julien, that doesn't mean we cannot use your lover to find out what Julien is searching for."

Asta, having reached the end of patience with the humans, yapped.

"Alright, darling. Some for you too." Katia proffered half a pancake with a dab of sour cream to the dog. Then she went back to her phone and found something. "Château Mont Rose re-opened a few months ago."

"Katia, I will help you if you help me. I am worried what to do about my brother Abdul."

"What about him?"

"He is visiting and I can't let him see Émile."

Katia sat back in her chair for the negotiations. Keeping her ladies happy meant giving a little. She had introduced Jawara to Émile Moser, Lausanne's current head of homicide, knowing he had a penchant for women of dark, exotic complexion. He paid for his exclusivity--full rent and spending money. He was a practicing Catholic with a wife, so marrying Jawara was out of the question.

"Tell your brother your husband doesn't want guests. You are in your honeymoon stage."

"My hus—?"

"I am sure Moser will play along if he should ever get wind, which he won't." Katia spooned sour cream onto another crepe and rolled it up.

"I don't think Émile wants problems."

"Your brother and lover don't have to see each other, do they?" Katia speared more half strawberries. "You've got Moser's picture in a frame on the mantel. If Abdul passes by, tell him Émile hates uninvited guests and that he is a very private individual."

"Abdul will see there aren't any men's clothes."

Asta padded over to the water bowl and then returned to Katia's feet. He watched his mistress patiently.

"Don't tell me Abdul will be left alone in your apartment!"

"He is on his way from Geneva. I told him about your travel agency."

"We haven't any clients yet." Katia's voice came out sharper than she would have liked. Blast it, she knew relatives would come scuttling from all corners! Some girls had stiffer spines than others when it came to dealing with moochers. Priorities were important.

"Be firm, Jawara, like your family was with you when they sent you out in the world as a maid. You owe them nothing."

Jawara shrugged.

"You are an intelligent woman kept by a powerful man of Lausanne. Protect that."

"I don't want to go back to the old life." Jawara stuffed a wad of crepe and strawberries in her mouth.

"The tour guide business will take off only if we don't go offering jobs with money I do not have. For what it's worth, I think Château Mont Rose should *be* on one of the tours. I would love to find out what is being investigated there. Crime lends a place appeal, especially if we can tell the story." Katia gave another wedge of crepe to the patient dog. Asta's tail thumped.

"You said that place was closed because of a murder."

"A teacher died there. I never said it was murder."

"Émile will tell me what investigation is going on over there if I ask. It can't be that important or he would be in charge. These crepes are delicious, Katia."

Katia felt sadness slip away. More the loss to Julien, not tasting her crepes. "Thank you, darling. Would you believe I was a schoolgirl at Château Mont Rose?"

"A boarding school? That must have been nice."

"I made a few friends, but the headmistress was scary. My roommates cried in their sleep."

"They were homesick?"

Katia thought so. She remembered dream visions of blood but left that out because some of it came true. The strawberries on Katia's plate now looked too red.

"We can't let nightmares control us," she said in a calm voice, carefully spearing a fruit.

Jawara smiled back with her perfect, pearly white teeth. No wonder Émile doted on her. Natural beauty.

"I promise to help you find out," the young Senegalese promised. "Because you have been a blessing to me."

Chapter 5

Séance in the Habana Bar

Phantoms of the past stole into Lauren's sleep.

A blasé, much-traveled grandfather deposits his gawky fourteen-year-old granddaughter on the train at the Gare de Genève-Cornavin. She hears his instructions, nods, and hugs goodbye.

Alone.

She feels she is an almost grown-up young woman, on her own, watching the pageant of Swiss villas sweep past.

A handsome, blond man waits in the tumultuous foyer of the Gare de Lausanne, oblivious to the white rectangle in his hands that cries out, "Lauren Briant, Little Girl from America, Come to Me before You Get Lost Forever."

She halts, amazed to have noticed the thin letters on the placard. Her gaze drifts down his slacks, settling on shiny, rust-colored leather shoes. His cologne, hinting at exotic, mature male tastes, perfumes the air, blending with the aroma of espresso and croissants from a café kiosk.

"Château Mont Rose?"

His is a smooth, diplomatic voice against the background of brisk footsteps, rolling suitcase wheels, phone conversations and the muted screech of a train slowing to a stop.

Lauren nods as a voice over the loudspeaker, *en français*, announces the arrival of the Brig train on platform 4.

By sleight of hand, the blond man conjures a business card under her nose. He whisks it away before she can read. The trick is a distraction, apparently, to snatch her suitcase and run. She chases him out to the street, wondering how a thief knew she was going to a boarding school named Château Mont Rose.

Lauren's angst evaporates at the shiny blue Jaguar. The man stows the luggage in the trunk. She settles against a leather seat redolent of cigars. He slides in and launches the Jaguar into the main thoroughfare. Her stomach lurches. He accelerates up a steep road with narrow curves, making her think of a World War I triplane pilot.

When she turns her head, he is the Red Baron, silk scarf flying in the wind, at the back of a two-seater. They both wear goggles.

She peers over the edge of the plane. Cows graze around tiny farms. Swiss chalets with their flower-trimmed balconies look like nothing so much as pastries with decorative frosting. Her fingers grip; she is conscious of the distance to the ground.

"Why don't you take this?" he mouths into the wind, passing her his card once more. Lauren tries to read the jumping words:

Monsieur Maxime Bonami, propriétaire

Château Mont Rose, *École de Filles*

Lausanne, Canton de Vaud, Suisse

Her breath comes more evenly as Monsieur Bonami, who this fair-haired man is, brings the triplane down for a landing. They brush the top of trees. Her laugh sounds giddy. The tires touch down and roll; the plane becomes once more a car.

It passes under a vine-covered arched gateway onto the cobblestones of the château's driveway.

Lauren barely has time to feel the ground under her feet when a spikey-haired woman grabs her hand and pumps, like a farmer desperate for water at the well.

"Let go!"

"*Parlez-vous français?*"

"*Oui.*" An unfortunate response. French rehearsed at school differs when under a blue sky in Swiss cheese land. Here, sheep dressed in dirndls offer slices of Emmental and Gruyère—as if Switzerland were a warehouse club.

"Baaaaah!" a sheep calls. Another holds a tooth-picked cube of cheese in its teeth for Lauren to try.

The single-person welcoming committee, sharpened titanium prongs of lacquered hair threatening to take out the eye of whoever is close, zips out a question *en français*.

"I don't. . . ."

"She speaks no French!" screeches Spikes.

Lauren knows "Spikes" is really Mademoiselle Terrieux, a teacher much feared.

"Who cares about French?" demands someone with a heavy Swiss-German accent. Eyes in a painted face with sagging jowls peer down from an upper floor window. It is the wax clown, Grock.

"Everyone, Monsieur!" retorts Spikes. "French is the language of love."

"It is the language of cold porridge," says the red mouth.

Grock grasps a violin stick. Arm and stick begin stretching toward the ground.

Spikes wraps her own arms, octopus-style, around Lauren. The violin stick plunges, stretching faster, downward.

Tapping heels herald Mademoiselle Wertheimer. "Remove your tentacles at once, Mademoiselle Terrieux, or be fired!"

Spikes jumps.

"Nor will you stab our new students, Grock, unless you wish to be melted by the cook and made into candles!"

The arm and violin stick retract upwards.

This younger version of Mlle Wertheimer says to Lauren, "I hope you will be very happy here."

"Aren't you forgetting to mention you will do everything in your power to see she is not?" asks Spikes.

Grock thrusts his head back out the window. "You are fortunate!" he calls out. "You have the nicest of all the teachers as the guardian of this floor. Her name is Mademoiselle Schwartz and she is going to teach you cold porridge. Her room is right across from yours. *Bis später!*"

The forms freeze and dissolve. Lauren is in her bedroom, but not alone.

"How much chocolate have you hidden under your blanket?" asks a doe-eyed woman with wavy chestnut hair pulled up in a twist. The moon streams in, highlighting escaped tendrils of hair.

Lauren thinks of the large chocolate bar under her bed, hidden in a shopping bag. Temptation starts with bliss, leading to pimples and pounds. For others, bliss can lead to death. If she can stop thinking about chocolate, will Mlle Schwartz not die? The teacher is still safe on the edge of the bed.

"Your earrings are beautiful."

Tapering fingers flutter up to the jewelry. "*Merci*." She touches her watch "Half past six—is the hour of. . . ." She mimes an invisible fork, moving it to her mouth. "Dinner. Yes? You come with me—half past six?" She points at the bedroom door, clasps her hands together, and lays her cheek against them, miming sleep. Her bedroom is across the hall, thinks Lauren.

The teacher walks out. Lauren tries to move her legs. The blanket might as well be a stone slab. It is not until the bell on the stairs rings to signal the dinner hour that she manages to lift her head—

"Lauren! Wake up, you're having a nightmare."

#

Three men and one woman sat on red leather armchairs at the Habana Bar of the Lausanne Palace Hotel. It was much too early for cocktails.

Hotel staff unhooked a rope barricade. Lauren and Rachel entered. Dark wood panels lined the walls up to the ceiling. Wine bottles lined shelves.

What was Paul doing here?

He sat next to a young man of swarthy appearance—perhaps Indian, Sri Lankan, or Bengali?

Rachel was busy nodding at a man, sharp of jawline, who rose as they approached. He looked to be in his mid-thirties, mildly tanned, with buffed, glowing fingernails. He might have a Ferrari stashed in the hotel's garage. Designer glasses hung from a cord around the neck of his corduroy jacket.

Rachel found her voice. "Lauren, Mr. Dominick Bentley. Mr. Bentley, this is the friend I told you about, the literary expert, Lauren Briant. Lauren, Mr. Bentley is our director and producer."

Dominick smoothed his sleek, coppery hair back with one hand. The locks erupted into curls at the collar. He had piercing eyes.

"All team members have permission to call me Dominick—at least while we film. After that, I will be Mr. Bentley again if you ever run into me, which you probably won't. I've already seen the guest list for Cannes. Hahahahahaha."

Rachel squeezed the corners of her lips up like she was being tickled. No one else reacted, least of all the big-boned young woman with wavy, dark hair. That stunner wore form-fitting pants and swung a shapely leg, attention on the phone in the palm of a hand. Her high-rise boots looked to be made of alligator skin.

"And this is Mr. Bentley's partner, Miss Stamoulos."

The female boss did not look up. Paul, meanwhile, looked flushed. Rachel stared at him and the young man next to him.

"This is Ajit, our tech expert," said Rachel, "sitting next to a *taxi driver.*"

"My cousin!" Ajit pat Paul on the back.

"You said your cousin was. . . ." Rachel frowned.

"—a programmer. He likes to pretend he is nobody." Ajit spoke with an Indian accent. The word "cousin" was apparently being used in some honorary or blood brother context.

"Are you *Swiss?*" Lauren couldn't help asking.

"*Bien sûr.*"

"Our conversations will be conducted in English," proclaimed Dominick, "as is normal for international teams." He nodded at Paul. "Of course we need a computer nerd. Your hiring is on spec—until I see what you can do. Are you any good at CGI?"

The stylish female with inky tresses thumped her phone onto the table. The group jumped.

She looked up, dark lined eyes seemingly capable of boring a hole through skulls. "I should have been introduced before these two jerks. Protocol, morons. Let's observe it from now on."

"I apologize. Lauren, this is Helena Stamoulos."

Lauren wanted to say Miss Stamoulos had already been introduced, but Rachel's eyes begged her not to.

"Ms. Stamoulos and Mr. Bentley are co-producing the show. They are the *Imagineers* behind the entire concept. That's a Disney term." Rachel's cheer sounded forced. "And Ajit has a great track record for catching paranormal episodes on film and audio recording devices."

"I use ancient hocus-pocus." Ajit's head wobble was very un-Swiss.

"Call me Helena," said the female producer.

"Yes, um, Helena—Mr. Bentley—Lauren is a wonderful writer and researcher. She could help in research and—"

"Enough jabbering!" barked Helena. "Tell that garçon waiter-chappie to get out."

"Can't I run for a piss?" Dominick rose from his seat.

"No. The chain needs to be formed now, this minute, or no money from me and no film."

"Is that what your crystal ball says?" He tapped on Helena's phone screen with a manicured fingernail.

"Dumb Ass Bentley, you have no clue about the other side. I would love to know how the spirits tolerate your presence."

Something about Helena struck Lauren as familiar. Had she met this person before?

Ajit beckoned the waiter, murmured in his ear. The latter served iced water all around, French rolls in a basket and butter balls in a silver dish on top of ice. Leaving, he switched off the lights.

"My God, it will take forever to get lunch this way." Dominick sounded peevish.

"You wanted to meet in the Habana Cigar Bar," said Helena. "Now shut up and join hands, everyone."

Cigars explained the base note. Rachel grasped Lauren's right hand. Paul was on her left. She accepted his hand, blocking the memory of the kiss. How had he got into this group?

"Close your eyes and concentrate!"

Lauren obeyed.

"Honored Guests," said Helena in a gentler voice. "Are we complete?"

Two seconds before, they had been morons.

"If you are satisfied, let us know." Helena's voice swelled.

The room felt like a swamp. Perspiration beaded on Lauren's skin. She could not fan herself with a menu or she would break the chain.

A chorus of voices responded, "Yes, complete!"

Her eyelids flew open.

Paul's eyes opened too. Rachel's were pressed tight shut, as were Ajit's and Dominick's. Hunched shoulders made the ring look like they were waiting for a flock of birds to land on their heads. Lauren quaffed a giggle.

"Will we be visited at Château Mont Rose? And at Chillon?"

"Mont Rose," moaned the voices. Their sound came from above, but no speakers were visible. Lauren heard a single voice whisper "Chillon" at her shoulder. She jerked.

"Let go!" said Helena, flopping her head down upon folded arms.

"I say. Are you alright? Blimey, it's hot in here." Dominick reached for his water glass. "Where in the hell did the ice go? Waiter!"

Lauren's eyes focused on the butter dish. The butter was half melted; the dish it was on floated in the melted ice-water. She picked up a menu and fanned.

Ajit dabbed his brow with a napkin. The waiter reappeared.

"Goddammit," said Dominick, "bring us fresh iced water, *tout de suite*."

"*Oui, Monsieur.*"

"Wake up, Thunder Thighs!" Dominick slapped Helena's leg.

"Tell me something," said Rachel to Paul in a low voice. She took a napkin, spread it on her lap. "Are you stalking Lauren?"

"No, I—"

"Have you *met* my cousin?" inquired Ajit.

"He drove Lauren to our hotel."

"I am not *stalk*—"

"Working as a team already," boomed Dominick. "Good. You might want to order vegetarian. The old girl recommends vegetarian to hone the psychic powers."

"The prehistoric cretin doesn't know what he's talking about." Helena was sitting up and giving an interesting performance, but not less so than Rachel and Paul, pretending not to know each other.

Chapter 6: Lauren's Interview

"Lauren, I need someone who will, among other duties, prepare the crew for meeting spirits we invoke." A piece of lobster lodged in Lauren's throat and she began choking.

Recovering thanks to water, she answered, "I thought you needed a writer."

"Preparing the crew and the audience to meet specific spirits is what I want the writer *for.* You heard voices just now, didn't you?"

"There are more spirits in a bar than anywhere else," said Dominick, with a raffish wink.

Helena scowled at him.

Lauren put her fork down. What was there about this tall, stylish woman with the bossy tone that tugged at the memory?

The Greek woman was tall and attractive if solidly built—nothing dainty there—and reeked of money. Her cropped black hair swung stylishly. The gold-rimmed glasses were emblazoned with a familiar designer emblem. The way Helena stared through those frames was disconcerting.

"Yes, I heard the voices."

"'She'll get the experience she needs as she goes along,'" said Dominick in a falsetto, "or she'll turn into one more basket case," he added, dropping the high notes, "like the others we've worked with—"

"Shut up," snapped Helena. "You don't understand the other side, Dumb Ass Dominick. I try to teach you, but you don't listen."

"Sure I do! And I surf the web for how-tos. I prefer all forms of *scripted* paranormal: Ch-Ching!" His arm pulled an invisible lever on a slot machine. He picked up his lager. "Cheers!"

"Lauren, would you please describe Mlle Schwartz to the group," Helena said, pulling her plate into her lap and stabbing a forkful of her own lobster salad. "Wonderful, isn't it? How often can you afford lunches like this?"

"At places like this!" added Dominick.

Never, thought Lauren. Lobster, never. At places like this, never.

"The crew needs to know the entity we will meet at Château Mont Rose." A speck of parmesan cheese was visible on the side of Helena's mouth.

"Start talking, please. You've lost your appetite anyway." Helena nodded at Lauren's barely eaten food.

"Remember the essay you got published?" Rachel prompted. "I told her about that. Go on, Lauren!"

Here was a surprise. Lauren had thought Rachel never read any story she wrote. Maybe the first line.

Dominick thumped his drained beer on the glass top table. "Lights, camera, action!" He cut his hand through the air and pointed at her.

"If anyone turns her into a basket case, it will be you," said Helena.

"Is this my interview?"

"Yes. Stand up and react." Helena wiggled her hand in the air like a gypsy dancer and then wiped the parmesan speck off her cheek.

"React" made Lauren think of the trick pulled on her with Grock the waxen clown. She didn't like being a guinea pig. On the other hand, if she got the job, she would be writing, not bagging groceries for a salary. She stood up. The unlit room pulled in around her.

"Mademoiselle Schwartz . . . was an assemblage of contradictions. She was a French teacher with a German-sounding name in a Swiss boarding school. She taught us the language with an artist's flair, drawing elaborate pictures on the chalkboard. She knocked herself out in each performance.

"She was feminine, and fluttery, and inclined to the dramatic. She wept or exploded without warning. I doubt many of us liked her at first. In truth, Mlle Schwartz had a difficult personality—"

"You can say that again!" Helena cawed.

Lauren chose to overlook the remark, continuing, "Mademoiselle Schwartz made all the girls stand up when she first walked into the room. We had to chorus, *"Bonjour, Mademoiselle."*

Rachel nodded.

"We rose to our feet like a herd of cattle. I don't know how she heard our greeting with all that stomping. Our desks were built on a tiered wooden platform so we could look down at her."

"That would have been a nice view from underneath." Dominick raised his refilled drink in salute. "Why are you calling this woman 'Mademoiselle'? Didn't she have a first name?"

"Her name was Danielle, but we were formal. Girls cannot call their teacher by her first name."

"Do I have to keep reminding you to shut up, Dumbass? Ignore him, Lauren! He didn't go to school."

Lauren saw a different expression on each face. Ajit looked affable; Dominick, oblivious; Rachel, anxious; Helena, overbearing yet interested; and Paul . . . unreadable.

"Mademoiselle Schwartz expected us to buckle down and absorb the French language. She devised tedious exercises. Once we had to underline every adjective in six chapters of *Le Petit Prince* for a single evening's homework."

"You vowed to burn that book at the end of the school year," said Rachel.

"But it was your idea to make a bonfire in front of the school gates of as many of the books as we could collect!"

Ajit nudged Paul with an elbow.

"We changed our attitudes about the book as time went on. *Le Petit Prince* is a classic."

"I'm not a big reader myself," said Helena. "I prefer movies. Anyway, all the best books have been made into films, right? No need to read nowadays. Keep going!"

"In the beginning, most of the students resented Mademoiselle Schwartz, but by the time Christmas rolled around, she had us laughing at her daily antics."

"Did *all* the students laugh with her?" Helena held her fork, prongs up, like a spear. Dominick drew away.

"N—no. I guess Mademoiselle Schwartz was harder on some people than others. She hated whispering. If she heard anyone whisper, her face turned a fuchsia color."

"Fuchsia?" echoed Ajit.

"Bright pink," explained Rachel. "Lauren could just say red." She dropped her eyes at Helena's withering glance.

"The transformation scared us. Her eyes bulged like marbles from their sockets. She screamed, '*Imbéciles! Imbéciles!*' and told us how we wore her poor nerves out. She wasn't the only teacher who acted that way. Sometimes we could hear the teacher in the next room yelling. We used to sit as still as stones, with hardly a breath between us because otherwise, Mademoiselle Schwartz would not stop shrieking. Except for one girl. . . ."

The tendons on Helena's neck swelled like piano strings under her skin.

"Do you remember the name of that girl?" Her eyes widened.

Lauren's throat went dry.

Oh no. It couldn't be.

Helena leaned forward to rap Rachel's hand with the knife butt. "Tell her!"

"Ow!" Rachel pulled her hand into her lap.

"Now!"

Lauren didn't want to hear.

Rachel took a sip of iced water, cleared her throat.

"You are here because of Miss Stamoulos. She asked for you."

The nasty hunch was about to blossom into a big, ugly truth.

"Don't you *remember* a girl named Helena Stamoulos at the château? In our class?"

Damn it. The memory had lain dormant in Lauren's psyche like eczema before erupting. There *had* been a Helena: a rich, metal-pierced bully with an addiction for carbs. That insufferable bitch had almost caused Lauren to bail from school the day after arriving.

Subsequent events had brought Lauren closer than anyone would ever choose to be to such a spoiled brat.

"Oh hell, dish the dirt already," chortled Dominick. He wore an amused grin, teeth bared like fangs. "Your old school chum is at the heart of this project. Our darling Helena has some sort of screw loose that enables her to. . . ."

"Shhhhh!" Helena backhanded the Englishman with a bit of muscle. Dominick moved his chair further away from hers. Facing the others, she said, "He's right. You can see I have special talents. Well go on, Lauren, describe the Helena you knew. . . ."

Paul and Ajit stared at her. So did Rachel. Lauren wondered if she was going to be publically flayed.

"She—you?—was our classmate."

"What did she look like?"

Lauren's hands trembled. "Black hair. Um, pretty?"

"Bull ca-ca," said Helena. "I looked like a cow. If you lie, you're off the team.

"You—"

"Say the name, *Helena*, like it's not me. It is a girl who doesn't exist anymore."

"He-Helena didn't understand how, *um*, high—uh—strung Mlle Schwartz was. Helena—she—*uh*, used to sit next to me, at least, uh, at the beginning of the fall semester. Rachel sat in front. Helena didn't, *uh*, didn't know—"

"Oh for God's sake, is she going to stammer for the next hour?"

Rachel paled.

Lauren might be putting her friend's job on the line, not just screwing up her own chance. She pulled herself together.

"Helena didn't know how to whisper. I don't know why, but when she was a girl, she just couldn't. She didn't know how to turn off her vocal cords. If she wanted something, like an answer to a question, or sweets I had in my pocket, she *tried,* but failed, to whisper. Her voice was always loud enough for Mlle Schwartz to hear. Sometimes I handed over every candy I had brought to class just so Helena wouldn't whisper too loud and get herself into trouble. But she didn't know when to stop talking. Mademoiselle Schwartz finally moved her to the front row. Even then Helena kept whispering too loud to the girls next to her. She received a lot of punishment."

Smooth-voiced or not, Lauren waved goodbye to the potential job. She felt played. Rachel knew the whole time whom they were going to meet. Her old pal seemed good at keeping secrets nowadays.

If Lauren wasn't hired onto the crew, and Paul was—how would she ever find out if he was the one who had rigged the quivering wax clown at Château Mont Rose? But then, what did it matter? Lauren didn't know if she wanted to go out with a liar. Still, she would be friends with a different liar, Rachel.

She had to finish this interview professionally, even if the words burned like coals off her tongue: "Helena was awkward, unsure of herself and a loner, despite having servants."

"Servants?" repeated Helena sharply.

"Girls who did what she told them to do. Not *friends*."

Helena considered the ceiling. "I guess you're right. What else?"

"She took offense. If anyone said the wrong word—and no one ever knew what that word was—she stalked off or had a tantrum. She was hard as a rock to be around."

Rachel winced.

"Even though she lived to offend, I think she wanted someone to pull her down a few notches." Lauren felt pumped into full-throttle masochism. As quickly as she thought of something, she said it: "Spoiled brats don't feel loved; that's why they keep pushing. They want to be punished. The administration did the opposite and gave her *carte blanche*. Helena could get away with murder in every place but Mademoiselle Schwartz's classroom."

The word "murder" might have taken things too far. Mlle Schwartz had been murdered. Rachel was pressing a water glass to her cheek, looking ill.

Helena studied her expensive boots for a half a minute before remarking, "My mother liked you when you had tea with us; did you know that, Lauren? She said you were good for me."

In one way, Helena had not changed at all: Lauren couldn't predict what would come out of her mouth.

"I was so happy to be able to introduce a real friend to her."

Friend? If one could mistake civility for friendship, which Helena clearly had done, then Lauren's politeness and tolerance had, in the end, resulted in Helena introducing her to a shocked and grateful mother. Mrs. Stamoulos had beamed over a teapot and cookies during that meeting.

The memory made Lauren neglect to tell the waiter she still wanted to eat her seafood salad. He swept it away. No one suggested dessert, but coffee was ordered.

"Rachel? Read the schedule," said Helena. "Lauren, sit down."

Rachel pulled out her device, opened a document, and began reading: "We meet at Château Mont Rose at 7 p.m. tonight for script review. Everyone except Paul and Ajit that is—they should be at the Château de Chillon by no later than 6 p.m. to set up the monitors, cameras, stuff like that. The rest of us will go to Chillon after the script review. The Château de Chillon authorities have given us the block of time from 8:30 p.m. until 4 a.m. to have the place totally to ourselves."

"Have we got our Frankenweenie gear?" asked Dominick.

Rachel acted like she understood what he was talking about.

"Yes, Mr. Bentley. Everything has been arranged. We just have to make sure we are done by 4 a.m. when the maintenance staff comes onto the Château de Chillon grounds."

"That should give us enough time to case out the place and catch some good footage," said Dominick.

Lauren hadn't a clue to how Helena and Dominick felt about her. Apparently, she was not going to be given one, either.

"Lunch is over," said Helena. "Let's get cracking, people."

#

Dominick's hand fell on Lauren's arm, preventing her from leaving the bar. Everyone else, including Rachel, walked out.

He fished inside his jacket, pulled out a folded paper.

"Sign this."

"A two-week contract," read Lauren aloud in a mixture of disbelief and relief. She did not realize how tight her brow had felt until this moment. She took the pen he offered.

"It will be renewed if I'm in a good mood, two weeks hence." Dominick took out his wallet and counted bills. "Here are your ill-got gains. Four hundred Swiss francs. Not my idea to pay in advance, but I have to go along with the peace treaty. Got a safe place in your bra? Show me where to tuck it in." He slid the wallet back into his inside jacket pocket, not seeming the least embarrassed at where his gaze was directed.

Lauren took a step backward. Why had Rachel left her alone?

"Not so fast." Dominick grabbed her arm. His mouth moved so close to her ear that when he spoke, warm breath blew gave her a deep shiver of revulsion. He was an attractive man, but—

"This is what I want you to do."

Lauren's spine tensed. She was ready to slap him, then abruptly had to resist the desire to laugh.

"Alright?"

"I *can't* do that!"

"You don't have a choice."

Somehow, Lauren made it out of the room with the money and without Dominick tearing up the contract.

Rachel was waiting in the hotel foyer. They descended together into the street.

"What did he say to you? Did he sign you on?"

"Yes."

"Did he say anything disgusting?"

"From a literary point of view, yes!"

"What was it?"

"He ordered me to write lies. And he stared at my boobs."

"What's so literary about your boobs?"

"Nothing. But he added insult to injury."

"Oh come on, show me a straight man who won't look at boobs. Dominick thinks all women are floozies. The perks that go with the job will make up for it. I'm delighted he signed you!" Rachel beamed.

Walking was liberating, as was Rachel's good mood. Lauren felt cheered. She could put "scriptwriter" on her résumé.

"Is four hundred francs for two weeks a good salary, Rachel?"

"Is that how much he gave you?"

"Yes."

"That's about 420 dollars, maybe a little less. You said for two weeks? "

"Yes."

"$840 per month is okay, depending on what else we have to pay for. Right now we don't have to pay for our room. Do realize how much the rooms are at the Lausanne Palace Hotel, where Dominick and Helena are staying?"

"How much?"

"One night at the Lausanne Palace Hotel would cost your two-week salary."

"I see." Reflected in a chic window of a clothes boutique, Lauren saw her steps matching Rachel's. Their arms were linked. The fresh air felt good on her cheeks. "I guess I have achieved the level of flunky."

"Me too. My salary is under $1000 a month as well. Let's not forget our bosses will cover hotel expenses and most meals. We were born flunkies, Lauren."

Born flunkies? Did Rachel, so proud of being public relations person to a ghost hunting team, really think of herself as a born flunky?

"Then why did our parents send us to boarding school?"

"To find rich husbands."

"That's so old fashioned!"

"Or maybe to learn French. All I know is the people we work for don't take buses or the métro. "

A cold wind rose from the direction of Lake Geneva, causing Lauren to withdraw her arm to zip up her jacket. She realized that Paul had not waited. He was nowhere.

A car honked.

"Lauren, look! It's Ajit."

"Is Paul with him?"

Ajit's head was tipped out the window. "*Salut!* Do you ladies need a ride?"

They were near Place St. François, the hub of the city's bus stops. The sun was still out but clouds were gathering. Rain clouds.

"If you are staying at Château Mont Rose," said Ajit, "you'll have a long walk in the rain." His gaze flitted to the sky. "I heard about the work on the transport system in that area. Get in."

"Where's your cousin?" asked Rachel as they got in the car.

"It's the weirdest thing," said Ajit. "He ran off so fast he didn't seem to hear me call his name. Doesn't show much gratitude for my getting him this great job."

The car engine sputtered into crotchety life and chugged uphill.

Chapter 7

Balls and Chains

A well-built African male wearing short dreadlocks and a light opaque brown jacket with zippered pockets sat in the driver's seat of a shining silver VW Golf compact. The car idled in front of a sleek apartment lobby, the dark glass exterior reflecting the vehicle's image. A mixture of awed relief and jealousy played over Abdul's face as he pushed buttons around the screen to the right of the steering wheel. His brow and jaw muscles rippled like stirred mercury.

"You turned on the GPS," said the dark beauty seated next to him. "Good. That is how you will find your way around."

"Why can't I take the Porsche? You have the keys for that one, too." Their words were a mixture of Arabic, Wolof and French, a dialect spoken in the city of Dakar, where the two had been raised.

"Allah forbid; that car is mine!" The gold rings glinted radiance from Jawara's swinging hair braids when she pulled away in consternation. Hadn't her little brother grown out of taking her things? Moser had given her the Porsche, and he would hit the ceiling if he didn't find it in the garage. For that matter, so would she.

The VW Golf belonged to Katia, who wouldn't be able to walk easily for a while, perhaps not even drive, not with a sprained ankle. Which ankle was it? Jawara's memory was short circuited nowadays. Too many things to think about. She would take Katia out in the Porsche if and when asked. Heck, she would let Katia drive the Porsche if she wanted, if her sprained ankle was the one not needed for driving. With any luck, the absence of the VW Golf would not be noticed. By the time Katia could walk easily, the Golf would be back in its normal position in the apartment garage. Jawara didn't want to stress Katia out by telling her she was lending the car to her brother.

"How did you get the money for the plane ticket to Geneva, Abdul?"

"I took the train."

"You can't take a train from Dakar!"

"I came from Tilburg." His expression reminded her of the old days when he was shorter than she and there was something she had yet to pry out of him. His gaze met hers then looked back at the dashboard.

Jawara crossed her arms. "Where is Tilburg? And where did you buy those threads? Your wardrobe consisted of beach clothes, from what I remember."

"They were a gift. Tilburg is in Holland."

"A gift from whom?"

"Damn, girl. You're not the only one who travels and you're not my mother!" His voice didn't raise, but he sounded peeved. When he was little, this was the voice he would use if she had found his hiding place but still couldn't see him fully. Abdul had always been good at finding places to squirrel away in when life was upsetting.

"*Maman* didn't tell me you went to Holland."

"Call her *Yaay*! You have become so toubab, so Western. I was in Holland only three days. *Yaay* doesn't know. She's busy."

"Why did you go to Holland? How did you pay to get there? Abdul! What is that ring for?"

"Crap." Abdul covered his left hand with his right.

"Show me!" They tussled over his left hand until Abdul allowed her to see.

"Fine, judge me, I got married."

Jawara's mouth dropped. "Married!" She looked at his face. Pleasure was not written there. Inconvenience, rather. "That's why you came to me for a job! Is your wife with you?"

"She's in Tilburg. If I get the job, she will come, she says."

Something in his voice prompted her to ask, "Do you want her to come?"

"I don't know," admitted Abdul. Now that his secret was out, he seemed more inclined to talk. "Do you want to see a picture?" He took out his phone, opened the camera app.

The picture showed a blonde woman with a festive wreath of flowers atop her head, deep laugh lines etched around her smile and eyes, and a bit of a sag at the jowls. The top of her head touched the top of Abdul's shoulder and they both were smiling.

"She's white!"

"Like your husband, girl."

"And she's old!"

"Like your husband, I say."

"Okay, I get it," snapped Jawara.

"Don't you care to ask her name?"

"What is her name?"

"Anneke."

Abdul had probably married one of the midlife single women from Europe who came as tourists to the beaches of Senegal in search of a stud. Long ago, Jawara had worried her little brother would hire himself out as a male whore, so she had made sure he learned to read, write and do well in math. Before his voice changed, he wanted to please her, the imp. He said he wanted to be a pilot. She had hoped he would be a teacher or work at a Western embassy.

Abdul had grown into a tall and good-looking young man, with a disarming, irrepressible grin and even, pearl-white teeth. For easy money, she presumed, he had turned himself into a cabana boy, rewarded for sowing his wild oats. Trading youth and beauty for the chance to escape poverty was the same choice Jawara had made, but she had forgotten about Abdul. She had pushed him out of her mind, maybe because Mama and Uncle Othman had sent her out in the world as a maid. They had forgotten about her too, forgotten about her as a human being. Why should she think of anyone but herself?

"There is one thing I need you to do, Abdul, and then you can use the car for a week or two and earn money as an Uber driver. You had better go to Geneva, where more tourists come in at the airport. In Lausanne, the transit system is so good that locals will not use you. The GPS will make it easy to get around Geneva."

"What about gas?"

Jawara gave him a wad of bills. Abdul would probably sleep in the car. If he had his wife's credit card, he could get a bed in a hostel. Let him sort it out. "You might find Switzerland too expensive for your liking," she said.

Abdul nodded. "Don't tell Yaay about the marriage yet. She thinks I came to work for you."

"Put that ID in the glove compartment."

The ID said Abdul was from the European Union, which he was now, being married.

"Your first stop is Château Mont Rose, are we clear?"

Abdul pointed at the dashboard screen. "Put it on the GPS. I'll get it out of the way so I can make some dough." He blinded her with his beautiful boy smile of joy, giving her a little pinch at the heart.

*   *   *   *

Detective Inspector Cloquet got off the elevator at the homicide floor. He stepped inside a main doorway and moved away from foot traffic.

"That's not a good place to stop. Someone might knock you down."

Light bounced off Moser's head, hairless as a peeled onion. Lucky for him, hair grew under his nose or someone might have mistaken him for a lamp post.

"I doubt that. This doubles as a weapon." Cloquet lifted the Malacca cane with its iron serpent head. Rheumatism from the gunshot wound in his leg was flaring from helping Katia about. He kept the cane in his car for moments of pain.

"I am concerned for your safety." Moser's flared nostrils and haughty eyebrows implied the furthest thing from concern. Wily tendrils crept out from those nostrils. At least two brushed the top of his mustache. Had she been there, Michèle would have closed her eyes in disgust.

"I'm looking for Paul."

"Yes, I saw him."

"You shouldn't have. He doesn't work for you."

"I didn't say I saw him in here. Don't take everything the wrong way. I feel for the kid. Homicide could use a top-notch programmer. I'm sure Paul would prefer getting his teeth into serious police work."

"The cases passed to us *are* serious."

"Spare me."

"I was surprised you didn't take this one. Nine deaths, five missing people. A specific Lausanne address linking them all. Sûreté is accountable."

Moser snickered. The officers at nearby desks glanced up.

"I always knew you were an Interpol puppy. Have you forgotten where our nation's borders lie? Those deaths occurred *outside* Switzerland. They looked like accidents to me. We have enough to do inside the country; we cannot police the entire world. There are ongoing terrorist alerts to attend to in Lausanne, not to mention organized crime rings and serial maniacs."

"Switzerland is an essential hub of European con—"

"*Pute*, Cloquet, I disagree with Interpol on this, if you haven't guessed. The deaths of nine travelers who *happened* to pass through Lausanne—"

"—all staying at Château Mont Rose—"

"—are likely coincidences. They may be caught up in a drug ring or the victims of food poisoning. There, I helped you solve the case. Find the sloppy chef."

Cloquet gripped the serpent's head. "You were the wrong appointee to head this office."

"Why don't you go into politics, Julien? You're good at running your mouth, if not your legs."

"Watch yourself, Moser."

"You blocked my transfer to Lausanne Homicide for years. Allow me to relish the victory." His nose tilted a little higher up into the air. More tendrils.

"You won't last long by misusing authority."

"Look in the mirror when you say that. We need a computer expert here in Homicide. Paul could help us stop real tragedy. You are on a wild goose chase, wasting Swiss tax dollars because of nostalgia over a little girls' school. We all know why."

Pickles and garlic sausage were heavy on Moser's breath, but that wasn't why Cloquet recoiled.

"If Paul is not here, I will trouble you no further."

"Don't think I don't care. An officer from my department has been assigned to your investigation." The volume of Moser's voice notched up.

Cloquet winced and raised the Malacca cane a few inches in a tight grip. "That's out of your jurisdiction."

"Commander Nor approved the request."

Cloquet knew Nor, the Lausanne station commander, from many years' collaboration. Nor hated whiners. Moser would come out of this looking stupid.

"Fine."

"Officer Papaux. Over here, please."

A young man Paul's age, but shorter and more developed in a hit-the-gym sense, bumped the corner of a desk, knocking off a stack of papers and a mug. The papers and mug fell to the floor. The weightlifter looked down at the mess. A female officer who had been sitting at the desk crouched to collect the papers. She shot him a baleful glance.

Papaux stepped over the puddle of coffee without apology.

"You are assigned to Inspector Cloquet's current case for surveillance purposes, as discussed earlier. You will report to me every twenty-four hours."

"Yes, sir."

Cloquet found himself staring at a saddle-like, flat-bridged nose with a fleshy tip. The fellow had a prominent forehead. Papaux returned the stare without emotion.

"Here's Nor's approval." Moser unfolded a paper retrieved from his shirt pocket. Apparently Moser had been planning to send the prizefighter along with the paperwork. Cloquet showed no reaction.

"Give him access to all files. He goes wherever you or Paul go."

"You risk blowing Paul's cover—"

"Take that up with Nor."

Cloquet headed back to the small department created after his disabling injury. *Divers*—Miscellaneous—dealt with crimes that could not be ignored for political and security reasons. Department chiefs like Moser made Miscellaneous necessary.

No longer able to run, Cloquet had been asked to show growth in computer skills. He accomplished this by hiring Paul, his sister Nina's boy, straight out of the Institut de Police Scientifique.

That son of a bitch Moser knew Paul had worked with the Onyx Intelligence Gathering System, which monitored (and intercepted) incoming data via satellite. Switzerland's position as an international meeting spot dead center in Europe made that kind of knowledge important to the highest levels of government. Paul had been offered a job with Onyx, but he chose to work with his uncle.

Cloquet looked over his shoulder. Where was Papaux? Maybe the fellow had stopped to help the female officer after all?

Arriving at the doorway to the former photocopy office, Cloquet heard an espresso beeper go off.

"*Mais enfin!* What took you so long?"

"*Salut*, Uncle Julien. Would you like an espresso?"

"*Non, merci*." Cloquet wedged himself past Paul to the second desk and chair. If Papaux showed up, he would have to stand in the doorway.

"Did you get onto the crew?" Cloquet leaned his snakehead cane into a corner where it wouldn't fall.

"The full report is on your desktop."

"Are you gaining ground with the two American girls?"

"Oh sure. They think I'm a stalker. Don't you want to read the report yourself?"

"I'd rather have it from the horse's mouth."

"You can have it from the horse's ass. I've lost credibility."

Detective Cloquet frowned. "How so?"

"First you had me pose as a taxi driver who is studying for a degree. Today the taxi driver has thrown his classes out the window for a job as a ghost-hunting programmer-technician. Even I would think I were a stalker if I didn't know me."

"Wanting to be hired onto an international film crew doesn't sound far-fetched. It sounds glitzy. Tell them your classes are all online, or you are working on your final project. You were driving a cab for extra income, but when your cousin Ajit offered you the chance to get paid for being a technical assistant, you jumped at the chance. Driving a taxi is not so impressive in the eyes of young ladies."

"That's what I told them two days ago." Paul drained his espresso.

"We didn't have options then. Now you'll be closer to all three of the women and able to persuade them to leave the château."

His words appeared to be falling on deaf ears. Paul's lips were pressed into a firm line under his mustache. Cloquet suspected the young no longer knew how to talk to each other. Technological devices had sabotaged romance.

"I believe I should tell Lauren Briant and Rachel Gordon the risk posed by their staying at Château Mont Rose," said Paul.

Cloquet's old swivel chair screeched with his jerk. Paul recoiled and knocked the espresso machine, which rattled.

"They'll throw you off the crew!"

"I'll explain Interpol's suspicions about Château Mont Rose."

"Don't do it, my boy. Your new employers will fire you. Plus that rich Greek woman will drag Moser into this. Which reminds me—"

"Moser already passed the case to us."

"Now he wants to discredit and shelve it." Cloquet looked up at the doorway. Papaux could be lurking in the hallway. "We've got a headache. Moser went over my head to Nor. He has decided to sic a tag-along on us."

"I thought he didn't like the case."

"He doesn't. The tag-along is for the purposes of discrediting. Moser wants to shut me down and absorb you into his department." He felt satisfied to see Paul pull his head back in consternation.

"I came here to work with you, Uncle Julien."

"Thank you. I will have that espresso."

Paul swiveled his seat, took out the used espresso packet and dropped in a new one. Within seconds the beeper went off.

"Papaux is the name of the officer," said Cloquet, taking the cup. "He should be here any minute."

"I have to go to the Château de Chillon this afternoon to help Ajit set up for filming tonight. I can't bring some stranger with me."

"You'll leave the girls *alone* at their old school while you're at Chillon?"

"They're women, not girls. You wanted me on the crew, and this is my assignment." Paul stood.

"Then *I'll* keep up the surveillance at Mont Rose. I should tell you about one other development. I brought a woman to stay with me at the château for one night. You can wipe that look off your face; it wasn't like that."

"Pardon."

"As it happens, she does run a brothel." Cloquet continued, "Her time was for sale. That is what I bought. I wanted to see what would happen with a female guest who had *never* been a student there."

Paul crossed his arms.

Cloquet sighed. "Katia says she *was* a student at Château Mont Rose over twenty-five years ago."

"Your experiment was for nothing then. Did anything happen?"

Before Cloquet could respond, a shadow attached to a thick body filled the doorway.

"See you later, boss." Paul slipped past Papaux.

"Sit down." Cloquet gestured to the vacated chair in resignation.

Papaux sat.

"Would you like an espresso?"

The prominent brow showed a subtle uplift of interest.

"Help yourself. I'll be with you in a moment."

Cloquet clicked on the desktop file and started reading about Dominick Bentley, a 35-year old British citizen who ran through prodigious amounts of money. He had a reputation for producing sexually suggestive "art" films.

Paul noted that disembodied voices were possibly wired-in sound. Hotel staff had offered no explanation for a heat surge in the Habana Bar. Ajit credited Helena Stamoulos with occult abilities possibly because she had hired him to hunt ghosts. Money purchased a good opinion and sometimes . . . complicity.

Cloquet printed the report out. Might as well give Papaux something to study.

"Read this, then we'll talk about the plan for tonight." The tag-along took the paper, his face a block of wood.

Then Papaux's eyes began moving like an old-fashioned typewriter carriage across the page. Cloquet had to suppress a desire to laugh.

Chapter 8

A Boy Named Mary

A thick stone wall surrounded Château Mont Rose. From her third-floor view, Lauren saw, beyond it, the outer edge of the forest's slim eucalyptus and fir trees. In those woods, Rachel and she had often gone to play medieval tunes on their recorders, wooden musical instruments similar to but predating flutes.

There was no leisure time to linger over such memories now. Whenever Lauren's gaze lifted from the laptop screen where typed words swarmed, she imagined Mary Shelley, author of the novel *Frankenstein,* outside on the grounds, brandishing a fist.

Lauren rubbed her temples, banishing the vision. She typed up seven pages of the script the revolting way Dominick wanted, trying not to scream.

Mr. Dominick Bentley told her that audiences expected *Frankenstein* to have been written by a male writer—specifically, the famed Lord Byron. It didn't matter how Dominick got the idea because once articulated, she realized it was as deeply embedded in his psyche as a tick on a dog.

"Impossible!" said Lauren. "Mary Shelley is the author of *Frankenstein.*"

"*Mary!* Why would parents name a boy 'Mary'?"

Dominick's sleek head tilted as if he were a Greek philosopher asking a logical question. His gaze was steady, one eyebrow raised. He was a good-looking man, if insane.

"Mary Shelley was a woman."

Dominick threw his head back in a single bark of laughter. "Oh hell, babe, no one thinks *Frankenstein* was written by a woman!"

"Excuse me?" Lauren could feel a headache starting.

"Your feelings hurt? Blimey, girls are so cute and sensitive. If you want to be a writer, you need a thick skin." He touched her forearm. "Feels thin to me. Soft. But thin."

Lauren snatched her arm away. "Haven't you seen *Mary Shelley's Frankenstein* starring Kenneth Branagh?"

"Why would I want to see a chick flick of *Frankenstein*?" Dominick laughed. "I prefer *Young Frankenstein.* Best Frankenstein movie ever. I'm not into black and white, by the way. People should keep up with the times."

Was he *pretending* to be stupid?

"Mr. Bentley, the original *Frankenstein* movie starred Boris Karloff. Most people thought of it as closest to the real Frankenstein book until Kenneth Branagh starred in *Mary Shelley's Frankenstein*—"

Dominick raised his hand in the air, rolled his eyes. "You can stop there, Sweetie. Sorry if this hurts your tender feelings, but I am not interested in hearing about a version of *Frankenstein* written by a woman."

"Why are you asking *me* to be scriptwriter if you hate women?"

"Hate women? Oh my God, tender feelings again. It's the opposite!" He stroked her chin and she jerked away. "Darling, don't get your knickers in a twist. Only a man could come up with a monster like Frankenstein. I don't know how this Mary chick got her name thrown into the mix. She probably slept with someone. Byron, most like."

Dominick seemed to take her speechlessness for surprise.

"You're a bright little Yank. Follow along . . . Frankenstein comes from Switzerland, right? Lord Byron was a prisoner at the Château de Chillon—also in Switzerland."

Lauren shook her head.

"You're prettier if you smile, babe. Remember, we will never know all the particulars. History is a hodge-podge. Bryon scratched his name in the dungeon wall at the Château de Chillon. I'll show you this evening."

"But that's—"

"Proof? I agree. Analysis has always been one of my fortes. Your job, doll, is to write a six-to-eight page script with Lord Byron center stage and Frankenstein at his side. Leave the girlies out of it."

Her hands trembled. "May I please say something?"

"Keep it short, poppet."

"Lord Byron was a great poet and womanizer. Even he wouldn't want you to leave 'girls' out of it."

"Oh really?" Dominick smoothed his hair. "Well, then, mention women in a sexy way. We want 10 minutes of dialogue. Did my girl Friday tell you I'm the director? The rest of the thirty to forty minutes will be CGI—and soundtrack. I want to evoke the ghosts of Frankenstein and Lord Byron."

Lauren had lost count of how many times she wondered if Dominick was sane.

"I'm betting my chips on Helena. She may be whacko, but that dame can call the dead back from a graveyard. She's the real McCoy with a bank account. Whatever she can't do, our techies will fix."

Dominick jangled car keys against coins in his pocket, stirring up a lot of noise. And friction.

Lauren decided she had just taken a job for a misogynist pervert.

"I'll pick you up at a quarter to 7. We'll go over the script and grab a bite. Don't want you having to spend your own money. Then we'll head with the rest of the crew off to Chillon."

Lauren did not believe any medium could call upon the spirits of literary characters. The film would be faked, just as the wax clown had been rigged, and she would play a role in this den of deception.

Unless she could write over Dominick's head, so as not to completely discredit Mary Shelley? Spending time alone with Dominick was another worry.

On the ride in Ajit's car, Rachel showed skill in not taking sides: "I know you can do what Dominick asks and still give the script dignity. He's not trying to insult you, Lauren; he's artistic. Don't take it personally."

"Have you seen anything he's filmed?"

"I'm just repeating what Helena told me."

"Have *you* seen anything he's done?" Lauren asked Ajit.

"Me? No."

Lauren fumed. "Why didn't you tell me Helena Stamoulos was your employer? I had erected a mental block against her memory for a reason."

"People change," said Rachel. "I didn't want you to judge hastily."

"And why did you keep the secret that Paul was part of the crew?"

"When Ajit told me he knew a wonderful computer tech guy, how was I supposed to know it was your taxi driver?"

"What a coincidence!" Ajit said.

If Rachel knew more than she was letting on, Lauren would have to find a coping strategy.

#

Back at Château Mont Rose, Rachel lost her patience. "Stop sulking! I got you a job, didn't I? A place to stay? A paid vacation?"

"I appreciate what you've done. But I won't write lies about famous authors, not even for a job in Switzerland."

Rachel studied her fingernails, then lifted her gaze, steady, to meet Lauren's. "People skew the truth all the time. Writers, reporters, teachers, presidents—they all tell lies about history, the news, whatever, to get what they want." She pulled a nail file from a makeup bag, adding, "I lied to get this job."

"How?"

"I said 'I have experience and I can do it' even though I wasn't certain. I've never organized a film or TV show before, but I like organizing my room. I'm not doing so badly. You like writing. You've been doing it forever. Relax. I'm sure you will find a way to keep your conscience at ease. I feel fine with mine."

Rachel did not stay long.

"Do you need anything besides a printer and paper?" she asked twenty minutes later, hand on the doorknob, purse strap over her shoulder.

"Paperclips and a stapler. Are you walking? What if it rains?"

"It doesn't look like it will rain. I won't go farther than La Rosiaz. Ciao!"

Alone, Lauren focused on Frankenstein and Mary Shelley. The Internet reminded her that Mary had come to Switzerland almost 200 years earlier with the 22-year old poet Percy Shelley, then a married man. Mary was not even 20 years old at the time.

If Lauren ran off with a married man, her parents would have plenty to say about the morality of her choice. For her era, Mary Shelley had been more than impetuous. She had scandalized all of London.

In Geneva, Mary met Percy's friend, Lord Byron. One evening during a storm when the group was gathered after dinner, Byron suggested they compete in writing ghost stories.

Lauren liked the word, "suggested." Dominick might be satisfied with it. If she wrote that Byron "challenged" the group, it could sound like Mary won. In Dominick's world, men won.

The more Lauren thought about Mary running off with Percy, the more she thought about romance. *Frankenstein* was supposed to represent the Romantic Era. Ironically, there was a lot about the Romantic Era that wasn't very romantic. Science, for instance. Mary's interest in science was at the core of the invention of the monster Frankenstein. Another non-romantic element was free love, which both Byron and Percy Shelley had embraced. Typical!

Free love was a male convenience.

Lord Byron, a man of great beauty, slept with whomsoever he pleased. Percy Shelley, wanting the same liberty, urged Mary to take another man as a lover. Poor Mary! To run away with the man of her dreams only to find he wanted to pimp her out.

The happiest time of Mary's life had been clouded by a ridiculous philosophy. *Frankenstein* was most likely a metaphor for that ugly conflict.

Lauren clicked "save" at the end of seven pages. She stretched and looked out the window. No fist-shaking Mary Shelley. Good.

Clearing her throat, Lauren read aloud:

"If not for the challenge made one evening in 1816 in Geneva by the famous Romantic poet, Lord Byron, to a group of friends that included Percy Shelley and his future wife, Mary, the story of Frankenstein would never have seen the light of day. . . ."

A rapping on wood stopped the flow of words. Was Rachel back?

"Hello?"

Silence.

 Lauren resumed reading. More rapping.

"Who is it?"

No answer. Lauren didn't feel like opening to a maid or Mlle Wertheimer, presuming the old woman had the energy to walk all the way to this room.

But if it were Paul?

"Hello?"

When no response came, Lauren's hand dropped from the doorknob. Grock the clown was out there, not a face she enjoyed encountering alone.

Lauren moved to the window seat where she could look out at Lake Geneva and the Savoy Alps of southeastern France. Unhooking the latch brought in a crisp breeze. Her thoughts turned to love. Poor Mary Shelley. No woman wanted to share.

Lauren wondered if Paul was dating a Swiss girl.

Would he have asked her out if he were?

At 7 p.m. Dominick was due to arrive and Paul was going to the Château de Chillon—unless Paul passed by at 7 p.m., as earlier arranged.

Would it look to him like she was flirting with Dominick?

Lauren paced to the opposite side of the room, turned, paced back. The confusion she felt might be similar to that felt by Mary Shelley in Switzerland when the future authoress found herself surrounded by Percy, Lord Byron, and Claire Clairmont, Mary's step-sister. Claire had accompanied Mary and Percy because she was in love with Byron. Claire had hysterics about Byron every day.

Friends could be burdensome. Rachel didn't have hysterics, but she was sort of a control freak. She was also kind, loyal, and funny.

A sparrow on the window ledge tapped its beak on the glass.

"Was it you I heard?"

The bird turned its little beak towards the estate wall as if looking for its mate. It turned back and tapped again on the glass, then looked up at her with its tiny head cocked. Once more it turned to look at the wall.

Lauren peered in the same direction. Her heart skipped a beat. She recognized the lady standing there. It was not a phantom Mary Shelley but a real Mlle Schwartz.

While both women were dead, the sight of Mlle Schwartz came as a shock. Lauren had not been thinking of her at all—unless subconsciously?

The teacher looked up at Lauren's window with wide eyes, mouth moving with unheard words. By degrees, she faded. So did the bird.

Lauren's gaze scoured the trees and the sky. Everything was normal if normal could be described as an absence of sparrows and dead teachers.

Shaken, Lauren opened the room's small refrigerator. A stash of Swiss Frey chocolate bars sat stacked on the top shelf. Rachel must have put them there. Lauren pulled one out. She hadn't had much to eat since breakfast— and a few bites of lobster salad for lunch.

She looked outside, saw no one, not even a bird. Lauren threw herself on the bed and ate a segment of the chocolate. It reminded her of the first Swiss chocolate she ever tasted, also provided by Rachel.

#

They were seated across from one another at a long, rectangular table in the school's dining room. The girls seated at the same table conversed in Spanish.

Rachel smiled at Lauren and asked, "You speak English?"

"Yes. I'm American."

"Same here. I'm from New York."

"California."

They shook hands across the table, exchanging names. The other girls stared.

"Are we being overly formal?"

"I haven't a clue," said Rachel. "Wait till you see the way dinner is served. It's different."

"How?" Lauren took a slice of French bread from the loaf in the bread basket and applied butter.

"The salad will come after the main course."

She was right. There was dinner, followed by salad, and then a wiggly gelatin dessert. Rachel tapped it with her spoon and the gelatin danced. Lauren asked the other girls where they were from. They named South American countries; then they reverted to Spanish.

"Someone at our table called us *'loca'*," Lauren said to her new friend on the walk back to the bedrooms. "What did we do that was crazy?"

"I suspect it was meant as a compliment."

When they got up to the first floor, a big girl with black hair and multiple face piercings was visible through a wide-open bedroom door. She was surrounded by mounds of pink pillows. Two girls flanked the doorway.

"A poster bed!" exclaimed Lauren.

"Please come in," said a petite brunette. "My name is Marisela and this is Carmen."

Carmen had frosted streaks in her shoulder-length hair. "We are from Venezuela," she said. "Would you like a caramel?"

Lauren and Rachel each took one from the box held out. Lauren found hers as hard as a rock.

The big girl in the poster bed did not look up. She wore headphones.

"This is the last day they let us watch movies in any language but French," confided Carmen. "Then if the teachers catch us watching movies in another language, we have to pay fifteen Swiss francs. Do you like the way I did my hair?"

"Did you do it yourself?" The hard caramel lodged inside Lauren's cheek made her words inarticulate. She looked for a wastebasket.

"Yes, I did."

Rachel spit the glob into her hand. "I just had my teeth straightened. So how can the teachers tell what language the movie is in if someone's wearing headphones?"

"They pull out the plug, fool," yelled the girl on the bed. She had detached the earphones and now ripped the plug out of the laptop. The volume blasted.

"Let's go," said Rachel, taking several steps towards the door.

"Wait—I didn't see you at dinner!" barked the black-haired girl.

Lauren's instinct was to walk right out as her friend had started to do, but Rachel had halted.

"We didn't see you either," said Rachel.

"That's because I took dinner in my room." The girl said with a snicker, turning down the volume.

Carmen and Marisela smiled at one another, but not much.

"We shouldn't have come in here and bothered you," said Lauren.

"Spoken like a smart moron, diddly doll face."

"Helena," began Marisela, "You might—"

"You spoke *my name!*" the big girl shrieked, cheeks turning red. "I am the only one who can tell people my name. Idiots! Leave me alone when I watch a movie. Got it? *Good, get out!*" She put her earplugs back in, reconnecting to the jack.

Marisela and Carmen exchanged a glance. Lauren was shocked. Why did they hang around such a person?

Lauren approached the poster bed and placed her hand over the screen.

"What the—!" The girl looked up.

"Why are you so insulting? We'll be polite to you and we expect the same in return."

"Or you'll call your mommy?"

"You don't know much about negativity, do you? It will come back and eat you alive."

Stunned by her own nerve, Lauren removed her hand from the laptop screen. She couldn't believe this girl—Helena—hadn't punched her. A handprint remained on the screen.

Helena found her voice: "Thanks for the advice, Einstein. I'll give that consideration."

Lauren hardly remembered getting down the corridor to Rachel's room.

"A few of these students have their own jets," said Rachel, lighting up a cigarette behind the closed door. "Or rather, their families do."

"I didn't come here for this." Lauren meant the treatment received from Helena, but Rachel seemed to think the reference was to cigarette smoke, for she opened a window. Lauren felt too agitated to explain. She wanted to be alone.

"Wait! You're upset!"

Lauren descended the staircase to the headmistress's office. She knocked so long and hard her knuckles began to hurt.

Then an adult was at her side, Mlle Schwartz. With French words, the lady coaxed her back up the stairs.

The official protest would have to wait until morning.

Helena stood in her open doorway with the authority of a quarterback, legs spread, wire dangling down from the earphones on her head, arms crossed. Mlle Schwartz acted as a buffer between the two, moving Lauren to her room.

From the end of the hallway, Rachel watched. She must have put her cigarette out.

Lauren felt rage swell. "I won't stay in a place with someone who calls everyone names!" she declared to everyone and no one in particular.

Mlle Schwarz nodded, but her accent was thick when she said, "You sleep now." Lauren wondered if she had understood.

Helena's brazen voice boomed. "Being stuck at this dump may not be so bad as long as there are shows like this going on." Anyone could hear her.

Mlle Schwartz closed Lauren's bedroom door with a sad smile and butterfly hand gestures. Then Lauren heard her lash out in French. It might be nice to know more French just to understand what the teacher was yelling.

A door slammed.

Within minutes, Marisela came into Lauren's bedroom. She swept the sweaters off the other bed, threw them into the closet. She gathered pajamas, toothpaste, and a bathrobe out of her closet. "Sorry about Helena. Be right back."

Imagine that! Marisela was her roommate.

Lauren lay wishing she was home, in California. The door opened. Rachel held out a bar of chocolate.

"Take this. I don't like this school either, but Switzerland is awesome. Just remember that boarding schools have some spoiled brats. There are nice people too. I want us to be friends."

After that, lights out.

The chocolate bar, a flashlight and a copy of *Wuthering Heights* helped Lauren escape. When the roommate slept, Lauren got up to pad out in the dark hallway and brush her teeth. She let the water run a long time. Despite Rachel's reassurance, Lauren thought she would call her mother the next day. Maybe there was still time to get their money back, and she could go home.

Chapter 9

Conference of Doctors

When Papaux let Paul's report drop back onto Cloquet's desk, the detective had to pin it down with a finger so it didn't slide into the wastebasket.

"Well?"

"I heard about it."

He couldn't have heard Paul's impressions from the luncheon because they had just been typed. Cloquet considered the fellow's dullness. Perhaps it was a façade.

He announced the need for a walk to clear his head and found the young man trailing him like a sheepdog. By the time they got three blocks away from the police building, it was apparent some bond of communication needed to be created with this new attendant or Cloquet might do something he couldn't explain logically in a report.

An uncomfortable pressure of acid reflux under his breastbone made him decide to duck into the nearest Lausanne café. Espresso on an empty stomach had been a bad idea. A cookie would have helped, but the tin had been empty.

A glass of effervescent water and maybe a small sandwich, of the kind that was attractively displayed under a glass dome on the tables, might offer relief. The sheepdog followed him in.

The café was pretty busy. Almost all the narrow tables were claimed by people sipping sodas and coffees, eating soup or sandwiches and chatting or reading phones. At the back of the room, someone held an old-fashioned print book. Only a few clients sat outside in the cold.

"Sparkling water, please. Papaux? Yes? Make it two."

The waiter withdrew and Cloquet lifted the dome to the sandwiches, gesturing for his companion to eat. The latter's forehead softened. Stubby fingers closed around two cheese and salami sandwiches.

"What is your first name?"

The response was hard to hear due to cheese, bread, and salami gnashed between teeth, a name that sounded like a cross between Louis and Leo.

"What?"

Lucas? Cloquet shook his head. Papaux would do.

"Do you feel you understand the case well enough?"

Papaux threw back his squat head with a gulp and paused to say, "I have to stay with you. Not participate."

A prize lemon, straight off the Moser tree! The glass dome, lifted again, prompted Cloquet to ask, "Would you like to order something more substantial?"

Papaux ordered a pizza with anchovies and sausage.

"No, thank you," said Cloquet, when offered a piece.

He worked on the threads of his thoughts as his companion ate. Château Mont Rose had a nasty past that was quickly turning vile. He must have spoken his thought, "Do some places attract evil?" Immediately after, there was a tap on his right shoulder.

An older gentleman with a thin long face like a greyhound and bright blue eyes met his eyes. He wore a plaid vest and blue corduroy pants that struck Cloquet for their quirkiness.

"I couldn't help but overhear your words. My name is Dr. Roland O'Barr." The good doctor spoke French with a Gaelic lilt.

"You're from?"

"Ireland. I am an anthropologist. I have traveled to a great many countries and ventured to a lot of out-of-the-way areas on this planet. To your question, I wanted to reply that quite a few cultures, including tribal people in the South Pacific and indigenous people of the Americas, would answer 'yes.'"

"My . . . question. About places attracting evil?"

"Yes."

"Do you mean geophysical places—or buildings?"

"Both. Natural sites or buildings, misused, can bring about a distillation of evil. It is a not uncommon concept to human civilization. Hard to prove, but just as difficult to disprove."

"I am more interested to know if anyone has proven it."

Knuckles rapped on the table top. Cloquet turned to his left. Papaux paused briefly in the midst of a chew, then his jaws resumed their turnstile grinding. Cloquet found a couple beaming at him and Dr. O'Barr.

"Anthropology, you say? Do you speak English?" said the gentleman, who seemed roughly Cloquet's age. His dress was not as lively as that worn by Dr. O'Barr.

Dr. O'Barr nodded.

"A little," said Cloquet.

"My wife and I are physicists. We understand French but don't do so well in trying to speak it. Dr. and Dr. Schimmel. Anna is originally from the Philippines. My name is Hans. I am from Germany." The fellow pulled out his card and handed it to Cloquet. It read as he had said: Dr. and Dr. Schimmel.

"There is an earth physics convention taking place in Lausanne, isn't there," said the detective.

"Precisely," said the female branch of the Doctors Schimmel, a pleasant-looking woman with one long dark braid running across a shoulder. On her head she wore a rust-colored knit hat.

"We thought we should tell you that the earth breathes," said her male counterpart. "It is alive."

"It breathes? What does it breathe?"

"Don't make it too confusing for this man and his son," reproached Anna.

Bewildered, Cloquet looked at Dr. O'Barr, who pointed his greyhound nose at Papaux. Good grief, they thought the lug was his son.

Papaux glanced up. "Is there time for ice cream? And tea."

"He has a healthy appetite," said Anna.

"What line of work are you in?" asked Hans.

"We—the young fellow and I—are not related. We do police work. Fairly routine stuff," lied Cloquet. "Why are you telling me the earth breathes?"

"We overheard your conversation about the possibility of certain geophysical areas attracting evil," said Hans. "It is ironic. Some of the more philosophically inclined scientists at the symposium like to discuss the potential of the earth possessing qualities of the soul."

"Is this a joke?" asked Papaux.

"Here's the waiter," said Cloquet, noticing the young male server standing near the Schimmels. They ordered tea and mille-feuilles. Papaux, holding his second-to-last piece of pizza in his hand, ordered tea and chocolate ice cream. Dr. O'Barr sipped his new soda and asked for the bill.

"When it comes right down to it, everything is energy–you, me, every part of the earth," said Hans. "That includes oceans, atmosphere, geosphere, and biosphere."

"If bacteria can grow on an electrode. . . ." murmured Anna.

"I'm not sure where you're going with that idea," said Dr. O'Barr to the two Schimmels. "This police officer was interested in whether places can attract evil. Or good, I would imagine. I told him many ancient peoples and some of their progeny firmly believe places can attract evil and still do."

"The elements of the earth parallel the chemical structure of human beings," said Anna. "Why would the earth, then, not have a soul?"

"Or countless souls," said Hans, "like mankind."

"Ancient cultures were aware and far more respectful of that potential parallel," said Dr. O'Barr.

"We wanted to give you a scientific point of view," said Hans. "The question is not so far-fetched. There are geo-physicists who discuss the earth from a moral, even spiritual, standpoint more often than you could imagine."

"Not all scientists eschew the concept of spirit," said Anna.

"I never imagined a conversation like this until today," said Cloquet.

"Science is a wonderful field," said Doctors Schimmel and Schimmel, smiling at each other.

"As is anthropology," said Dr. O'Barr, tilting his long thin face to catch a sunbeam against one cheek.

Cloquet watched Papaux wolf his ice cream and drain his tea in record time while the scientists and anthropologist on either side exchanged their reasons for being in Lausanne. Cloquet heard O'Barr say he lived in Lausanne, and sure enough, when he produced a card, a local address was printed.

Yet Cloquet was distracted, not just by consideration of what to do about Château Mont Rose but how to get rid of the lug or fret that he was stuck with him for the rest of the night.

#

At half past six, Lauren heard what sounded like the pointy toe of a shoe kick at the base of the door.

"Who is it?"

"Me."

Lauren opened to Rachel, toting bags.

"You should have called." She took the printer box from her friend and hefted it onto the bed for unpacking. "I would have come downstairs."

Doing so would have meant passing the wax statues on her own, but Rachel would have been right at the bottom of the stairwell. This growing phobia had to be quelled.

"Too many things to carry. I couldn't reach my phone."

Lauren hooked up the printer and made copies of the script, then ate one of the oranges Rachel had brought.

At a few minutes before 7 p.m., Dominick arrived with Helena. Lauren was relieved to see them enter together. Rachel said hi from her bed.

"Don't mind us, girl Friday," said Dominick with a dismissive wave of his hand.

Helena threw herself into the one cozy armchair. Lauren perceived with regret the contents of her makeup case were on full view on the desk, acne cream laid next to the concealer. How had she forgotten to move that stuff?

"The wax displays are great," Dominick said, pulling the straight-back chair away from the desk. "Much better than I expected. Is there one of the dead teacher?"

Lauren's stomach flinched. The last thing she needed was a waxen image of Mlle Schwartz. She wanted to remember the teacher fondly, not grotesquely.

"Later, Igor," said Helena. "We have to prepare for the shoot tonight. Lauren, are you ready to read out loud? We need to hear it. Stand there—yes—by the window and read the script. Wait." Helena turned to Rachel, who tapped on her iPad. "What are you doing?"

"Enticing ghost-lovers."

"Perfect. Okay, Lauren," rejoined Helena. "On your mark, get set, go."

Lauren read for about thirty seconds.

"Ah! Quite!" The exclamation was one of many; Helena didn't clarify what she meant and Lauren, with a few stops and starts, got used to the outbursts and read aloud until the finish.

Meanwhile, Dominick considered the items on the desk, picking up whatever he pleased.

Lauren tried not to get distracted. When she put down the script, Helena said, "I like that year—1816—and the freakish weather that kept those famous people all close together. But let's leave out the part that comes right after."

Lauren's spirits sagged. Did Helena have objections as early as the second sentence?

"The queen is referring to the group having orgies and taking dope," said Dominick in an offhand manner.

"Oh." Lauren ran her finger down the page. "I didn't write 'dope'—it was laudanum."

"Liquefied opium is dope."

"I didn't write 'orgy' anywhere."

"Sounded like an orgy to me." Dominick wagged his eyebrows. The action was both charismatic and annoying.

Lauren shuffled through the papers. Was she losing her mind? She couldn't find anything like that.

"He means the hallucination," said Helena, "I want you to omit that part."

"Are you kidding me?" cried Dominick. "That was the bloody best part. Leave the tits in. I expressly told our writer to put tits in."

Rachel, head down, obsessively typed onto her iPad. Lauren felt irrational resentment at the WiFi industry. Where was Rachel's voice to help her understand what Helena and Dominick were talking about?

"Excuse me," said Lauren, "I wrote that the Romantic poet Shelley thought he saw Mary Shelley sprout demonic eyes in place of nipples. I know that *could* sound racy. That is why I tried to be careful with the wording. Here it is."

She cleared her throat and read, "Mary Shelley sat with the others in long sleeves and full-length gown, modestly dressed. However, because her husband, Percy, was experimenting with laudanum, he suffered a shock from his own fevered imagination, which caused him to run out of the room. This hallucination, seen in the person of his future wife, foreshadowed--"

"Maybe it should be Lord Byron who sees the tits," interrupted Dominick, rubbing his chin. "It's his ghost we're calling up, after all."

"I don't want to communicate with dead perverts," said Helena. "Take it out."

Lauren was dazed. "Take out the hallucination?"

"Yes. Dominick is right; it's too distracting. We are supposed to focus on calling out for the ghost of Frankenstein," said Helena, crossing one leg over the other, setting off a swinging leather boot with sparkly heels and decorative chains.

"Dr. Frankenstein?"

"No, the monster."

"Who's going to believe in a show calling for the ghost of a literary construction?" Lauren muttered. No one would have heard her a moment earlier, but the room had suddenly grown still.

"I hope you didn't write your skepticism into the script," said Helena.

"Frankenstein was a real construction to Byron—and the world," said Dominick, with glacial overtones.

"I just meant the spirit of Frankenstein's monster cannot be called because he was not a person. He's more of a—Halloween character."

Dominick's face looked as friendly as a hammer. "And little girls who played with Barbie dolls a couple years back aren't really writers even if they *can* type. Explain what "director" means to her, Helena."

"It means he decides all the details as we go along. Film is an art form, after all." At "he," Helena nodded to indicate the Brit.

"Hold on." Dominick fished in his canvas bag, pulled out a book. "I thought a college graduate would understand this," he said, waving the paperback at her with menace. "It just goes to show how useless diplomas are. Let it not be said I am an impatient man. I have no objection to giving a few pointers." He held up the book cover.

Lauren caught the word *Frankenstein* before Dominick began flipping through pages.

"In the film industry, we have an *obligation* to our audiences to do research," Dominick said with the authority of a humanities professor.

Lauren's mouth opened; Rachel's warning glance told her to shut it. Tight.

"I marked the page this afternoon. Here we go," Dominick said again, raising a finger into the air.

He cleared his throat to read aloud: "'When Mary Shelley took a local legend based on truth and crafted fiction from it, she'd made Victor a tragic figure.'"

Dominick surveyed his audience with eyes wide and brows raised as if he had made a major intellectual point. No one spoke.

Frowning, he said, "Look, Victor was the Swiss scientist who created Frankenstein, for everyone's information—Victor Frankenstein. He gave the monster his own name. My point in reading this to you is that the 'Mary' you are so in love with," Dominick raised his chin so he could slide a disdainful gaze down his long patrician nose at Lauren, "*stole* a story from history. I'll wager she took it from Lord Byron; that's why the word *local* is used."

"Do you know what the word *legend* means?" asked Lauren lightly, avoiding obvious notice of the hiss Rachel made when she sucked in breath through clenched teeth.

"Don't push me, missy. Legend is history." Dominick snorted.

"May I see that?" asked Lauren, careful to be polite.

"Certainly." Dominick handed over the book.

"This is *Dean Koontz's Frankenstein*."

Dominick nodded with satisfaction. "Koontz is a famous bloke, isn't he? More than one person can write about a figure in history. I thought you would appreciate that Koontz is a Yank like you."

"Dean Koontz is a fiction writer. This is a novel. Have you ever heard of—"

"Pizza?" crowed Rachel so brightly Lauren could not hear her own last word, "Wikipedia?"

Rachel's stabbing gaze could have killed a small pet. Hopefully, she would never decide to raise hamsters. Lauren handed the book back to Dominick and sagged onto her bed. There was no other place to sit.

If Lauren had thought her work was over for the night, she was wrong. A pizza was ordered and eaten, but her slice sat on a napkin untouched. She had to type, revise, print out, and read aloud new, newer and newest drafts.

The two producers agreed on nothing. Whenever Helena said, "Bravo," Dominick snarled, "Chick flick gibberish!" Then Helena told him he had the discernment of a two-toed sloth or she lost interest, squinting at the walls as if trying to look through them.

After the script had been so much debated Lauren was no longer sure of what was really going to be read on film, Dominick stood. "I must go downstairs and make some calls, in privacy, before we leave, Ladies. Need to sharpen my ice skates while I'm at it." He took his coat and left.

Helena pumped her chain-swishing boot in the air. "I liked your Frankenstein analysis, Lauren. It will work if we can be patient with Dominick. He's the fretful, artistic type. Sensitive. Sometimes he's an asshole, but you will see he's a dedicated director."

What an enigma Helena was.

"I also like what you wrote, Lauren," said Rachel.

"You were right. Lauren is skilled." Helena chimed in. "She's better than I remember from our English classes. Mainly I remember you both as the only true friends I had—but Lauren most of all—with occasional kindness from that shy girl, Ayesha. . . ."

"The daughter of the ambassador from Pakistan," said Rachel. "Lauren and I went out to tea with her during spring break."

Tired, Lauren listened to them talk, recalling girls whose faces she had forgotten until hearing their names again.

"Even though it was Rachel's idea to hire you onto the crew," said Helena. "I couldn't forget you, Lauren. You wrote funny stuff! And you told Mademoiselle Schwartz off in French class! That was the best day ever."

Rachel smiled like a Girl Scouts troop leader who had engineered a happy reunion between best friends forever.

"What day was that?" was all Lauren could think of to say.

"One of those days when Mademoiselle Schwartz was screaming we were idiots and imbeciles. You said what I was thinking."

"What we were all thinking," added Rachel. "You told her she couldn't yell at us and if our parents knew, they would be furious."

"I did?" Lauren felt eight years were slipping away.

The unwelcome vision of a distraught Mlle Schwartz picking up and flinging a stack of books from her desk onto the floor, then racing out of the room, invaded her brain. The teacher's sobs had been audible from the corridor.

"Why did so many girls stare at me?"

"They admired you," said Helena.

Really? The girls had looked at her like her foot had drop kicked a kitten across the room.

"Rachel, do you remember saying I shouldn't have done that?"

"You did make the *teacher* cry."

"She deserved it," said Helena. "Schwartz was a mean bitch."

Why did Helena want to communicate with the ghost of someone she thought of as a 'mean bitch'?

It was funny how people could glamorize the past. There had been little heroism in what Lauren had said, and on the occasion, she had felt very alone.

After staring at her like she was a murderer, the rest of the class had a whispering party. The South American girls got out their nail files to make use of unexpected self-improvement time. Any one of them could expect to win a beauty pageant, in Lauren's opinion.

Rachel leaned forward. "Do either of you remember Mademoiselle Villot?"

Helena cocked her head. "The name sounds vaguely familiar."

"She was not only Mademoiselle Schwartz's best friend, she was her lover. When Mademoiselle Schwartz ran outside the classroom, Mademoiselle Villot came in and gave us an assignment."

"I remember Schwartz never called us names after that day," said Helena. "She still hated me, though."

"I don't think Mademoiselle Schwartz hated you," said Lauren, a light shiver running over her skin. How unnerving it had been to imagine seeing Mlle Schwartz outside the estate wall! "Some teachers are just strict. She made us laugh, don't forget."

"I don't remember that," said Helena.

"Do you remember the day she took us to her room and showed us her sculptures?" asked Rachel.

Lauren didn't answer. The idea of Mlle Villot being Mlle Schwartz's lover struck a raw nerve. She didn't have any problem with a teacher being gay, straight or celibate—but Rachel had summoned another disturbing vision that had lain buried.

"What's wrong?" asked Helena.

"Nothing."

"Your face isn't saying 'nothing.' What's on your mind?"

"I don't know how to say this."

"Just open your mouth and talk."

"Why do you want to communicate with a dead teacher?"

"Because she *was* our teacher!"

"You hated—I mean—didn't like her. At all."

"True."

"Is your interest in calling upon her spirit solely for the sake of making films about ghosts?"

Helena pursed her lips. She looked away. At length she said, "Not with her."

"Do you want to punish her?"

"No!" burst out Helena. "Maybe I'm sorry she's dead. It is tragic to die so young, and of a food allergy! Teaching kids is hard, and I was a brat. Okay, teaching *me* was hard. I know that now." Helena's cheeks had flushed pink. "Maybe I want to say I'm sorry."

Rachel and Lauren exchanged glances.

"For being difficult?" Lauren asked.

"Yeah."

"Helena, Mademoiselle Schwartz didn't die of a food allergy."

"She didn't?"

"No. She was murdered. Poisoned."

Helena nearly fell off her chair. She grabbed Rachel's forearm. Lauren saw the pressure points on Rachel's skin go white.

"Oh my God! Why do you say that?"

"We thought you knew."

"I didn't." Helena's voice rasped. "Who murdered her?"

"That's the thing. . . ." Lauren felt another chill, into her bones. She eyed the windows, but they were latched shut. "We think it was murder by accident. We—Rachel and I—followed clues during that period."

"Sleuthing around," said Rachel, removing her arm from Helena's grasp.

"You need to tell me what you know," said Helena. "This could affect the séance. If Schwartz thinks *I* killed her, she'll never answer."

Rachel's eyes reflected the irony Lauren felt. For a period of time, almost everyone at the château had thought Helena was the murderess. Did Helena know that?

"It was the second day at school for me," began Lauren, "when I learned something about the Bonami marriage—and how much Madame Bonami didn't want to be part of Château Mont Rose. I took a book to the graveyard across the road. I was reading under a tree when three people entered the graveyard. They wanted to look at Château Mont Rose from the vantage point of the hill that the graveyard is laid out on."

"Okay," muttered Helena.

"They were an American couple and a lady with a Swiss-French accent. The American guy was older and wanted to buy the school so that his wife could learn French in it."

"You don't have to buy a whole school just to—" said Helena, "unless—oh, never mind. Go on."

"I was trying to stay hidden, but I dropped my apple. It rolled down, and they saw me—asked me if I liked Château Mont Rose. I was really homesick. I told them 'no' and that I wanted to go home."

Rachel's eyes flashed with remembrance. She gave the barest nod.

"Then the lady who I thought was the real estate agent—a stylish blonde—told them not to pay any attention to me. The couple started walking away, but the blonde looked like she wanted to slap me.

"After that, I left the graveyard because I thought I would be bothered again. Maybe that angry-looking blonde woman would come back. I wanted to be alone."

Helena's eyebrows went up but she said nothing.

"I decided to go into the nearby woods of birch and firs." Lauren pointed at the window in the direction of the forest. "I found a stream and a little, secluded patch of grass above it. I was shielded by bushes so in case anyone came by, I would still have my privacy. I lay down there to read and doze.

"But a man and a woman came for a picnic. They brought a blanket, a basket of food, and a bottle of wine. The woman had a sketchbook. The man stripped down to his skivvies and she began drawing him."

"You were spying!" broke in Helena.

Lauren felt a rush of heat up her neck. "Not on purpose. I was there first."

"Spying, Lauren!" echoed Rachel.

"They invaded my privacy," said Lauren. "I had to see who they were."

"I would do the same thing," said Helena. "Can't trust anybody."

"The lady wore a straw hat with her hair swept up under it. She was turned from me. I could see her back, which was half bare because of the kind of sundress she wore. I recognized the man, however. It was Monsieur Bonami."

"You knew who Monsieur Bonami was on your second day at school?" asked Helena.

"He picked me up from the train station."

"Oh, I see. My folks have an apartment in Montreux. Mom drove me here."

"What changed my mind about not wanting to leave Switzerland was how much I understood when the man and woman talked to each other. I understood more French than I thought I would. Monsieur Bonami said he was bored. He went into the stream, cupping his hand to get water to drink. Then he went over to the lady and squirted water down her neck. She jumped, but she was laughing. She called him '*Un monstre.*'"

"Pretty easy word in French, *monstre,*" said Helena.

"That was when I recognized Mademoiselle Schwartz."

"So what's your point?" asked Helena. "We knew she was an artist."

"The point is he put his arms around her, picked her up and laid her down on the ground. She acted like she was struggling, but she wasn't."

"You kept watching?"

"Through the leaves of a bush."

"Voyeurism," said Rachel.

"Would you have stopped?" Lauren demanded.

"Hell, no," said Helena.

"And then?" asked Rachel.

"I told you about this a long time ago, Rachel. He threw her underwear up and it caught on a tree. She started exclaiming, "*Ah, oui; ah, oui!*""

Rachel chuckled.

"And then I was embarrassed," said Lauren. "I didn't want them to see me there."

"Sure, sure," said Helena.

"I tore into a mad dash. Monsieur Bonami yelled, 'I know who you are,' but he couldn't have known. I was wearing jeans and my hair was in a ponytail."

"That would describe every other girl in the school," said Rachel.

"Exactly. The next day, when you and I were going out to La Rosiaz, we overheard Mademoiselle Wertheimer and Monsieur Bonami having an argument in the salon."

"I do remember that."

"Mademoiselle Wertheimer was really upset. She said she had worked at Château Mont Rose all her life and couldn't go somewhere else. Monsieur Bonami said he knew his wife wanted to sell the school so she could buy a nightclub in Vevey. And he said it would be over his dead body—or hers."

"So it wasn't an argument about Monsieur Bonami having sex with Schwartz?" asked Helena.

"No," answered Lauren.

"Monsieur Bonami promised Mademoisellee Wertheimer her job was secure," added Rachel. "And I explained to Lauren that the blonde woman in the graveyard must have been Madame Bonami, his wife. She was the one who signed me into this jail when my dad brought me."

Helena looked curiously at Rachel. "You thought this school felt like jail?"

"Of course."

"Me, too!"

Chapter 10

Female Passions

Lauren held the bedroom door open for Helena.

"I expect both of you downstairs, quick," Helena said, glancing back at the Americans. "I'll go find Dominick." She sashayed down the hall, chains swishing on her boots.

"Where's the rest of the crew, Rachel?"

"They're at the Château de Chillon, setting up. They needed an hour or two to run electrical cords to electromagnetic devices that record ghost phenomena. And Lauren?"

"Yes?"

"Be careful about taking dates with Dominick."

"I didn't—"

"He's Helena's."

Lauren flushed. Rachel made the strangest assumptions. "What are you talking about? That guy is the most—"

"They're a couple. They may not be in the same room at their hotel, but that's only because Helena likes her space. They're solid."

"Why does she call him 'Dumb Ass'?"

"Because she's Helena," Rachel waved her lipstick in the air. "I'm telling you this after receiving a warning from her—a text message. She said for you not to take Dominick's comments or private invitations seriously. She likes you; don't ruin that."

Lauren repressed the urge to defend herself. "It is going to be hard having two bosses who contradict each other. I swear I never—"

"Every couple has its dynamics." Rachel dropped her lipstick in her purse, smacked her lips. "Try not to fight with *him*. Fighting with Dominick is Helena's private domain. They find it titillating. If you fight with him, she'll view that as trying to arouse him."

"Oh, great. Now I cannot disagree with him without being considered competition." She considered the pizza. Even cold, it might be better than nothing.

Rachel was out the door.

"Wait; Slow down, please!" Lauren cried, leaving her untouched slice of pizza congealed on its paper plate.

Dominick and Helena were waiting in the front seat of the SUV. As soon as Lauren and Rachel got in, Dominick revved the engine and took off. The radio played jazz and no one spoke. Drops of rain pattered on the windows and roof.

Looking out into the evening sky, Lauren felt a sense of guilt. A lot of remembering aloud had gone on in the last half hour. Still, Lauren felt she had neglected to do justice to the true spirit of Mlle Schwartz. Someone had to speak up for the dead.

At 14, she hadn't really understood the teacher except to recognize the woman had an entertaining, dramatic, and often tempestuous teaching style. Lauren had learned to speak French thanks to Mlle Schwartz's efforts. Now, at 22, she felt it was inevitable that M. Bonami should have fallen for Mlle Schwartz. Beautiful, cold Mme Bonami had wanted to sell the school while romantic and artistic Mlle Schwartz epitomized its spirit.

Maybe Mme Bonami was the superior beauty in a Swiss spa sort of way, but Mlle Schwartz had been more passionate about the meaning of the school. By the time winter thawed into spring, the whole class—always with the exception of Helena—was terribly fond of the teacher, her dramatic story-telling at the blackboard, and her dreaminess.

On mornings after downpours of rain or blankets of snow, Mlle Schwartz entered the classroom with huge, brooding eyes, floated over to the large windows looking out on the garden, responding with grace to the girls' chorus of "Good Morning, Mademoiselle." Then she tapped on the window panes so that the sparrows, looking ill-prepared in their downy feathers to repel the cold, stopped worm-hunting and lifted their tiny heads at a tilt.

Mlle Schwartz could not refrain from exclaiming, as if she had never seen them before, "*Ah, les petits oiseaux*! Oh, the little birds!"

If the sparrows could take up their day's tasks in a chill environment, so could Mlle Schwartz. Opening *The Little Prince* with a pensive smile, Mlle Schwartz asked for volunteer readers. After that, the teacher commented on some meaningful aspect of the book. Her favorite subject was the rose's love for the little prince:

"The rose didn't want to be as mean as she was. She wanted the little prince to love her, but she didn't know how to win his love—so she was cruel."

The GPS interrupted Lauren's thoughts. The voice was a female's. "Turn left onto Rue du Bugnon/Route 1," it directed.

Dominick turned.

Goosebumps rose on Lauren's skin. The voice on the GPS belonged to Mlle Schwartz. Lauren shivered and zipped up her jacket, burrowing into the neck scarf. Switzerland was experiencing the coldest spring in 100 years, people were saying.

Lauren needed to keep her thoughts on the script tonight. All that talk about a dead teacher was stirring her imagination.

So much writing, trying to please Helena and Dominick, had worn down her nerves. At least she had avoided the bald lie, "Lord Byron was the author of *Frankenstein*." Lauren had tried her best to aim a subtle message at intelligent listeners.

"Merge onto Route du Simplon/Route 9" directed Mlle Schwartz's voice from the GPS.

#

Lauren wondered at the strength of the wooden bridge the SUV crossed when Dominick turned in to the parking lot of Château de Chillon. The bridge looked ancient, but it held the vehicle's weight. This time.

"It is hard for me to imagine ghosts in places as busy as castles," Rachel was saying. "Especially when the castle has modern lighting, cameras, and interactive touch screens. Not to mention a 21st-century bathroom."

"Those features are only in a few rooms," said Helena. Dominick was parking. "Besides," said Helena, "spirits aren't driven away by technology. What makes you think they would be? Spiritual energy is attached to places. Have you ever thought about how many people have died on earth? That leaves a lot of opportunities for spiritual residue."

Lauren thought "spiritual residue" sounded like some sort of thick, sticky stain.

"This castle gives concerts and stages Halloween, Christmas and Easter events. There are always people here," said Rachel. "It is hard for me to imagine it haunted. Honestly, I had to pressure the staff for a time we could come without being surrounded by actors or a cleaning crew."

"Same thing back home," piped up Dominick. "My parents live in a few rooms of the family manor. The rest of the place functions as a tourist draw and a public clubhouse. People are always around. Local teenagers are the worst, spraying graffiti or having it off on the grounds."

"When spirits remain above the grave," said Helena, ignoring the last remarks, "They are unaware of most of us, with some exceptions. They come closest to specific individuals at night, with the goal of rubbing their torment off onto the psyches of the most receptive humans."

"God, I love it when she talks like that," said Dominick, his voice husky.

Lauren began to wonder if Dominick had paid her enough. Rubbed-off torment sounded unpleasant.

"Don't worry," whispered Rachel. "All you have to do tonight is read and act scared."

"No contagious torment?"

"Not enough to insure against." Rachel pulled down her cap. "There should be some food inside. I arranged a delivery—cold cuts and such. You must be hungry."

Lauren heard her stomach growl and wondered how long it had been doing that.

They got out and passed along the entry into the first gateway, which Rachel said was 15th century. The castle was lit all the way around the outer walls. There was no Paul standing to meet them at the gateway. Ajit, however, emerged from the shadows to help carry things.

"Don't go down into the dungeon," he warned when Lauren stopped at an open door inside the castle courtyard. "It's not lit. Wait until we all go down together. Up this path!"

"Oh, right." Lauren had assumed they would enter the first doorway. She was a little distracted, expecting to see Paul every minute. He would show up eventually. She was surprised at how much she wanted to hear an apology from him for making the wax clown seem to move. She was having difficulty passing Grock in the hallway at Château Mont Rose.

They arrived in the Grand Hall of the Count, an expansive room with slender black marble pillars and shimmering checkered wall tiles. Four windows overlooking the lake were topped by four-leafed clover designs. Lauren could hear the lake water lapping against the foundation of the castle at a distance.

Dominick wanted to get every crew member on camera. Rachel had the first turn. She stood under a coffered wall ceiling dating back to the fifteenth century and read almost in a monotone from Lauren's revised text:

"Built on a rock jutting out into Lake Geneva and connected to the mainland by a wooden bridge, the oval-shaped Château de Chillon has guarded access to central and northern Switzerland for a thousand years. Erected for vigilance, security, and beauty, it was meant to shelter its inhabitants from harm and attack. What no one ever foresaw was that one day it would spawn that most hideous of all monsters, known by the name of its creator, Frankenstein."

Dominick said, "Cut!" and told Ajit to turn off the two floodlights that made Rachel look "waxen."

"Waxen is good. We want 'creepy'," said Ajit.

"I want dark and foreboding," said Dominick. "These floodlights make the women look like lemon popsicles. Dimmers are warmer."

Ajit panned the camera when Dominick pointed at Lauren. She smiled and Dominick scowled. When she went deadpan, he cheered up.

"Action!"

"Few people realize the tie that was created, on this rock foundation, between the most chilling creature to haunt human imagination and the world's most romantic lover, Lord Byron. Byron was the close friend of Percy Shelley, husband to Mary Shelley. To understand how that tie brought about the creation of Frankenstein's monster, we must descend into the Château de Chillon's formidable dungeons."

"Cut! Not bad. Your voice is fine, I think. Since you *had* to work that woman's name in, I hope we've got her tits worked in too. Which one of you gals is doing the nude shot?"

"Leave them alone, Dom-Dom," snapped Helena, from a corner seat.

"How about this: one of the girls lies on top of a wooden table and unzips her jacket. No shirt or bra underneath, leaving the jacket open. Or we can cut two holes and pull her boobs through. It will be very tasteful."

Dominick sniffed at the lack of response.

"Is it just too bloody cold for you girlies? Cold makes tits pointy and hard."

"Would you shut your pie-hole?" exploded Helena. "Try to remember we are targeting a predominantly female audience."

"We need the blokes watching as well. I am trying to save this film!"

Lauren could have sworn she saw Helena mouth the words "Don't worry" over Dominick's head.

Dominick took a few moments to watch the playback on Ajit's camera. Then he decided they should descend to the dungeon. "We need that shot of Lord Byron's signature etched into the column over there," He pointed, then asked, "Hearing anything yet, my hairy-chested mystic?"

"I hear a donkey braying," replied Helena.

"Ajit, take the rear; film us going downstairs and upstairs," said Dominick. "Damn, there are a lot of steps in this place. Who has the map—girl Friday? Keep your headgear on, everyone. No extra flashlights; the blue lights are sufficient. Lauren can finish reading the dungeon segment and then Helena will do her stuff. Let's get a move on."

"Or our blood will freeze," murmured Rachel.

"Rachel," said Helena, her voice as authoritative as Dominick's, "viewers won't understand how amazing this castle is without an approach by lake during the day. Dom-Dom, are you listening? No highway shots. Also, I am not sure Rachel should be introducing. I think Lauren should read the entire script."

"I am the director," said Dominick. "And you are the psychic."

"The psychic with the money," retorted Helena. "You have to listen to my suggestions."

"Sadly, yes. I can do that in my sleep."

"You want a fight?" Helena stalked up to Dominick. They began bickering.

Lauren took advantage of the moment to whisper to Rachel, "You should get Ajit to film the oubliette hole where people were thrown into the dungeon."

"It's covered in glass," Rachel said. "Just do the writing, okay? We already have two directors."

"Sorry. I didn't know."

"It's okay," said Rachel. "You know how many times I've been here? Every summer, growing up. Then, two days ago, before you got here, I had to come out with Ajit and Dominick for a prep tour."

"Not Paul?"

"No, I did not meet him until today, Lauren."

"Where is he?"

"God, how should I know? Maybe he got lost. The castle is hard to navigate, even for people who work here. It seems simple but it's all staircases up and down, never ending. It's bigger than it looks when you first walk in. Anyway, if you have any more directing ideas, tell Helena. Or Dominick. Whichever of the two you think listens best."

"Neither one."

"Bingo."

"Rachel, do you know if Paul—"

Helena let out a shriek.

"Uh oh," said Rachel. "She's going into a—"

"Yes!" screamed Helena, extending her hands up towards the ceiling. Then she dashed out of the Grand Hall.

"After her!" cried Dominick.

Ajit and camera followed producer and director.

"We're going to traipse all over this castle after her, that's how it works," blurted Rachel. "We had a dry run the day before you got here. It's more exhausting than going to a gym."

"Ladies, you are following?" asked Ajit, his head reappearing with the camera, which he aimed at them. He gestured for them to hurry. "Get in front of the camera!"

"You're too tall for some of these doorways, aren't you?" Lauren asked.

"I have to be careful, yes. People were smaller in the Middle Ages."

The clump of Helena's high-heeled fashion boots echoed. Everyone else wore rubber-soled canvas shoes or boots. Each member of the group—except Ajit, whose hands were full—had a handheld flashlight in addition to headgear with embedded light.

They followed Helena, single file. She moaned softly and her fingers brushed the stone walls.

"See the cameras Paul and I installed earlier?" whispered Ajit. "There's more than one type of device."

Lauren didn't know where to look.

"Green lights." Ajit pointed up at a corner.

"Where is Paul?" asked Lauren.

"He is working from the main computer," said Ajit. "We were lucky that guy on the Chillon staff, Vanni, helped us prep today. We had to move some of the wires around this afternoon because not all the outlets work."

"Talk about ghosts," said Rachel.

"Was anyone murdered here?" Lauren asked.

"That's a good question," said Ajit. "Ask it again and sound more scared."

Lauren's second attempt was drowned out by Helena calling out for Lord Byron.

"Lord Byron! Lord Byron! Touch us! Show us your spirit!" screeched Helena. She continued calling for Lord Byron up and down staircases, the rest of them following, until Lauren squeezed Rachel's shoulder.

Rachel shrieked.

"Sorry, Rachel!"

"What do you want?"

"Where are we going?"

"Helena's using her psychic powers to find the dungeon."

"I thought the dungeon was at the beginning of the castle, where we first got in."

"There are maps at the front desk," said Ajit.

Dominick's voice, coming from just ahead, sounded irritable: "Helena, do you know where you're going?"

The words "Dumb Ass" bounced against the dark walls, followed by "You broke my——." Squabbling followed. The crew stopped so that Helena and Dominick could argue.

"That settles it," said Ajit. "Let me call the night guard to help us out." He turned off the camera, pulled out his phone, and hit a name on his call list.

"I don't think your phone will work in a castle. I did pick up a map, actually," said Rachel. She fished in her jacket pocket.

"Hey, Vanni," cried Ajit, making Lauren jump. "We're in a really dark corridor! Sorry to disturb you, man; you watching football? Who's winning?

Okay, listen, we're kind of lost. . . . A number? We just passed a plaque that had '18' on it."

"It was 28," said Rachel.

"Might be 28," repeated Ajit. "The last courtyard? I don't know."

Lauren rubbed her arms. "May I see the map, Rachel?"

"We're looking for the dungeon," said Ajit. "but the clairvoyant, um," he lowered his voice, "doesn't know where we're going."

Dominick and Helena were still arguing, but they seemed to be distancing themselves to be more private.

"Do you see a numbered plaque in this room, Rachel?" asked Lauren, using her flashlight on the walls.

"No," said Rachel. "Ajit! Lauren! I can't hear the bosses. Do you?"

Ajit said a few more words and put his phone back in his pocket. "Miss Stamoulos?" he called out. His cry echoed.

There was no reply.

"Fine time for the group to get split up," he grumbled.

"Look, I'll run forward and tell them to wait." Rachel said

"The dungeon is in the other direction," said Ajit.

"Okay, you two wait here?"

"Alright," agreed Lauren and Ajit.

For a few seconds, Lauren saw Rachel's beam bouncing against a stairwell wall. She heard Rachel call out, "Mr. Bentley! Helena—Ms. Stamoulos!" The words echoed and abruptly stopped as if swallowed by the stones.

"Castle acoustics," said Ajit. "Past a certain point, you can't hear people although they might be really close."

Lauren, seated, and Ajit, leaning against a wall, waited at the top of a staircase.

"I should keep filming," Ajit said, holding up the camera. "There might be floating orbs."

"You've done this before?"

"It's my profession."

"True. You did say so at the restaurant."

"I have never hunted ghosts on film. This will be a first."

"On film, can't tech people just bounce floating orbs in with computer programing?"

"Paul could, easily," said Ajit.

"So if floating orbs are fake, what are we actually looking for?"

"I never said floating orbs are fake," responded Ajit. "Although CGI can fake anything nowadays. Miss Stamoulos, in my opinion, has very real paranormal powers."

"I think there *is* something to paranormal manifestation, but let's get real," said Lauren with an indignant shiver. "Lord Byron didn't die here and Frankenstein's monster is fiction." Rubbing her arms was barely warming her. She stood up.

"You know what I think?" returned Ajit. "Helena will end up contacting some other spirit that *does* reside here."

"Have you seen proof of her powers? Aside from the restaurant episode?"

"I saw her last year on stage," said Ajit. "She spoke to individuals in the audience and gave them messages from departed loved ones. People were crying and hugging each other."

"You seem to believe in her," said Lauren. "As long as she doesn't contact a creature from the black lagoon, I'm ready to see what she can do."

A wave of cold wafted around them. Lauren's teeth began to chatter.

"Are you chilly?"

"I'm freezing because I am not moving. When is someone going to come back?"

"Any minute. It's a big castle. Why don't you move around? That will warm you up."

Lauren nodded. He was right. She went down the stairs, stomping her feet, trying not to think of spiritual residue. She was about to walk back to Ajit, who sat on the stairs holding his camera aimed at her, when she heard the sound of someone approaching from another direction.

"Finally! Who is it?"

Whoever it was walked heavily.

Rachel didn't usually drag her feet. It had to be Vanni, the fellow Ajit had talked to. Lauren swung her flashlight beam in the direction of the approaching person, hoping she wasn't blinding anyone.

Then she shrieked.

An over six-foot figure dressed in tatters shuffled towards her. The creature's forehead went up about a mile, high and pale, eyes gleaming murky white. It hunched to get through a doorway. When it straightened, the arms reached out for her.

"Ajit," Lauren croaked. She could not hear her own voice. She flattened herself against an ice-cold wall.

The camera was working. The little green light told her so. She tried to swallow, but darkness and approaching horror paralyzed the action.

Last thing she knew, her legs folded.

Chapter 11

Collision Course

Having consumed a dinner of microwaved beef and potatoes, Cloquet stretched his legs out on the faux leather couch in his living room. Mercifully, he was alone. Papaux had agreed to go home and wait for his call. After their lunch, Cloquet had been inspired to remind him that the dinner hour was close. The tagalong muttered something about stopping at a gym and a Chinese restaurant.

The window of the detective's living room overlooked the Parc de Valency. His Russian Blue cat, Johnny, named for French singer Johnny Hallyday, sprawled half on, half off, his lap—furry limbs in a yoga pose. A detective show beamed out by Radio Télévision Suisse 1 filled the large flat-screen TV. Part of Cloquet's brain followed the story.

The rest was actively engaged with the ghost-hunting crew. Cloquet craved data from Paul and kept looking at his phone on the coffee table.

Johnny did not move when Cloquet responded to the awaited beeps and saw the message:

Strategy on dangerous ground.

Merde. What did he mean? *Come on, boy!* He couldn't text Paul back without raising suspicions with the crew currently at Chillon. Someone else might see Paul's phone.

The inspector's thoughts were at the old school. For all its fine interior woodwork and ivy-covered stone walls, Château Mont Rose had struck the inspector during his recent two-day investigation as a place gone toxic.

His hand fell on Johnny's head. He rubbed the tomcat's ears. It purred. Cloquet thought of the time he was called out on a bone-chilling spring night. Eight years ago. Light had streamed out the open front door as his squad car pulled up. A steel gray-haired woman stood at the top of the steps, folded hands pressed up against her bosom. She introduced herself as "Mademoiselle Wertheimer, headmistress."

He nodded acknowledgement.

She peered at him coldly. "Monsieur Bonami and his wife are much shaken and have repaired to their private residence."

Cloquet's eyebrows lifted. A teacher just dead, and the proprietors had run off?

Mlle Wertheimer sniffed. "I hope the corpse will be removed swiftly, for the sake of the school."

"You are worried about the resident students witnessing a traumatic sight?"

"Oh. That, too, of course."

Cloquet pulled himself back to the present. There was no point in trying to watch the end of a program he couldn't focus on. He turned off the TV, gently shoved Johnny off his lap, and got up. He had promised to take care of matters at Château Mont Rose. Better go now and evade the lug.

He threw his dinner tray in the garbage. Johnny looked up from his kitty dish.

Cloquet tossed a handful of dry nuggets into Johnny's plate. The cat glanced at the food and back at its human. It meowed. Johnny wanted wet food.

"Later." Cloquet put on his coat and fur hat, then descended to the apartment garage.

His heart skipped a beat. A dark hulk leaned against his car. Same shape as the lug.

"What are you doing here?"

"Waiting." Papaux straightened and his foot sent something rattling across the cement floor.

"Didn't we agree I would text you?"

"That's what *you* said. Not my instructions."

Cloquet got into the driver's seat with a mutter.

At Château Mont Rose, the little bell on the front door set off a jingle. "Stay down here," said Cloquet, not surprised when the lug followed him up the stairs anyway.

Surprise, the concierge desk was empty. A standup placard with a clock face read: "Will return at. . . ." The moveable hands showed 9:30 p.m.

"*Bon Appétit,*" said Cloquet.

"Is there a restaurant here?" asked Papaux.

"I was being sarcastic. Thought you ate."

Papaux grunted.

Certain doors had proved difficult during his last stay. Now with added implements to his lock-cracking gear, Cloquet moved up to the second floor. The grandfather clock chimed in the foyer.

A bump, cry and crash made Cloquet whirl, grab the handrail.

The waxen general was on its face, lifted arm askew, the same statue that had broken Katia's fall. Papaux looked at it in clear annoyance, like an ungainly bird awakened by a rodent.

Cloquet brightened. "This goes into a report, Papaux. Damages like that cost the department money."

"Aren't hotels insured?"

"A police warrant does not cover destruction of goods through clumsiness."

"Clumsiness? I didn't touch it! It aimed itself at me."

"*Pardon?*"

Cloquet might have believed Papaux if not for noting the lug's proclivity to collision.

"You think Moser will swallow that?"

Papaux looked doubtful.

"I could really use you at the concierge desk, Papaux. When the concierge comes back, you show your badge. Ask him where's he's been, why he left the place unstaffed. Then get him to show you the downstairs layout, where the kitchen is. . . ." Cloquet tried to say *kitchen* without inflection, but he was counting on the lug's appetite. "You do that for me, we can work something out with the destroyed wax statue in our report."

Papaux nodded, backed down the steps.

A previously locked door on an upper floor opened for Cloquet's instruments. The room's hidden pearls included a chaise lounge covered by a dirty dust cloth. The detective lifted the cloth to inspect the fainting chair, sneezed thrice. He prodded the cushion of the lounge with his gloved hand. The stuffing was old and squishy, decomposing goose feathers.

There was a sturdy French antique armoire that might have been beautiful if not covered in a solid film of grime. No covering cloth there.

Cloquet inserted the thin backbone of his new lock cracker into the armoire's keyhole. The device sprang teeth to fit. He heard the click, set the teeth to hold, and turned. The armoire gave off a splitting crack, like a large walnut opening. Time and weather had melded the door to the inner frame.

Tiens, here *was* something!

His flashlight outlined the contours of a human form under a draping cloth. His breath caught. A statue? Lack of odor was reassuring, but one never knew.

He pulled off the cloth and breathed. The form was of a girl in a dark, flowered dress. He prodded her, feeling ridiculous, with the lock-cracking device. The hair and clothes were stiff, waxen. But of course.

The flashlight showed the girl's eyes gazing straight out into the room, perhaps for the first time in years. Why wasn't this figure on display?

There was nothing else. Cloquet closed and locked the doors of the wardrobe, then the door to the room. He moved down the corridor.

He took the last flight of stairs, up to the third floor, just under the tower. Waxen figures stood haphazardly, sometimes in the center of a passage, making it easy for none but the slender to slip by. He managed by moving slowly, without touching them.

He had never liked wax figures. Fifteen years earlier, on a visit to London with Michèle, father and daughter had joined the queue of tourists in front of Madame Toussaud's wax museum. Michèle had seemed to enjoy the visit in the way young people liked horror films.

 Someone had scattered these wax figures about the hotel like confetti. Flesh-colored statues revived a dead building about as much as embalmed pharaohs had enlivened the pyramids.

Swiss actress Ursula Andress greeted the detective at a turn in the corridor. He paused. The bikini-clad James Bond beauty with the wax knife flat against her thigh looked like she had just emerged from the waves. Cloquet resisted the impulse to touch.

Another locked bedroom door opened. Another armoire stood next to a single bed. Both pieces of furniture were covered with dust cloths. A desk covered with nothing but dust stood against the far wall. Cloquet pulled out the desk drawers, sneezing. No hidden bottoms. He turned to the armoire, which opened to his device with the bang of a miniature cannon.

It took a moment to register the baby cradle standing within. Cloquet threw aside its lace covering and shone light upon the waxen face of a newborn. Skin crawling, he hastened to re-shut the armoire.

Who made wax babies and hid them?

The last unplumbed space was the tower. He had seen a padlock on its door during his last visit. Tonight that padlock was missing.

Turning the knob did not open the door, however, so the lock-pick had to be inserted, and its teeth clicked. When Cloquet tried the knob once more, the door opened outwards, into the hallway, leaving very little room to squeeze around.

Standing still, he noted faint light glowing at the top of the staircase. He guessed this light came from moon beams.

"Hello?"

He did not really expect an answer, yet he got one.

"Come up the stairs, Inspector," called out a woman's quavering voice. "You have taken a long while to get here."

Chapter 12

In the Name of Art, Love and Theater

Paul was furious. He pulled at the upper portion of his head.

"Leave that alone!" scolded Dominick in a cheerful voice. "We have to film more than that bit with you and Lauren. And it was brilliant. Good show, old man." Dominick was clearly pleased with the contrived disaster.

"You told me she would be prepared."

"And she was!" Dominick smoothed his sleek hair back, looking clueless.

"Hey Paul, you've got to breathe slowly," said Ajit, with concern. "You're going to hyperventilate."

"*Merde!*" Paul felt like punching Dominick in his chiseled jaw.

"She prepared the script," said Dominick. "We worked it all out. Took hours. I was careful not to tell her about you."

"Me neither," Ajit confided in an undertone. "That way she would have the right reaction. I am sure she will understand when she wakes up." Ajit's gaze was on his replay screen.

Paul groaned.

"Wish you made that sound while approaching," said Dominick.

"I just recorded it," said Ajit. "Easy to work in later."

"Splendid."

"*Espèce de. . . .*" Paul's hands went up to his neck to work off a bolt. The glue was strong.

A fellow wearing a tight-fitting turtleneck sweater danced up and slapped Paul's fingers away. He shook the riotous mop of dark curls on his head and brushed the pencil-thin mustache under his flared nostrils. "*Mais, non!*"

This was Vanni, who a second time pulled Paul's hand away from the bolt with surprising strength for one of such slender build.

"Pleeeease don't wrinkle your brow like that. Unless--," Vanni paused, rubbed his own eyebrows upwards with his right pinky, "unless you're going to film again on this minute! The director says you must be frightening. Too much frowning leaves lines. Ah, see, your eyebrow—the one I made— is crawling away like a bug. Let me squash it down . . . ."

Vanni licked his right thumb and thrust it upon a lump planted over Paul's real eyebrows. The motion reminded Paul of his mother licking her handkerchief and using it to rub dirt off his cheek when he was little. Vanni was so affectionate he looked like he wanted to give Paul a mama's kiss, too. And a little more besides.

"Don't resist, Paul," said Helena, head tilted, expression intent. "Cooperate, please. Tonight, art and spirit are powerful in this castle. I can feel a force calling me." Her body swayed like a dance instructor's. "The disembodied can misuse our energies unless we control them."

Paul would have preferred his energy to be focused on his laptop, where he could tease out evidence. He had found and opened email boxes of Château Mont Rose victims, tracing links from forums to functioning email addresses. Pay dirt was finding recent invitations sent in the last few days. He had been on the verge of manufacturing un-invitations to those same recipients when called away to be groomed as Frankenstein.

Instead of preventing new visitors and figuring out how to save the girls already involved, Paul had caused Lauren to faint. All the blood had drained from her face before she crumpled to the floor. She could have a concussion. When she discovered who did that to her, she would hate his guts. Great.

This was by far the worst idea Uncle Julien had ever had. What was wrong with the truth? Now it was too late.

"There's really no reason to be upset," said Vanni in his sing-song voice, tracing swirls on the oversized prosthetic chest Paul wore.

Paul brushed Vanni's hand away, grabbed Ajit's jacket front. "Why didn't you warn her? What is she going to think?"

"You should not worry about what she thinks," cried Vanni. "She is not thinking at all. She is unconscious. But do not undo all my hard work on your handsome face!"

"She had to react naturally, friend," said Dominick, leaning in to answer. The director's closeness brought up a whiff of garlic despite Paul's four extra inches from the Frankenstein boots.

Vanni added, "Explaining is not going to help her understand why you scared her into terrible shock!"

"Would you shut up?" barked Dominick at him.

"Of course, I shut up," said Vanni. "And I give her a little something for relaxation, in the name of art, love and theater."

It took Paul a second to register the meaning of Vanni's words.

Rachel emerged through a door on the other side of the now well-lit chamber. "Why isn't Lauren okay? She acts like she can't hear me even though her eyes are open."

"What do you mean?" asked Helena.

"He gave her something to relax her," said Ajit with a nod at Vanni.

"She was hysterical," said Vanni, throwing his palms up.

Rachel frowned. "Did you put something in the drink?"

"Don't worry!"

Everyone except Dominick turned to stare at Vanni.

"She woke up crying, verrry upset!" Vanni was sputtering. "I couldn't watch her suffer." His slender hands fluttered like flower petals blown off their stalk.

"What exactly did you give her?" growled Paul.

"A glass of port; *c'est tout.*"

"A glass of port won't hurt," said Helena in a decisive tone. "Vanni has been helpful. That is the message I am getting."

"A couple of drops of Paregoric, which is tincture of the poppy seed in the port, was what I give," said Vanni. "I had that from my wisdom teeth's removal. Then I give some refreshment. Yes, maybe alcohol, but not on an empty stomach, never, never. The nice young lady is not crying now, not angry. Peaceful like a dove."

"Shut your trap," said Dominick, "you, on the double payroll, I'm not signing your check if you yack the night away."

Helena laughed. "I wouldn't take checks signed by Dominick, crew members. They'll bounce."

"We'll get some more Frankenstein shots now." Dominick looked irritable. "Paulie boy, get your Frenchy buttocks over here. That scene was worth it, even if the girl sleeps the rest of the night. Helena, my darling ball and chain, where are you going?"

"To talk to someone."

"Not without me!" Dominick turned to Rachel. "Got a camera? Your torch? Good. We need more footage. Frankenstein, keep up. "

Rachel slapped Paul on the back. "You heard the boss."

"Remind him I'm Swiss."

"Like Frankenstein?"

"I don't know what Frankenstein was."

"He was a little of everything," said Rachel. "Like the Swiss."

#

Stretched out on a chaise lounge under a soft feather quilt, Mary Shelley blinked her eyes at the filigreed brass peacock tail spread open to shield against sparks jumping in the fireplace. What a very pleasant, protective peacock, headless though it was. No doubt getting its bottom cooked.

Mary pulled her legs off the couch and pushed aside the quilt. She put her feet on the ground and stood up, feeling wobbly. She had to find Percy to tell him about the peacock. Maybe he would write a poem to celebrate its courage.

There were still more brownies on the tray, the bottle of port beside them. Mary took another brownie. That's what happened when a young lady missed most of lunch and all of dinner. Chewing, Mary looked down at her legs.

It was a shock. She swallowed too fast and coughed. A glass of port was needed to help swallow down the lump. Someone had dressed her in men's trousers. Or—were these her riding pants?

Mary lifted her right leg. No, good gracious, this was a pair of men's pants, curiously blue, not riding britches at all. Nasty fabric, neither velvet nor silk.

There had been an Italian gentleman in the room a while earlier, before she got so full of funny dreams. Polidori? Polidori was Lord Byron's good-looking Italian physician. He never could fix Lord Byron's crippled feet but he made mouth-watering brownies. Where had he taken her dress?

Percy would know. If Mary found Percy, she could ask him to question the physician.

She swayed out of the room, like Alice tumbling down the rabbit hole. After a series of dizzying turns, she came to a halt. Here was a low-ceilinged kitchen, with a long workspace at center. For anyone else, it might have been a completely dark room in a castle, but the young woman whose bloodstream was full of a complex mix of chemicals saw pots and pans hanging from hooks overhead.

At the far end of the room sat a woman from the past (though not one belonging to Mary Shelley's), head lolling on her arms. She wore a net on her hair and a cooking apron over her dress.

"Oh it's you girls," said the woman. "You made too much noise to be cockroaches."

Mary smiled. Girls? The astute woman must have perceived she was, like Frankenstein, made of assorted entities.

The woman groped in her apron pocket for a tissue. Used-up tissues were strewn all over the table at which she sat, and her eyes, Mary thought, looked as bloody orange as a sunset.

"I thought no one else wanted to eat, so when the door creaked, I said to myself, 'It's my husband come to kill me. I had best just sit still and get it over with. Then I lost my nerve and looked up. Thank heaven, it's only you two."

The woman blew her blotchy tomato nose in the tissue. The sad chuckle turned into a sob.

"Why does your husband want to kill you?"

The question welled up from a boarding school memory.

"In revenge. He thinks I killed her." The cook for Château Mont Rose shook her head over the weight of her words.

"Where is he? Has he threatened you?"

"He's always on the grounds, somewhere, maybe at our cottage at the back. I dare not go home tonight. He's probably sitting at the door with the shears or the hoe. One of those tools would do just fine to hack through the soft skin of a poor woman like me."

"Monsieur Fourmon, the gardener? Is that your husband?"

"Who else? We were hired as a couple. I am always in here, cooking. He is always traipsing about the grounds."

Mary took over, deciding she would like to find Percy.

"Don't leave, girls," pleaded the cook. Some reasoning part of Lauren's memory knew the lady was addressing Lauren and Rachel.

Madame Fourmon continued: "Before you came in, I thought I would go out of my mind and run shrieking into the night."

Good cooks were so hard to get, and a house with a writer needed a cook. (Mary Shelley firmly took over.) She should try to appease this poor demented creature. Maybe the woman would find some lovely port in her cupboards and offer her a glass. There was a small chance she also had brownies.

"What affrights you, dear woman?"

"That murdered teacher!" said Mme Fourmon. "She was a wanton vixen, making eyes at him all the time. Didn't that puff him up! How many mornings did I walk out to fetch things that had been forgotten in the grocery order to find my old Don Juan prancing about in front of her classroom window!

"'You're going to kill the plants from walking on that bit of garden so much,' I told him. He called me a jealous old woman with no gratitude. What about him? If I weren't such a good cook, the Bonamis would never have hired us as a pair. No one wants to hire a lonely male gardener in a school for young ladies. Hiding in the bushes, fantasizing. . . . Oh, my nerves. . . would one of you girls have a little cigarette?"

"I might be able to find some snuff, but Percy hid the cigars," said Mary.

"Never mind," said Mme Fourmon. She pulled a cigarette from her sleeve and lit it on the stovetop. "Mademoiselle Schwartz *may* have died of poisoning. They haven't done the autopsy yet, but it *looks* like poison." Smoke swirled out of her mouth like fog—or lethal gas in an execution chamber.

"She died after eating the food *I* prepared. My goose is cooked." Mme Fourmon groped in her apron pocket for a tissue, blew her swollen nose like a horn.

"Did you poison her, Madam?" asked Mary.

"Who are you?" asked the cook.

Was she Lauren or Mary? So hard to decide!

"No, of course I didn't poison her," said Mme Fourmon. "I was too busy making a feast to think about poisoning someone. Eggs in aspic, shoulder of lamb with fresh mint sauce, cream-filled berry tarts to please Madame Bonami. Did you know she is diabetic? I had to make her mint sauce and tarts differently from the rest. Monsieur Bonami provided the sweetener; he always does, orders it special for his wife. It's supposed to taste like sugar but M. Bonami told me it causes stomach upset for people who aren't diabetic. Severe upset. He warned me not to try it. You can bet I wasn't going to, not with a warning like that!"

Mary thought that made perfect sense.

"Imagine going through life without sugar. A person might as well not live. Then I had to contend with that bad girl, Helena, sneaking into the kitchen again, as if I don't send up enough food to her room. Why should one girl get such special treatment?"

Lauren/Mary nodded, sat down on the floor.

"Luckily for me, Mlle Wertheimer was close at hand and got that bad girl out. Such awful face piercings! I can't cook and deal with problem children." The cook puffed at the cigarette, screwing up her round face in its smoke. "Do you know what my husband yelled at me an hour ago? 'You always hated her!' I believe he thinks I did it."

"Don't say that. He must love you," said Lauren. And it was, for a moment, the most she had felt like herself in the last half hour.

Then Mary stepped back in, wanting Percy, shoving Lauren out.

"You might have at least offered me a chair."

She jumped unsteadily to her feet, leaving the suspected murderess to stew in her misery.

#

Ajit was in charge of the energy-detection equipment, spread out over at least a dozen rooms of the Château de Chillon. The device he now held in his hands had nothing at all to do with cold spots or low-frequency recordings. It was a high-tech metal detector. While he thought his chances of finding gold bullion hidden in one of the world's most famous castles were pretty slim, the quest for buried treasure was a growing addiction. He was excited about his chances at Château Mont Rose, a place where the walls might have never been opened.

Ajit had experience with the paranormal, but his attitude towards ghosts was one of secret frustration. In his opinion, the dead were generally unhelpful.

Unimpressed by orbs of light showing up on film or slamming doors that made his clients jump, he wanted a useful ghost to show him where treasure was hidden. There had to be loads of metal money boxes squirreled away in old mansions if the departed would kindly point out where.

He held the assembled detector in his two hands and scanned the wall, crooning, "Come out, O Noble Spirits and reveal your secrets. . . ."

\#

Rachel used her bathroom break to check up on Lauren and found the room empty. She looked at the fireplace, the bottle of port, the bottle of pills, the marijuana brownies, the empty chaise lounge and finally turned round to Vanni, who had accompanied her to his theatrical prep room. It was all she could do not to grab the port bottle and bash him over the head.

"Of all people on earth," she said, "you chose Lauren to give morphine, marijuana, and alcohol to. Without asking anyone. Without asking me."

Vanni drew himself up. "You make Vanni's kindness sound like a crime. Mademoiselle Lauren, she is not a little baby, yet she was hysterical. Your people scared her. I had to do lightly with her nerves. She would not stop the crying and shaking."

"Are you trained as a nurse, buddy? Lauren can't take all that. You don't know her. She is more sensitive than anyone I know."

"Then why did you let them scare her?"

Rachel looked away. "I mean she can't ingest drugs and alcohol."

Vanni took the bottle from her hand. "Your French is not so good. Read the label. This is not morphine. This is 'tincture of opium,' made for me by my good friend in theater. Morphine is for car-wreck patients in the hospital. For the dying."

Rachel felt her bubble of patience pop. "You fucking idiot. Don't get snooty with me. You can't give drugs to other people even if you do self-medicate. Some people are allergic. What if you kill her? What if she has a heart attack or gets dizzy and falls off a balcony? "

Vanni had evidently not thought of that. He used the support of his hand to lean on a table, face blanched. "She will not be dead!" he vowed. "I myself will find her."

"You had better pray she is alright or I will sue your sorry ass so painfully you will wish *you* were dead. I know Swiss law. You'll spend the next ten years in a prison. Get going."

\#

Lauren was showing Mary Shelley her boarding school, which had unaccountably swollen, snakelike, into a labyrinthine medieval castle. Escorting the great writer around was easy, given they inhabited the same body. Knowing what room they were in was another thing altogether. It had to be spring break because the hallways were dark and the girls had taken most of the beds off on holiday with them.

Lauren led Mary through the dank grass outdoors. Outside they came upon the gardener, Monsieur Fourmon, scratching at the earth. For about two seconds, Lauren thought M. Fourmon looked a lot like Ajit. When she shook her head, she saw only M. Fourmon, the gardener who had worked at Château Mont Rose when she was a boarding school pupil.

The man jumped.

"Bonjour, Monsieur Fourmon," said Lauren. "This is Mary Shelley, the woman who wrote *Frankenstein*."

Mary Shelley became tongue-tied.

"Forgive us for disturbing you, Monsieur Fourmon," continued Lauren. "Our teacher has died. We know that you were her friend."

M. Fourmon removed his gardening hat and held it next to his heart. "I recognized you as Danielle's girls."

Lauren nudged Mary and winked. M. Fourmon had called Mlle Schwartz by her first name!

He blinked watery eyes. "She was a lovely, vibrant woman, a romantic and true lover of nature." His gaze followed a butterfly that flitted about like a beam of red light.

A lump swelled in Lauren's throat, but Mary took a step backward.

"You had better get out of here," warned M. Fourmon, "or that bitch will kill *you* next."

\#

Ajit shoved the metal detection tools back into his bag. He didn't know which had unsettled him more—the freaky one-sided conversation with Lauren, who had acted like he was talking to her when he wasn't—or the gnawing at his conscience now for allowing her to stagger away alone. Clearly, she was out of her mind. If something bad happened to her, the potentially lucrative evenings at Château Mont Rose might never take place. He had to catch up.

Chapter 13

I Thought You were Dead

Detective Inspector Cloquet climbed the creaking staircase. He did not know who was up here. The female voice had been neither winsome nor ugly, as neutral as a wall. For a split second, his heart leaped up before him in hopes of finding his daughter, Michèle. Belief in the unseen offered that trap and sometimes he fell in, glad to lose himself.

Just as swiftly his heart regained its steady plodding. He breathed a resigned sigh. The many séances sat through with little satisfaction had eroded hope of clinging to a relationship with his lost child. If he was ever lucky enough to meet Michèle again, it would be in a better place, God permitting, after he was dead. A Catholic priest, a Jewish rabbi and a kind Muslim imam had all made that plain enough. His own advice to himself ran along the lines of helping the living now and not being an emotional sap.

The detective paused midway on the stairs, holding the thin wood rail on his left side and getting a good grip on the SIG-Sauer P225 pistol in his pocket with his right hand. His cane was wedged snug up into his left armpit. He could walk without it, if need be. He liked the security it gave him as a secondary weapon. As for the gun, well, he didn't really think he was going to be shot, but life was full of surprises.

He was sure the rooms in the tower were not part of the Duvanel residence. According to paperwork filed on Château Mont Rose, the caretaker and his mother slept in the cottage behind the swimming pool, once used by the school gardener and his wife, Monsieur and Madame Fourmon.

Who would Cloquet find tonight at the head of this tight staircase?

The last three steps brought him into view of the long, slant-beamed attic illuminated by no more than moonbeams. A form sat erect in an armchair by the far window. She did not get up.

"It has been a long time, Detective. Please come forward and sit down."

"It is so dark in here," he said, trying to swallow away the tightness in his throat. He had an idea of the woman's identity now, as unlikely as it seemed. In a couple of seconds, he would be sure whether he was in the presence of Château Mont Rose's former headmistress.

He remembered calculating Mlle Wertheimer's age right after the inquest into the death of Mlle Schwartz. Canton files offered a birth certificate with a date of 1902. Impossible, he had thought. She was far too fit. Someone had typed in a 0 instead of a 2, perhaps. 1922 or 32, maybe. She couldn't have been born in 1902.

"I think best in the dark."

The detective used his cane to swipe at the floor, feeling for objects he might stumble over. He came without incident to the couch near the woman and lowered himself. The furniture was lumpy under his bottom; no decent support remained. A spring arched into an inner thigh, but he ignored it, not wanting to act the role of the twitchy schoolchild. He peered at the woman's form through the darkness. Wisps of hair played at her skull. Cavernous shadows hollowed her eyes.

"I thought you were dead."

"Deceased in prison, you mean?"

"Yes."

"How morose you are, Inspector. I was released after three years. Good behavior, of course. Don't forget I turned myself in."

"You did do that."

"Thank you for remembering. I cared."

The detective tilted his head. Caring meant warmth, something she did not show. "About. . . ?" he asked.

"I didn't want the students killed. You must remember; you arrested me. I reported Maxime Bonami's plan to abandon the two American girls on the most dangerous ski run in the Swiss Alps. They were so naïve, so easily manipulated, he would have gotten away with it if not for me."

"I had forgotten the owner's first name, Maxime. *Oui,* if not for you, the girls would have perished on that mountain slope. I never understood why he found such lengths necessary."

"The fool thought they knew too much."

"Did you have such fondness for the girls you felt compelled to save them?"

"I had and will always have high regard for the reputation of Château Mont Rose, Inspector." She sniffed. The sound came out like a mouse squeaking under a cat's paw. Cloquet took a moment to collect himself.

"What are you doing back here, Mademoiselle Wertheimer? I would have thought you would go to your own family." In his head, he asked, "How can you be here alone? Who is caring for you?"

"Château Mont Rose was run by the most beloved friend of my life, Jeanne Bonami, the aunt of Maxime Bonami. *She* was my family, Inspector. She and I were very young women when we made a pact to devote our souls to this institution. Can you not feel her presence? I know she is here. That is why I am."

"I cannot say I do," said the inspector. He felt uncomfortable with the headmistress's words. He would not like to think his daughter's soul was stuck in a building, which is what Mlle Wertheimer was saying about her deceased friend. "Are you here as an employee or a resident? The legal status—"

Mlle Wertheimer threw her head back and laughed like a girl.

The hairs on his arms stood on end. Bumps rose on his skin.

Moonbeams crept through the smoky tendrils of hair on the woman's head. She spoke now in a calm voice: "Inspector. I just told you this is my *home*."

"In what capacity—"

"Inspector," Mlle Wertheimer interrupted, her voice suddenly hoarse. "Don't waste my time. It is limited. You see how it is with me."

That was what he couldn't see.

She lifted a claw-like hand. "You have been invited up here to receive a warning. Malicious spirits are meddling with Château Mont Rose."

Detective Cloquet was careful not to react.

"One evil spirit, in particular, is known to you. The murdered teacher."

"Mademoiselle Schwartz? You call her evil?"

"Yes, her *damned* soul. That is how it is when women die young, with disordered, selfish intentions."

Talk about a grudge. The former headmistress had never sought to hide her feelings about Mlle Schwartz. That teacher had been having an affair with the married owner of the girls' school. The old crone had nursed her disapproval all these years. Maybe prison had pushed her over the edge.

"You will agree, Inspector, the young do not know what we, the aged, discover. Life is all fantasy, all the waiting and dreaming. One is as alone at the end as one was in the beginning. Significance comes with a lifetime commitment voluntarily made to something greater than oneself. For me, commitment was to the purpose of Château Mont Rose, an institution built to tame girls, just as your purpose has been devoted to the public weal."

The detective nodded, not willing to debate. He had to hear all of whatever she wanted to say.

"Mlle Schwartz's spirit is not resting in peace," she continued. "Because she wanted too much. She is still here, her desire keeping her soul on earth."

"What proof do you have?"

"You think I am making up a story? Are you aware that people who have stayed at this hotel are dying or disappearing after their visits?" The old woman sounded smug.

Detective Cloquet thought there was only one way she could have come by this information. She possessed insider knowledge. Mlle Wertheimer might be going back to prison before long, despite her advanced age. He cursed himself for not being wired for sound.

Hope sprang up: if Papaux was listening from the narrow staircase, an anomaly as unlikely as global warming stopped in its tracks, he might bless Moser and kiss the lug's cheek.

"How do you know this unless you're part of it?" he retaliated. "Were the victims hypnotized to commit suicide?"

"I know from dreams and visions, Detective. Oh, but you look disappointed!"

How did she see his expression in the dark? He could barely make out her face, let alone her expressions.

"The château grants me knowledge through dreams and visions. I believe the spirit of Mlle Schwartz hypnotizes former students after they check in as guests. She curses them with her malevolence."

"How could Château Mont Rose tell you this?"

"It does. No doubt Schwartz blames former students for the frustration of her desires. Teachers are like that, easily embittered. They make the choice to educate the young, then gnash their teeth because they cannot bear the commitment."

There might be some truth to that.

"Schwartz's vain goal, to crush the school's reputation, has remained a malignant energy she left in this world."

Cloquet watched the wasted form labor for composure, exhausted by her show of passion. Someone must have told her about the deaths. She had concocted the rest of her spiel out of long-nursed hatred.

During his career, Cloquet had known people to hate others irrationally. People like Moser, for instance, denigrated the incumbents they replaced. Jealousy was ambition's fuel.

"She aims at former students," added Mlle Wertheimer, "and at present is trying to influence two who are current guests. Two Americans."

Cloquet allowed his shoulders to relax. He did not believe he was onto a lead or a confession. He faced senility here, in extreme form. The Duvanels presumably took care of her. Given her presence and the time-worn furnishings in the often-locked tower, Wertheimer resided right here. If she had lost her marbles, she constituted an annoyance to guests. Maybe that was why there had been a padlock on the tower door on his last visit. She had her bad days and good.

"On no account, Inspector, should anyone believe a word from the— you will call it 'ghost'—of Mademoiselle Schwartz. Hers is a demonic presence. To believe any messages she might convey will lead to ruin—death or worse."

This elderly woman who had once talked about nothing but school reputation and student pedigrees sounded like an old gypsy. He half wondered when she would offer to serve tea and read the leaves. Eyesight finally adjusting, he noticed a single electric burner on a sideboard.

Mlle Wertheimer leaned back in her chair and said, in a rasping voice, "I am tired, Inspector. It is my bedtime. You may leave now."

"May I turn on a lamp and have a look?" he asked, with more formality than necessary. He really didn't care what she answered.

"Of course. That's your job." When he turned on the lamp, he saw her eyes were closed. Her head rested against the side of the winged chair, a crocheted lap blanket pulled across her knees. He opened her armoire. Dresses and shoes emitted an aroma of mothballs and eucalyptus. The door to the small adjacent room was closed. "May I?" he asked, wondering if she was awake.

She was.

"There is nothing inside but an upright piano."

He opened the door and found she was right. There was nothing else save very cold walls.

The sound of Mlle Wertheimer lightly snoring made him depart without a goodbye. Her body had gone limp in the chair. He began his descent, leaving alone a woman whose lifespan had been at least five times as long as Michèle's.

#

On the eastern end of Lac Léman[1], in one of the great halls of the stone castle of Chillon, Paul watched Helena's back arch and her head roll from one shoulder to the other. He had never seen anyone bend a neck so far backward and breathe. While Dominick filmed, she continued her movements, reminding Paul of Cirque de Soleil contortionists or, more to the point, traffic victims whose lifeless bodies sometimes resisted extraction from automobiles squashed into accordion shapes.

Struggling with disgust, Paul wondered if Helena's head were unscrewing and might soon drop to the floor.

"The medium is channeling," said Dominick.

So that's what it was. During the three days Paul had walked, run and climbed after Helena, he had known she was physically fit, but he had not suspected this level of suppleness and control. Perhaps people had to be athletes for spirits to use them? Dominick's tongue ran over his lips while filming. Here was a director who appreciated weirdness.

"Ask her a question!" he commanded.

"Who are you?" asked Paul.

Helena straightened. Head high, she walked rigidly in the direction of a window. She pivoted. "*Bonjour, Mesdemoiselles!*"

Paul lifted his eyebrows, displacing the moving bug.

Good Morning, Young ladies? Where did Helena think she was?

"I have a lesson for you. Be attentive." Helena said primly. Her French was clear and articulate. Paul had not once heard Helena speak with an accent this good. She preferred English, and her Greek origin was always apparent.

"Girls, you must memorize my words and follow the instructions precisely."

"*Oui, Madame,*" Dominick cheeped.

---

[1] Lake Geneva

"I am *Mademoiselle* Schwartz," corrected Helena. "And I am addressing two individuals in particular."

Paul didn't feel she meant Frankenstein's monster and a cheesy director. He watched Helena reach upwards with her index finger to trace letters upon a window pane. The writing went slow and was impossible to make out.

To fill in the gap, Dominick panned the camera to the monster, Paul, who did nothing.

Dominick snorted in frustration, panned back to Helena. She pointed at whatever invisible message she had just written.

"Follow these instructions and you will not come to harm. *La leçon est terminée,*" she said, and with the briefest smile, crumpled.

"Bloody hell," cried Dominick. "Go on, Frankie, take my camera and find the others." He placed the camera on the wooden table and dropped to his knees by Helena. "We'll be along as soon as she can stand and walk—if we're lucky. Last time she fainted on a stone floor, she sprained her ankle."

"Okay."

"Hold on, new plan! It looks like she'll be out for a long time." In proof, Dominick pulled up one eyelid on the unconscious woman, shaking his head. "You find the others and tell them to wrap up whatever they are doing, and then wait for me or for you in that makeup artist's room. After that, you get your arse back here on the double and help me carry her. Got it, Frankie?"

"Uh-huh. And my name is Paul."

#

Ajit was on the chase. He was amazed at how swiftly Lauren covered ground without any helmet on her head, which meant without a light. If she had a torch, or "flashlight" as the two American girls kept calling torches, hers was not on. She had rushed into the dark like a bat. He, conversely, found himself stumbling, in spite of the light on his cap and the one in his hand, over the wiring lines he and Paul had unrolled hours earlier when daylight from the castle windows made it possible to work in each room.

The few times Ajit caught up to the sound of the young woman's footsteps, feeling sure she was but a foot or two ahead, he would reach out and find nothing. Then taps or steps echoed from a new direction. Sound bounced in the castle, confusing him.

"Wait for me, okay?"

No answer.

Women. You couldn't reason with them, sober or st̶o̶. ̶ felt ready to give up when he caught sight of Lauren passing under a̶.̶

"Dammit! I mean, Miss, aren't you cold? Stop! Lauren. . . ."

Ajit rushed after her and found himself alone at the top of a descending staircase. Frigid air rushed up, seeping through his clothes. The stairwell ceiling was an arch; he could reach up and touch the icy stones. From the darkness below, he heard the waters of the lake hitting against the castle foundation.

It was the jailors' entrance to the dungeon. Bitter chill clung to the stale exhalations from this place of former despair. Ajit's ears pricked at a shuffling of feet, and he saw a small orange glow in the gloom. Finally! She had turned on her torch.

"Hello down there. Lauren?"

The orange glow bobbed.

He was about to descend when a voice behind him called out,

"Caretaker! I have need of your assistance!"

He turned around. Here was Lauren.

"Will you help me find my husband?"

Her words didn't make sense, but it was her.

"I will remunerate you for your trouble."

The hairs on the back of Ajit's neck bristled. A quick glance down the staircase revealed nothing. No orange glow, nothing but inky darkness.

Worse, it took energy to wrest his seemingly cemented foot from the first step of the staircase.

Flipping ghosts.

"Yes, I'm coming," he called, irritated to see she was already far up the path.

#

Meanwhile, Ajit's abandoned black bag of equipment waited in the empty chamber above. The zipper opened and shut. One floor higher, unmanned cameras in ancient servants' quarters caught orbs of light, floating without purpose.

In the Great Hall, whispered children's voices spiked the auditory recorder.

Yet the worst place, by far, for ghost hunters alone at night at the Château de Chillon, was the abandoned dungeon. There, sluggish remnants of misery, like flatfish on a sea floor camouflaged by sand, waited for anyone in search of residual torment.

#

In a distant corridor, Rachel allowed Vanni to lead her in an independent hunt for Lauren. Rachel's phone had gone dead; it was useless.

"I don't know why it died so fast. I charged it."

"Mademoiselle, some castles suck away the energy of electronics at night," said Vanni. "Give me your hand. There is a courtyard underneath us. I don't want you to fall."

Rachel let him take her hand to cross the open-air passageway.

"I can't see anything over the edge."

"Please, do not lean on these handrails, Mademoiselle. They are 900 years old or more. Maybe sometimes repairs are made. Not when I am here, though, I never see any repairs. The wood might crumble."

Rachel at once let go of the handrail. She didn't much like holding Vanni's hand, so she pulled hers away and stayed near the stone wall.

Their helmet lights went out at the same moment.

"Stay near me, Mademoiselle."

"Why did the lights go out?" Her flashlight still worked.

"I do not know. If you do not want to hold my hand, stay close."

"Okay."

She followed the sound of Vanni's footsteps until she realized he was walking faster, leaving her behind. Her heart climbed up to her throat. The world was as dark as charcoal.

"Vanni?"

"Here I am." She felt his fingers grope for her hand, allowed him to hold it. They moved forward swiftly. When they crossed short bridges which Vanni assured her ran over vast, dark space, the planks reverberated. Rachel thought she might puke.

"Are you sure Lauren is this way?"

"What?"

She repeated her question.

"Oui, oui. Time is money, eh? You Hollywood people—*impaziente,* no? I am helping you, please remember it. You said that maybe—"

Rachel cut him off. "I am worried about my friend. Don't negotiate with me until we find her. And not even then. We could waste the rest of the night walking around this castle."

"*Oh là là,* there is nothing to fear. In the morning, twenty people will come: Staff, actors, all speaking different languages. They will find your friend Lauren if we do not. Then I have to work again, do makeup for the actors. I am good at so many things, I—"

Rachel blurted, "Stop! We need to focus on finding Lauren."

"I see her in the security monitors."

"*Saw.*"

"Yes, saw. I know where she is. Where she was. Do not worry. I am sure." He gave a high squeal and pointed, lifting onto his toes. "There she is, *et voilà!*"

Rachel shoved past Vanni and ran to Lauren, who sat on a short stone wall under the open air ramp.

"Oh my God, Lauren, are you alright?"

Lauren wrested her arm from Rachel's fingers. "I beg your pardon, Miss. You are wearing pants."

"Lauren, it's me, your best friend. At least in Switzerland, I am."

"Claire?" asked Lauren, sounding huffy. "My best friend? You always say that but it really isn't so. You seduced Percy. Now you're after Lord Byron, and to be blunt, he doesn't want you. No, I would not say you are my best friend."

Rachel turned to Vanni. "Oh, Crap. She's lost her mind. She thinks she's Mary Shelley. It's your fault, you idiot."

"Who is Mary Shelley?"

"A famous author from the 19th century. Lauren was writing about her."

"Why, thank you," said Lauren. "You do me too much credit. I'm really not famous."

"How much stuff did you give her?"

"I feel rather dreadful," said Lauren, holding her stomach.

"You need to lie down," said Rachel.

"I need Percy." Lauren covered her face with her hands and slumped. Her plaint was muffled: "I have been grossly affronted. Someone has taken my dress. And yours too, it would seem."

There was a short bout of weeping, then Lauren looked up at Rachel. "I am with child and my husband doesn't even know."

"Um, *Mary*, I don't think you're pregnant."

Lauren's reaction was violent. Her spine straightened and she cried, "The impertinence!"

"Okay, okay, maybe you are. If you'll please sit here, calm, with this gentleman—"

"Dr. Polidori?"

"As good a name as any. You sit here like a good girl with him and—"

"Lord Byron's doctor. Claire, you always forget the names of the men who won't paw you."

"Yes, well, we'll talk about that later. If you stay with . . . Dr. Polidori," Rachel pulled Vanni forward, "I will go get Percy. Your husband, the great poet, right? Just don't move. Polidori—"

Vanni grinned. "I am Polidori?" He seemed amused.

"Yes. Can you do that? I'll be right back. Give your flashlight to me."

Vanni handed over his flashlight and sat down close to Lauren. "Do not be sad, Mademoiselle," Rachel heard him say. "I, Dr. Polidori, will sing for you."

Chapter 14

Hide and Go Seek

Intent on Dominick's most recent command, Paul clumped along faster than he probably should have on such unwieldy lift boots. He almost ran into Rachel, despite the fact she carried two flashlights. They halted just before colliding.

"There you are!" Rachel sounded relieved. "Paul, you must help Lauren. In Vanni's makeup room. Can you come with me? No wait—in about ten minutes? I have to get her there first."

"Of course. What's wrong?"

Rachel aimed the light at his face. He tried to smile diplomatically and felt his eyebrows wobble.

"Lauren is out of her mind. It is Vanni's fault, but I think you can help. After I get her back to the makeup room, wait about ten minutes before you come. Knock first. We'll sneak you in and get you cleaned up. Lauren really shouldn't see you again as Frankenstein. You look too gross."

Perhaps the smile hadn't helped.

"I don't know how long you're going to be able to hide my identity as the monster," Paul said. "She's bound to find out it was me."

Rachel's light was blinding him. He squinted. The fake stitches dug into his skin.

"The Frankenstein act wasn't my idea," Rachel said. "You think Lauren will be happy with *me* when she discovers I allowed her to be terrified out of her skull, possibly causing lifelong scars?"

Here was a nasty forecast.

"If you thought scaring her would cause lifelong trauma, then why—"

"How the hell was I supposed to know you would be so good at frightening people?"

Damn.

"On the other hand," said Rachel, "It is possible she will never remember how terrorized she was this evening."

"How could that happen?"

"She could go into denial."

"The event is on film," Paul reminded her. "To be aired internationally."

"True." Rachel finally dropped the light beam. "But it won't be aired for a while," she said, "and Dominick might not use that part."

Paul gave a bitter laugh that ricocheted against the corridor walls. "I think that's exactly the kind of scene Dominick will keep."

"Shhhh! If you help me with Lauren, she might forgive you for scaring her *if* she ever finds out. Now I need you to play a romantic role."

"*I'm* not the one who should be forgiven." Paul retorted. He suddenly realized what Rachel was asking. "I thought you disapproved of me as a romantic interest for your friend."

"I said 'play' a romantic role, as in make-believe."

"Will Lauren appreciate make-believe in the morning?"

"You sure are touchy. Did you have a hard childhood or something?"

Paul held his tongue. "Listen, Dominick says we are done for the night, but he needs my assistance carrying Helena. If you will be so kind as to take his camera, I'll finish up with him and then return to the makeup room."

Rachel took the camera, not asking what was wrong with Helena. No love lost there.

"Meet you in Vanni's room in ten to fifteen minutes, then," she said, leaving him alone in the dark.

Paul couldn't find Dominick or Helena where he had left them. He circled out through the courtyard and saw the director, struggling with a still-unconscious Helena in his arms. Paul grabbed her under one armpit.

"Bloody hell! Take the legs if you don't mind."

Paul lifted Helena's muscular legs. She was probably a couple inches shy of six feet. Only with platform shoes had Paul been able to look Helena and Dominick level in the eyes. Still wearing the wretched high shoes, he stepped cautiously.

Paul helped one employer transport the other down to the front gate of the Château de Chillon. They crossed over the small bridge leading to the parking lot and stopped at the SUV, breathless.

"There is a key in my left jacket pocket," said Dominick. "Let down her legs, get it out and open the door."

Paul unzipped the pocket, found the key and pressed the remote button.

"Now recline the passenger seat."

Paul did so.

"Get her legs again."

Huffing once more, Dominick staggered forward with the unconscious woman, setting her partially onto the seat.

"Crawl in from the back and pull her up. So we can get the door closed."

Paul crawled in, grasped Helena under the armpits and pulled as Dominick shoved.

"I hope she's not hurt," said Dominick, when Helena was in. "I would say it was a great night. We got some unbeatable footage." He looked into Helena's face, brushed her hair back.

"Balls, she's still unconscious. I'd better get her to a clinic. There's the other car for the rest of you."

"Do you know where the nearest clinic is?" asked Paul.

"I have the address stored on the GPS."

Paul's opinion of Dominick crept up a notch.

"She's always hurting herself when she channels."

"Then she should stop."

"Not my golden goose! She knows the risks and injuries that come with spook territory."

Paul's opinion slid back down.

"Tomorrow, Bloke," called Dominick from the open car window. The SUV ground over the asphalt and screeched off to the highway.

Paul turned around to walk back into the castle and his eyes froze on the car he and Ajit had driven—their shared car. The lighting around the walls of the Château de Chillon bounced a glow upon the dark lake water and the car, and helped to define the glimmering form of a lady.

Where had she come from? The lady looked as if she had stepped out of an old black-and-white silent movie.

Nausea unsettled Paul's gut. He could see through her.

She stood erect, chin high, hair swept up on her head with two gold combs gleaming in the coils of the tresses. Her filmy dress stopped at the knees. Shadows stood in for eyes. She didn't open her mouth, didn't move. Paul's queasiness increased.

He took a step forward. Then another. Her image grew grainier. His hand touched the car hood. She disappeared.

"What the?"

Paul clopped around to the back of the car, got on his knees, peered under. His stomach settled, but his heart sank. He walked to the lakeside. There was nothing on the water, no floating dress. He beamed his flashlight at the surface, looking for bubbles.

Not a trace.

Lake water lapped at the foundation stones of the great castle, but no cry for help thrust itself up with the sloshing waves. Paul cast one look over the lake and gave up. He had heard of police officers developing psychological problems. Still, he had not expected them so early in his career. He clumped back into the castle, where the thick walls deadened all sound.

At his knock, Rachel cracked open the makeup room door.

"I'm here."

"You look like hell. Come closer."

Paul shuffled forward.

"Lauren thinks she's Mary Shelley," Rachel whispered.

"Who?"

"That's what Vanni's drugs did to her."

Rachel sounded angry. Maybe he shouldn't ask who Mary Shelley was.

"What do you want me to do?"

"I want you to wait three minutes so that we can move her to the poster bed with the curtains, which I will close. That way we can sneak you past so Vanni can get you out of makeup and costume, back to normal. After that, you play along."

"Play along. How?"

"Call Lauren 'Mary' for starters. Act like you are in love with Mary."

"You don't want Lauren to remember who she is?"

"I know what I'm doing," said Rachel glaring.

"Who is Mary?"

"Weren't you listening when Ajit filmed Lauren's introduction in the Count's Grand Hall? He said you were watching us via computer."

"That must have been the same time Vanni was doing this to me." Paul lifted his ragged-coat monster arms.

"Hmph. Mary Shelly *was* the author of the novel *Frankenstein*—the writer who dreamed you up." Rachel snickered.

"How is that funny?"

"You don't look like any woman's dream man."

Paul narrowed his eyes.

Rachel resumed, "Lauren is sensitive to substances like alcohol. She rarely takes a sip of something alcoholic and she's allergic to some medicines. Whatever Vanni gave her may be too much for her to recover from. What will I tell her folks if she suffers permanent brain damage? I might have Vanni arrested."

"The Swiss police won't help you," Paul blurted. "It is not as easy as you think. Our country has twenty-six different drug policies, one for each canton."

"Twenty-six?"

"Each canton votes on its own policies. Besides, Switzerland has embraced the four pillars."

"What are you talking about?"

"It is a drug policy that has helped reduce dependence by de-criminalizing usage and approaching addiction therapeutically."

"Vanni gave an innocent girl hallucinogenic drugs!" Rachel's face reddened.

"Vanni gave his prescription drug to a girl who accepted it. No judge will blame him." Paul could tell that was not what Rachel wanted to hear. "Look—I promise to call Lauren 'Mary' tonight."

"Thank you," said Rachel in a curt voice.

The sound of weeping swelled from inside the room.

"Your name is Percy Shelley; that's Mary Shelley's husband. 'Mary' wants 'Percy' to come to her. That is why she's crying," explained Rachel. "There's a chance Lauren might accept you in that role after you get cleaned up."

"Is Percy a nice guy? I won't be another monster."

"Percy Shelley was a famous poet."

"I don't write poetry."

"Did I ask you to?" Rachel rolled her eyes. "God, I need a cigarette. Just pretend to be Percy Shelley for one night. Try to leave a good impression so she doesn't have nightmares for the rest of her life. Because if she does, that will be *your* fault. I'll be right back." Rachel slammed the door.

Paul gave a low Frankenstein growl.

#

Minutes later, Vanni was stripping clothes and goo off of Paul in no particular order. He liberally applied baby oil, dropping used cotton balls onto the floor. Soiled balls dotted a pile of rags, clothes, and plastic neck bolts lying upon on a drop cloth on the floor.

"Hurry!" hissed Rachel through the archway. "I said Percy is worried about her."

That was not far from the truth. Paul hoped he would never have to hear a young woman go into blind, shrieking hysterics at his approach ever again.

"*Mon cher*," murmured Vanni, his breath tickling Paul's ear, "Why not step into my portable bathing tub? I have hot water. It's a wonderful experience, *à la médiévale*. You may bathe like a king of the Dark Ages. I will rub the stitches and bloody spots off with a soft washcloth and baby oil."

"We don't have time for him to take a bath," snapped Rachel, who was listening.

"Do you want Mary Shelley to see her Percy with blood stained into the skin of his neck?" asked Vanni indignantly.

"You mean the red stains won't come off?" Paul peered into the mirror.

Rachel poked a finger into Vanni's chest.

"Do you know how much trouble you are in, Mister? For giving drugs to my friend?"

"I give you the word of Dr. Polidori—she will be fine by morning!" Vanni lifted his brows imploringly at Paul.

"I don't need a bath. I can get one at home."

"Our pretty boss says 'fast.' You need my hands to clean away the glued-on stitches—"

"Listen, Monsieur Whatever-your-last-name-is," cut in Rachel.

"Bombello," said Vanni.

"Bombello. Stop schmoozing and *leave Paul alone.*"

Paul appreciated Rachel a bit more.

Vanni sucked in a breath. "I have been *most* helpful to Monsieur Paul and Mademoiselle Lauren. You *need* a makeup artist! I can make any one of you into an angel or a – a dragon – just like in the movies."

"We aren't going to need a dragon."

"Monsieur Dominick wanted a Frankenstein. Always he will want someone to look very sad or more beautiful." Vanni talked with his hands, and one fluttered to Paul's head where it got batted away.

"*Scusa*! If Paul does not wish me to help, he can be alone. But it will take him longer. He needs. . . ."

"Would you shut up?" Rachel yanked Vanni away by the arm.

Paul made haste.

#

In the cottage behind the swimming pool of the Château Mont Rose estate, Virginie Duvanel sat up in her bed, brow furrowed. The clock read 2 a.m. Sounds from the sitting room made her grope for her bathrobe in the dark.

She grabbed an iron rod in one hand, just in case the noises weren't being made by Jean.

Out in the corridor, she breathed easier. There was nothing to fear. Virginie's once-lethargic son was awake, seated on the stool placed in the middle of the sitting room, working on his project.

"You should be sleeping, Jean. Do you expect me to staff at 8 a.m. all by myself?"

"I'll do it. Don't I always?" Jean's pile of wax, into which he had worked pigment and resins, was heaped over two cookie sheets, one on the floor and one close to his reach on a small table. Before him was a life-size armature of a female figure, the layers composed of wax kneaded onto plaster-soaked burlap draped over wire mesh.

"Mademoiselle Wertheimer has not decided about the others you made yet. Why not wait for her decision?"

"It's not up to her," said Jean. "The château needs these."

Was the château talking to *Jean*?

"I had a vision." The stool creaked as Jean shifted his weight to turn towards his mother. "I saw a female warrior from Greek mythology."

Virginie did not believe in a "vision" inspired by the movies. The Grecian face staring over her head seemed familiar. She wanted to go back to bed.

"You know you've been smearing wax into the carpets?"

Jean snorted.

A wave of indignation swept over Virginie, leaving her drained. The effort to keep the château clean took a great deal of energy. "You could help me polish, clean—instead of wasting your time with all this."

"I understand. You need more help."

"Yes."

"It will come. Patience, *Maman*."

Nothing worse than a know-it-all child. Jean was a dear boy, but he was, *après tout*, a boy. Fortunately, the château tolerated him. Little did he know how lucky he was not to have been aborted by his silly teen mother.

"You'll sleep soon?"

"Of course. Just a little longer, then I'll go to bed."

Virginie felt eyes burn into her back as she retreated to the bedroom. Pivoting on a whim, she saw Jean's shifting derriere under the creaking stool. He faced away. The only other pair of eyes in the room belonged to the waxen Greek woman.

#

Drifting in and out of sleep, Mary had worked herself into what her philosopher father would have termed "a state." She felt overwhelmed by all the tragedy in life, culminating in her solitary situation (alone with a bunch of friends who, in their unquenchable egotism, marred what should have been a delightful stay in Switzerland). She could barely see Percy for the tears in her eyes when he finally appeared next to her on the medieval bed.

"Darling," she said, lifting her head. "You took so long! I thought you had left me for. . . well, it doesn't matter. I know what happened."

"You do?" asked Percy.

"Yes, Percy. She *does*," came Claire's voice from behind the curtains at the foot of the poster bed. "Give Mary some Kleenex."

Mary wondered what Kleenex was. A handkerchief was what she needed.

"What?" asked Percy.

"Tissues."

"Oh." Percy pulled one from a fancy box. "Here you are."

She took the peculiar soft paper and dabbed her eyes. Percy had returned! He ran away so often. All kinds of people—creditors, admirers, and wanton strumpets like Claire—pestered him, chased him away from her. If only Papa would make a healthy bank transfer, then Percy would not be hounded like this.

Yet here he was, and he loved her. He wrote to her once or twice a day when they were not together, on paper (stronger than that limp thing soaked now with tears) filled with verse and eloquence. His heart was hers. Tears welled up again.

Percy wiped her cheeks with another limp paper. "Don't cry."

"Oh, my darling!" Mary sat up, rested her head on Percy's chest and heard the beat of his heart. "Hold me!"

His arms went around her.

"Percy," murmured Mary. "I sorrow that your wife killed herself. You must feel horrid. Yet. . . now we can be legally married. What joy! The mountains. . ." her voice trembled with emotion, "will kiss high heaven and the waves shall clasp one another!"

Claire's voice again pierced the rapture.

"*Mary* needs to go home to bed."

Claire was so irksome! Mary was already in bed. She glanced at it. Admittedly not their proper bed at the rented cottage. Mary did not want to make love on a bed that might belong, who knew, to some strident person— like Claire—who might wish to crawl in with them. Mary would rather go back to the cottage.

"Let's go home, Percy," whispered Mary. "It has been a perplexing evening. I am so sorry for you, darling, and for myself too. We must console each other."

"Hear, hear. Let's go home," said Claire.

Seriously, the only way to get Claire out of the bedroom was to make sure it was Mary and Percy's own. "You'll recite a love sonnet to me tonight, won't you?" She nibbled Percy's ear, and her hand found its way inside his shirt to caress his bare chest. A wave of desire swept over her. "Percy, let's go home *quickly*!"

Percy groaned.

Chapter 15

A Message from the Spirit World

Detective Cloquet descended the grand staircase to the first floor, just above the *rez-de-chaussée,* ground floor, of Château Mont Rose. It was a little after 11 p.m. He paused at the château's empty concierge desk and saw neither Jean Duvanel, Papaux, nor any other living being. Dead waxen stares slithered down the back of his neck.

"Papaux?"

No answer. Maybe the concierge had taken Moser's assigned snoop on a tour of the kitchen? The reservation book, with its blank open pages, suggested there was no pressing reason for Jean Duvanel to return to his post unless the fellow wanted to retrieve the paperback lying in a half-open drawer. Cloquet thumbed through a few pages, dropped the book back in. Science fiction.

The Duvanels' dwelling was the cottage behind the swimming pool. Cloquet buttoned his wool coat up to the throat, tugged his fur hat down to cover his ears. These early spring nights did not yet suggest the passing of winter. Quite the contrary. He set off briskly around the side of the château, exhaling crystalized clouds.

A single lamp post illuminated the path turnoff to the swimming pool and tennis court. Several lamp posts stood dark. He directed a beam upon them, found their casings broken.

At the end of the path, light streamed out from low-set cottage windows. He shoved his gloved hands in his pockets for warmth, one clutching the pistol, and stole forward.

At the gate, Cloquet ducked under a tree. The window curtains had not been drawn. Jean Duvanel's apron-tied back was to the window. What was he doing? Was Papaux in there? Cloquet crept along the fence for a better view.

Cloquet watched Duvanel work on some sort of statue for a moment more, then the inspector walked up to the door, pushed the bell.

Heavy creaks sounded from the cottage floorboards. The front door opened a few inches. Jean Duvanel peered out.

"What are you doing back here?"

Cloquet pulled out his badge, realizing Jean recognized him as a guest. "Lausanne Sûreté. An armed assailant has been reported in the area. It is a case under investigation and activity was spotted in this garden just a while ago."

Jean Duvanel's expression was troubled. "That's why you were at the hotel? Why didn't you say so sooner?"

"I had my reasons."

"But just now activity was spotted? From an armed assailant? How come I don't hear a helicopter?" Jean Duvanel looked up.

"There are officers spread throughout this neighborhood," said Cloquet. It wasn't a total lie. Papaux was somewhere around here. "May I come in for a moment? I'd like to make sure no one has slipped in."

Jean Duvanel did not move to let him pass.

Cloquet decided to throw out his net. "Sûreté is looking into the connection between certain recent visitors to Château Mont Rose and their subsequent disappearances—or possible deaths."

Duvanel seemed as if he hadn't heard. "Don't you cops go out in pairs? Why are you alone?"

"My partner is checking out the parameters."

"The hotel is fine. It's secure."

"How can it be? No one is at the front desk. You are aware, Monsieur, that it is illegal to leave a hotel unstaffed with its front door unlocked? Moreover, there is no registered security system for this hotel at City Hall."

"The place is *not* unstaffed. Besides, I locked the front door. Only the side door is unlocked. There's a buzzer that rings all the way back here in the cottage in case guests forget and come to the front door where they can't get in. But I tell them about the side door."

"Will you please let me come in?"

"What for? You want to talk about people who visited Château Mont Rose and got in trouble with the law and disappeared? People disappear all the time," said Duvanel.

"Let's say, then, that we are talking about deaths occurring approximately two weeks after visitors *to this hotel* crossed the Swiss border on their way home."

Duvanel guffawed. "What the hell? You are giving me two different stories. Travelers who left Switzerland and died on their way home—and armed assailants in the area? If you don't have a warrant to stake out this place, get out, or I'll call the police on *you*."

"I told you—" Cloquet began, feeling foolish, and glad Paul was not there to hear him.

"*Des conneries!*"

Sheer frustration caused Cloquet to wedge his foot and cane into the door opening just as Jean Duvanel moved to close it. "I can get a warrant," he warned. "Under any pretext I choose." I want to know why you're so nervous, why you're perspiring so much on a cold night."

Duvanel's gaze shifted to Cloquet's ear. Something very hard came down, on the back of his head, and Cloquet's world dissolved.

#

Rapping woke Lauren. Rapping on her cranium. She tried opening her eyes to see who was doing it, to make it stop. The cursed eyelids were overlaid with lead. Pounding continued. Grimacing, she forced the eyelids—tentative use of the fingertips and brute determination—to break open. The lids screeched like metal covers dragged off a sewage system drain.

She winced at the stabbing pain of foggy morning daylight on her pupils. There were no curtains, nothing to close. She turned her head and the pounding continued—from within her skull.

"Ooooh."

There was a mound in bed, two hands' span from Lauren. Locks of russet brown hair cascaded over the adjacent pillow, suggested an identity. The setting was baffling. At Château Mont Rose, Rachel and Lauren had separate beds.

Surprises requiring mental activity did not help the headache. Lauren lifted her sand-filled arms, pressed a thumb into either throbbing temple. Her gaze traversed the bedroom, a job not without its penalty to her agonized brain.

"Rachel. Are we at the Château de Chillon?"

Rachel did not stir. Lauren observed that the four walls of the room did not look medieval. Where were they? She would have to muster more energy to get her friend's attention.

"Rachel, wake up. Please. My head feels like a time bomb. I need aspirin."

The mound muttered something indecipherable. How sad. What was the use of a friend who couldn't wake up in an emergency?

With a whimper, Lauren took better stock of the surroundings. On a night table, she found a water bottle labeled "Pure Swiss" and a glass beside it. Lipstick on the rim looked like her lip gloss color. She didn't remember a thing about sitting on this bed or drinking water at any point before this horrible morning.

Nonetheless, water sounded rational. Lauren poured herself a glass. Then she tapped Rachel's shoulder.

"Stop poking my boob."

"Oh, sorry! Do you have aspirin?"

"Yes."

Despite the hopeful word, Rachel needed to be jarred into locating the blessed pills. Lauren prodded, "What are we doing here? This isn't Château Mont Rose. "

The muted sound of a doorbell and male voices filtered under a door.

"Hold on," said Rachel, sitting up with a grim expression. "Good morning to you, Mrs. Shelley." She dragged a purse up from the side of the bed, shoved her hand in and stirred the bag's contents with unpleasant noise until pulling out a plastic bottle of white pills. "American." She shook out four, gave Lauren two. "Swiss probably make better stuff, but that's all I have."

"Thanks. You're a life saver."

"I know."

Rachel took two, lay back down, and pulled the quilt up to her nose.

"I don't know why you call me Mrs. Shelley. I'm just writing about her, that doesn't mean I think I am Mary Shelley."

"It doesn't?"

This sounded like the beginning of an argument, which Lauren preferred to avoid. "Is that a bathroom?"

"You would know. You used it last night."

"I must have amnesia. Where are we? Why aren't we at Château Mont Rose?"

Rachel's squint indicated she had taken out her contact lenses. "Look, you locked that door last night," she said, gesturing, "and put yourself and your husband to bed. We are here by some weird arrangement between you and Paul. I have never felt more like a third wheel in my life. I didn't get to switch places with Paul until he unlocked the door. That was probably when you fell asleep."

Lauren's jaw dropped. "What do you mean, my husband? Switching places? Is this a joke? Is this . . . Paul's apartment or something?"

"His apartment."

"Please, Rachel. Why are we here, really?"

With a sad smile, Rachel patted Lauren's hand. "You did a good job on the script, which we all heard last night. After reading it, you got really upset."

"What do you mean, really upset?"

"Um—you spent half the night thinking you were someone else."

"I don't know what you mean."

"It might be because that idiot Vanni gave you some of his prescription meds along with other stuff."

"What?"

"He was trying to calm you down."

"Why?"

"You—seemed upset." Rachel avoided Lauren's eyes. What was she not saying?

Lauren's head hurt so much it was hard to talk. "Please get to the point."

"It's not as bad as it sounds," said Rachel. "What guy wouldn't be flattered on a woman he likes insisting on her conjugal rights?"

Lauren stared.

"You thought you were Mary Shelley. And you thought Paul was Percy Shelley. Do you remember a little?"

"Not even a shred. Are you making this up?"

"No, sorry. You believed you were married. That's why you locked me out of the bedroom. Kept calling me Claire."

Lauren paled. "I. . . locked you out. Do you think. . . ?"

"Do I think Paul took advantage of the fact that you were out of your mind?"

Lauren looked at her friend coldly. "I don't like this story."

Rachel chortled. "You were ranting that Lord Byron was a bad influence on Percy because Lord Byron was sleeping with his own sister."

"Lord Byron *did* sleep with his own sister."

"I guess when a person lives in the past, as you do, realities get mixed up after too many intoxicating substances." Rachel got out a pack of cigarettes from her purse. "I think I hear Ajit. I wonder if he has last night's footage."

Lauren wobbled in the direction of the bathroom. Memories of the night before were lumbering back.

#

Seated in front of his computer monitor, Paul carefully watched two scenes he felt certain would upset Lauren.

"The one with Helena is a message from the other side. It's got to be important." Ajit peered at the balcony. "Hey, Rachel is smashing her cigarette into your balcony floor. Don't Americans use ashtrays?"

"I'd rather Lauren wasn't handed this information with her morning coffee."

"Did I hear the word 'coffee'?" Rachel stepped through a glass door. "I like this. A balcony with two entries." She shut the door behind her. "Brrr. Lauren is in your shower. I hope that's alright. And me borrowing your bathrobe. You don't mind, do you?"

"No." Paul forced a smile.

Rachel considered Ajit. "Wow. You must not have slept. You look terrible."

"Wish I could say the same to you," Ajit answered.

"Yeah, thanks. Mmm, coffee. Don't get up. Just tell me where the mugs are."

"The cabinet to the left of the window. Third shelf from the top."

"You have milk or cream?"

"In the refrigerator."

Rachel came back out sipping from a white mug Paul never used. It had been in the back of the cabinet. Dammit, why couldn't this nosy woman take one of the blue mugs given him by his mother? They were right in front.

Sitting down, Rachel read aloud from the stoneware: "D-A-R-D. Is this your special baby mug? Your first word or something?"

"I'd forgotten I had it."

"Is DARD a Swiss-French swear word? Enlighten me."

Ajit lifted his gaze from the computer screen. He and Rachel waited.

"It's a computer programming term."

"I've never heard of it," said Ajit.

"I've forgotten what it means. Is Lauren herself this morning?" Paul returned Rachel's stare.

"She has a headache but at least knows what her real name is." Rachel took another long sip. "Good coffee."

"The message on this film is meant for Rachel and Lauren," said Ajit.

"What message?"

"From the spirit world," said Ajit.

"I think I should see it first, before Lauren. She had a big enough shock last night."

"Okay," said Ajit agreeably, looking at Paul, who nodded. "The message part is freaky, especially after what happened with that—that thing I was chasing at the Château de Chillon—"

Ajit had the attention of both. He described chasing Lauren through the castle, seeing her descend into the dungeon. "I came to the conclusion that it was a paranormal entity who took on Lauren's likeness. Sadly, I didn't get any of my chase on film."

"Maybe it is just as well," said Rachel.

"However, we got other stuff. Dominick hasn't even seen what I am about to show you. Ready?"

Rachel and Paul nodded.

The muted sound of water running through pipes to the bathroom shower assured Paul. Lauren wouldn't be walking out. He settled back in his chair.

In the film, Helena made the bizarre movements Paul had witnessed in person. They watched her write on the window pane with her finger.

Ajit touched the keyboard, bringing up a program that changed the colors. "Paul did this for me. See? Helena was writing with the trace oils in her skin."

"Go close up to the window pane, then freeze," said Paul.

"It's hard to read," said Rachel, leaning forward.

"We printed out stills." Ajit pulled two sheets from the printer.

"'*À Mesdemoiselles Briant et Gordon,*'" read Rachel.

"*Quittez la Rose avant qu'il ne soit trop tard,*" continued Paul.

"Leave 'the rose' before it's too late?"

"Yes."

"What rose?" asked Ajit.

"I would imagine Château Mont Rose," said Paul.

Rachel looked down at her coffee. "If Helena was channeling the spirit of our teacher, the message sounds straight from the book she loved, *The Little Prince.*"

"How so?" asked Paul.

"There's a rose that the little prince loved. Mademoiselle Schwartz used to make a big deal out of that relationship. She said the rose didn't want to hurt the little prince with its thorns, but had no choice."

Ajit's eyes had closed. He was asleep sitting upright.

"I really don't think there's anything paranormal about that scene," said Rachel, shaking her head. "Helena was probably giving us a message pulled from her own subconscious. She sees herself as a thorny rose."

Ajit reopened his eyes, now bloodshot. "You think Helena wasn't really channeling?"

"I'm not saying Helena can't do it, but I think she fakes things at times. The voices at lunch the other day were too hokey."

"It wasn't convincing enough?"

Paul looked sharp at his cousin. "You asshole."

"Hey," Ajit blinked his red eyes. "Even real mediums need help. It is just that spirits don't come quite on command, but they DO come. Take a look." Ajit opened a different film clip on screen.

In it, Lauren skipped, then paced, to and fro in a dark corridor, turning in anticipation.

"She thought Rachel was approaching," said Ajit.

"We don't need to hear it." Paul tapped the mute button.

On the monitor, Frankenstein drew near to Lauren. Her jaw dropped. The whites of her eyes glistened. She collapsed mutely to the ground.

"Look at that woman," Ajit said, "behind Lauren."

Seated on a stone bench off to one side was the misty form, which solidified (somewhat) into a woman with upswept hair and dangling earrings. She crossed her legs.

"A white ghost," whispered Ajit. "Almost always female. Very rare. They appear when they can draw on the emotional energy of those around them."

"Do you recognize that . . . that specter?" Paul asked Rachel. He rubbed the hairs on his arms down.

Rachel, frozen, at last found her voice. She nodded and said, "Mademoiselle Schwartz."

It was the same woman Paul had seen by the car.

Chapter 16

Rachel the Inquisitive

When Lauren emerged from the bedroom, the monitor ran optical fantasies, bright lines in multiple colors making geometrical shapes.

"Good morning," Paul said, with a welcoming smile.

"There's coffee!" said Rachel, raising a white mug with red letters.

"Would you like me to pour you some?"

Lauren nodded, followed Paul to the kitchen.

"Don't use his baby mugs," called Rachel.

"Do you like milk in your coffee?" Paul took a carton from the fridge, pushed a sugar bowl on the counter close to her reach.

"Yes to milk, no sugar, and thank you." She watched him pour, took the offered spoon. "I don't remember coming here last night."

"Did you have a shock when you woke up?"

"I woke up with a headache. Thank you for the water bottle next to the bed."

"My pleasure." Paul dropped sliced bread into his toaster. "Do you want something for that headache?"

"Rachel gave me aspirin." Lauren took a sip. "The caffeine should do the rest. But thank you."

"Do you remember Vanni giving you some pills when you didn't feel well?"

"I remember a guy named Vanni, but that's about it. My memory is fuzzy."

"He gave you a mixture of things. He's talented but imprudent."

"He is the curly haired Italian guy who works at the Château de Chillon?"

"That is correct. He might be Swiss Italian. Dominick left early with Mademoiselle Stamoulos—Helena. She also was not well."

"Did she get sick?" asked Lauren.

"Dominick said she often gets hurt after an attempt to channel spirits. We four were left to get home together and you were not yourself."

"So I heard." Lauren stared down into her mug of coffee, wishing she knew if she had done anything to warrant humiliation.

"It was hard for Rachel to manage you all alone. Drugs can do that."

"I have never abused drugs in my life!"

"Some people think they're doctors. Vanni won't be doing that again, not after the threats Rachel made. He'll probably send you flowers."

"Is there anything . . . for me to apologize for?" Lauren asked, with effort.

"Not a thing. I am delighted to have you as my guest. Is the caffeine helping?"

"It's starting," she said. Paul didn't strike her as a liar. Lauren leaned over the sink to better see the view from Paul's kitchen window. Old buildings stood shoulder to shoulder like soldiers, most with wrought iron balconies and modern store fronts underneath. Ceramic and wood flower boxes with geraniums decorated the balconies.

She wandered back into the living room; Paul followed with toast and jam. Rachel talked on the phone.

"That was Dominick," said Rachel.

"How is Helena?" asked Lauren.

"She hurt her elbow. We're going ahead with filming at Château Mont Rose tonight. There won't be anyone there but us. Right now Dominick and Helena are having a champagne breakfast."

"I didn't see anyone else there yesterday," said Lauren. "Helena booked the whole place? Why two nights?" She spread some toast with butter and jam.

"Dominick said Helena wanted two nights 'just in case.' I admit I worry about cost-effectiveness."

"It's not your money," muttered Ajit, spreading jam thickly. "Why worry?"

"My job is to worry," said Rachel. "If more money is spent than is made, how long can the company last? Dominick wants to review Lauren's script before we start filming this evening."

"I haven't written it yet. Is Helena going to call out for the spirit of Mlle Schwartz?"

"Probably. Dominick wants Lauren to give Paul an outline of her ideas *before* we start filming."

Lauren put her coffee down. "How will I know if Dominick approves of the script?"

"He'll tell you as we go along."

"Most computer programmers working in film have the benefit of a storyboard beforehand!" said Paul.

Rachel shrugged.

"Better than driving a taxi, right?" said Ajit, yawning. He lay down on a floor mat, disappearing from view.

"One more thing, Lauren," said Rachel. "Dominick says not to make Helena look bad."

Lauren sat up straight. "Come on, Rachel. Get real. Helena was arrested for murder!"

Rachel was stony faced. "I know. You will have to lie."

#

Lauren and Rachel waved goodbye to Paul at the driveway to Château Mont Rose.

"Did he strike you as distracted?" asked Lauren.

"You're imagining things. Maybe he has to do a few loads of laundry. Guys hate that."

The concierge sat reading and eating a croissant.

"*Bonjour*," said Lauren.

He glanced up and grunted.

"I wonder what happened to Mademoiselle Wertheimer," said Lauren, keeping pace with Rachel's quick steps.

"She probably died in prison."

They were at their bedroom door. "She didn't check you in?" asked Lauren, frowning.

Rachel let them in and faced Lauren. "She checked you in?"

"Yes! She must live here."

"Impossible."

"I swear it." Lauren felt her pulse quicken.

"Lauren . . ." Rachel hesitated. "Did you talk to her?"

"Of course I talked to her. She didn't hear very well. She had a hearing aid. "

"You're sure it was her?"

"I wasn't sure at first. She's tinier now, shrunken and hunched over."

"So it might have been someone else," said Rachel as if they were debating.

"When did you start distrusting my ability to recognize people?"

Rachel took a moment before mumbling she was sorry. Not much later, she had picked up her purse again.

"Are you going somewhere?"

"You need the quiet. Helena wants me to go over to her hotel."

True, quiet was good for writing, but the thought of being left solitary with the wax statues outside made Lauren feel sick. As soon as Rachel left, she bolted the door.

#

Rachel stood on the visitors' side of a reception desk at the Lausanne Sûreté. The uniformed female officer, looking to be in her mid-thirties, spoke in English.

"It is impossible. There are hundreds of officers in this building. I cannot find one whom you met so many ago when you were a teenager."

"This man is a friend of my dad," said Rachel. "I have one of his cards." She passed it over. It certainly paid not to clean out one's wallet for eight years.

"Detective Cloquet used to visit my father in Les Diablerets." The fiction sounded plausible because "Les Diablerets" rolled off Rachel's tongue fluently as if she had spent every summer there. And she had.

The female officer answered in French.

Rachel flinched. Listening to the language was lovely. Speaking correctly was a pain in the neck.

Rachel mangled her reply in French.

The officer returned to English. "If he is a friend of your family, then I can tell you he is convalescing after an accident. Detective Cloquet is at Clinique Cecil, Avenue Ruchonnet 53. Will you go by taxi?"

"No, bus."

"The métro will get you there too. The clinic is an old pink building, used to be a hotel. You should ask him for a new card if you do see him." The officer passed the frayed, faded bit of paper back to Rachel. "Detective Cloquet is not head of Homicide anymore. Have a nice day."

A childhood accident on a New York underground train that derailed in the borough of Queens, New York, had left Rachel paranoid of the metro. There was no way she was going underground. She hopped a bus.

The expansive pink building looked posher than a hospital. Carrying her purchased bouquet of flowers, Rachel walked past the nurses' desk. Locating the name Cloquet at first was difficult until she retraced her path and found room 412. Rachel stepped in through the doorframe and pressed her back against the wall.

There were two beds, separated by a curtain. Male voices indicated a visitor at the far bed. She peeked around the enclosure of the closer bed. The thin man lying there was not, she thought, anything like the detective she remembered.

The male voices picked up in volume. Foot in midair, she almost fell over.

One voice belonged to Paul!

The other male voice was deeper. Did Paul know Detective Cloquet?

A cart rolled down the corridor. Rachel moved closer to the skinny sleeping man and lowered herself quietly into the chair next to his bed.

Her original goal had been to find Detective Cloquet and ask him if Mlle Wertheimer was alive, out of prison. Lauren's comment had shocked her.

Now she had a second pressing question: what was Paul doing here?

The voices conversed in French. "I do not know where--*mumble* – is," said the deeper voice. "It was perhaps he who struck me. Why—*mumble*—me? You must find out."

"Why would you be assigned an assistant who attacks you, Uncle?"

Uncle!

"Moser probably told him to put me out of my misery. I wouldn't be surprised."

"Uncle Julien, the police are supposed to uphold the law."

"People do strange things to achieve their career goals. Paul?"

"Yes?"

"Are the girls staying at your apartment tonight again?"

". . . tonight begins the—*mumble*--at Château Mont Rose."

"*Mumble?* Like in prison?"

"People who hunt ghosts *mumble mumble*. No one comes in; no one leaves."

The thin sleeping man next to her was having leg spasms. *Oh shit.*

". . . . Monsieur Dominick Bentley, your cousin, Ajit, and our three young ladies, Helena Stamoulos, Lauren Briant and Rachel Gordon. No others?"

"No one else but me."

What the hell?

"They must be protected."

"*Ma fille,*" said the thin guy, no longer asleep. His rheumy eyes blinked up at her.

She sucked in a breath.

A trickle of drool ran down the side of this old codger's stubbly cheek. His fingers reached out and clamped her wrist.

"*Ma fille!*" he crooned.

Rachel gave a high-pitched shriek.

#

In two steps, Paul ripped the curtain aside.

"*Ma fille!*" bleated the elderly man.

Rachel stood up fast; the chair behind her toppled. She tried pulling her hand away, managing instead to drag the skinny fellow up to the rail guard so that his nose pushed against the bar. He was no bigger than she, yet his grip snagged her like seaweed on a fishing hook.

"Tell him to let go!"

Paul touched the old man's shoulder. "Calm down, friend. It's alright. This is not your daughter." He had to pry the man's fingers off Rachel's wrist.

She jerked away.

"We are very sorry," said Paul.

"I was looking for Detective Cloquet!"

"Then announce your entrance, why don't you."

"How interesting to find you here," snapped Rachel as Paul pulled her past the curtain. "You turn up everywhere, just like a rash."

Paul wondered how much she was going to botch up his investigation.

"May I present Mademoiselle Rachel Gordon?"

She stuck out her hand.

"Alors," murmured Cloquet, smooth as glass, reaching out to clasp it. "What a pleasure to see you after all these years, Mademoiselle Gordon."

"Thank you. These are for you." She offered the flowers to the detective.

Paul stepped forward to put the flowers on a side table. Then he shoved his own hands into his pockets and leaned against the wall.

"I'm sorry to find you in the hospital, Detective. What happened to you?" Rachel nodded at the dressing covering half of the patient's head.

Cloquet lifted a hand to his skull. "I had a blow to the cranium."

Paul left off tapping his right foot upon the floor. "You've got a concussion."

"Quite mild. Policemen get those in the evening and go to work the next morning."

"Detective Cloquet, does Paul work for you?"

Here it came.

"He is my nephew."

"And he works for you?"

"She was eavesdropping," said Paul.

"I looked up the word on your mug," said Rachel. "D-A-R-D."

Paul wished he had thrown the mug away. Cloquet darted a reproving glance.

"Let me read the definition from my iPad. Please bear with my bad pronunciation." Rachel cleared her throat. "DARD: A terrorist-fighting unit."

"All Swiss men are required to have military training," said Paul.

"You are avoiding my question. You and your uncle were talking about us, the ghost-hunting crew. Do you think we're *terrorists?*"

"Of course not," said both men together.

After a moment's pause, she asked, "Then why are you spying on us, Detective?"

"We are not spying on you," said Cloquet.

"Some people would call it that. I heard you say we needed protection. Does the whole crew need protection? Or just Lauren and me?"

The inspector's face was as ambivalent as the gray sky outside.

Paul gave Rachel credit for managing her impatience—to the best of her abilities, he thought. She waited all of five seconds.

"If you won't answer that, then tell me what you feel you need to protect us from."

"Let's back up a little. You've asked several questions," said Cloquet, adjusting his position. "Paul is one of the most capable young men to come out of the Canton de Vaud's police academy. It is my great fortune he has chosen to work with me. That is why I assigned him, undercover, to your case."

Paul's attention shifted from Rachel to his uncle. It was the first time he had ever heard Uncle Julien praise him so unreservedly.

"If I had known Paul was a policeman," said Rachel, "I wouldn't have suspected him of being a stalker. Why did he say he was a taxi driver?"

Cloquet winced

"You didn't say what he is supposed to be protecting us from."

"There have been, regrettably, some deaths associated with Château Mont Rose."

"You mean the death of Mlle Schwartz?"

"Deaths, plural," said Paul. "And a few disappearances."

"Recently?"

"Since the establishment has reopened, some guests have died quite soon after leaving the hotel. After they crossed the Swiss border. And disappearances, since Paul brought those up."

"Those guests may yet be in the country," said Paul.

"But you can't find them," said Rachel.

"Not yet. Now would you kindly explain why you wanted to find *me*?" asked Cloquet.

"Our old headmistress is back at Château Mont Rose. Lauren—you remember her—says that Mademoiselle Wertheimer checked her in when she arrived."

Cloquet nodded. "Mlle Wertheimer is living at Château Mont Rose."

"She was an accomplice to murder!" Rachel's cheeks flushed. "If *she* is out of prison, then where is Monsieur Bonami? Aren't *those* the people you should be protecting us from? They should be behind bars!"

"Paul, pour me a glass of water if you don't mind."

"Does Switzerland routinely let murderers out of prison?" demanded Rachel.

Paul would have given anything to retort, "No more than the USA," but the water seemed to go down Uncle Julien's windpipe. Paul slapped him on the back and offered a tissue.

"Those two *killed* our teacher!" cried Rachel. "Maybe they're kidnapping or killing hotel guests."

Cloquet held up his hand to calm her. "I too believe your teacher was killed." He coughed a little and said, "However, events did not take place quite in the way you seem to recall. Monsieur Bonami and Mademoiselle Wertheimer were responsible for putting poison into a tart intended for Madame Bonami. That poison was disguised as a sugar substitute, for Madame Bonami suffered— no doubt still suffers—from diabetes."

Rachel crossed her arms and pursed her lips.

"Madame Bonami did not ingest the poison and today lives outside of Switzerland."

Rachel blurted, "Mademoiselle Schwartz ate the diabetic tart by mistake and died. Lauren and I knew about the poison. We knew a lot about the Bonamis and Mademoiselle Schwartz's affair with Monsieur Bonami. We *know* what happened. These people are murderers."

"No, they are not murderers. That tart was not eaten by anyone. If it had been, the taster would have died."

"Mademoiselle *Schwartz* died."

None of this was news to Paul; however, it was intriguing to see how much Rachel cared about a teacher who had died years ago. He wondered if her emotions had been stirred by seeing Mlle Shwartz's ghost.

"The coroner stated your teacher died *not* by poisoning but by smothering—asphyxiation," explained Cloquet.

"Smothering? Like under a pillow?"Rachel seemed at a loss. "You— you—arrested Helena Stamoulos at the time; could *she* have. . . ."

"I pulled Helena out of the school at the time to put any other suspect off guard. The measure was taken to protect the three other students left in the school during that spring break—yourselves and a young lady from Pakistan. Mademoiselle Stamoulos at the time was a troubled teen. I was not sure how deeply she was implicated through her own bad attitude toward Mademoiselle Schwartz."

"Who was the real killer if not Monsieur Bonami or Mademoiselle Wertheimer? Could it have been Helena? How was Mademoiselle Schwartz asphyxiated?" demanded Rachel.

Paul watched his uncle wiggle a finger under his head bandages, scratch, and blanch. His skull wound was tender. The movement helped distract Rachel.

"Oof." The detective pulled his hand down to his lap. "Mademoiselle Gordon, no murder was ever officially proved, even if one was intended."

Rachel's face flushed. "You just admitted you believed our teacher was killed. . . ."

"I did. But I could be wrong. Château Mont Rose closed. A company took over the estate's title. Sometimes I wonder if the house itself—"

"Uncle. . . ." interrupted Paul.

"A detective's life is very frustrating," said Cloquet, turning his head slowly to look out the window. "Not all cases are tied up neatly. Mlle Schwartz was asphyxiated while seated in her chair at the luncheon. Her death certificate gave sudden onset asthma as the reason for cessation of life. Despite the truth of the tart being poisoned, neither she nor anyone else died from it. Many police cases close unsolved."

"Is Monsieur Bonami in prison?" Rachel's voice faltered. "He tried to kill Lauren and me!"

"But he did not succeed. Alas, Monsieur Bonami was never held accountable for endangering you two girls up at Zermatt's most dangerous ski run."

"And he conspired to murder his wife," Rachel choked out, aggrieved.

"Monsieur Bonami spent six months under psychiatric evaluation. He had well-paid lawyers. Today he lives in Geneva."

"No prison?"

"Not the kind he should have been in."

"Detective Cloquet, is Paul watching out for us?"

"For all foul play, including kidnapping and—you'll pardon me—the female slave trade. We have our eye on Mademoiselle Wertheimer and all other characters of interest."

"Is Helena Stamoulos a person of interest?"

"Yes."

"And that is why Paul was maneuvered onto the ghost-hunting crew?"

"The opportunity presented itself," said Cloquet, gaze returning to meet Rachel's worried expression.

"And Ajit? Is he a detective? Like Paul?"

"No, he isn't," interrupted Paul. "Ajit's passion is ghost hunting. He thinks I am what he says I am, a computer programmer who works as a taxi driver. In order to remain 'undercover,' my friends and family can't know."

Both men watched for her response.

"Thank you," she said. "I won't bother you anymore, Detective. I hope you feel better." Rachel pulled the strap of her purse up over her shoulder.

"Mademoiselle Gordon," said Uncle Julien. "Paul will be able to do a better job if his identity is not given away. If I cannot rely upon your discretion, you may come into grave danger."

"I'm sorry Ajit isn't a cop too," said Rachel with a half-hearted toss of her head. "And I promise not to say a word."

Chapter 17
How to Punish a Teacher

At Château Mont Rose, the morning's thick mist transformed, with distant rumbling, into light spring rain, drizzling then pattering against the window panes. The night before, antiquated water radiators had kept the room cozy. By day, the cellar boiler stood cold and Lauren shivered as she typed wearing her coat, trying to remember events in the classroom of a dead teacher.

There had been a palpable homesickness etched into the faces of the girls and wafting through the château corridors, dense as the thickening fog drifting over Lake Geneva. Some girls were so confused by longing they cried for the imagined warmth of their mothers' kitchens, forgetting who had paid to send them away.

Onto that stage stepped Mlle Schwartz, a passionate young teacher who cajoled the girls into learning a new language, teaching them about thorny roses and little birds intrepid in the melting snow.

For her pains, Mlle Schwartz was murdered.

Every so often, Lauren stopped to rub circulation into her arms and challenge her memory. Hadn't the students learned to love Danielle Schwartz? Most had, but not Helena. Helena's growing animosity towards the teacher erupted daily, like inflamed acne.

One cold morning, Mlle Schwartz did not come out of her bedroom. No one really noticed her absence at breakfast, but in the classroom without a teacher, the girls' whispers grew in volume into loud conversation and laughter. Finally, Mlle Villot, the teacher from the next classroom, marched in on her short legs. She slammed her stick on the desk and gave an assignment and a warning.

Then she went to look for Mlle Schwartz. The latter's bedroom door was not locked. Mlle Villot entered it and discovered Danielle Schwartz, alive and humiliated, lashed with rope to her bed. A faint smell of urine wafted into the air.

In the investigation that followed, Mlle Schwartz's bottle of water was found to have been laced with sedatives. Someone had entered the teacher's room during the night. The intruder tied the drugged woman's arms and legs with the kind of knots that tighten when a victim struggles to get free. When the drugs' effects wore off, a gag rag muffled her yells.

Mlle Schwartz managed, by squirming, to free her mouth from the rag. Still, her cries were not heard for the thunderous clopping of girls' feet and the shrill peal of the morning bell in the corridor.

Hoarse from yelling, Mlle Schwartz simply waited to be found. When that finally happened, she took a half day off while Mlle Villot pounded back and forth in her sensible shoes between the two classes until lunchtime.

No culprit was ever named.

Helena's proud smirk grew bolder.

From that day on, the relationship between Mlle Schwartz and Helena was strained beyond reconciliation. Helena flashed her guilt like a badge of honor. Why did Mlle Wertheimer not remove Helena from Mlle Schwartz's classroom?

On the days Helena deigned to attend class, she could be found, arms folded and book unopened, unrepentant. She studied when she felt like it—usually never. She whispered to girls seated near her. Mostly they ignored her.

Perhaps the attendance of Marisela and Carmen upon Helena in her bedroom was enough to relieve Helena's natural loneliness. Or maybe it was not. Lauren knew, deep down, that the young Helena put up so many walls she was her own prisoner.

Lauren rubbed her arms. Good grief, how could she leave out the Greek girl's war with the teacher? There was only one way to approach the script: a former bully who had tortured her teacher was now a psychic who wanted to tell a ghost she was sorry.

Lauren took the thermos kettle to the bathroom sink to fill with water. Teeth chattering despite the warm sweater and thick socks, she put the full kettle into its holder. The red light came on. A glance at the window ledges assured her there was no sparrow. She sat back down and remembered.

The shift in Lauren's relationship with Helena began with gifts. The Greek girl sent tokens down to Lauren's bedroom in the hands of Marisela or Carmen, whose expressions indicated Lauren had joined the club.

A lovely cologne was followed by a new wallet in hues of burnt orange. Were these things Helena didn't want? Lauren wrote brief words of thanks on little cards with pictures by French painters, as her mother had taught her. Marisela or Carmen took the cards back to Helena.

The kettle whistled. Lauren made herself a cup of Earl Grey with powdered creamer. Then she took it to the window and leaned against a wall to sip and contemplate. The rain had stopped and a fistful of sun rays splashed over the lake. The brightness revealed the French Alps for several minutes, then clouds and grayness returned. It was too early to say if the rain was over.

Too early, as well, to decide if Helena's transformation from metal-pierced bully into a stylish clotheshorse meant at least a degree of true inner reformation. She brawled constantly with Dominick. If there were the slightest relapse to the sneaking bully of their teen years, Lauren would go back to California and her grocery store job. She drank half the tea, her gaze on the lake view, then returned to her script.

She could have been working anywhere from ten to twenty minutes when floorboards creaked.

"Rachel?"

She waited for a skeleton key to turn in the lock. When it did not, Lauren's gaze slid down and froze on the narrow gap between door and floorboards.

"Oh my God."

Some sort of guck was seeping into her room from under the door. Lauren approached the small mess. There was no odor, but it looked like brownish slop. Any moment it would seep into the Berber rug.

She leaned forward, opened the door, and peered out.

"Hello? Something spilled on the floor and it is going to ruin. . . "

Her breath halted, just like that. Her brain begged to shut down. Here was Grock the clown, losing his legs and pelvis in goo. The statue careened, tilting in his own melting wax. Bloodshot waxen eyes bulged wide, and the clown's mouth sagged open in protest.

The hallway air was cold, but the wax figure bubbled. A single shot of hot wax splattered up onto her skin.

"Help! *Au Secours!*" Lauren pivoted, thinking of the towels in her bathroom. She slipped and fell into the mess. Wax had oozed up to her toes.

She yelled, tried getting up, slipped again. Her scream rattled doorknobs in the dark hallway. The hot wax scalded and stuck to her skin.

Whimpering, Lauren began crawling. This time her arm slipped from under her and melted wax plugged a nostril. A yet higher-pitched scream reverberated through the dark, lifeless corridor.

Grock's face, outside the bedroom, was nearly level with hers. He had melted down to his waist. His eyes rolled in their sockets, one angled at her, the other aimed at the ceiling. A bubble popped on his ruined lips.

Eyes wide, Lauren made a decision. She scurried out of the room, to the hall floor runner, past Grock. She must have cried or yelled from the hot, thick goo, but once on the rug, the pain was less because the fibers soaked the substance.

Other statues were melting too. Wax dribbled and bubbled at every base. Feet and in some cases, legs, had dissolved into pools of steaming wax. The middle part of the hall runner offered some respite, and she used it to scurry to the staircase.

But the stairs were worse, for a statue melted at the top of the landing as did others placed along the turns. The glopping sound of wax, dripping down the steps of the grand staircase, echoed.

Lauren reversed direction and rushed back into her room, taking a great leap over a puddle. She kicked the door shut. She would be trapped, but there were no waxen statues inside. Dropping upon the closest bed, she took stock. Her skin was red and raw. The bedspread was sticking to her. She pulled it off her skin where it stuck to her skin and got cool towels, wet from the sink. Wax was all over her boots and clothes, but that didn't seem to matter as much as surviving.

The mirror over the sink reflected a bright red left cheek and nostril. A welt grew in the center of her forehead. There was wax in her hair. She wet a towel with cool water, used it as a compress. Then she got the phone (it now functioned) and dialed Rachel's number.

"What's wrong? You sound terrible—"

"Call the fire station! There's a fire on the floor under this one. The wax statues are all melting. I'm in danger."

"Oh my God! Can you get out?"

"I'll try to climb out of the windows. Rachel, make the call!!"

Chapter 18

Villa Cygne

Villa Cygne was the name of the house that stood next door to Château Mont Rose. Virginie Duvanel, love child of Villa Cygne, grew up in contemplation of its illustrious neighbor. Like the girls who lived at the boarding school, her roots were in a foreign land.

Before Virginie's conception, her Italian mother, Gina, arrived in Lausanne seeking housework. Madame Déculotté of Villa Cygne hired Gina for her sedate demeanor, so different from the bubbly young residents next door who snagged her husband's roving eye.

Without being aware, Gina worked her female charm on Monsieur Déculotté. Her proximity was irresistible. After the conquest—both parties privately blaming the other—Gina continued to polish, primp and prime Villa Cygne, concealing her growing bump until the morning she gave birth in an upstairs bathroom.

The baby might have gone back to Italy to live with its mother *toute de suite* except for Gina being run over by a car piloted by Madame Déculotté. The latter was sent to prison for her lead foot.

Monsieur's sister moved in to watch the helpless baby; together they pried open the heart of Monsieur Déculotté. He did the necessary "adoption" paperwork. Meanwhile, Monsieur Déculotté divorced the murderess and found a replacement bride who took over raising the love child.

At Villa Cygne, little Virginie grew up noticing older girls from all over the world come and go at next-door Château Mont Rose. She learned to distinguish carefree Americans from fine-boned Venezuelans who peppered their Spanish with laughter. She admired the serious, blonde German fräulein and the dark-eyed, chauffeur-shadowed maidens from the Middle East. These magical girls walked by her home in pairs or trios. Sometimes she ran into them having tea and pastries in parlors down in the La Rosiaz suburbs or central Lausanne. She dreamed of being one of them and nurtured the illogical hope that Papa would enroll her.

The new Madame Déculotté had different dreams for Virginie and her own daughters. She engaged a seamstress to teach Virginie practical skills. By the end of Virginie's compulsory Swiss schooling, she was free to spend the day stitching up silk and satin party dresses for her little sisters. Madame Déculotté did not neglect to relate the disgrace of Virginie's birth to her daughters, whenever the need arose. When Virginie and her sisters got into fights, the younger girls bombarded her with reminders of a low-born mother.

Papa stayed out of these quarrels.

At the age of sixteen, Virginie sought refuge with a young Swiss engineer by the name of Thierry Duvanel, fresh out of L'École Polytechnique. She met him at a discothèque. Papa financed their marriage as his wife was keen for Virginie to leave.

For some reason, Virginie's failure to conceive a living child led Thierry to bitterness and heavy drinking. He acted as if he had a kingdom which needed an heir, though no kingdom existed. He blamed Virginie for making him less of a man.

M. Déculotté made one more attempt to brighten his first child's life: he bought an alteration shop in La Rosiaz. This he placed it in Virginie's name at the town hall. To celebrate, Thierry gave up engineering. Virginie worked hard and paid all their bills. In this manner, a father's good impulses led to worsened circumstances.

One day, a pregnant girl from Château Mont Rose came to the shop for alterations on several pairs of pants. During a fitting, she blurted, in hysterical sobs, the secret of her womb, which the young mother declared she could not keep. Madame Duvanel, as clients called her, was touched by the news of an unwanted spark of life. She considered the impact a child might have on Monsieur Duvanel if he could be persuaded the babe was his own. A true life as a family might begin. Thierry might go back to engineering.

For months Madame Duvanel play-acted at pregnancy. The performance was made simpler by her husband's drying out in rehab when the schoolgirl was due to deliver. The newborn was transported to the alteration shop in a suitcase. Thierry Duvanel came home to an eleven-pound baby whose forehead he anointed with fine Scotch Whiskey. Monsieur Duvanel was committed to prison some years later for a hit-and-run while driving drunk.

At least little Jean, the suitcase baby, had a home and a Swiss name.

Virginie passed her reverence for Château Mont Rose on to her son, and it was Jean who got them the job as caretakers when the old school was transformed into a hotel-museum.

#

Early morning found Virginie arranging a breakfast tray with a fresh flower next to the blue teapot. The old lady for whom the tray was destined ate very little and shunned the traditional Swiss breakfast of strong coffee, warm

French bread, cheeses, and jam. She preferred a soft boiled egg with a small bowl of muesli.

Virginie held the tray with one hand and opened the door to the tower with the other hand. She used the free hand to grasp the rail so she did not trip. It was a wonder old Mlle Wertheimer could get up and down this steep flight on her rickety legs when it was her turn to sit at the concierge desk.

The elderly woman didn't have to work. Jean could do it; so could Virginie. Mlle Wertheimer staffed infrequently, when she felt like it, so what was the point? Of course, Virginie conceded that Mlle Wertheimer needed to get fresh air and sunshine and not stay cooped upstairs. Occasionally, Virginie came upstairs to dust and found no old lady. Mlle Wertheimer demonstrated she was still capable of going out to find her own fresh air.

"Good morning, mademoiselle." Virginie placed the tray on a small table, which she pulled closer to the elderly woman.

"Good morning, Virginie. Did you have a visitor last night? I heard a commotion."

"A police officer was looking for a prowler in this area. The officer harassed Jean, who was working on a sculpting project."

"How rude of the officer! Château Mont Rose must be working its inspiration on Jean." Mlle Wertheimer prodded the flower in the vase to stand upright. Her meddling made things worse.

"You approve of Jean sculpting?" Virginie felt surprise.

"Of course! Now, tell me about the officer."

Virginie shrugged. "Jean spoke to him at the front door. Then, as the officer was leaving, someone sprang on him, hit him on the head. Jean heard him fall and I called an ambulance."

"Police officers must know the dangers inherent in their job. There seemed to be a number of people walking outside the building."

"Paramedics."

"You did the right thing. We don't want any prowlers at Château Mont Rose."

"Thank you, mademoiselle."

Mlle Wertheimer's mouth, wrinkled like a purse pulled shut by string, was full of oatmeal. Virginie left her to enjoy breakfast and the cooing of pigeons under the attic eaves.

Two hours later, Virginie found the tray sitting on the floor, just by the staircase door. Sometimes she had the ungracious thought that if the old lady was spry enough to bring her dishes down one flight of stairs, she might bring them all the way to the kitchen.

#

Paul avoided a fire truck blocking the Château Mont Rose driveway. He left his car outside the estate gate. A woman's giggle floated from the side of the vehicle. He halted at the rear of the fire vehicle, out of view.

"That tickles!" (Small gasp.) "I'm fine! Nothing is broken."

"You ripped your pants and scuffed your skin."

Paul stretched his neck to peer around the back of the fire engine. A fire fighter about his age, squatting, pulled off one of Lauren's boots. Another fireman, big and buff, stood close.

"I didn't see any swelling. The bruise needs cleaning."

"Lean on me; tell me if it hurts to walk." The more muscular fire fighter had an arm snug around Lauren's waist. They began to move—bodies touching. This was far more attention than any non-fire victim needed. There was not a trace of smoke. Paul presented himself to view.

"Where's the fire?"

"False alarm," replied the squatting fireman, who rose, still holding Lauren's boot. "Our captain and two of the crew are inside, completing the investigation."

"Paul!" Lauren broke away from the arm of the powerhouse. "Did Rachel call you?"

"Yes," said Paul. He looked at the building. Rachel had called, commanding him to telephone the fire department. Ripped ivy leaves and long, torn branches lay on the ground. The shrubbery did not look singed.

"No fire is always better than fire," said the fire fighter with the boot. "Captain Soutter told us to examine the casualty."

"I'm not a casualty." She took her boot.

"Mademoiselle, you fell."

"I escaped. Now I want to sit down."

Paul strode up the hotel's front steps, past the wax Jung.

"You don't have clearance!" cried one of the firemen.

Paul didn't want to flash his detective I.D. where Lauren would see it. The captain was inside; he was the person to show his I.D. to. Paul dashed past the empty concierge desk. The wax figures argued against any fire having taken place.

What had possessed Lauren to tell Rachel the house was ablaze and then climb down the vines from a second floor window? She could have broken her neck.

A firefighter with stripes on his uniform descended.

"Captain Soutter?"

The man was tall, fit, late 30s or early 40s, a bit of gray in his mustache. "Yes. Who are you?"

Paul pulled out his badge. "Sûreté."

"Why is Sûreté involved?"

"I made the call reporting the fire."

Captain Soutter frowned. "You! What was your intention, Officer?"

"I was told there *was* a fire."

The fire chief stared. "Explain yourself."

"My boss told me to call it in—not my boss at Sûreté—I mean the people I am working for undercover." Paul made sure there was no one listening. "Sûreté has infiltrated—"

"The ghost-hunting crew?"

"Yes. How did you know?"

"Word gets around." Captain Soutter paused. "So what's your investigation really about, a meth lab?"

"No. A string of deaths tied to this place of business. Detective Inspector Julien Cloquet is my direct superior."

Capain Soutter lifted his eyebrows. "*Certes*, I'll be in touch with Detective Cloquet. Someone is going to be fined. We thought the place was burning down."

Paul nodded.

"Was it the girl outside who fell off the vines? Did she claim there was a fire?"

"She's not the boss and I really don't know who the fire report started with," Paul lied.

Captain Soutter shifted the equipment higher up on his back. "It will come out in the inquiry." He continued his descent.

A loud voice Paul recognized—Helena's—greeted Soutter at the bottom of the stairs.

"Are you the fire chief?" She was smiling. "There doesn't seem to *be* a fire!"

Captain Soutter grunted.

Helena was being charming. "I think I can explain what happened, Captain. It is not at all unheard of for a fire to break out in one dimension and not in another. Perhaps as a forewarning, a memory, or a symbolic statement. My crew is investigating paranormal phenomenon in this building."

The captain turned to look at Paul, who translated Helena's English.

"The person who called in the fire," said Captain Soutter, "failed to specify which dimension to look in. Is the person who first reported the fire employed by you?"

Helena assented.

"*Très bien*," said Captain Soutter. "Since this is your crew, there is a paper I need you to sign. You may call it a bill in any dimension."

#

Lauren waited on a stone bench under a flowering garden trellis. Sun rays hit the blossoms and bright green leaves. Her gaze fell on a caterpillar slithering along a branch, a flower as its goal.

The two firemen, flirtatious or not, had made some chauvinistic cracks in French that stung. Blondes couldn't be trusted to light their own cigarettes, for instance.

Lauren didn't smoke. Wounded pride had made her unable to think of a snappy answer. That was not a good sign for a writer. Rachel would have had one. The two had introduced themselves, but she had decided to forget their names.

If there had been a real fire, the water pumps on the fire engines would be working. The wax Carl Gustave Jung stood looking out the front window as unperturbed as the day she arrived. Her nose could not detect the slightest hint of acrid smoke residue.

How could wax melt without a fire? Why didn't they see what she had seen? What was wrong with her?

Something flicked her shoulder, like a finger tap or clump of dirt. She looked around for an insect, a dragonfly or ladybug, which might have flown into her.

She saw a male gardener digging near the wall. He was uprooting seedling scrub brush and snipping the branch shoots off small trees. Of course, it was easier to uproot growth when the soil was damp from rain, which had drizzled all morning.

The gardener's movements seemed stiff. Perhaps he was old and his joints hurt. Gray locks stuck out from under his cap. This was the first staff member Lauren had seen apart from Mlle Wertheimer and the concierge.

"Monsieur?"

She stood up, keeping most of her weight on the right foot. Her left foot had twisted under her when she landed, so there was some tenderness.

She approached the gardener. "Monsieur, May I ask you a question?"

The skin of his neck crackled when he turned his head.

She halted.

His eyelids went down in a slow blink. They reopened millimeter by millimeter.

"Monsieur?"

The gardener turned his head back again, the crackling resulting in a neck tear. The hand gripping a tri-clawed weeder went up in the air. It crashed down into the wet earth. The gardener's head joggled.

A second blow of the weeding arm detached the gardener's head by half.

Lauren turned, trampling the flowers, oblivious of her tender foot.

#

Emerging from the side entrance of the château, Paul caught Lauren in her wild race. In his arms, he could feel her heart galloping. The panic in her wide eyes made his own heart jump.

Chapter 19

A Taste for Fine Things

The car near drove itself. Damn, it was fine, like honey, like a fish feast in Dakar. God, he missed the sautéed sea fish in Mama's home cooking. Here, he ate a lot of hamburgers and pizza. Okay, Greek food too, but was he Greek?

Europe was different than Abdul had dreamed it. The people didn't eat better, not even with all their money! *Wallahi,* they paid a lot for food. Unless a fellow ate fast food every day (he did), there was also a big difference in price rates.

In Senegal, great food was served in the street, at a reasonable price for locals and a few notches higher for tourists. Abdul's favorite Senegalese meal was Thiebou dieune, which anyone could find at dozens of stands but Mama (Yaay) made it best--rice cooked in spicy, garlic tomato sauce and smoked fish broth. To the rice, she added whatever fresh vegetables she found that day-- eggplant, cabbage, carrots, red pepper, sweet potatoes, and parsley. Yaay placed the big platter of spicy rice on the floor, vegetables and sautéed fish in the center, and everyone sat around the platter. Hot sauce and cut limes waited close at hand. As a special touch, Abdul's mama sprinkled crispy fried rice on top.

Abdul's finger itched to squeeze fish and spicy rice and a bit of vegetable into a tight ball and pop it in his mouth right this minute. Why was he so hungry?

He tapped his phone to play an album by singer Youssou Ndour. His nerves calmed. A little patience was what he needed. And lunch. Too bad Anneke had never tasted Thiebou dieunne. Yaay would have paddled him if he brought such an old white lady home. Ideas about money came with Jawara's big checks, when Abdul saw how much they bought after Yaay cashed them. Any young man stuck in Senegal would think the same: Find a way to get to Europe. Anneke, visiting the Senegal beaches, offered him that way and now, look!

Damn, this car was like fine rum. Cognac, that would be a Porsche, but he could be patient. Senegal was not going away; it was waiting for him. He pressed down on the accelerator, driving up the hill to Pully. He hoped Jawara would give this car to him. She had a rich husband. Abdul would make her remember she also had a little brother.

Anneke's car back in Tilburg was 12 years old. As soon as he saw the clear coat peels and dents in the door, he knew he had to do something. He was a man who needed a fine set of wheels, even if the wife gave him Louis Vuitton luggage and made him half owner of their condo. A man didn't leave the sun and sea for all this damp coldness unless there were bluer skies ahead. Abdul could see himself as a Pigalle model. He told Anneke. Make it happen, woman.

The GPS interrupted Abdul's fingers, tapping to the music: "In fifty meters, pull over to your right." Why did his fingers clench the steering wheel? Why did he brake before a bus stop? There a lady stood curled over her cane like a bent, half-used candle, peering at him. The skies above her grew somber with gathering dark clouds. His eyes felt cold. He was shocked. Why had the car stopped? The ancient one plucked her way forward with the cane, towards his open window.

"Young man, take me to Château Mont Rose," warbled this little woman through the open window in an old seagull voice. Bird caw or not, her face had the color of a dead fish, not something one he would buy or eat. Fish that had gone bad, with clouded eyes and gray gills.

Her hand was on the door handle. He hit lock but the door opened easily, letting in cool air and her somehow human frame unfolding onto the passenger seat like a disease. Shit.

"Turn off that noise."

"Get in the back," Abdul sputtered, turning the music off.

"No." She closed the front passenger door, put on her seat belt. "Drive, Abdul."

He put on his blinker to get back into traffic, petrified at his obedience. "How can you know my name?"

"Easy-peasy, Abdul. All the dots are connected."

"I don't have to—," he began and then felt a little ashamed because she was old and that was not the way the teachers at the madrassah had taught the little *talibés* to treat the elderly. The woman did not seem irritated. Her head was nodding up and down and sideways like a time-ravaged marionette.

"The car knows where it is going."

What a hell of a strange thing to say. And she was right. He was not directing the car, not following GPS.

"Are you a djinni?" His voice was shaking.

"A creature made of smokeless fire?" she answered, considering. Her head continued to bob, but not in a way he could interpret to mean yes or no.

The wheel that Abdul was gripping suddenly came off in his hands. He was no more steering the car than his passenger was. With a cry, he attempted to re-attach the wheel and to brake. Nothing he did made any difference to the car, which drove along at a reasonable pace, following the road.

"Is it a smart car?" he cried.

The old woman was practically choking from laughter.

"The car belongs to the château now, Abdul," she said when she caught her breath. "Yes, yes, put the wheel on top of the mount."

The car sedately turned right before the wheel felt attached to the mount. It drove onto a cobblestone driveway, also without being managed, and came to a stop.

"I am not created out of smokeless fire," said the wrinkled mouth. "Nor, would it seem anymore, of flesh and blood. Like you, Abdul, I have made a trade. I have given some part of my soul up for this world."

The slow smile that showed two ragged rows of little yellow teeth made his heart skip a beat.

"As long as you are in this city, you will be at the call of the château. I don't have to explain anything to you because you have it all in that handsome head, don't you!" She lifted her stick-like arm and touched a waxy finger to his temple.

He nodded, eyes widening.

"It will be a good thing. The château is not angry with you. You are not one of its former students. However, you are linked through your sister. More importantly, you are driving a car belonging to a former student who needs punishing."

What kind of people was Jawara mixed up with?

"Be a good boy and go get your first client at the pizzeria down the road, the way you came up. That tourist will give you a tip because he is American."

Abdul nodded, speechless.

"When you are done with that client, you may return to the pizzeria. The owner will have your dinner of Thiebou dieune ready."

Djinni or angel, she didn't have to say that twice.

#

Lauren sat quiet as a mummy during the ride to Vevey, a small town near Lausanne on the shores of Lake Geneva. She was glad when Paul gave up trying to chat. The excursion helped distance her from the freakishness of her morning. She wondered if crossing the Swiss border would banish the nightmare completely.

Paul pulled into the parking lot of an elegant historic-looking building. The sign proclaimed *Les Trois Couronnes,* The Three Crowns.

"This is the kind of luxury hotel a beautiful young woman like you would be expected to stay at. You fit here better than this car does; that's for sure."

Lauren smiled at his comparison. Paul was right about his car. The old black Audi was like a broken tooth among the sharp, gleaming rows of Renaults, Mercedes and Alfa Romeos.

"I thought you had only a moped."

"My moped is newer than this vehicle. Ajit and I share this car, so it isn't totally mine."

"I know this hotel," she said.

"You've been here?"

"No, but I've heard of it."

The 19th-century façade boasted elaborate windows and balconies, trimmed and decked with open Venetian shutters, wood filigree, and wrought iron.

"Why did you bring me here?" she wondered aloud.

"Let's say I have a special relationship with the place."

Lauren allowed Paul to escort her through the foyer, leaning on his arm to take the weight off her left foot.

"Does it hurt?"

"A bit tender, that's all."

Les Trois Couronnes had framed pictures of a past when visitors came in carriages, the men in top hats or bowlers, accompanied by women wearing bustles and carrying parasols.

"I wish I could have seen this place then," Lauren said. "I love the different-colored marble and the chandeliers."

A hostess led them out to the lakeshore terrace. Most tables, under broad sailcloth umbrellas, were empty. The afternoon sun glared in Lauren's eyes so that she couldn't read the menu. She fished in her purse for sunglasses.

"Can't we sit near the water?" Paul asked the hostess.

"I'm sorry, sir, those are set for dinner. We are at the end of the luncheon service."

"I am Henri Junod's brother."

"That is why I seated you at all." Frost blew off the woman's imperial smile.

"Did you want to be near water because of my reputation for conjuring fire?"

Paul laughed.

"I never *thought* I was delusional," she admitted.

Before Paul could respond, a waiter arrived, so he said, "Please tell Henri it is Paul and we'll have two of 'the usual'."

The waiter collected their menus and left.

"Who is Henri? What is 'the usual'?"

"Henri is my older brother, the head chef. 'The usual' is whatever he has left over from lunch."

Leftovers turned out to be veal served with fresh asparagus stems drizzled in hollandaise sauce. As they ate, Paul left the topic of fire alone. He told her instead about the boathouse that had once been underneath the hotel's terrace. "In that time, there was no embankment. The waters of Lake Geneva, or *Lac Léman*, extended right to the back of the hotel. Deliveries were made by boat through stone arches."

"Like in Venice!"

Lauren was just thinking about describing the wax gardener when a man wearing a chef's hat appeared, pulled up a chair, and sat down, eyes sparkling.

A waiter was right behind with three demitasse cups of espresso.

"Was it exquisite?" he asked, point blank, as if he knew her.

Paul answered: "*Bien entendu!* Henri, I would like to introduce you to Lauren Briant, my colleague."

Henri rose halfway from the seat, took Lauren's hand to kiss. His face was fuller than Paul's, his hair darker and wavier with a few silvery hairs threaded around a rather more leonine head. Still, the family resemblance was obvious.

"Do you drive taxis, Lauren, or are you a computer-engineering student?"

Lauren hesitated. Paul hadn't told his own brother about landing a new job?

"I am a writer for a film crew. Paul is on the crew as well—with his cousin Ajit."

"Ah, Ajit, that scamp. May I ask what kind of film?"

"The subject is ghost-hunting."

"Ghosts are becoming big business," said Henri. "First Ajit and now you?" He was looking at Paul, who did not grin back. Lauren felt some tension but then Henri deftly began telling hotel ghost stories, concluding, "How many deceased visitors actually appear at *Les Trois Couronnes*. I wouldn't know, for I am always in my bed at night, sleeping."

"Do you sleep at the hotel?" asked Lauren.

"No. I have a flat." The rain abated

She blushed. Well, of course he did. What a stupid question.

Paul was quiet as Henri took his departure. To Lauren, he said, "I look forward to seeing you again." The brothers embraced affectionately, making Lauren feel her perception of tension had been in error.

Returning to the Audi, she exclaimed, "*Daisy Miller!*"

"Who?"

Drops of rain dampened the pavement. "That is the title of a book set at this hotel." She ducked into the car. "The novel was written by Henry James."

"The opera *Faust* was composed here," Paul said, igniting the engine. "Do you enjoy opera?"

"Sometimes."

"Ah. Then I won't break into a Puccini aria. Not everyone reacts well. Are you ready to go back?"

"I guess so."

His hand slammed the horn when a car cut in front. "Zut. She's talking on her phone while driving. It's illegal."

"Where are the police when you need them?" asked Lauren.

Paul looked startled.

"Did you finish writing the script?" he asked.

"Yes, and it is full of truths. Maybe that's what has unhinged my mind." Her voice betrayed angst. The phone rang from inside her purse.

"Must be Rachel. Hello?"

She had been talking to Paul in French; in the same language, she heard, "Lauren Briant? I have something to tell you."

It was not Helena or Rachel, but it was a woman.

"Who is this?"

"Mademoiselle Schwartz."

The phone slipped from her fingers, bumping down the side space between car door and seat. Lauren fished the device out with a shaking hand.

"Hello?"

There was no one there.

"The mountains get in the way," said Paul.

"I don't think mountains are what made the call drop." Lauren held the phone in front of her face like it was a bomb needing to be defused. "My phone was fully charged. Now it says no battery power."

"You can recharge in your room."

Had he heard? Her phone had been fully charged. If she told him what the caller said, he would drive her to the nearest psych ward. Melting wax statues because of a fire that didn't take place, a dead teacher outside a school wall (who also knew how to make calls) and a cracking wax gardener were her repertoire of new secrets to be guarded against the world's discovery.

Lauren felt she was losing her mind.

Black clouds billowed overhead, and thunder clapped. Rain poured out of the sky as from an immense cauldron. The car slowed to a crawl.

"The storm is happening to both of us, isn't it?"

He gave her another sharp look. "I wouldn't have slowed down if it weren't."

Lauren hesitated before saying, "The firemen didn't believe me, you know."

"They were happy to save you."

Was that jealousy?

"You heard about the melting wax I saw?"

"Of course."

"I want you to feel my arm."

He glanced at her.

"As evidence."

He pulled the car to the side of the road. "We're very close," he said, and she knew he meant to the Château although they were also close to each other, cut off from the world by water. She held out her arm.

"At the time, it burned. It doesn't hurt anymore. Like it never happened, but the wax is there. You can feel it."

He hesitated. Lauren took his fingers, swept them over her skin where wax remained.

"Pull some out."

"That will hurt."

"I don't care."

He tugged a little, pressed the wax between his fingers. "It *is* wax. I never said I didn't believe you, Lauren. I'm the one who called the fire station. Rachel asked me to."

"When I fell on the ground into the wax, I was crying from pain. How could I have imagined that? But the firemen said the wax figures did *not* melt." Lauren dropped her gaze. "What's wrong with me?"

"Maybe," said Paul slowly, "we should be asking what is wrong with Château Mont Rose."

Rain washed over the car rooftop and windows.

"Helena thinks the building is haunted, perhaps by your teacher who died. I also heard Helena say she thinks you have psychic abilities."

"She does? Is that what you think?"

"I don't know." He focused on the wheel. "Science teaches us there is more to heaven and earth than meets the eye."

Whatever was the matter with Château Mont Rose, others would feel it soon. Lauren would not be alone. This was what they had all signed on for, as ghost hunters.

"Why is Helena letting Rachel and me *sleep* there if she believes it is haunted?"

The rain abated and Paul, shaking his head, restarted the car. "Why didn't she book herself in, too?"

"It probably has something to do with Château Mont Rose not having room service."

They pulled back into the flow of traffic.

"Until two days ago, I thought this was just going to be a vacation. When Rachel offered the potential of a job in Switzerland, it was like a dream come true."

After a pause, Paul asked, "Did you leave a boyfriend in California?"

"There's no one like that. My parents are there. And my brother."

A moment later, Paul changed the subject: "Did your teacher die *inside* Château Mont Rose?"

Lauren began to explain the circumstances when Paul slammed on the brakes. The car skidded and swerved. Lauren's feet pushed against the floorboard, and her hand clutched the armrest.

The vehicle squealed to a stop in a shower of mud.

"Are you okay?"

She nodded.

Paul got out. "*Ah merde!*"

The Audi had hit a massive fallen tree branch. It had a nasty dent in the fender. Tree parts wound around the car's axles.

They were about twenty yards from Château Mont Rose's front gate. Lauren walked towards her alma mater in the drizzle.

\#

Stretched out on her bed, arm thrown over her forehead, Lauren looked up into Rachel's face. "Can you say that again?"

"The letters D.S. were carved into the trunk. Big. Fresh, like they were just done. Ajit saw it when he helped Paul move the tree."

"It was a huge branch, not the whole tree." Lauren looked up at the windows, where rain continued to patter. "D.S. doesn't have to mean Danielle Schwartz. How do you know a Doctor of Science didn't carve the letters after a night of drinking?"

"I don't. But given the circumstances of this place. . . ."

What Rachel considered a big deal felt to Lauren like the least in a string of freakish occurrences.

"Do we get to rest now?"

"Yes. Helena said it would be hours before we start. Try to sleep if you can because we'll be up all night. Are you okay lying there by yourself? I'll be over here on my own bed."

Lauren nodded. Rachel was being nice, treating her like an invalid. Lauren had not mentioned the phone call from Mlle Schwartz. Perhaps Rachel knew about it already. It would be like Dominick to get a French-speaking actress to pretend to be their dead teacher and put Lauren on edge. She wasn't going to mention it if Rachel didn't.

The whole crew was on Lauren's suspect list—even Paul. She couldn't really trust anyone.

"As long as I can see you, Rachel, I think I'll be alright. If I notice the walls or floors oozing, I'll let you know. Or you can let me know. It might be your turn next."

Rachel did not look enthused.

Chapter 20

Alors?

Detective Cloquet stared at the hospital ceiling, promising himself a beer when released. The nurses would tell him not to drink as long as he took painkillers. Doctors and nurses liked to insinuate chemical threats to his liver. Psychological and physical threats in a detective's career posed, by far, the greater danger. An evening beer helped him cope. He knew where to draw the line.

After all, Michèle had been killed by a drunk driver.

He had slept over four hours. Looking at the clock on awakening, he was surprised to have been allowed the long snooze. That was a good sign. When he first arrived at the hospital, a nurse woke him from sleep every hour or less, asking for his name, address and other statistics—typical concussion procedure. The long nap meant he was out of the woods.

#

Worn out by emotions, Lauren snuggled under the duvet, facing her friend so that when she opened her eyes, she could see Rachel on the other bed. Wind-flung raindrops pattered erratically on the windowpanes. Fluctuating weather and reality had marked the last two days. Re-entering Château Mont Rose after the late lunch, Lauren found the wax figures as untouched as new candles. Their waxen eyes mocked her delusion. She almost wanted to scratch at them with her fingernails. How childish.

Paul and then Rachel had hinted at Helena's conclusion that Lauren was receptive to psychic phenomenon. Helena would speak to Lauren about her vision tonight. There was nothing to worry about. Such were the assurances given by Rachel, Lauren reflected, feeling drowsy from lunch and emotional exhaustion.

Behind her closed eyelids, images shuffled by as if on a pack of playing cards snapping across one's fingers. She dreamed of Château Mont Rose.

Standing between office curtains barely opened, Mlle Wertheimer stares at the two American students emerging from the estate's back garden. The headmistress's form and color blend in so well with the drab curtains Lauren almost doesn't notice her.

"Don't look up."

Of course, Rachel looks even though she is practically blind without her contact lenses, which are upstairs next to her bed. "We haven't done anything wrong!"

"I wouldn't be so sure about that."

Mlle Wertheimer meets them at the château's front door. "Come into my office!" They follow meekly.

"Sit down!"

The padded and studded armchairs are meant to seduce parents. A scent of stale eucalyptus cloys the air. The heavy curtains have been drawn.

Mlle Wertheimer studies them, aided by a giant-sized microscope on her desk. Each girl sits in an arm chair, ensconced between glass slides.

"How dare you," the headmistress says after a repulsed glare at either girl, "disturb the gardener or any other person on my staff? I forbid your sniffing around the estate like a couple of pubescent bloodhounds. The police—not schoolgirls—investigate murders."

"The contract our parents signed does not allow you to forbid us," blurts Rachel.

The signed contracts for the two Americans materialize on the headmistress's desk. Mlle Wertheimer knits her brow. "I should find some activity for you. Alors. . . ."

In French, this word runs along the lines of "so" or "well." Mlle Wertheimer can make it mean anything. It can mean, "Stop crying" or "how empty your head is!" It can also be flung into people's faces like a soiled handkerchief.

"There is an exercise trail up in the woods. You shouldn't go back to America without partaking of our national pastime. It will show you why we Swiss are so healthy. I will find someone to take you."

Mlle Wertheimer has morphed into a travel brochure.

"One more thing." The headmistress leans forward. "Inspector Cloquet, head of homicide from the Lausanne police, has pulled Helena out of school."

Lauren and Rachel blink like two bears roused from their caves in mid-winter.

"Alors," says the iron matron, slapping the word down like a brick, "let us find someone."

She snaps her fingers. They find themselves in the staff room.

"Alors, Mlle Terrieux!"

Spikes raises her porcupine head from a book, stills the crossed, swinging leg.

Lauren and Rachel huddle together.

It is no use. Within seconds they are huffing behind bobbing shoulders and marching legs. The woman's unflagging energy is an assault on normal human beings. Spikes strides like a Roman centurion. She sneers at students getting on a bus, never fails to raise a hand to speed them on their lazy way.

"It's about time you two got some exercise."

Rachel, a poor mole without spectacles whom Lauren must lead by the hand, mutters invectives.

Spikes pivots on the balls of her feet to hike in backward propulsion. "Anything wrong?"

"Pleeeeeease slow down," Rachel begs.

Lauren thinks the exercise trail might be amusing with someone else. At every so many yards, or meters by European estimation, is a sign, directing the participant to perform a certain exercise. At some spots, equipment is on hand. They crawl through a tunnel, hop over arranged logs, shimmy across a monkey bar.

At the end of the trail, Rachel collapses under a tall birch, pulls out a cigarette pack and lighter.

"Smoking is a repulsive habit," says Spikes, arms folded. "Especially for a girl your age."

Rachel blows a smoke ring, then holds out the cigarette. She examines it like an insect picked out of the fallen leaves.

"Smoking will turn your teeth brown."

"Then they'll match my hair."

"It will kill you, stupid girl."

"Mademoiselle Schwartz was killed without smoking," says Rachel. "The odds on dying young around here are pretty high."

"The weak die first." Spikes' eyes glint.

Leaves rustle overhead. Lauren considers how nice it would be to get away from this woman, never see her again in nightmares or memory.

"Mademoiselle Schwartz died because someone killed her," she says.

"Mademoiselle Schwartz was a perfect example of weakness. Look at that pathetic drivel she served you students: The rose loved the little prince! But the rose had her thorns and did not know how to keep from pricking her loved one.'"

"Don't make fun of the dead," says Lauren.

"All she cared about was cutting a poetic figure, playing around with paints and clay. That bimbo didn't have the sense of a ten-year-old."

Spikes grabs the cigarette from Rachel's lips, squashing it into the pliant ground.

"When I inherit that dead bitch's burden and you're under my tutelage, I'll show you what real study means."

Lauren says recklessly, "I guess not many people will show up at Mademoiselle Schwartz's funeral."

"Oh, but I intend to go." Spikes scampers off.

Lauren opened her eyes, surprised to find her hands tightly clenching the bedspread and not feeling at all rested.

#

"You're back."

Paul had entered Uncle Julien's corner of the hospital for his second visit of the day.

"I found out that La Société Chantal Étoile is listed as owner of Château Mont Rose. La Société also owns at least a dozen vineyards in this area, two restaurants and three nightclubs. Its financial holdings are at the Credit Suisse bank. Members of the board of directors live in various countries. Madame Bonami is one of them."

"The divorced Madame Bonami?"

"The very same."

"I thought she didn't want anything to do with the place."

"Château Mont Rose came to her in the divorce proceedings."

Uncle Julien gave a low whistle. "What about profits? Has Château Mont Rose had any to report in eight years?"

"None."

"You verified the holders of a numbered account," said Uncle Julien. "Do your hacking capabilities extend to transferring funds out of the same accounts?"

"Impossible."

"Keep that poker face. It may come in handy. Paul."

They both smiled.

"What about Papaux?"

Paul knew that question had been coming. "He hasn't been home. He hasn't been at Sûreté. They say he is with you. His car is parked outside your apartment building."

Uncle Julien frowned.

"I searched the roof, basement, and hallways of your building—and his own apartment house." Paul cleared his throat, before adding, "He's not in the morgue."

When there was no response from the patient, Paul dangled the keys to his uncle's car in the air. "Ajit is waiting for me downstairs. Your car is in parking lot C. You'll find your cane in the back seat." Paul passed the keys, a small cardboard box, and the stall ticket to the detective. "Your laptop is set up and it's in the car. I didn't know if you were going home or had other plans. Just click on the owl icon. I made the program user-friendly."

"What about the cameras?"

"All connected. Click on the owl. You'll get every room we wired."

"How many rooms does that come to?"

"As many rooms as I could find cameras at headquarters."

"Did you have problems?"

"Multiple requisitions. I jumbled them in the database. I'll have the system cleared out and the stuff back in place before anyone can fix that."

"Let's hope so. Sound?"

"With every camera."

"What did you tell Ajit?"

"I told him my wiring made things easier. I also told him I'd only be up here ten minutes to hand over your car keys. He wanted to come up and say hi."

"You'd best get along then. What time does the show start?"

"Lockdown is at sunset."

"Paul?"

"What?"

"Look for him. Papaux has got to be in there."

#

Sitting up, Lauren looked across the room and thought of awakening Rachel. The dream had dredged up a day she had managed to suppress for several years.

After the hike with Spikes, Lauren and Rachel had gone down to the police station to report Mlle Terrieux as a potential murder suspect. A nice, fatherly detective listened and took notes. Wasn't his name Detective Cloquet? He told them to come back if they had any more insights or gleanings.

They had at least one other idea, in fact, but like know-it-all teens, kept it to themselves.

"Rachel?"

Still sleeping.

Would Rachel remember how much of their own detective work they had done?

The girls went from the police station directly to the Bonami villa, thinking to determine whether the owner's wife was truly diabetic.

Madame Bonami answered her door wearing creamy tights and a lush angora sweater with plunging neckline. She looked like a movie star.

"What do you want?" No one could ever accuse her of being warm or friendly.

They stammered inane excuses for being there. Chilled by the wind at the open door, she let them in out of the rain, grudgingly. Everything around Mme Bonami that was not white was a mirror. No paintings were on the walls. Beauty was present in her own reflected, shimmering form. She led them to a cream couch in a white salon and cried, "Marianna! Take their dirty things away from them and get them something to sit on!"

A maid brought short plastic stools and placed them on the marble tiles. She took their coats.

Lauren babbled her fear of developing diabetes and rattled off a list of symptoms she believed she had.

"Why in the world are you asking me about this?"

"We heard you have diabetes," said Rachel.

The woman scowled. Even that was attractive. "Who said so?"

"The cook," Lauren and Rachel answered in unison.

"Oh really." She stared at them. "Whatever possessed you to come to me instead of to a doctor? You two are a couple of little liars."

"No," protested Lauren. "We're scared."

"Of what?"

"The murder of our teacher," cut in Rachel. "It's made Lauren sick."

"That's stupid. The murderess is a Greek girl named Helena. She was taken into custody by the police this morning. Marianna! These girls need their things."

Lauren and Rachel, following the maid to a side door, looked back to see M. Bonami, who had just entered, seize his wife and slide his hands up her sweater. Surely he knew the girls were there.

Had he known she watched when he and Mlle Schwartz were in the forest? Was he acknowledging that Lauren was a voyeur?

Or had Mlle Schwartz's death given him renewed interest in his wife?

Lauren got up off the bed and looked at her reflection in the bathroom mirror. She picked up her hairbrush. Using it, she went to her laptop. There was nothing left to do about that awful period but read the moments of Mlle Schwartz's life and death recalled for this evening's script. If Mlle Schwartz's spirit showed up, they would deal with it.

Chapter 21

A Ghost Teacher's Lesson

Lauren's typing might have roused Rachel, but it could as easily have been the rattling of the shutters. The rain had stopped, but wind continued to rise and fall in sporadic gusts around the building, ferreting into crevices and rustling through ivy like it was searching for something.

"Good evening."

"I slept. Did you?" Rachel's voice was thick.

"Yes. I dreamed of our year here."

"Did it inspire you to write something else?"

"Yes."

There was a loud knocking at the door. Rachel got out of bed and opened.

Helena entered, took a stance like a gunslinger, legs apart and arms crossed. She was an imposing figure in black.

"I need to speak to Lauren alone. Get out."

Hair mussed and clothes rumpled, Rachel grabbed her jacket without objection. She stepped into the hall, closed the door behind her.

Jangling with metallic accessories, Helena sat.

"Still writing? Dominick is on his way. Before we hear the script, I thought I should talk to you."

This was it. Helena was going to explain the nasty hallucinations. Lauren leaned back. "Okay."

Helena crossed one black leather ensconced leg over the other. "Did you know Mlle Schwartz took advantage of me?"

Seduction? Money? Lauren's eyebrows climbed.

"Yes, she channeled through me yesterday."

Ah, paranormal usage. "We weren't even here yesterday."

"Her spirit followed us to Château de Chillon. The proof is on film."

"Was I supposed to see that before writing?"

"Not necessarily. You can see as much of the footage as you want after the reaching-out is accomplished. Or you can wait until Dominick does his splicing magic. You may have a completely different feeling for Château Mont Rose by then." Helena nodded and tapped her long fingernails on the desk.

Lauren waited for some mention of her own strange visions.

"I hope you aren't frightened by the paranormal."

"No," Lauren wasn't scared exactly. Worried about personal sanity was closer to how she felt.

"You're not crazy, Lauren."

What soothing words, even from Helena.

"I would like to apologize for the fire trucks."

"Hey, I'm delighted about that fire you saw. We are in a very real presence."

"Really? Whose?"

"Mademoiselle Schwartz, silly. We have ties to no other presence in Lausanne."

"We have ties to the school."

"It's a building."

The outer window shutters were seized and shaken by a fierce gust. Lauren had to raise her voice to be heard: "How does the presence of Mademoiselle Schwartz explain the melting wax figures I saw this morning?"

Helena held up a knowing hand like a stylish Chinese sage. "Everything is explained by the *sequence* of paranormal events. Schwartz's spirit took over my body at Château de Chillon last night in order to make me write a message on the window. She warned you and Rachel to leave the 'rose.'"

"Meaning Château Mont Rose?"

Chains swished on Helena's leg. "Yes. You have the sight, you see. Schwartz's spirit thinks you're too weak to endure it. It's true some people snap. That's why she's been trying to scare you off."

This interpretation was unexpected.

"Everything I have witnessed is from the spirit of Mademoiselle Schwartz? She wants to scare me?"

"I encourage you to be strong. *I* believe in you, Lauren. Have you ever read the *Tao Te Ching*? It says, 'When I let go of what I am, I become what I might be.' Schwartz was wrong about me when I was a teen; she thought I wouldn't change. But I let go of who I was and became what I might be. Now her spirit is wrong about you. The poor woman died unenlightened."

Lauren had witnessed Helena's sociopathic bullying tendencies years earlier. Mlle Schwartz had not been the least wrong about how messed up Helena was then. Even if Helena had matured into a rich psychic who read philosophy and could restrain her anger, she was not necessarily a spiritual analyst.

Since that would be the wrong observation to make and still keep her job, Lauren said, "Mademoiselle Schwartz has been exposing me to weird visions to insinuate I am weak?"

"Those weird visions are a promise that there will be more than abundant psychic phenomenon." Helena's eyes glowed. "Imagine how an audience will respond to our reaching out to the spirit of our own dead teacher! I'm counting on you to show backbone."

The chains threaded through black loops on the jeans, vest and steampunk jacket swished as Helena stood. She had put studs into her bottom lip and through her nose in the last couple of minutes. The medium was beginning to resemble her former teenage self.

"Do you like my look? I want to make sure Schwartz recognizes me."

"She must have recognized you yesterday at Chillon," reminded Lauren, "if she channeled through you."

"She recognized a medium, not necessarily me, Helena."

"You do remind me of the old days."

The wind gave a penetrating howl.

"Just remember I am really not that girl. Not anymore."

\#

Detective Inspector Cloquet could have checked out of the hospital *without* staging a dramatic event. However, departing quietly would have involved a lot of medical questioning and possibly a letter of complaint to the Lausanne Sûreté. He had been told to stay put for 48 hours of evaluation. Officers were supposed to obey their doctors.

All Cloquet had was a mild headache. The nausea was gone. He was too hard-headed, hairline fracture or no, to be confused. He remembered enough of the assault to form his own ideas about suspects.

There never had been a prowler around Château Mont Rose. Cloquet's assailant was someone who lived on the estate, and it hadn't been Jean Duvanel. It had to be someone spry enough to lift an iron rod and strike. He doubted elderly Mlle Wertheimer could wield a tool with that much force. He had Duvanel's unseen mother in mind. Housekeepers did a lot of weight lifting as part of their job, didn't they? They heaved vacuum cleaners and furniture around.

Cloquet wanted to exit the hospital without hassle. When dinner finally arrived, the inspector ate the appetizing bits off his tray. Finished, he pulled the small box Paul had brought him out of his bag of clothes. Crisscrossing rubber bands kept it from opening. He ripped a page out of his portable notebook, jotted down a few words, folded and put the message on his pillow.

Something scratched in the box. He removed the rubber bands.

"*Bah*! These are the only circumstances in which I can appreciate you creatures."

Cloquet slid the top off the box and tossed the cockroaches under the curtain partition. At the same time, he kicked over his wastebasket and cried, "Oh disgusting!" His finger pressed on the nurse station button.

"*Bon Dieu*, where did those cockroaches come from? What the hell is happening to this hospital?" He shouted, to be heard in the hallway.

A wail erupted from his roommate's bed. Cloquet felt sorry for upsetting the sick old man, but it couldn't be helped. Two staff members appeared.

"There are cockroaches here. We could get food poisoning!" Cloquet closed himself into the bathroom.

That left the poor roommate complaining aloud. The staff members, audibly accusatory, could be heard hustling around the room, stomping, and slapping.

Cloquet wore his bathrobe over pants and a T-shirt. The slippers would have to stay on. The hunt was on inside the partitions. He slipped out with his clothes in a bag, cane in hand, and filed down the hall until he found another restroom. There he stripped off his bathrobe and changed the slippers for real shoes. The head bandage went into the towel disposal. Dressed like a visitor, he was bothered by no one and exited the building.

A half hour later, Detective Cloquet sat with a blanket over his legs on the couch at home, watching Jean Duvanel on his laptop monitor. The hefty concierge was moving from room to room, fitting keys on his master ring into locks.

It was strange no one on the crew had told the man to get out. Duvanel passed close in front of the camera, a film of sweat visible on his brow.

Cloquet marveled at the camera reception and computer set up. Paul had brought him into the 21st century. Cloquet could see the dust on the dressers, mantle pieces, and wax figures, as well as cobwebs hanging from many a ceiling though he could not see into the darkest recesses. The building was old, so it had incandescent lighting rather than modern fluorescent bulbs.

He clicked back to the home screen of the software program, which offered 15 boxes for him to choose from, each featuring a view from an individual camera in a sidebar.

Duvanel appeared in a new square. Cloquet enlarged it. The concierge's erratic roaming stood out in contrast to Ajit and Paul, sedentary in Mlle Wertheimer's old office. Cloquet had noted both nephews, the biological and the adopted, on either side of a very large desk. Each was absorbed by a laptop monitor.

Did they know Jean Duvanel was roaming? Cloquet couldn't call or text Paul without making Ajit curious.

Duvanel was upstairs in one of the rooms containing an armoire. The concierge inserted a skeleton key. A microphone picked up the creak of the armoire door opening. Duvanel's footsteps receded.

"*Zut!*"

Duvanel seemed to have gone somewhere with no camera coverage. Cloquet felt certain it was the other room with an armoire. Why hadn't his nephew cornered the fellow?

He took a sip of freshly opened cold beer. He didn't feel sleepy, but beer could lead in that direction. He should be drinking something else. In a moment he would get up, make a small sandwich, and after that, coffee. Now he clicked on a box showing one of the American girls holding a paper.

#

"In 1855, Château Mont Rose took its place in history as the first girls' boarding school in Switzerland," read Lauren. "For approximately one and a half centuries, young girls from all over the world passed through its gates."

Dominick opened his mouth, and Helena squashed her hand over it.

"Madame Jeanne Bonami purchased the estate in 1955. She decided that *The Little Prince,* written by Antoine de Saint-Exupéry, held a metaphor that represented the school's mission. In that book, the little prince told of his love for a rose who hurt him. The flower didn't know how *not* to be mean because she was born with thorns. That rose symbolized the girls who boarded at the school."

Dominick's tongue poked through Helena's fingers pressed over his mouth. Lauren faltered.

Rachel, typing on her iPad, did not look up.

"You asshole," said Helena. She wiped her hand on her shirt. "Nobody would think you're over thirty. Keep reading, Lauren."

Dominick grinned.

Dominick's nonsensical comments stopped Lauren every thirty seconds. She wished Helena hadn't surrendered.

"Imagine the lucky blokes who lived with all those young flooding female hormones."

"Would you shut up and let her read?" hissed Helena.

Lauren got through another page. To her surprise, Helena seemed thrilled about being featured in the script.

"I didn't realize I was so pivotal!"

Dominick, on the other hand, was not pleased. "That script may piss off the ghost."

There was a knock. Vanni tiptoed in, dark glossy curls tumbling into his sparkling eyes. Rachel must have brought him on the team. He held a platter of sliced, air-dried beef.

"A gastronomic specialty of the canton of Valais," Vanni said, leaving the platter on the center table. Pickles, grapes, and cheese were tucked around the curls of beef.

He exited and returned to place a basket of fragrant rye rolls on the table. His third entry brought a bottle of Fendant wine and another of Evian water along with five long-stemmed glasses on a tray.

"Take one glass back," said Helena, interrupting the recitation. "The writer will eat later."

"Oh—I'd like some water, please!" Lauren's throat was parched.

Vanni left the glass and hovered near the door, awaiting Helena's final command.

"Come back and do Lauren's makeup in twenty minutes. She looks unhealthy. Is your name Vanni? Go eat your dinner now or you won't have any other chance."

Dominick, Helena, and Rachel dined while Lauren read aloud. Her hunger grew. It was hard not to be swayed by the odor of the delectable beef, cheese and rye rolls, and the smell of the wine. Thank God for lunch with Paul. That meal was likely going to have to last her until morning.

"A very fruity vintage," said Dominick, pouring out the last drop of the bottle. "Do we have tea?"

"The food would have tasted better on a boat," said Helena.

"On the contrary," said Dominick. "Pheromones have seeped into the mold and mildew of this building. There's no better accompaniment to a good wine than pheromones."

Then Helena and Dominick began bickering about the food and the script, contradicting each other. Lauren took notes, scratching most out as the two producers squabbled. Finally, Helena dropped her napkin on the table.

"That's it. Let Lauren finish the revision. We have to get ready. This evening's encounter will be emotional. I need to meditate for fifteen minutes at least." She seized Dominick by the elbow and towed him out of the room.

Rachel stacked the empty platters and moved to retrieve a used wine glass on a windowsill. She laid it on top of the dishes.

"You're not leaving?" asked Lauren. "Can't you stay here with me?"

"Rachel!" called Helena from the corridor. "Get out here, *tout de suite.*"

"I'm sorry." Rachel carried the platters and glasses to the door. "You're a writer in the film industry now. Can you get the door?"

Rachel passed through with the cluttered tray.

The door yanked itself out from Lauren's hand and slammed shut on its own.

"I didn't do that," said Lauren quietly. "I didn't."

Chapter 22

Grock Lives Here

The text from Paul indicated that he and Ajit had known Duvanel was sneaking around. Paul was on his way to chuck him out on his ear. No sign, yet, of Papaux. Lockdown was imminent.

If Paul failed to find Papaux, a team would have to be called, and Cloquet would have to explain the mess to Moser and Nor. It would be a real shit storm.

Cloquet absentmindedly rubbed his cat's ears. At least Johnny didn't try to walk on the laptop, which had been an annoying habit since Cloquet had first brought a computer home. Training with a rolled newspaper had done the trick.

On impulse, Cloquet logged into police records for the canton de Vaud. He had an idea. He wondered if the former students who had gone missing from the hotel had criminal records.

He couldn't quite believe how right his instinct proved. In records spanning two decades, five of the missing had been cited for offenses as teens, ranging from disorderly conduct in town and marijuana usage to child endangerment (one girl gave birth and tried to "hide" the infant in a bathroom waste basket).

It was Swiss policy to quietly deport rich law-breaking teens. In their respective countries of origin, the young people underwent due process of law. With a clean slate, they might return to Switzerland after a certain elapsed time period—the longest enforced being five years. Their wealthy families sometimes owned Swiss timeshare apartments, had numbered accounts, skied on Swiss mountains and kept the fondue restaurants in business.

Yet Cloquet could not understand why any single person, let alone five, would want to return to a place with painful memory associations. He personally avoided the entire canton, and certainly the stretch of mountain road, where his daughter's life had ended.

The damage some of the more inconsiderate teens inflicted on other people, even on the reputation of the boarding schools that were responsible for them, left scars. That was the domino effect. Pain had ramifications.

Did places not resonate with the horror of events? Cloquet had felt a sense of gloom when passing once through Berlin, whose history spoke for itself. People said the same of parts of Russia.

Château Mont Rose had been in business for 150 years when it closed in the aftermath of Danielle Schwartz's death. Misdeeds by students had chipped away at its reputation before that event.

Could the château be calling girls back to punish them?

He felt ridiculous for having the idea.

#

A knock sounded on the door once, twice, thrice.

"Fraulein," called a voice. "Fraulein Briant, I bring your dinner. Fraulein Stamoulos sends me."

Lauren removed her headphones. She had been listening to Baroque music. She hoped the person in the corridor with the phony German accent wasn't Dominick.

"Come in."

"The door is locked, Fraulein."

It couldn't be. She hadn't locked the door, not wanting to touch its knob. The word Helena had used—"backbone"—floated up in Lauren's memory, so she rose, stiff and determined.

The opening door revealed an artfully made-up face level with her own. Black lips grinned, revealing yellow teeth like corn kernels on a cob. The white field around the mouth was outlined in a red, heart-shaped line.

Grock the clown stood before her, holding a tray of food.

Lauren staggered back. "What do you want?" she choked out.

The wide-eyed waxen eyes did not blink. The inky pupils contracted and one eyebrow lifted. "*Vy* are you speaking Spanish?"

"I'm speaking. . ." she began, but her vocal cords had constricted. She fought to make a sound: "English."

The clown hit one heel against the other and squared his shoulders. The brows furrowed, and a bit of eyebrow broke off. It fluttered down and stuck on the oversized jacket resembling plaid wool.

"Ich bin nicht Englische!"

Lauren knew that meant he was not English.

"Stay away, you *damned* hallucination" was what she wanted to say. The words that crept out were "What *are* you?"

"I am a bicycle rider."

Lauren shoved the door shut. The slam was satisfying for a brief second. She took the quilt off her bed, pulled it around her body, over her head, and perched on the mattress corner. Her heart beat hard. She clutched the quilt in two hands and began rocking.

Rapping on the door recommenced. Lauren rocked.

The other side could leave her alone.

"Mademoiselle!"

The knob was turning. The door opened.

Dark, shiny curls appeared, and then a face. It belonged to Vanni.

He put the tray down. "Mademoiselle Lauren, *ça va*? You are fine?"

"I don't know."

"Ghost-hunting is hard for you." Vanni's voice was gentle.

She felt his arms around her, around the quilt. It was a hug. She almost sobbed.

"Do not worry, Mademoiselle."

Then he let go, stepped back and bent down to look at her again through the quilt peephole.

"I keep imagining things," she blurted.

"Ah. You think I do not know? I, who work in a big dark castle where many people have died horrible deaths from torture? Vanni *does* know. I prepare myself carefully for Château de Chillon at night."

Goosebumps rose on her skin despite the warmth of the quilt. Maybe she wasn't cut out for dallying with departed spirits.

"A castle is supposed to be romantic. They always were for me, until now." As soon as the words were out of her mouth, Lauren realized nothing had ever been romantic about Château Mont Rose except its name.

Vanni looked sympathetic. "Do not be so sad and serious."

"How do you prepare yourself?" She hoped he would not bring up alcohol or drugs.

"I make a pact with the castle." His voice was solemn. "I promise Vanni will not harm the castle if it will not harm Vanni. And of course, I ask *le bon Dieu* to protect me."

"A pact?"

"Yes. If I see things, I let them go. Like wild birds. I let them fly away. Vanni refuses to carry the baggage of the castle's memories."

Lauren frowned. Vanni's method of talking about himself in third person was disconcerting.

"Can you please say *I* and not *Vanni?*"

He smiled and nodded in agreement. "Since being a little boy, I make this agreement with any castle I am in. Mademoiselle, I was born in a castle."

Lauren's fingers released their tight grasp and the quilt slid off her head, settling around her shoulders.

"Much better! You do not need to walk around like a monk with a blanket covering your face. I am here to make you so pretty all the dead spirits of Château Mont Rose will say 'please' before they try to scare you."

She tried to smile.

"*Per favore*, sit in front of the mirror." He gestured to the plate of food.

While she nibbled, he used the brush on himself, touched up his glossy locks with vigorous strokes, then admired his reflection.

"Is it my turn now?"

Vanni nodded, pulled the quilt completely away from Lauren, and tossed it on the bed. He plugged in the curling iron and set to work brushing her hair while describing pacts made with castles.

"Out loud?" Lauren asked.

"Out loud is better. You think something made of stones and mortar can read your mind?"

Lauren didn't want to know that answer.

"If you make the pact sincerely, you will be able to endure the truth.

"What truth?" she wanted to ask, but something stopped her. It was the reflection in the mirror. When she did not rely upon it—when she looked directly up at Vanni—all was well. But when her gaze flashed to its shining surface, the reflection of Vanni was no longer wearing snug jeans or form-fitting vest.

The reflected person she saw moving around behind her wore baggy pants and a grossly oversized plaid wool jacket. It was the clown, Grock.

#

Paul was upstairs and flustered. He couldn't find Duvanel.

Electricity did not work on most of the third floor, and Paul was glad he had brought his flashlight. It would have been impossible to see into the corners of the east-facing rooms without illumination. Dusk had so far advanced that a person could stand unmoving in certain corners and barely be noted.

Duvanel must have slipped by him. When Paul returned to the top of the staircase, frustrated, and peered over the balustrade, he saw the bald head retreating down the stairs.

"Stop!"

Looking up, Duvanel made a rude hand gesture and sprinted.

Paul cursed. He took the steps down two at a time. His head knocked the wax general's upheld arm, but he didn't hear any crash behind him. A brief feeling of surprise erupted: hadn't Uncle Julien said the statue was damaged? That thought was chased away by astonishment that an out-of-shape guy like Duvanel could move so fast.

Dominick's voice echoed from above his head: "What's all this running? I need the crew ready for lockdown. No one leaves! Do you hear?"

Midway down the hallway in pursuit of Duvanel, Paul heard Ajit call his name. He kept going. Outdoors, he raced fifty meters, just in time to see Duvanel slam his own front door shut.

Paul caught his breath, feeling warmer in the outdoor evening air than he had inside the château. The cottage lights went on.

There was no use interrogating Duvanel now. A running man was one thing, but a person on home turf felt safe and belligerent.

"Blimey, it's about time," said Dominick from the balcony. Paul climbed wordlessly under his gaze up to the first floor. Rachel, Helena, and Ajit were all in the office, waiting.

"No one leaves again for ice cream or to see their mummy. Lock the doors and bring me the keys."

"What if there's an emergency?" asked Rachel. "You saw what happened last night. Helena was unconscious."

"Conscious or unconscious means nothing," said Helena. "If my body, my outer shell, is unresponsive, it is because my spirit is traveling."

"Leaving Chillon for the clinic last night was necessary," conceded Dominick. "But we had good footage. I will make the decision about emergencies. Helena is just too important--"

"I know." Helena looked pleased.

She probably had no idea how heavy she was to carry to a car.

"No stopping tonight," she said. "Even if you think I am in a coma, understand it is a trance. I'm communing."

The Englishman's face had gone broody. "Where is that script girl?"

"Getting made up, Mr. Bentley," said Rachel.

"She doesn't have to look like a bloody princess. We'll be filming with infrared cameras. Eyeshadow won't show. All she has to do is wear the dress. "

"Not for the introduction, Dummy-Dom," said Helena. "Why are you acting like a cat on hot bricks? I could do with some aspirin." She rubbed her neck.

"Aspirin," Dominick snapped his fingers. "And ginger ale. Girl Friday, arse in gear!"

Rachel nodded, moving.

Paul wondered if Uncle Julien was watching, and if so, what he thought of the team's irritable moodiness. It was everything Paul could do, himself, to resist giving in to inexplicable querulousness.

#

Seated before the vanity table, Lauren felt a charge of fear zap down her spine.

"You're not looking at me, Fraulein."

She addressed Château Mont Rose under her breath.

"I used to live here. I'm sorry I wanted to leave at first. I was young and missed my mother. After making some friends, I began to like living here. I liked learning French."

"Fraulein." The voice pierced like an icicle. "Do we not have some business between us?"

"I left because the year was over."

"If you vill pleez look up, *Fraulein*!"

Abruptly Lauren felt stupid, talking to a building. "Oh dear God," she prayed, "If there is nothing to make friends with—please protect me from lurking evil."

"Do you like your hair, Mademoiselle?"

Vanni's voice was his own. Lauren looked at the mirror. Above her head of well-coiffed hair, she saw the eyes of the young man twinkle in cheer.

"I do. Thank you."

"You are welcome."

"I was following your advice."

"Is it working?"

"I guess we'll see." Lauren started to rise.

"Not yet!" Vanni pressed her back down with two hands. "You must wait for me to bring the delicacy you will be wearing tonight."

Giggling, Vanni ran out the door, left it ajar. Lauren's gaze hung there. He reappeared before she could panic, wearing his own tight jeans with the Gucci insignia, boots, velvet vest and curly mop of hair. He held a large, fancy shopping bag.

Lauren breathed easier.

"It was necessary to make your hair match this delight before showing it to you." Gaily, he extracted a box from the bag: "May I present to you. . . ."

He unwrapped tissue and pulled a long gown of eggshell chiffon out of the box, dangling it before her. Creamy lace edged the pearl-beaded bodice and sheer long sleeves. Yards of shimmering fabric spilled out from the folds they had been in.

"Is that a wedding gown?"

"*Oui, oui*! Yesterday we—I—take your measurements while you sleep." Vanni wiggled his shoulders. "We are the same size, you and me, almost like sisters."

Lauren looked at the mirror to see if Vanni had morphed yet. He had not. She found *that* exciting in a nice, dull way.

"Why would Dominick want me to wear a wedding dress?"

His shoulders lifted. "You are beautiful. Perhaps he wants to—to marry you to the château—symbolically?"

"That sounds weird."

"See the veil? With pearl beads. It would make anyone who wears it beautiful. Mademoiselle, you are fortunate."

"How does that gown work with Helena's heavy metal look?"

"Who am I to explain the genius of directors?" Vanni's eyes were moist. "Scenes must be in many different flavors. Tonight Mr. Dominick prepares a magical feast."

Vanni laid the dress neatly out on Rachel's bed. Lauren hoped he was right about genius, for they were all stuck with Dominick. She couldn't remember anything beyond the first hour or so at Chillon. She wondered dully what had been filmed there. Rachel would show her.

"We put it on you later, mademoiselle? To make you happy. . . ."

Lauren thought he might burst into tears from joy.

"Shall I walk downstairs with you?"

Since Vanni was still Vanni, she agreed.

\#

Cloquet had dozed. The beer and painkiller had relaxed him more than he needed. He moved Johnny off his lap, went to the kitchen. Back at the monitor with coffee and a sandwich, he found one of the 15 boxes was blurry from a moving figure.

It was a girl wearing a rather dark floral dress, exiting a room. The glimpse of her profile struck him as familiar. Then in another box, signifying her entry into another room, the same girl looked up at the camera. She disappeared for a second and then he saw her eyes, close and cold. She must have found a chair to climb. Suddenly a fingertip came straight onto the camera lens. It pressed and rubbed, leaving a smear like butter.

Or wax.

He lost her. He did not know where she went after that, at least not for the moment. Cloquet clicked on the headmistress's old office. The room was crowded and sound came through. (Cloquet blessed his talented nephew.) Ajit held a camera, Paul sat with an open laptop, and Bentley talked (nonsensically) and gestured. Cloquet recognized the three young women, but not a young man with dark curly hair. Bentley finished blabbing and the group dispersed.

Chapter 23

A Dress with a Mission

Lauren leaned against the wood column. It blocked the wax figure of Carl Gustav Jung from the camera, by Dominick's specific direction. He wanted the focus to be on the girls' school of earlier days rather than the museum that had taken its place.

A spotlight beamed directly into her eyes.

"Can you turn that off until I start reading?"

Ajit cut the light.

Helena, whispering with Dominick, glanced at Lauren. She jerked her head and threw back her shoulders as if she had received a shock. "I feel an aura. Perhaps several. We must begin."

"Lights!" said Dominick.

Lauren raised one hand as a shield against the renewed glare, held the script outstretched to Rachel. She would speak from memory. The words had etched themselves into her brain.

Rachel took Lauren's papers, apprehension on her face. Probably she worried that Lauren would screw up the reading. But Lauren knew she wouldn't. She wished Rachel would believe in her.

Paul and bright-eyed Vanni peered down from the upstairs landing.

"Makeup!" cried Dominick, snapping his fingers.

Vanni barreled down the stairs, patted Lauren's forehead and nose with an oversized powder puff that he tucked into a pocket of an apron, and pulled out a comb to poke at her hair and re-arrange her bangs.

"Now the clapboard, Vito."

Vanni grabbed the clapboard from the stairs. "My name is Vanni," he said, with a toss of his curls. "I am *not* Vito Corleone." He indignantly slapped the two parts of the clapboard together. The device was old fashioned, with chalk- scrawled words.

"Don't look serious, girlie. Look sexy. Action! Take one," said Dominick.

Thrown by the command, Lauren stammered.

"Cut!"

Rachel shook her head.

"Why 'cut'?" asked Helena.

"Where is the damn dress I paid for?"

"I thought I nixed that idea! You got a wedding dress? How stupid do you want her to look?"

Rachel covered her eyes with her hand.

Lauren wondered if the strange pearl-studded gown upstairs was going to cause problems.

"You asking why she isn't wearing a wedding dress proves you don't believe I'll get in contact." Helena fingered a metal eyebrow piercing. "I can tell you're trying to manufacture a 'white lady' ghost, Goddamnit, Dom."

"I always have plan B, woman. Channeling doesn't come on command. I've seen you calling out for spirits too dead to budge. We're going to get the illusion, on film, of a virgin bride being deflowered."

Was the man mental? Lauren looked wide-eyed at Rachel, who shrugged.

"Let's try believing, shall we?" Helena said. "She can wear the dress later, if you insist."

"Start where you left off, kid," said Dominick. "Don't be so depressed looking. Stick out your chest. Action; take two."

Ignoring him, Lauren said to the camera, "When Mademoiselle Danielle Schwartz was hired to teach at Château Mont Rose, she assigned her students *Le Petit Prince*, a story about love and tolerance. Yet in her first spring at the school, this popular teacher was murdered. An investigation conducted by the Lausanne police sent the perpetrators to prison. Tragically, the crime shattered the boarding school's reputation. A century and a half of good work was destroyed.

"Today, the establishment has reopened as a hotel and museum. Tonight, the former students of Danielle Schwartz are gathered together at Château Mont Rose for a special purpose. The celebrated Greek psychic and thorniest of all Mademoiselle Schwartz's roses, Helena Stamoulos, will attempt to make contact with the spirit of our murdered teacher."

"Cut."

Helena wore a sad smile. "I was the thorniest rose!" There was a catch in her voice.

Then Dominick cried, "Action," and Helena began calling out in a resonant voice, with her eyes rolling backward in their sockets, for Mlle Schwartz to appear.

#

Via satellite, the comment that "the Lausanne police sent the perpetrators to prison" released darts into Cloquet's conscience. The truth was *no* human being had been named as the teacher's killer. Neither Madame Bonami nor Mlle Schwartz had eaten the poisoned tart. Maxime Bonami had been indicted and sent to jail for plotting to harm the three schoolgirls who were now in the ghost-hunting crew at Château Mont Rose.

It had been a short incarceration.

Monsieur Bonami's intelligence and charm had worked wonders on the prison psychiatrists. Certain numbered Swiss bank accounts must also have benefitted, for Bonami was today a free man.

Danielle Schwartz's case file stated that the woman died of natural causes. Cloquet had shared that fact with Rachel, warning her not to repeat it to her friend Lauren. To do so would put them both in greater danger than they currently faced.

Cloquet watched the group form a circle around Helena.

"Join hands," Helena commanded, closing her eyes. "O spirit of Danielle Schwartz; we were your students, your roses. Our thorns scratched you, but *we* did not take your life."

No sooner had Helena finished her appeal to the unseen spirit than a loud rumbling sounded, coming through Cloquet's laptop. It reminded him of students' feet pounding down the staircase on one of his visits when girls had returned from spring break.

He could not figure out what caused the sound now, but structural vibrations were certain when a large painting disengaged from the wall and clattered down the staircase.

"Break not the circle!" cried Helena. "Oh roses of Mlle Schwartz! Break not the circle of thorns."

A female asked, "Was that Mlle Schwartz's spirit?"

"Yes," Helena replied.

"She seems angry," someone said.

Cloquet scratched Johnny's head, weighing the moment to interfere. He was more worried by the strange girl who had smeared two camera lenses than what might be contrived vibrations. Paul had doubtless silenced his phone but would be on the lookout for any text, in code, Cloquet felt important enough to send.

#

Virginie Duvanel had remained in the tower well past the dinner hour, at Mlle Wertheimer's request. The elderly woman seemed troubled with so many noisy interlopers on the premises. She ate birdlike from her tray, ignoring the housekeeper who sat on the other side of the darkening room. With night came enough moonlight streaming in through a window for the brittle movements of the gripped fork, stabbing and lifting morsels to the mouth, then dropping them back into the plate again, to be fully visible.

Virginie did not care if the old woman really ate or not. She liked being close, the sense of belonging. As a girl, Virginie had climbed a tree in her father's yard and looked over the estate wall. She remembered seeing the headmistress clap her hands at the front door. All the girls in view stopped what they were doing and listened. Now it was Virginie who listened.

When she was not serving Mlle Wertheimer or overseeing household tasks, she liked to imagine herself young, enrolled at Château Mont Rose by Papa. Papa today was sequestered in a care facility, but she liked to think of him as vibrant and concerned for her.

The illogic of being a Swiss-French girl in a school where students learned French eluded Virginie. She fantasized about Lausanne shop clerks allowing her to sign her name when purchasing pretty clothes like soft angora sweaters and high-heeled boots; that was how she had seen boarding school girls dress on their way to town. She imagined young men, nicer than the one she had married, escorting her to restaurants and bringing her chocolates on Valentine's Day.

Such daydreams were easy within these walls. She never knew at what turn in a hallway a fairytale life would flicker into color, complete with sounds and scents, enveloping her in its sensual reality, making her giddy with delight.

Mlle Wertheimer was done with her meal. Virginie blinked at her, eyes refocusing. How long had the old woman sat, unmoving, on the other side of the dark attic room?

"*Alors.*" The word was a beacon of light. "You have been a very good young lady."

Virginie's heartbeats quickened joy straight to her fingertips. When fifty-five-year-old Virginie heard kind words from Mlle Wertheimer, she felt like a brilliant and beautiful pupil.

"Unlike certain other girls from Château Mont Rose," said Mlle Wertheimer, "who misbehaved. They were incorrigible, were they not?"

"Oui, mademoiselle. They were reprobates."

"As if Château Mont Rose counted for nothing." Mlle Wertheimer tisked. "*Bien entendu*, we expect the rose to scratch us with its thorns, don't we, Virginie?"

"Oui, mademoiselle. If we are not careful."

"The wise gardener handles the rose with care for the thorns, does he not?"

"Indeed. Otherwise, the flower must be nipped in the bud."

There was a short silence.

"You are witty this evening," replied the old headmistress. "If only you had been a real student."

Virginie squirmed. She did not like to be reminded she had not been.

"Young ladies should not interrupt. I *know* girls. They have been my career. I hope, Virginie, you have been as successful with your son. He needs to be loyal."

"Of course, mademoiselle."

"But he does not always listen to you, does he, Virginie?"

"Yes, he d—" Virginie caught herself. Young ladies did not contradict. "He is not disobedient, mademoiselle, just distracted."

"Boys," said Mlle Wertheimer. She prodded the word out of her mouth like a bit of moldy fruit. The moonlight disappeared behind clouds, leaving the room in darkness. "They are trouble. You say your boy is devoted to Château Mont Rose? We will see. Jeanne Bonami *thought* her nephew was devoted to the ideals taught at Château Mont Rose. "

"Yes, mademoiselle."

"Males get away with all manner of trouble; females may not. Are there more naughty girls here tonight?"

"Oui, mademoiselle."

"These people have stirred up the château."

"They are a film crew, mademoiselle, hunting for ghosts."

"What ghost do they think to find?"

Virginie had thought Mlle Wertheimer knew, but she said, "They are looking for the ghost of Danielle Schwartz."

Mlle Wertheimer gave a strange hiss. Virginie shifted in her seat, waiting for directions.

"Pay close attention. If one of the others tell you to do something, you must not question."

"But. . . . they are not—" Virginie groped for a word and settled on "—roses."

"No. They are the thorns. Now we wait."

#

Solitary in the château's main office, Paul read Uncle Julien's text message. If anyone crept in and looked over Paul's shoulder, the words read as a phone bill.

The code reminded Paul that the former headmistress lived in the building, presumably in the attic. Uncle Julien said he must be on the lookout for a girl in a dark, flowered dress, perhaps a maid, not to be confused with Virginie Duvanel, who lived in the cottage at back.

Technically, there wasn't supposed to be anyone in the château tonight except the ghost-hunting crew.

A decrepit old woman in a tower was not a problem, but the unknown girl who was wandering around upstairs, smearing camera lenses, had to be smuggled out and questioned. Why was she sabotaging the ghost hunting?

Paul found the two smeared camera boxes on his monitor. Irritated, he considered how he could find the girl and get her outside without Dominick finding out. Short of knocking the fellow unconscious, Paul did not see how he was going to wrest the keys to the doors off him.

The solution appeared in the next message. With a formal thanks for paying his bill, the decoded statement revealed Uncle Julien had keys for every door in the building, including the main gate. He was on his way.

With the phone set on vibrate, Paul turned his attention to the camera control panel. He deactivated the cameras he would pass under.

He rose as Vanni entered the office, and asked, "Aren't you supposed to be out there?"

Vanni looked dejected. "Helena says only the 'roses' of Château Mont Rose may stay in the foyer. Anyone who is not a rose will make the dead teacher unhappy. Dominick told me to leave, but *he* is hiding so he can watch. " Vanni slouched across the room.

"They *are* the bosses."

"*I* could have been a rose. You think I did not wish to attend a school like this?"

"It was for girls, Vanni."

"My heart weeps to be left out." Vanni lowered himself on the couch, picked up a fork and poked at the food platter.

"Was anyone hurt when the painting fell?"

"No. Your cousin Ajit, he could have been squashed by a statue, rocking, but he held onto it and did not get hurt."

"That's good. What about the ladies? Lauren . . . how is she?"

"Well," Vanni held the fork like an orchestra conductor a baton, raised his black eyebrows to meet the curly mop. "She may be a verrrry little bit not herself."

"What do you mean?"

"She does not see Vanni in every direction she looks. There are different personalities inside, here," he touched his chest with his clenched fist, "struggling to get out." Vanni put down the fork and set his elbows on his knees, chin on the upturned palms. "I want to be her friend."

Annoyed by trying to understand Vanni's meaning, Paul said, "I'm sure Lauren knows you are her friend."

"But she is afraid of how this place interprets me and it scares her. Do you suppose because she was a student here, she is being punished?" When there was no answer from Paul, who stared at him, the Italian continued, "I tell you what I think. Château Mont Rose—" he enunciated the name like a medieval courtier, his hand sweeping in an arc to indicate the whole building, "is *not* a true castle, yet it was once a home for the world's 'princesses.' It must have a hurt pride." He popped two grapes in his mouth. "Resentment is not healthy. I want to be a rose, but I do not take revenge."

"I'm sure you don't."

"Buildings have feelings too. Castles--they feel proud or angry. In Italian, we say, *"Che Dio distruggerà, ha prima fanno impazzire"*—Whom God will destroy, He first makes mad. Why do you think *le bon Dieu* will destroy the entire earth before the great Day of Judgment? To humble it, when it goes mad."

Paul felt unprepared for the apocalyptic turn of conversation. "Listen, don't worry about Lauren. Just relax for a while." He started to leave but Dominick blocked the doorway.

"Stay right where you are, old man. Give the dolls a minute for their séance. I told Ajit to put the camera on a tripod and get out of the room. We can watch through the computer monitors."

Paul exhaled his frustration. Dominick sat at one laptop and Paul, with Vanni breathing down his neck, resigned himself to the other. When Vanni wandered back to the coffee table for more grapes, Paul clicked on the upstairs camera boxes. He found a third camera lens smudged.

The *bitch*.

"That's it, baby," muttered Dominick at his monitor. "Bring on the beasties."

Paul clicked on the séance box and saw Helena straining, head lolling and jerking, with her arms stiff. Rachel and Lauren held her hands.

He clicked on a fourth upstairs screen. The girl in a dark dress approached the camera and found something to climb on. A finger pressed itself upon the lens and rubbed until the box was an opaque blur.

Chapter 24

Lauren Sees a Shrink

Rachel had been gripping Helena's hand for a good ten minutes. It brought back an odd memory.

When she was thirteen, her mother took her to see Madame Zavlasky, a popular New York medium. Mama wanted to contact Grandma Sari, recently deceased. Madame Zavlasky's head had rolled backward on her shoulders much as Helena's head rolled backward now. Grandma Sari's voice, not sounding quite as Rachel remembered it, had warbled out of Madame Zavlasky's mouth. So far, nothing but entreaties came out of Helena's mouth.

Rachel wondered if Mlle Schwartz's voice would spring from Helena's lips. Would the words be comforting like Grandma Sari's? Mama had cried when Grandma Sari said she missed everyone, mentioning things only family members could have known unless the medium had done preliminary homework. Grandma Sari ended with wishing them a Happy Hanukkah.

That was when Rachel asked Grandma Sari, in Yiddish, if she was happy. Madame Zavlasky did not answer; her body went limp. The medium then raised her head from the table and announced Grandmother Sari's spirit had left the room.

Rachel concluded Madame Zavlasky did not speak Yiddish.

Helena somehow struck Rachel as the real deal. Should Mlle Schwartz start speaking through Helena's lips, Rachel expected French. Since Helena's French was none too fluent, speaking in that language would prove spiritual contact, as well as a need for subtitles on the end film product.

What Rachel didn't expect was an invisible hundred-pound steel harness to drop onto her shoulders. Her knees buckled and she fell.

At ground level, no further weight pushed down unless she tried sitting up. Rachel pulled her legs around and straightened them. The carpet smelled musty. She looked up at her companions and tried to speak.

Panic overwhelmed her. 23 years of age and she was suffering a stroke? All she could move was her eyes.

Lauren had disappeared from view with the sound of a bag of potatoes being dropped. By effort that made her head pound, Rachel turned her face a few inches. There Lauren was, eyes closed.

Rachel wished Helena would notice them.

Viewed from the floor, the Greek woman had gained in stature, although her posture was peculiar. She was bending backward over the balustrade, which creaked and groaned.

Where in the hell were the men?

#

Vanni peered over Dominick's shoulder, not Paul's, thank heaven. Paul was already irritated enough at not being able to go upstairs, grab the girl, and get her out. Maybe he should point out the smeared sidebar boxes on his computer screen and suggest he go investigate.

"Nom de Dieu!" said Vanni.

"What?" Paul looked at the foyer scene.

Dominick's hand, attaching itself to Paul's jacket, prevented him from jumping up. "Helena specifically didn't want us to interfere. She's a big girl."

"Very big," cried Vanni. "The balustrade is collapsing!"

Paul wrenched his jacket free and ran from the room.

The foyer landing was glacial. Paul seized Helena's wrist. At the same instant, he felt a force push him into the balustrade. He braced his legs and called out. A man grabbed hold of his waist.

Helena was yanked away from the railing just as the wood balustrade broke and swung into the air. Helena, Paul, Dominick, and Vanni fell backward, away from the gap, each on top of the other. The camera, on a tripod, stood running, unaffected by gravity or any other force. Ajit was nowhere to be seen.

"Oh my God, that hurt. I'm glad . . . you broke in." Helena crawled to the wall farthest from the staircase.

"As soon as I saw you in danger, I came running," lied Dominick.

Vanni was slapping Lauren's hand and cheek.

"Your dead teacher was quite the trollop, wasn't she?" said Dominick. "Come back into the office."

Helena allowed herself to be led away.

"Can you get up?" Vanni asked Rachel.

She proved she could, groaning. Lauren seemed asleep.

"Mademoiselle Lauren does not look so good," said Vanni, gesturing to Paul. "Except for the makeup and hair, *bien sûr.*"

"She's breathing," said Rachel.

Lauren's breathing was shallow. Paul got water, but the effort of sprinkling Lauren's face, shaking her, and calling her name brought no response.

#

In his apartment, Detective Cloquet made a last-minute check, clicking on every screen. Paul had texted the news Cloquet could plainly see. The lockdown was too dangerous to continue. One of the young Americans, Lauren Briant, was unresponsive, a perfect reason to terminate the group's activity. Unfortunately, Paul's cover would be blown.

Cloquet intended to drive to Château Mont Rose and unlock a door through which his nephew could smuggle out the teenage girl who had been smearing camera lenses. After that, if the young American woman, Lauren, had resumed consciousness, the lockdown might continue. Cloquet could follow events from outside in his car. He had WiFi provided by his Sûreté-issue vehicle.

The bottom two screens on Cloquet's sidebar showed the front door and salon window of the Duvanels' cottage. Enlarging one, Cloquet saw Jean Duvanel pushing something into the neck of the statue he had been sculpting earlier. Cloquet zoomed in.

They were tacks or nails, making him think of voodoo.

Cloquet studied the tall wax figure dressed in a toga. It was an uncanny duplicate of Helena Stamoulos.

#

For years, Jean Duvanel had avoided taking initiative. He had seen what it did to his old schoolmates, loading them down with dreary jobs, nagging wives and complaining children. Initiative led to toil.

That was not the life he wanted.

However, he had not realized initiative and inspiration were linked. Inspiration, when it came, was sharp and vivid. It conveyed images in waking or sleeping dreams. The very first of those images was of himself and his mother applying for two positions at Château Mont Rose.

Once he and *Maman* were hired, inspiration multiplied. Mother and son moved onto the Château Mont Rose estate. Checks arrived for which not much exertion on Jean's part was required. Images filled his head and he quenched his thirst for them like a desert nomad at an oasis.

For instance, as wax statues began arriving, Jean Duvanel's hands itched to try out sculpture. It did not feel like work. His first few attempts were junk, but he was patient. At last, he had achieved a masterpiece.

He realized his sculpture looked exactly like that attractive but loud woman who had stomped all around the building this morning when the firefighters arrived. She had screamed at people. What was her business screaming at him? The château didn't need her, but it had inspired him to sculpt the loud woman's form before he had ever seen her. Astonished at the likeness, he believed he had the right to do as he wanted with the wax figure.

Jean pushed in another tack. He was not supposed to kill the recipient of the curse. He meant to drive the human to her fate while the château would keep the beautiful, unspeaking image of her.

#

Holding his violin, Grock the clown grins at Lauren with lifeless, waxen eyes. "Shall I play for you?"

A second voice interrupts. "She needs to stay in the collective unconscious where she is resting."

"Ze collective unconscious is not restful, Doktor," says the clown, flopping his long shoes on the floor. He circles around like a hyena.

"Grock, I beg to differ. Take your simpleton act away from my consulting room. I need to be alone with the patient."

Lauren can see everything, even her diaphanous self. Her psyche is pinned to a couch like a butterfly to a mounting board.

The doctor, a bespectacled man in a dark, three-piece suit, approaches. "Allow me to introduce myself, Fraulein. I am Carl Gustave Jung. I am going to sit in my chair behind you," he says, gesturing with a pipe, "so that you do not focus on me as we talk." He moves back and sits. "I want to get to the bottom of your trouble with Château Mont Rose."

Lauren asks, "But where is the 'collective unconscious'?"

"It does not have an address, Fraulein; It is a psychological place of knowledge. In that place, all roles of human beings exist. These roles appear in our subconscious as we develop."

"Dr. Jung, are you made of wax?"

There is a little pause of silence before Dr. Jung answers. "I am not made out of wax in the collective unconscious."

"Are you a hallucination?"

"That word is as appropriate as any other."

"Will you help me?"

She can hear him scratching with a pen on paper.

"I will help you interpret your dream. Please describe it to me."

But this is it, she wants to say. In her dream, she is talking to a wax figure of a Swiss psychoanalyst.

Jung says, "We need to hear the messages of our dreams and waking imagination. By analyzing these experiences, we reintegrate our different parts."

This makes some sense. If Lauren wants to reconnect to her body, she has to reintegrate the parts. "I will tell you my dream," she says. Anxiety washes over her. How can she admit she is afraid, without making things worse?

The clown, shuffling around with his floppy slippers, pipes up, "Be careful, little girl. Herr Doktor's patience has a limit."

"I am dreaming that I am talking to you, Doctor Jung, and that a terrible wax clown is in the room. He scares me."

"Ach, so. Children are afraid of clowns."

Doesn't Dr. Jung see she is a full-grown woman?

"Dr. Jung, is Grock a hallucination?"

"Who?"

"Grock, the clown. He knocked on my bedroom door this evening. I keep seeing him as a wax figure. I saw him melting this morning."

There's that pause again, long enough to think he will not respond. "He who has a head of wax should not walk in the sun," Jung says finally.

"He wasn't walking in the sun!" Lauren argues. "He is with us in the room—you just spoke to him!"

"This is your dream state, Fraulein." The doctor's voice is ambivalent.

"What is the purpose of the clown showing up when I am *not* dreaming? I saw him tonight in my bedroom." Lauren hears Dr. Jung rocking his chair. "Dr. Jung?"

There is a low snicker. Grock says, "So many questions!"

"Hush!" commands Dr. Jung. "Young woman, surely you know why clowns exist. They punish bad children. You must have done something very bad when you lived at Château Mont Rose."

#

Virginie Duvanel waited a long time upstairs in the dark with the old woman seated on the far side of the room, neither one of them saying a word. The pigeons cooed and rustled under the eaves.

Her bottom was sore. She wiggled into new positions, crossed her legs, and let her mind drift. There was no television to entertain them. Virginie could not remember Mlle Wertheimer ever watching television, not even to take in a documentary or the news. There was certainly no such thing up here as a computer or a CD player. Virginie wondered if the old woman became so caught up by memories she needed no other stimuli. Or did she see dreams of herself played out on the walls like Virginie did? No one who had tasted that joy would be interested in anything else. Virginie's heart sped up as she thought of her addiction. Surely the château did not offer such pleasure to her alone?

Someone played piano up here from time to time. Virginie heard the tinkling of music when she walked down the path to her cottage. She assumed it was Mlle Wertheimer.

Out of the dark, Mlle Wertheimer croaked, "There are not any ghosts here to communicate with."

"Oui, mademoiselle," said Virginie.

"What kind of devices do these people have?"

Devices? Mlle Wertheimer surely did not mean vacuum cleaners. Virginie cast about in her mind to identify objects she had seen.

"Flashlights and cameras, mademoiselle."

"What kind?"

"The kind they hold in their hands. And headgear, with cameras on them, little ones. I saw those things when I snuck into your old office."

"No one saw you?"

"I used the secret panel door."

Mlle Wertheimer did not like to be reminded that the past, when she used her office and the secret panel door, could not be revived. The office had been turned into a salon for the hotel's guests.

Finally, the night clouds split and moonlight streamed in. The old woman's locks of powdery curls looked like the dust balls swept from under beds. The old woman's eyes resembled two sink drains. Virginie stifled a giggle.

Guilt followed. If Château Mont Rose could read Virginie's thoughts, it might say she didn't belong, due to disrespect.

"Be a good girl, Virginie, and make sure," said Mlle Wertheimer, as if she had a glimmer into Virginie's ideas. "If you want to belong to Château Mont Rose. Do as you are told. Now go."

"Oui, mademoiselle." Standing up, Virginie heard her knees pop. She wanted to collect the dinner tray, but was rebuked.

"You can take it later. Go."

Chastened, Virginie went down the narrow staircase too fast. One foot rolled forward on the point of her shoe. She managed to catch the side rail with both hands, but banged her hip bone. Mlle Wertheimer did not call out to inquire if she was alright. Virginie should have realized the château could hear her thoughts. She took a moment, smoothed out her skirt, and felt gingerly with her feet until she got to the bottom. She rubbed the sore hip bone and closed the door at the bottom of the stairwell.

Sounds drifted up from the crew. She padded down the third-floor corridor in her flat shoes. "Make sure," she whispered to herself. A scratching sound caught her ear. It could be a rat.

The scratching increased in volume at a corner room. Virginie pushed the door open and looked in on an obscenity.

A dark-skinned young man wearing headgear worked, scratching with a tool, at a crack between two boards. He stopped, shined a light close up, and ran his fingers over the wide crack. Then he stuck a large blade into the wainscoting and levered. Splintering resounded.

Outrage swelled in the chambers of her heart. All the years of effort by housekeepers and carpenters were to be defiled by this verminous intruder?

The human rat was in front of an open window. Smudges on the window panes from wax fingers showed one of the helper statues had opened the window in readiness. Human rats could be encouraged to jump ship.

Virginie saw the straight line she should take. She burst in, at full speed, arms outstretched to thrust the thief through the window.

She caught Ajit off guard.

Chapter 25

Mlle Wertheimer's Old Office

Rachel leaned out of the first-floor bathroom window, cigarette dangling from her fingers. Illicit smoking in this bathroom had calmed her as a teen. Any teacher marching down the corridor looking for a student to yell at had to respect the locked door and the flush of the toilet.

Her hand was trembling when she placed the tip of a new cigarette on the burning end of the first one. She threw the old butt in the water-filled porcelain bowl. How embarrassing to have chewed out Vanni for doping up Lauren when here Rachel was, needing her own nicotine fix.

Maybe they shouldn't have come back to the château. Disasters seem to follow Helena despite her wealth. Rachel had not appreciated the look Paul had given her when Lauren wouldn't respond just now. But damn it, it was hard finding a promising job nowadays, even with a business degree. How could an undercover Swiss detective working for his uncle understand that?

When Rachel asked what the hell they had just endured, Dominick told her to hold her tongue. Helena made some incoherent remark about the instability of Mlle Schwartz's spirit. As she spoke, the boss was slapping at her neck like she was in a mosquito-infested jungle. Dominick pulled Helena's hand away, and anyone could see angry red bumps all over her neck. Dominick said bugs must have been in the carpet and made Rachel get out repellant and a tube of hydrocortisone cream from their supplies.

She exhaled smoke out the window into the night air, watched it billow and disperse. The message on the window pane had warned them to "leave the rose." During the séance this evening, they had been attacked.

Why would their teacher's spirit warn them and then attack them? The first action was protective, the second, malicious. Rachel thought about how Mlle Schwartz had barely mustered enough energy to emerge as a wispy form in the footage taken at Château de Chillon. Even so, Rachel had recognized her. She inhaled on the cigarette. Was there any chance Ajit had spliced some old film in? That was pretty far-fetched. He had never heard of Mlle Schwartz until being hired on the crew. Where would he find a private video of Mlle Schwartz?

Minutes ago, Helena had told her not to worry about Lauren's "trance state." It was so weird to think of Lauren having psychic powers.

Rachel took another drag. Her thoughts were going around in circles. She had to set a limit. If this night did not turn out well, if anyone got hurt, she and Lauren should discuss calling it quits. There were other opportunities for an interesting career, right?

Rachel just couldn't think of one.

Resisting the desire to light a third cigarette, she turned to throw the butt into the porcelain bowl and froze. A moment earlier, the toilet bowl had been clean save for a single floating butt.

Under her uncomprehending gaze, at least fifty charred cigarette butts floated in the toilet water.

\#

Paul saw the female rush at Ajit, who stood like a ball in front of a pool table pocket. Ajit would go through the window, which was wide open.

Paul cut in front of her and grabbed his cousin's legs. The female pushed Ajit, but he did not go through the window. Instead, the three struggled. Fingernails ripped into Paul's cheek. He landed a right uppercut—and the woman went limp.

Ajit punched Paul in the following split second. Stars and nausea made Paul roll away.

When he came to grips, Paul sat up, saw the ripped wall paneling.

Ajit held a flashlight on him. "That was a mistake. I thought you were her." He nodded at the woman.

A rag was stuffed in the woman's mouth, and duct tape was plastered from one ear to the other so she couldn't speak when she awoke. Blood dribbled from her nose. Ajit had secured her hands and was doing the same to her feet.

"Where did you get the duct tape?"

"My bag of tricks. I am always prepared."

"A little too prepared, Ajit. Why are you digging into the wall?" Paul gestured to the damage.

Ajit shrugged.

Paul studied the tied-up woman. Could this crazed older woman be the head housekeeper? She didn't fit the description of the girl in a flowered black dress.

Her eyes opened. A yell was muffled behind the rag.

"We have to get her out of here."

"I'll say!" agreed Ajit, closing the window through which cold gusts surged. "Dominick said there was no one in the building. Should we tell him about her?"

"Then he'll blame us. Does she work here?"

"I think so—I saw her earlier while waiting for you. I thought she left. You should have been here helping me; that's what you're getting paid for."

Paul didn't think Ajit would mention the woman's presence to Dominick. It was too closely associated with his mining the walls.

Paul pulled out his phone to text.

"What are you doing, man?"

"Uncle Julien. He's a cop. He'll know what to do."

"Are you nuts? Dominick and Helena don't want any outsiders here, certainly not the police. You're going to lose our jobs for us."

"We have to get her out," said Paul. If we ask Dominick for a key to get out, he'll ask why and then we'll have to show him this woman. She'll mention you vandalizing the place. Can you say 'lawsuit'?"

"Shit," said Ajit.

"What were you doing, treasure hunting?"

Ajit avoided Paul's eyes. "Uncle Julien doesn't have keys either."

"Maybe not," said Paul. "But he is a crack locksmith. The police have their tools."

Paul's phone vibrated.

"*Formidable*," said Paul, reading the text. "He's in the area. Help me, Ajit." He grabbed the woman under the armpits.

\#

Lauren blinked and the room teetered. When it stopped moving, she recognized Dominick, feet propped on a small tapestry footstool, his mouth sucking on a cigar he held between three fingers. The end fanned bright orange.

She sat up and recognized Mlle Wertheimer's old office.

"Well, good morning, cupcake. How was your trance?"

Lauren grimaced. Lingering nightmare images hovered at the periphery of her memory. When she tried to grab at them, they turned to puffs of smoke.

"Men don't mind visual weirdness, especially on the female form. That's a director's secret, of course." Ashes fell from Dominick's cigar onto the office rug, and he rubbed them in with the toe of his shoe. "I had the greatest fun listening to you—and watching. Recorded as much as I could."

"What did you record?"

"Your ramblings. You talked in your trance."

"I don't have trances." In a smaller voice, she asked, "What did I say?"

"Shall I play it back? Or do you just want the highlights?"

Why had Rachel and Helena left her alone with him?

"You saw the owner of this boarding school shagging your teacher, for one thing."

Lauren felt her face grow warm.

"You watched an illicit tryst by a stream. Panties were thrown in the air and you nearly had a heart attack. What a little cutey you must have been, all pimples and knees. I'll bet that fellow, Bonami, wanted to wring your neck."

Alone time with Dominick was a negative.

"Where's Paul?"

"Hell if I know. You got a thing for him?"

"That's none of your—"

"Everything's my business," snapped Dominick. "It's in the contract. Funny you didn't mention Paul. You were making confessions to a doctor, saying 'Monsieur Bonami' was the most handsome man in Lausanne. No one would ever guess that an innocent-looking babe like you has voyeuristic tendencies. I do wonder what Paul will think."

"You're not going to play the recording for anyone?" Apprehension coiled around Lauren's stomach.

"Anything obtained during lockdown is legit for the film. It's in the contract you signed. I am in your debt." Dominick waved the cigar in the air as he spoke, grinning.

"We're supposed to be ghost-hunting. Helena wants—"

"Shadows of the past come in all different forms." Dominick leaned forward, offered her his cigar.

"Yuck."

"No? You've given me proof I was on the right track. The school owner was an exhibitionist. He made love to the teacher whose ghost you three women are so hot to drag out of the grave."

Vanni burst in to crouch next to Lauren and put his hand on her head.

"She is awake!"

"That she is," said Dominick. He twisted open a brandy bottle, poured into three paper cups. "Let's drink to Château Mont Rose."

"Merci!" Vanni accepted a cup.

Lauren shook her head.

"Suit yourself." Dominick tossed his brandy back in a gulp, and then he poured another shot. "Cheers." He lifted the cup. "Gianni?"

"Not Gianni. Vanni."

"Giovanni, take the young lady upstairs. Get that bridal gown on her. Don't forget the veil. Text me or call out at the staircase when you're ready. Let's say fifteen minutes?"

Glad to leave the office, Lauren took Vanni's arm. When they got to the first landing, she halted.

"What is wrong, Mademoiselle Lauren?"

"It's not that I don't think the bridal gown is beautiful. . . ."

"But, Mademoiselle?"

"I don't trust Mr. Bentley. I'm not sure what he has in mind."

Vanni nodded. "Not to worry, *ma petite*. Let Vanni—myself—take care of everything."

Lauren held back. "One more thing. I—I really can't pass that wax clown at the end of the hall. Do you mind if I close my eyes and let you lead me?"

Vanni's expression softened further. "Ah!" He nodded. "Do you have trust in Vanni? No matter what you see or hear?"

"I think so. You have a kind heart."

"Then keep your eyes tightly shut. Do not open them, not even to peep. Keep your arm on mine, *chérie*, I will get you past. We must be strong. Though this place is not big like Château de Chillon, it could have an appetite to swallow us both."

Lauren wondered what happened to making friends with the château. She held onto Vanni's arm, not opening her eyes when the padding of his sneakers shifted, at some point down the hallway, to the tinkling of bells with every floppy step.

#

Rachel found Helena standing outside the bathroom. The Greek woman prodded Rachel to go back in.

"We have to keep our voices down," said Helena, closing the door.

Rachel avoided looking at the toilet bowl.

"My spirit guide, an ancient Greek general named Alcibiades, says Mademoiselle Schwartz's spirit is trying to keep us away from connecting with the real force animating Château Mont Rose."

"Why would she do that?"

"Mademoiselle Schwartz was unstable and egotistical. She doesn't want us to be here. Look what she's doing to my neck." Helena moved to the sink, turned on the cold water, and looked at her neck in the mirror.

"I'm confused," said Rachel. "I thought you wanted to commune with Mademoiselle Schwartz."

"That was the original plan, but I have a new idea. Even worse news is she wants to be Lauren's spirit guide."

"If Mademoiselle Schwartz wants to be Lauren's spirit guide, why would she shove us all to the floor?"

"You mean try to kill us?"

"Kill *you*," corrected Rachel. "Lauren and I were pushed down."

Helena stuck one hand in the cold water. "She doesn't want us to make contact with the real spiritual entity at work here. She always was a selfish bitch."

Rachel felt a distinct sensation of teenage déjà vu.

"So we're done for the night?"

"Not on your life," said Helena, dabbing her welts with dripping fingertips. "There is a force here. Alcibiades made his plan of attack clear: he counsels us to ignore Schwartz and do to Château Mont Rose what he did to the hermai."

"Am I supposed to know what that is?"

"The hermai was a symbolic statue in ancient Greece," continued Helena. "You haven't seen it?

"I've never been to Greece."

Helena winced and turned off the water. "When the general was alive, he defaced it. He broke off either the head or genitals on the statue, maybe both."

"Was this general thrown in prison?"

Helena gave a deep sigh. "Rachel, how would I know? He had to take away the statue's power. People were worshipping it."

"No one is worshipping Château Mont Rose."

"Really? Worship comes in many different acts."

Rachel thought about that for a moment. It made sense.

"So you're going to break something?"

"Of course not. I'm not going to break anything. Alcibiades is wrong."

Rachel stared long and hard at her employer's reflection in the mirror. Every time Helena words started to make sense, something went askew. "Your *spirit guide* is wrong . . ?"

"I will become 'one' with the château," said Helena. "Then I'll get the *real* story. We'll become famous."

"You don't want to listen to, um, Alcibiades?"

"I don't listen to everything men tell me to do," said Helena. "Even if they *are* dead."

Rachel smiled. Her employer sounded reasonable once more.

Chapter 26

Mystery Girl

Standing in misty night air cold enough to warrant a lined jacket and fur cap, Detective Cloquet oiled the hinges of Château Mont Rose's main gate before opening its padlock with the copied key. The last thing he needed was for the creak and whine of the big gate to announce his arrival.

The gate swung open without squealing. He put the oil can back in his trunk, closed the lid gently. The detective's laptop lay inside the car, hidden under a newspaper. He left his cane on the back seat.

Inside the boundaries of Château Mont Rose, his skin crawled. Just a silly feeling, brought on by memories and the weather. He trudged over the wet stones, cold seeping through gaps in clothing down his neck, his breath pluming out warm and visible. As he got to the side door, a text message vibrated on his phone. The boys were waiting inside. He got the door open without a problem.

"*Salut,* Uncle Julien," whispered Ajit. His arms held a woman's legs, duct-taped together, feet clad in sensible flat shoes.

Clearly, this was not the expected young woman. Paul supported Virginie Duvanel under the armpits. Cloquet recognized her from her ID picture. Her hands were bound together over her waist, the mouth gagged and duct-taped. Her gaze raked over Cloquet's face like a cat's claw.

"Thank you for coming, Uncle Julien," said Paul, as if they didn't meet every day.

"You are welcome," said Cloquet. "Was it necessary to tie her up?"

"She tried to kill me," said Ajit in a hard voice. "I'd like to drop her head on the walkway."

"Let's hold off on that. Put her down."

Ajit and Paul complied.

"What happened?"

"She came running at me, tried to shove me out an open window. *And* she bit me! Paul was witness."

"Paul and I can get her to the car," said Cloquet. "When you are finished with your crew duties, you will have to come down to the station to file a report."

"Go back inside before Dominick notices we've breached security," urged Paul. "I'll be right in."

Ajit held his hand up, sideways, to the inspector's view. "See where she bit?" Spitting on Virginie, Ajit turned on his heels and left.

"Where is the girl?" asked Cloquet.

"I haven't found her yet."

"And Papaux?"

Paul shook his head again.

The captive struggled, tried yelling.

"Stop fussing or you will go to prison, Madame. You have broken enough laws tonight," Cloquet scolded.

She stopped struggling.

"This group of people have paid for their time at Château Mont Rose," Cloquet said. "You assaulted a crew member, which is at least a misdemeanor, more likely a felony if attempted murder can be proven. Unless someone can persuade the young man not to press charges, this may be your last night as a resident of the premises."

Cloquet shone the flashlight briefly into Virginie's face, which had blanched in fear. "If you have detained any other visitor to the château in your cottage or on this property, I will find out. I am now going to remove your gag if you can be calm. Do you promise?"

Virginie nodded.

Cloquet undid the mouth gag. She kept her word.

"You are the mother of Jean Duvanel?"

She nodded.

"Your first name is 'Virginie?'"

"Oui."

"Remain in your home, with your son, until you hear from me again. Release all persons who do not belong in your dwelling."

The flashlight cut back across Virginie's worried face. She bit her bottom lip with her teeth.

Cloquet nodded at Paul, who sliced through the duct tape and then ripped it off. Virginie did not utter a sound.

"Compliance, Madame. Help her up, Paul."

Paul steered Virginie to the walkway, then let her go, unsteadily, on her own. They watched her swiftly enter her cottage.

"I don't have a gun," said Paul. "Even if I had one, I can't sit out here watching to see if she comes back out, but I aimed a camera at the house so you can see from your laptop if you brought it."

"I did. You take this gun." Cloquet pulled out a semiautomatic pistol.

"I didn't bring one because I wouldn't be able to explain it."

"Hide it. Paul—"

"Yes?"

"Don't stop looking for the teenage girl *or* Papaux."

#

In the corridor, Helena gasped, "Help me," and threw her arm around Rachel's shoulders. It was like being caught by a sagging bear.

"Get me into the office."

They did not get so far. Helena collapsed upon the rug on the main landing where the balustrade had broken, just outside the tiny hallway leading to the office. Dominick heard the noise, came out.

"Zip me up."

"I wish I knew what was happening," muttered Rachel, pulling the zipper on Helena's black leather body suit up to the neck, over the welts and swollen flesh. Dominick knelt on Helena's other side.

"So it's plan B?" he asked.

"Yes. We'll need the bag."

The bag turned out to be a small, heavy backpack. "We cannot speak about what we are doing," Dominick told Rachel. "Copy me, but don't talk about it to the others. Not even if Ajit comes out of the office and sees us. And where is the Frenchie?"

Rachel didn't know. She watched Dominick plant a kiss on Helena's lips; the latter closed her eyes and lay quietly. Dominick tucked her hair into a black cap. Then he set to work, extracting items from the backpack.

Imitating Dominick, Rachel warmed wax with a low wattage heating instrument, applying the softened product to Helena's exposed skin. Dominick inserted drinking straws snipped very short into her mouth and nostrils. Then Helena's face was plastered in wax.

When he sat back, Helena was cocooned in wax and leather.

"Go get Lauren for the next scene," he said.

Nodding, Rachel rose and kept her eyes averted from the wax figures, feeling more than a little uncomfortable. Light glowed at the baseboard of the bedroom door. She walked faster, knocked, and Lauren opened.

#

Once Paul re-entered the building, he moved quickly, looking for Papaux and the girl in the dark, flowered dress. He ran up the back staircase, stopping in one of the last rooms he had seen the girl. An empty armoire stood with its door hanging open. The camera was still in place, perched on a sconce. He investigated and found a dry substance caked over its lens. Wax.

Back out in the corridor, he came to what appeared to be the staircase to the tower. He flung open that door, releasing a heavy, fetid odor of mildewed wool and dust. The toe of Paul's shoe knocked against the first step, but his flashlight showed a huge gap in the staircase. No one lived up here.

Paul descended to the second floor. There was no young woman in any of the rooms—and no Papaux either. The female must have escaped downstairs. Paul caught up with Ajit on the landing near what looked like a human cocoon of Helena in black leather. The two cousins stood over Helena for a confused moment, looked at each other, then silently entered the office.

When asked, Dominick refused to give any explanation other than "Helena's in her chrysalis stage."

Ajit got some ointment and bandages out of the medical box and put it on his hand wound.

Sprawling in the office chair, Dominick sucked on his cigar. After a few minutes, he said, "Paulie boy, you'll be a star tonight. That script girl has a thing for you; She told me all about it. But you'll have to film along with Ajit until I need you to act."

Dominick was no Cupid, so what was he up to now? However, he had warned them, when hired, that at any moment they might need to take directions in front of the camera. It was contractual.

Vanni's voice floated down the hallway:

"Ready!"

Dominick tamped out his cigar and gave directions. Paul and Ajit gathered cameras, additional headgear, and moveable lighting.

"Make sure extension cords are all hidden. Don't let Lauren out of the bedroom yet," Dominick called down the hallway.

The lamps made the facial features of the wax figures leap to life. Jean-Jacques Rousseau winked, Burckhardt scowled. A schoolgirl averted her gaze. Paul had to remind himself he had nerves of steel. Shadows could play tricks.

"Let her out," yelled Dominick, as if Lauren were a bull.

Paul crouched by a statue, holding a camera.

"Leave on the face veil! No tripping, girlie. Giuseppe, stay behind the door. I want the young virgin alone on the screen."

The bride floated eerily in the direction of Ajit, who stood in the middle of the hallway. Paul thought Lauren must be cold in the crepe and lace gown. She held a spray of silk flowers. Dominick kept up a flow of suggestions:

"You are not sure, pretty little caterpillar—do you want to do this? Do you want to give yourself to a man who might be a scoundrel, a cheat? Someone who has betrayed you by frightening you?"

Paul frowned, but kept filming. What was Dominick doing? Behind the timidly approaching bride, the wax clown leered. Paul hadn't remembered it having such a black hole of a mouth or such chiseled, sharp teeth. Still, the bride held her head high.

"Good girl, not a word. You are the ghost bride who will experience the surprise of the flesh."

Dominick's arm rose in the air like a choreographer's. "You are the walking dreamer," he cried, "and to know you will taste your long-held desire makes you tremble."

The director slithered along the wall now with a camera in his hand. He cried, "You, Frenchie—put that camera down. I want you to start stalking the bride. Move along the side, like I am doing, behind the statues, then creep out behind her."

Paul left his own camera hidden against a pair of wax feet. At least Lauren could hear what he was being asked to do. It would not be a surprise to *her*.

"You, doll-face, notice the stalker!"

The bride came to a halt, perceived Paul.

"That's it, poppet, you are nervous and excited. You, the stalker-bridegroom, catch her!" Dominick commanded.

Paul spurted, put a hand on Lauren's arm.

"What? Not like that! Like this," cried Dominick, shoving Paul aside. He seized Lauren by the waist, roughly pulled up her skirts. The two fell to the floor.

"No, no, no!" The cry reverberated through the halls, but it didn't sound like Lauren's voice. "I forgot to shave my legs!"

The bride's naked legs were covered in curly dark hair. Strange for a blonde.

Dominick panted. "Oh how kinky! Are you fellows filming?"

"Yo," said Ajit, gesturing with pointed finger at his camera.

The bride threw back the veil. The face was Vanni's. The cross-dressing bride slapped Dominick's face, hard.

"You must *ask* before touching!"

Out of the corner of his eye, Paul perceived a woman in a dark dress disappearing down the staircase. From where had she emerged? Making a split second decision, he pursued her.

"I did not give permission for anyone to leave!" yelled Dominick.

Chapter 27

Dominick Gets Mad

Sitting before the bedroom vanity mirror in which her own image, at least, remained unchanging—no painted skin, no plaid vest—Lauren heard her name bellowed from the corridor. She turned, hand poised on the back of her chair.

"We'd better go out. Dominick sounds impatient."

"Doesn't he always?" Rachel put out her cigarette and closed the window.

They linked arms to walk out.

Dominick, Vanni, and Ajit waited on the landing. Dominick was running his hand through his hair as he sputtered. Lauren listened until the quiet, supine figure of Helena drew her attention.

She and Rachel stopped at the edge of the Turkish rug, looked down on the still figure in amazement.

"What happened to her?"

"This was her plan B," said Rachel. "I helped Mr. Bentley apply the wax to her skin."

"The cap is waxy too."

Rachel sucked her breath in sharply, dropped to a crouch. "Someone has been messing with our work. Mr. Bentley! You said it was important for Helena's hair to be tucked in. Look—it's been pulled out on one side. Helena, did you do this?"

Lauren moved aside to let Dominick have room to see.

"Get it through your head," he told them, "she's in a trance, so she can't answer. In the state she is in, she wouldn't be able to pull her hair out of the cap."

Vanni also leaned over the wax-cocooned woman. The long bridal veil he wore spilled over the unconscious woman's face.

Dominick pushed the veil off Helena. "Do you mind, Mario?"

Vanni held two fingers above the straws sticking out of Helena' mouth and nostrils. "She is breathing."

Dominick snorted. "Why wouldn't she be?. We weren't discussing whether she was breathing."

"The hairs, they were ripped from her scalp," observed Vanni, touching around the cap. "You see? There is a little blood."

"But she seems alright," said Rachel.

"Blimey. . . . " said Dominick, sounding rattled although he forbore castigating Vanni further. "You, girl Friday, tuck Helena's hair in—and—" his hand gestured at the office, "do some first aid. Get that bag we used. Make sure no skin is exposed to air that is not covered in wax. Have your girlfriend help."

Lauren was glad Dominick didn't say anything about Vanni in the bridal gown.

"Wasted time," groaned Dominick. "Still, the camera must have recorded whoever did it." He looked up. "If one of you has something to confess, now would be a good time. I am going to review the footage. See the camera?"

He pointed to the one on a tripod, aimed at Helena.

No one spoke.

"Better to admit tampering with the mistress of ceremonies now than to have me watch the evidence."

They looked at each other uneasily.

Dominick shrugged. "I'm just saying. Stupid thing to do, really. Maybe one of you thought Helena had hundred franc bills tucked under her cap?"

He rolled his eyes in frustration. "Fine. Crews!" He shook his head. "You, Valentino, go take off that damn dress. Tall cameraman, whatever your name is, check to see all the equipment in the various rooms is functioning. Get your Frenchie cousin's arse to help you—or this will be his last gig on my team."

Ajit nodded.

The group began dispersing.

"Oh, and *girls*," said Dominick, baring his teeth in a parody of a smile.

Rachel and Lauren froze, attentive.

"Don't imagine for an instant I found humor in your little stunt. *Decide* which of you is putting on the wedding dress or—you'll be needing airfare home to Oklahoma."

He slouched away to the office, grumbling, "Bloody Yanks."

Lauren and Rachel exchanged a somber glance.

"Oklahoma?" asked Lauren.

Rachel tipped her head and shrugged.

They gave Dominick a little distance before following him, fetching the backpack and returning to the landing where Helena lay alone. Rachel pulled back her cap to inspect the site of injury. "I don't see any blood," she said.

"Are you wearing your contact lenses?" asked Lauren.

"Yes, of course. It is just so dark."

"We can see where her hair was pulled out of the cap. That's the spot. I'll clean there." Lauren dabbed with antibiotic ointment. Then Rachel tucked Helena's hair back under the cap. Rachel applied hand-warmed soft wax to the edge where cap met skin.

"What's the point of all this?" whispered Lauren when they had finished.

"I don't know." Rachel kept her voice pitched low in response. "Helena told me her plan was to commune with Château Mont Rose."

"By pretending she's a wax statue?"

Rachel put a finger to her lips, gesturing at Helena.

"It reminds me of a Houdini endurance stunt."

"I don't think that's what she's doing."

"Can she hear us?"

Rachel shrugged again. Lauren considered the quiet figure breathing through straws. "Helena, you are doing a great job of ignoring us."

"She is," agreed Rachel. "I mean, you are, Helena."

There was no reaction whatsoever from the wax-and-leather-clad woman.

Lauren stood up, waited for Rachel to do the same. "As upset and angry as Dominick may be," she said, choosing words with care for the ears of her female employer, "you've got to admit he has a reason to be annoyed. There isn't a lot of drama involved in this scene. A sleeping woman covered in wax doesn't exactly sound like high-rated viewing fare."

Rachel looked at the tripod-based camera. "I guess not."

"Too bad Dominick can only think in terms of sex."

"That just makes him a typical male. And maybe that's what males want to see, in five hundred different settings."

"Rachel." Lauren tugged her away, towards the bedroom, muttering, "I can't film the scene he wants. I was hired as a writer. Besides, the script I wrote was about reaching out to the spirit of Mademoiselle Schwartz, not about being a mauled bride."

"You have to trust them a little."

"Them? Helena and Dominick? They're--"

"Don't say it."

Lauren pressed her lips together. They walked, gazing at the carpet runner.

"I just won't do that scene with the bridal gown!" Lauren sputtered.

"I can't fit into your dress, Lauren," Rachel shot back.

"Think of a solution. You can't expect me to be filmed doing God alone knows what in order to make our debauched director happy?"

"It's not my job to think of script solutions," said Rachel, her voice breaking. She seemed close to tears, and they weren't whispering anymore. Luckily, Dominick was out of earshot, as was Helena.

"Haven't you read about actresses being psychologically scarred by maniacal directors?"

They were at the door to the bedroom, Grock standing next to them in the shadow.

"Maybe this job isn't for us. I've been thinking about that."

"I do have an idea, something film worthy." Lauren felt the darkness of the corner where the wax statue stood stretching forward to touch her. "I'll tell you inside the room."

Rachel tried the doorknob. "Why is it locked?"

"Vanni, open the door please," Lauren called, allowing her gaze to creep over to the shoes of the wax clown. So long as the long, floppy slippers were in the hallway, they couldn't be inside the room as well.

Could they?

She held her breath, squeezing her eyes shut. Then a little voice argued with her: she had survived Vanni's transformation more than once, hadn't she? It wasn't his fault.

The door handle moved.

#

The bright light coming out of the salon caught Paul's eye. He was already stupefied by what he had just witnessed: the liquefaction of the wax girl in the dark, flowered dress. She bubbled out under the front door in the foyer, making him pause in shock. Then she was gone.

He had stood for a moment, uncertain of what he had seen, until noise and lights pulled him forward. Here, on the entry floor, was a full salon of pretty young ladies having a party. Every lamp in the room was lit. And it just couldn't be.

Paul believed he was caught between two hallucinations. There was no time to come to grips with either one. His throat was dry as chalk. In front of his eyes, four young females seated on a couch in the salon laughed and chatted. All they had to do was look up to see him.

Or was that wrong? A voice within him clamored for explanation.

Who were these girls? If the melting girl was wax, were they, too?

Paul turned his head to look at the statues lined up in the foyer. They remained motionless. A waxen Carl Gustave Jung stood, as ever, looking out the foyer window.

The lilting laughter was unnerving. Paul stared. He realized he was sweating. His nerves were on fire. He had to do something. If he barged into the salon demanding IDs, how would these females react? Would he slip into unconsciousness? Would it be like a nightmare from which one sprang up awake, heart racing, but in all other respects normal?

There was only one way to find out. He was ready to step in front of the party when he recognized a face. A fifth young woman had just sat on the arm of the couch, chatting with fervor, roses of life in her cheeks.

It was his deceased cousin, Michèle.

#

Detective Cloquet crushed a considerable number of flowers, forgetting where he stood, when he saw the form solidify, taking shape out of bubbling slime that had oozed from under the front door of Château Mont Rose.

The door itself never opened.

The object grew, achieving the height and form of a human-sized blob. The blob refined itself before his eyes. Within moments, a teenage girl in a dark, flowered dress took his breath away. The shock hit like heartburn.

Cloquet took deep breaths. Through night-vision binoculars, he spied something grasped between the girl-thing's fingers. They seemed to be strands of hair. Cloquet thought again of voodoo when the girl-thing took the path to the back garden cottage. He had to intercept.

He moved out from the security of the tree, tracking the moving form. A familiar pain flared up the bad leg, but he ignored it. The creature did not turn around.

Cloquet caught up, threw his left arm around the girl thing's chest. His elbow pressed against her back. She—it—was warm and soft, but not like a human. He yanked the thing close against him with a stranglehold under the chin.

Correction—it would have been a stranglehold if the waxen thing could breathe. Cloquet seized the hand holding the hair. He clamped hard with his fingers, but the girl's waxy hand half slipped out of his grasp. He tried anchoring his fingernails into her wrist. Let her scream, if wax people screamed.

The fingernails slid in like a knife into a rotten apple. There was no firmness, and she was still hot. The entire hand detached at the wrist—still moving. Cloquet's heart skipped a beat. "*Mon Dieu*," he said, choking on the words without dropping the hand.

The fingers writhed. He stuffed the moving thing in his jacket pocket, zipping it shut, fighting the urge to be sick. With his other arm, he kept pressure around the cooling girl torso. Though the wax creature was hardening in the night air, it left a film on everything it touched.

The pressure he exerted to restrain the wax girl was, ultimately, ineffective. The damaged humanoid, neck oddly skewed, slipped out of his grasp. She loped away, resembling a kindergartener's first modeling attempt, chest folded backward like moth wings. The creature reached the cottage door and melted down under it, into the house.

The lump in Cloquet's pocket flopped around like a fish. Cloquet searched his other pocket for a lighter. He seldom smoked, but he carried a cigarette lighter. The fingers inside the pocket gained firmness and contrived to poke at his belly. He unzipped the pocket, plunged his own hand down upon the waxen one. His other hand held the lighter. When he pulled out the hand, he saw that the thumb and forefinger were still pinched upon the dark strands of hair. The other fingers attempted to claw at him.

He held the lighter flame as steadily as possible under the wax hand.

When the fire sizzled into the wax, the hand went into spasms. As he moved the lighter so the flame lapped and caught all its surface, the thing writhed, smoked and dripped. He held it as best he could. It was like roasting a marshmallow for which he did not have tongs.

Wax dripped onto the cement pathway. The smell coming from it was acrid and coppery, a mixture of rancid roast pork fat and Sulphur. In the dim garden lamplight, he imagined he saw veins and charring bones. When his own hand burned, he let the dripping lump slip to the ground. Getting down on his knees to see it, he prodded the blistered wax thing with a stick.

It moved. Grabbing a nearby brick from a flowerbed, Cloquet slammed the waxen hand remains into the pathway. When he was done, he felt a throbbing in his temples. He was hot and spent from exertion.

The cottage shades were drawn, but he felt watched. He trudged back to his car in the lane, greatly depleted. If he put petroleum jelly on his skin at once (there was a tube in his glove compartment), his hand might not hurt so much tomorrow.

#

Virginie passed through the front door and small salon to her bedroom, seeing all too clearly how Jean was defacing the new statue he had made. She retrieved the iron rod and came back out, waving the metal in the air. Anger at the young man she had raised made her forget the humiliation just endured.

She hadn't expected to attack that young hoodlum who was breaking holes in the wall of Château Mont Rose. However, she had known it was the right thing to do, just as she knew now that Jean needed to be chastised. Sometimes she didn't understand what she did. All her impulses were directed by devotion to Château Mont Rose.

"Have you lost your mind, shameful boy?"

"*Mon Dieu, Maman.* Put the rod down."

"Stop ruining that statue. It belongs to the château."

"I'm the one who made it. It's for a specific purpose. In fact, I am helping—"

"I said stop!" Virginie screamed, striking him across the buttocks. She knew it must hurt, though not half as bad as she had hurt the detective's head the night before. Jean's buttocks had lots of cushioning. She would use more clout if he didn't listen.

Her son jumped away, bumping a small table. His cheeks jiggled, turned red. "You can't do that to me. I'm a grown man." His hand jutted out to grab the iron rod. They wrestled for it. "*Maman*, let go. I'm your son," he said. "You don't know what you're doing."

The rod was wrenched out of both their grasps. The Grecian form, descending from its stand, caught Jean in the gut on an upswing. Virginie gasped and staggered back. That breath was expelled from her by a sharp whack in the diaphragm on the rod's backswing. Instant torment swept over her. She felt Jean's head hit against hers. Then, blackness.

When she came to, the Grecian statue was gone and her lungs hurt to breathe.

#

Lauren sat on her own bed. Paul was across from her, at the vanity table, with his back to the mirror. Vanni lay in full bridal attire upon Rachel's bed.

Rachel had taken refuge in the only comfortable armchair.

"Come with me upstairs," pleaded Lauren. "I think I might be able to reach out to Mademoiselle Schwartz in the tower."

Rachel looked incredulous.

"You're the only person who can film my effort," said Lauren. "You're the only one of us who will be tolerated."

"After what I just told you?" said Paul to Lauren. "If you insist on reaching out to Danielle Schwartz, let me come with you. I think *I* will be tolerated."

"I see we're keeping secrets," said Rachel, arching a brow.

"It's not like that," said Lauren. Paul had confided to her what he had seen in the foyer. When Lauren admitted, reciprocally, that Vanni was metamorphosing into a clown in front of her eyes and she thought she had heard Mlle Schwartz's voice on her telephone, Paul had urged her to convince Rachel to pack up and leave.

"We can't do that. Not yet," she had told him.

He didn't understand, and she needed to explain why they had to stay, not just to him, but to Rachel as well. Considering that Vanni had helped Lauren be strong in difficult moments, his presence in the bedroom made sense.

"It has occurred to me," said Lauren, "that we haven't made contact with Mlle Schwartz tonight. Other things have happened, but not that. I know it's scary," she added, seeing Rachel was about to speak. She lifted her hands.

"Alright, I'm listening," Rachel acquiesced.

"I have reason to believe we may yet contact her, but we have to do it on *her* terms. I have poured my heart into this script, which does homage to Mlle Schwartz, a gifted and devoted teacher."

"Why does Mademoiselle Lauren believe she can contact her teacher?" asked Vanni from Rachel's bed.

"Because I am the one who saw our dead teacher, Mlle Schwartz, outside the garden wall," Lauren replied, looking at him, then at Rachel and Paul. "I was looking out the window this morning. She was looking back at me. And if I could see her out the window, why shouldn't I be able to contact her inside the château? Mlle Schwartz was an artist. She would understand the need to reach out to her for the sake of art. My script is my art. At least you have to let me try. I think she will respond."

"Helena mentioned Lauren has channeling abilities. Maybe it is true," said Rachel.

"It wasn't Helena who should have been reaching out to Mlle Schwartz. They were enemies," said Lauren.

"It should have been you," said Paul.

Lauren nodded. "Thank you! I must try. Rachel, come upstairs with me and film my effort. At the very least, it will prove we tried—"

"But why doesn't he come with us? He can hold the camera." Rachel jabbed a thumb in Paul's direction.

"Paul didn't know Mlle Schwartz. I have a gut feeling her spirit won't speak to or show herself to anyone inside the château but students who liked her, who were her friends. Think about it: of the total crew, that means only you and me. People who were never students here have been traipsing all over these lower floors tonight. As for Helena—well, we both know she was Mlle Schwartz's enemy, at least from among the student boarders. Helena was practically shoved off the balcony a little while ago by an invisible force. That's got to tell you something."

"And we were treated like welcome guests?" asked Rachel.

"A distinction was made."

"Where precisely upstairs do you wish to go?" asked Paul.

"The tower. It was the best place in the building for me."

"Why, if I may ask?"

"For one thing, because there was a piano. I took music lessons in the small room that held it. That place was an escape—with music. Mlle Schwartz understood the arts; that was her form of escape too. "

"You won't be able to ascend the tower staircase," said Paul, shaking his head. "I saw it. Too many steps are broken."

"So much for plan C," said Rachel.

"With respect, I would like to see for myself," said Lauren.

"Let's say Paul is talking about the wrong staircase," said Rachel, "or hope grows wings on your feet. What are we supposed to do about Dominick?"

"He wants me to take off this dress," came Vanni's voice, sulky. "But I can't do that with all of you here." He sniffed, smoothed his eyebrows. "You all know Mademoiselle Lauren will not put it on when I take it off. Someone must pay homage to so much beauty." Vanni let his two hands make a long sweep of recognition at the delicate gown with shimmering beads. "Would one of you please pass me my makeup case?"

"I'm not playing the bride," said Lauren. "That's final."

"It could mean the end of our gig; you realize that?" said Rachel, handing the case to Vanni.

"If one shot is all we have, we should take it right now." Lauren stood. She could see her confidence having an impact on Rachel. "Dominick could call us out any minute. I want to avoid direct confrontation."

"I'll wait out on the landing," said Paul. "To keep an eye on Helena and distract Dominick if need be."

Lauren smiled at Paul. He was being so supportive.

Vanni coyly waved the three of them out with one hand and searched with the other among his eyeshadows, brushes, and lipsticks.

Lauren and Rachel left Paul on the first-floor landing. They tiptoed up the staircase as swiftly as they dared. On the third landing, they could hear Dominick's voice below. At the distance, it was faint.

"Paul will have to deal with him," said Rachel. "I hope this doesn't take too long."

"Here's the door." Lauren pressed her ear to the wood of the tower door, then jiggled the knob.

"This corridor smells kind of stale," said Rachel, looking around the narrow gray hallway and straight down at her feet. "Have you noticed the carpet is sticky?"

"It's old."

Rachel lifted one of her feet. "Ewww. Does old carpeting decompose?"

"You stepped into something. I wouldn't worry about it."

"Disgusting." Rachel tried wiping the bottom of her shoe against a wax figure stand. "Yuck. Lauren, what are you doing?"

Lauren turned the knob again. The door was stuck.

"Okay, you tried. Let's go downstairs."

"Rachel, hold on." Lauren kept turning the knob. "We used to come up here all the time. Give me a chance." Rachel's jitters felt catching—or perhaps it was a sense of rule-breaking that came from boarding school days.

Suddenly Lauren felt reckless. She hadn't a clue how to reach out to a spirit, yet presumed she knew. What would she do up here?

The knob clicked.

Incredulous, she opened.

Rachel's chin pressed against Lauren's shoulder. They both looked in.

"I never really liked this part of the building," whispered Rachel, "not even when we got to paint boxes on a Saturday morning here instead of being imprisoned in a classroom study hall half the day. Too much wind—you hear it? The basement was better. That's where we had ballet lessons with Madame Berger."

"You went to dance class more than I did. I guess New Yorkers prefer the underground," said Lauren. "I practiced piano almost every day up here." She heard the wind wailing, buffeting the tower. It did not make her at all anxious. She felt a lifting of worry from her shoulders. "Do you hear piano keys playing?"

"You're imagining it. And you're wrong about me liking the underground."

"Can you film me going up?"

With a resigned sigh, Rachel lifted the camera. "Let me hold onto you so I don't trip," She gripped the waistband of Lauren's jeans with her free hand.

"I don't see any hole in the staircase," said Lauren. Her foot felt firm wood. "Is there a second staircase somewhere?"

"You're the one who came up here every day. You would know better than I do."

"Then this is the only one," said Lauren. "Paul must have been on a different floor."

A sticky sound came with Rachel's footstep. "My shoes are ruined!" she muttered.

"I swear I hear a Bach three-part invention." Lauren climbed. Piano music floated to her ears. She knew the piece by heart, or at least, had known it in the days when she played it frequently. Her skin tingled. She hadn't needed to wonder how to make contact with Mlle Schwartz! Contact seemed to be happening on its own.

"Keep on filming, Rachel."

"The recording light is on."

"Then the sound will be recorded too." Proof that the music was really playing, Lauren thought. The whole world would hear it on playback.

"Yes. Our conversation in a dark, gloomy staircase will have viewers riveted."

#

Paul sat in a winged chair against the wall, knowing his expression was tense, brooding. One elbow was propped on an arm of the chair; his chin rested on his fist. He did not straighten up to greet Dominick when the Englishman re-emerged from the office. Helena lay quiet on the rug in front of them both.

Dominick looked down at her. "That's about as exciting as watching paint dry. Bugger this. I want to re-do the bridal scene with Lauren. Or Rachel. One take with each. Whoever is sexiest wins."

"Lauren and Rachel went to another part of the building to film Lauren's attempt to reach out to the spirit of their teacher."

"Well, that's just . . . how do you say 'shit' in French?"

"*Merde.*"

"That's just *merde.*"

"*Merde* has a second meaning," said Paul.

"How much meaning can shit have?"

"It can also mean 'good luck.'"

"Leave it to the Frogs," said Dominick. "I need a drink." He went back to the office.

Paul thought about having a hot coffee. Uncle Julien must be wanting the same thing about now, to warm up and wake up. And why didn't Ajit come out of the office?

"Ajit?"

No answer. Paul pulled out his phone, tried texting. No luck. Ajit's camera was on the concierge desk. *"Merde."*

He crept down the staircase. Damn, morphing château! It must have pulled Ajit somewhere. Ready to see girls laughing in a lit room, Paul saw nothing. The foyer and salon were dark and empty, save for the rigid wax statues.

He felt gripped by the certainty that if he stared long enough at the waxen form of Jung, the psychoanalyst would turn around and speak to him.

Paul averted his gaze. "Ajit?"

There was no response. He did a short tour on the ground floor. Then, with clenched jaw, Paul took the stairs back up to the first floor, two at a time.

He peeked into the office. Dominick was alone there, glass in one hand, bottle before him, staring into space. He could have been part of the museum collection but for the burning cigar he held.

Ajit was nowhere to be seen.

Paul went down the corridor, knocked softly at Lauren and Rachel's door. "Vanni, are you alone?"

Grock the clown expelled stinking breath. Paul recoiled

"Yes, *caro mio*, do you want me?" came a voice from inside.

"No, I mean, please stay in there. I'm looking for Ajit."

Paul grabbed Ajit's camera as he passed the concierge desk and climbed the staircase to the second floor. He paused on the landing. "Ajit?"

A wax gypsy turned its head. Paul told himself it was the moonlight streaming through window panes that caused the illusion. Then he reminded himself he had seen Michèle with a party of girls. Dead Michèle. His flesh crawled. There was only one thing to do—drag the whole crew out, even if he had to break his cover.

He opened the first door he came to, used the flashlight, "Ajit?" No one, not the slightest movement. Second bedroom door. Nothing. He avoided looking straight into the face of any wax statue. "Ajit?"

"Here," came a muffled voice. *"Paul? I need some help."*

Paul stepped through a third door. A torrent of wind struck him like a sumo wrestler. It slammed him against a wall, camera around his neck, and the door shut. The gale flattened him like so much grease.

It hurt to open his eyes, so he kept them pressed shut. "Ajit!" The name was sucked into the storm, and Paul's ears hurt from wind. Another hallucination, and this one chafed like hell.

Chapter 28

Ajit's True Calling

Ajit was back in the place where he had earlier been thwarted by
Virginie; his crowbar levered once more into the wainscoting. The paneling
responded with a rippling crack. Splinters leaped into the torchlight beam.
Thicker planks, yellowed and mottled, rested between Ajit and his prize. He
could hear the coins and bank notes cheering him on through the pores of the
old wood.

Old striped wallpaper from above the paneling hung in shreds. He worked
on opening the hole wider. Soon he dropped the tool, peering into the breach lit
by the torch.

The metal detector had warbled its lullaby of treasure. Now he spied a
rectangular-shaped carpet bag. Ajit reached in, but the object was farther away
than it looked. The crowbar dispensed with more decaying wood, extending the
opening into a long, uneven hole running to the floor.

Ajit let the crowbar go and mopped his brow. Then he got down on his
side so that one arm and shoulder could enter through the break. His fingers
plucked at the carpetbag but he could not grab its handle. He needed two
hands.

The moment he had so long dreamed of had arrived. The Swiss were
notorious hoarders. Look at all those numbered bank accounts! With two hands
reaching in, he grasped what felt to be, inside the carpetbag, a heavy trunk of
gold or silver bullion. He tugged. The bag with its treasure inched closer. He
had to brace his toes against the running board.

Another pull brought the treasure through the rupture he had created
in the wall. At the same instant, splinters shot from the wood like army ants.
They moved, burrowing into the bare skin of his exposed arms.

Ajit shrieked. He tried to brush the splinters away. Brushing caused
fiery pain. The splinters burrowed, alive, growing legs and pincers and mouths.
They crawled up under his rolled sleeves, to his biceps and armpits, slithering in
like cactus needles. He screamed. The splinter mouths ate, leaving pin drops of
poison in their feces.

His eyes rolled upwards. His legs jerked. The last sight he had, eyes
cracked open, was of a clown's face, peering out from the hole in the wall,
nodding and grinning.

#

Seated outside Château Mont Rose in his car, Detective Inspector Cloquet had the laptop open. Bouts of wind assailed his vehicle like vagrants with rags, extracting a donation by force. "Clean your windshield for five francs, Monsieur?" He jerked his head up repeatedly, not sure what he expected to see in the dark empty street or, when he looked down again, on the laptop screen. Agitation rubbed away at his patience. The gusts of wind kept breaking satellite connection.

It was ironic that his old-fashioned police car phone, dependent on radio signals and attached to the dashboard, was more reliable than his mobile device or laptop.

His last view was of a group of girls partying in the downstairs salon of Château Mont Rose. Each time the picture disappeared, he waited to reconnect, hoping the next view would show the salon dark and empty.

On the contrary, the same girls reappeared, dressed in clothes that could have been purchased yesterday or a dozen years ago. Their T-shirts, hoodies, ripped jeans, leggings and short skirts could be seen on any street in Lausanne.

They simply should not have been present tonight at Château Mont Rose.

On the two or three occasions the picture lasted for more than thirty seconds, Cloquet zoomed in. He told himself the illusion of pores in any girl's skin was made by the impression of an orange pressed on the soft wax. The peachy hue of life was suggested by a light addition of watercolors. These were wax figures. When they moved, their hair swung stiffly. The lips smiled, but without sincerity.

Their merriment was a hollow charade.

A semblance of girls' voices was unconvincing. Their laughter so grated upon the detective that he hit the mute button.

He was killing time, waiting for his nephew's summons.

What else could Cloquet do but stay calm? He was still unsure about wax figures that came to life. He played with the idea that he had burned his hand all on his own, with his lighter. He had no real proof to show of battling a wax figure. However, the pain of his hand was real.

He was in two minds about whether to divulge his wax creature encounter to Paul. Maybe his nephew had run into a similar experience? If so, wouldn't Cloquet have received a text message?

He had to trust Paul's responses and inner resources. Detectives did not panic. Nor should he.

Cloquet rubbed the bridge of his nose with thumb and index finger, waiting for the reconnection. He was just about to put the laptop into standby mode when the reconnection showed a different girl walk in front of the camera. His hand froze in the air over the keyboard. It was Michèle.

Right behind her followed the only man in the room, setting off titters among the girls. His muscular arms flexed. His face came close to the camera. Cloquet found himself staring at a saddle-like, flat-bridged nose with a fleshy tip and a prominent forehead above it.

Papaux smiled broadly, pulled Michèle close, his arm around her waist.

"You see, Cloquet?" he said, to the camera. "She's ours now."

#

"Mademoiselle Schwartz?"

"Come in, child," said a voice in a singsong Swiss-French accent. "We have been waiting for you. For both of you."

Lauren heard Rachel gasp. Across the room, two figures were seated against the window. Their faces were not visible. Clouds parted and the moon's beams spilled, like forked hay, over the threadbare rug.

"Come closer, girls."

"Who is that?" asked Rachel, her voice sounding nearly strangled.

"Shhhh. Do what she says. Keep filming. " Lauren crossed the room, Rachel in her wake.

 Lauren felt giddy. This was it. Helena had been right! She could make contact.

"We are alone, Mademoiselle Schwartz," said Lauren. "No one else is with us. Who is the person with you?"

A clap of thunder rent the air.

"I can see you are alone. That is good, young ladies. Do you not see my face?"

Lauren stopped short. Gathering clouds extinguished the moonlight. It was a blustery night; maybe the clouds would be pushed away in a moment? There seemed to be enough light from her headgear and flashlight, where she stood, to make out the hazy features of both seated spirits. Butterflies beat their wings in her stomach. Her legs turned to quivering reeds.

Lauren began to doubt the spirit's shape was tall or elegant enough to be Danielle Schwartz. Did spirits return in withered forms?

The butterflies disappeared. Lauren should have realized.

"Mademoiselle Wertheimer?" she sputtered. That was no spirit. She had seen her downstairs. Oh no! "And Mademoiselle. . . ."

"Terrieux," muttered Rachel.

Exploding thunder joggled the château rooftop. The shapes were silhouetted as a bolt of lightning ripped across the night sky—especially the head of spiked hair. Their flashlights allowed Lauren to see the two women well enough. Mlle Wertheimer presented the same shrunken caricature Lauren had encountered at the concierge desk.

"But I thought. . . ."

"You were looking for Mademoiselle Schwartz," said Mlle Wertheimer. "But isn't this better? Château Mont Rose is so glad to have you back, Lauren."

"You don't understand. I am looking for Mademoiselle Schwartz's spirit."

Another clap of thunder shook the tower walls.

"And you found ours."

"I didn't know you lived up—"

"*Live?*" Mlle Wertheimer turned to Spikes. "It is a sort of life, this selfless habitation, wouldn't you agree, Mlle Terrieux?"

"Indeed! I had no sensation of when my mortal life stopped and the château took over." Spikes' voice did not have the same spidery weave as the ancient headmistress's. Hers grated like a steel brush.

"Let's get out of here," muttered Rachel, bumping at Lauren's leg with her knee.

"Wait." Lauren knew there was more than these two awaiting her. "What about that music? Who is playing?"

"Lovely isn't it? It's from your old piano room," said Mlle Wertheimer. "Go on, open the door."

"Yes, do," said Spikes, with an alarming grin.

"Yes, do," said a third voice, from several feet away.

Lauren felt a crick sting her neck from turning it so fast.

"It's Mademoiselle Villot," said Rachel in a tone of shock. A sheet of rain hit the windows. The light on Rachel's headgear lit up the stodgy figure seated on an upright chair. Lauren wouldn't have recognized Mlle Villot if Rachel hadn't said her name. Knowing Mlle Villot was here made Lauren feel certain of whom she would find at the piano.

Why was Rachel so shocked? Mlle Villot had loved Mlle Schwartz. Why wouldn't she return to the château if her darling friend's spirit was here?

"Don't worry," said Mlle Villot. Under the filmy light, her large eyes appeared to be flooded with tears, much as they had been for weeks after Mlle Schwartz died. "You will find something you like in that room. Or should I say, *someone* you like—someone beautiful."

"Mademoiselle Villot is correct." Mlle Wertheimer inclined her head, hands folded on her lap. The old woman had raised her voice, Lauren thought, to be heard over the torrent of rain and the Bach piano music.

"Let's go, Lauren." Rachel let the camera hang around her neck. She had stopped filming. She tugged on Lauren's arm, at the elbow. "We're outnumbered. It's an ambush."

"I have to look in that room," said Lauren, jerking her elbow free. "Mademoiselle Schwartz is waiting. You promised to keep filming. This will make us famous, just like Helena wanted."

"And do you promise we'll go then, after you look?"

"Yes. Stop nagging."

"She's waiting for you, Lauren," said Mlle Wertheimer.

Lauren heard the music of the three-part Bach invention float to her ears. It sounded better than when floating down the tower staircase. The notes were more fluid, like warm honey on toast or the happiest baby birds to ever be born. Was Mlle Schwartz playing for her? She sprang forward in the dark, remembering exactly where the knob was, and flung the door open.

Rachel had the camera to her eye as promised, but she cried. "Don't believe what you see, Lauren. It's a lie."

Lauren's jaw dropped. Lit candles suffused the tiny room with golden light. The lovely pianist's fingers flew over the keyboard. Lauren was hardly aware of the rain or howl of wind outside. She was enchanted.

"It can always be this way, Lauren dear," said Mlle Wertheimer from across the room, her words ringing like little bells. "You may remain forever at the height of your grace and splendor. Listen to yourself play. You are exquisite."

"Wonderful," chimed in the two teachers, clapping.

Lauren didn't hear them. Her eyes were absorbed by her own image, playing with a skill she had reached perhaps a half dozen days in her life because she was apt to grow lazy, wasn't she, and forget to practice. Life changed people, distracted, drained and tore them down.

"This isn't what you came for," Rachel said, her tone steady, serious. "You came to find Mademoiselle Schwartz. Look, Lauren. The room is empty. Nothing but candles on an old, broken-down piano."

"The room is not empty. Don't you see who is playing?"

"These demons are taking over your mind. Wertheimer used to mess with our heads to make us feel bad or work too hard. Did you forget she went to *prison* for conniving to send us off with Monsieur Bonami?"

"She did?"

"So that we would fall to our deaths on a dangerous mountain slope! Break our necks skiing down the black run. We would have died. Wertheimer was an accomplice to premeditated murder."

"But I turned myself in, you ungrateful young woman. I saved your lives," Mlle Wertheimer declared, calm and cool. "Château Mont Rose caused me to see the error of my ways. It was the institute's reputation at stake!"

Lauren was glad when Rachel faced the headmistress; she wanted to listen to the music. Besides, Rachel was repeating herself:

"You conspired to kill Madame Bonami and then you conspired to kill us. The Swiss government put you in prison."

Would she stop talking? Rachel's hand fell on her shoulder.

"Lauren, look at me!"

Lauren shrugged off the hand. "Shhhhh!"

"Château Mont Rose has gone rotten, Lauren, evil. You're not communing with anything beautiful; you're falling for a trap."

Rachel clearly wouldn't understand the paranormal if she tripped and fell into a bathtub of it.

"What do you see in that room that I don't?"

Finally, a little open-mindedness!

"I see myself." Lauren pointed. "Right there."

"Bullshit. You are nowhere but right next to me. That stupid room is freezing and empty."

"People can become blind to the beauty before them," called out Mlle Villot from the corner.

"Lauren is sensitive to what is real for her and for Château Mont Rose. Certain young ladies serve as symbols of the institute's golden era," said Mlle Wertheimer. "The château has chosen Lauren."

"She doesn't want to be chosen," cried Rachel. "Neither of us do. We refuse. We're getting out of here." Rachel tugged on Lauren's arm. "You need psychological help, Mademoiselle Wertheimer. I'm surprised they let you out of prison."

"Mademoiselle Gordon." The name reverberated throughout the room. A crack of thunder followed.

The piano music stopped and the image of the player grew translucent. That glowing but less tangible young Lauren turned to look at the group.

Mlle Wertheimer's voice swelled with the thunder: "Mademoiselle Gordon, you are a thankless creature. You are invited to leave us—alone."

Outside, another lightning bolt lit the sky, but farther away. Something else, not thunder or rain, bothered Lauren's ears.

"Rachel, what is that noise you made just now?"

"That was the storm," said Mlle Wertheimer.

"Don't listen to her, Lauren. It's my boots." Rachel's voice teetered on the edge of hysteria. "I'm standing in melted wax and so are you. Don't you feel your feet getting warm? The wax is in my socks. My feet feel gross and slimy."

Lauren put her fingers in her ears, massaged, and popped them out. Then she lifted her feet, testing. She had to tear her gaze off the dimming image of herself seated on a piano bench, to look down at her boots. Were they wet? Saturated? She wasn't sure. Her feet felt sort of numb although they did not hurt.

"It was hard to hear you. All I could hear was piano music."

"Do you hear this?" yelled Rachel, glopping forward to slam her hand down on the piano keys, over and over. The keyboard sounded horribly out of tune.

Lauren clapped her hands over her ears, looked at the piano bench. "Where did she go, that other me—" She looked in vain at the walls for her dissolved self.

Rachel's words were urgent: "What you wrote for the ghost-hunting scripts, Lauren, was really good. You're talented. But you won't get a chance in hell—and trust me, that's what this is—to do what you chose to do if you listen to Wertheimer. The piano music you said you were playing, I couldn't hear. This bitch's voice, I can. You didn't want to be a professional pianist. You chose to be a writer. Don't give up now."

"Throw that nasty little hoodlum out, Mademoiselle Terrieux," ordered Mlle Wertheimer. "You were never the right type for this place, Mademoiselle Gordon. I knew it from the first day I saw you, but I had mercy. Now I see my grave mistake. You are a bad influence, just like Danielle Schwartz."

Lauren heard the insult to Rachel, but her gaze was riveted on the piano and its bench. Where had her younger, but more beautiful mirror image gone?

"We have to leave," declared Rachel, "now!"

Lauren felt a hard ache behind her eyes. It came with changing her mind, seeing things as Rachel described them. She allowed Rachel to close the door of the tiny room. It was a lovely room, but too small to confine her spirit for eternity.

The forms of Mlle Wertheimer and Mlle Villot, like two old chickens perched on the other side of the dark attic room, tilted their heads. Conversely, the looming figure with spikey hair marched with suction noises through melted wax towards them.

"But Mademoiselle Schwartz. . . . " began Lauren, feeling confused.

". . . is banned from this establishment," called Mlle Wertheimer pulling back her thin shoulders, lifting her chin.

"You can't ban a spirit," said Rachel.

"You don't think so?" cried Spikes, her laughter menacing.

"Château Mont Rose banishes whom it pleases," said Mlle Wertheimer. "We are but its willing servants. It has now chosen to banish you, Mademoiselle Gordon. Lauren, say goodbye to this joke of friendship. She wanted to cripple you."

Avoiding Spikes, Lauren and Rachel had backed themselves to the head of the staircase. They peered down at it.

Where the staircase had been, a gaping chasm yawned.

Chapter 29

A Storm in a Teacup

Paul didn't realize how stiff he was from squatting, balled up, arms over his head. The fabric of his jacket sleeves chafing his ears reminded him of the moped-driving goggles stashed in his left-hand pocket. He had to practically unlock a joint to pull his arm down and put them on.

Standing, he fought against the torrent of wind to move to his right. When that proved futile, he struggled to the left. The squall opposed him, no matter which direction he chose. To the left, his hand eventually found the door and its knob. The quest probably took ten or fifteen minutes.

The doorknob resisted as stubbornly as a soldered metal pipe.

Bless you, Uncle Julien, thought Paul as he pulled out the pistol. He aimed at the bolts around the knob and fired off a round.

No sooner had he wrenched the knob off and the door open than the gale died inside the room. He had been locked in a long, bare storage closet. The gusts had come straight out of the walls, whipping his cheeks raw. He could have sworn the wind was peppered with grains of sand.

No evidence of debris remained.

Paul wondered how Ajit, the great paranormal know-it-all, would explain this episode. For a fellow who claimed to be acquainted with the deeper mysteries of life, Ajit didn't seem to be interested in much other than tapping on walls to find stashed-away bars of gold. Maybe Paul didn't know his cousin as well as he thought.

The realization made Paul gasp and run to the staircase. But of course! Ajit had snuck back to his absurd treasure hunt!

Paul took the stairs by two again, racing to the corner room where he had earlier saved Ajit from that crazy older woman. He looked through the doorway and perceived such dark stillness that he thought the room empty until his torch found Ajit in a half-fetal position on the floor, arms stiff and outstretched and stiff. Damage to the wall proved his cousin's recent activity.

"Ajit?" Falling to his knees, Paul tried to determine what was wrong. He slapped on Ajit's cheeks, to no effect. Paul aimed the light at his stiff arms and found both hands and arms were puffy, swollen. He looked closer. "Zut!"

Splinters stuck out from his skin like cactus needles.

A box-shaped carpet bag sat just outside the break in the wall. Paul used Ajit's metal detector to shove the bag back through the gaping hole. It was heavy and did not make it all the way in on the first shove.

Paul thought about using his foot to shove it sideways when he noticed dripping. Perhaps rain had seeped in?

The dripping was from the inside of the rupture. It could be leaking pipes, but the substance was thick, almost gooey. On the ground, it pooled dark red.

The wall seemed to be bleeding.

Paul felt sick to his stomach, but he fought it, pushing the carpet bag further inside the hole. Then he removed the camera strap from around Ajit's neck and fished out his own Swiss pocket knife. It had tweezers. Ignoring the bleeding wall, Paul began plucking the barbs, one by one, from Ajit's inflated wrist, half expecting air to hiss out. The light from Paul's headgear was just sufficient for the job.

Ajit moaned.

"Stay still."

Dots of blood welled from the wood filaments exiting from Ajit's arm. Coagulated puss oozed out too, from where the larger splinters had lodged. Paul knew he was using up precious time, and refused to think about what the wall was doing. The swelling of Ajit's arms suggested a toxin, the threat of which he had to minimize with all possible speed.

After much diligent plucking, Paul was as finished as he could be in this place. He had done his best. Dozens of dots and slivers remained under the skin. There was nothing he could do about those.

Ajit groaned and shivered, but he was awake, alive. Paul wished he had hydrogen peroxide. He patted his cousin's cheeks.

"Don't be patronizing," moaned Ajit.

"*Eh bien, mon vieux.* We have to move, find the women and get the hell out."

"Did you take out *all* those fucking splinters?" Ajit wouldn't look at his hands.

"All the ones I could grasp with tweezers."

Ajit's eyes locked on the wall and he moaned. "Holy God."

A man's head was visible in the narrowing hole; the eyes blinked. It was a face Paul knew by his uncle's description and from having passed him, a face possessing a saddle-like, flat-bridged nose with a fleshy tip and a prominent forehead disappearing to view.

The wall healed over the moving mouth of the man, who repeated, "Come on, boys; come and get me!"

Paul dragged Ajit up. Neither mentioned the metal detector on the floor. While Paul was plucking out slivers, the metal detector had bent, slowly, into a pretzel shape.

#

It had been five years, barring home video clips, since Detective Inspector Cloquet had seen his daughter move, smile, or show any of the innumerable sparks of life that make the corporeal human body into a beloved, vibrant companion. Nor had he expected to. She was dead.

Watching footage of their little excursions, *en famille*, had been painful right after the accident. He carefully made copies of the video clips, fearing to lose what he might never be able to bring himself to view again. Those filmed scenes were the only proof the inspector really had to show that his daughter had once lived, not counting her photos, degrees and sailing trophies, books and clothes.

Cloquet knew the most tangible part of Michèle was in his own heart. When he had been summoned to identify his daughter's body after the mountain road crash, the mangled corpse was not what he wanted to remember as his beautiful daughter. The coroner assured him death had been instant.

Then head of homicide of the Lausanne Sûreté, Cloquet had managed not to crumple in front of officials into the useless piece of broken fatherhood he became later, at home. In the coroner's office, his eyes had turned red and his steps had faltered, but deep breathing, which he had trained himself to do for years, helped him sign the papers to get the grown child's unrecognizable remains home.

And buried.

Michèle was today in an expensive coffin under the ground. Correction, her cadaver was in that coffin. Cloquet did not believe her spirit or soul was underground or even destroyed. If the human body converted to other forms of energy, it stood to reason that the animating factor—that thing people called the soul or spirit—went somewhere else. To a merciful God, he hoped.

Where her spirit had *not* gone was into this enigma moving around on his laptop screen. Someone could have got their hands on his video clips, stolen the footage through hacking, the way people stole IDs, and then photoshopped the material to hypnotize him.

Or—Cloquet shuddered—what he saw now was the same kind of creature he had tried to destroy, made of wax.

The girl was smiling at him as if she knew he was watching. She looked exactly like Michèle before she died. And Papaux looked as he had the last time Cloquet had seen him, in that very building, but it couldn't be Papaux. Not really. Something bad must have happened to Papaux.

Feeling his face flush, Cloquet wondered what message this generic Michèle had for him. Why would a figure of Michèle appear on the detective's laptop screen?

To distract me.

Cloquet shoved the laptop aside and jumped out in the rain.

#

Dominick came back to dull sobriety with a shock. It was not the hissing or smell of hot fibers that roused him; it was the strangeness of pleasure ending in pain. Trembling, he pulled his lips away from the strange-tasting mouth. No sooner had he reached his peak of pleasure than he realized this was not Helena's true face. What had she done to herself?

A bleating erupted from his throat, the kind of sound he would have ridiculed in anyone else. The creature's eyes, inches from his, had as much life as a pair of marbles. This wasn't Helena's warm, musky-scented skin. He knew he was guilty. He had chosen not to notice.

This *thing* was hideously strong. Her arms clasped like octopus tentacles, rubbery and unforgiving, around the small of his back, pulling him closer. He couldn't pull away.

He realized the pins plunged in this creature's neck were not a kinky dog collar or Gothic necklace as he had imagined at first.

The pins looked like—oh bloody hell, what was that word for what aborigines wearing dreadlocks in American swamplands did? Voodoo? Sticking pins into a replica hurt the real person. Dominick remembered the welts on Helena's neck. He had to get away from this damnable thing.

The female facsimile blinked dead dirt eyes. In appalling discomfort, it took Dominick another moment to realize a good deal of the heat in the room emanated from the rug. Its fibers were smoldering. He had dropped his whiskey glass. His cigar—he blocked that thought. He always left his cigar in an ashtray. Most of the time.

Tiny flames seared and popped in the carpet under his gaze, snapping like baby teeth.

Who bloody cared what had brought on a fire? Damned old Swiss buildings and their old faulty electrical wiring! He had to escape, find Helena, and get the hell out.

Dominick punched the face in front of his, surprised to feel his fist bend the nose. Pounding and pushing, he wrenched himself away from the waxen Helena doll and staggered to his feet. Every part of him that had pressed against her stung in the air like it had been brush-painted with acid.

His skin throbbed. He needed water.

The Helena replica walked the fingers of one hand over her bosom, She moved her hips, oblivious to the smoke and plumes rising from a burning stack of magazines. She was a goner.

Dominick grabbed his clothes, thought for a moment about using them to beat out the fire, then realized he would have to run into the street nude. His gaze avoided the creature splayed on the couch.

He ran out, groaning. Why weren't the ceiling water sprayers working?

The true Helena was not on the landing where he had left her. Had she got up on her own? Had she awoken, seen him with that *woman thing*, and misunderstood?

Impossible. When Helena put herself into a trance, she had a hard time coming out of it.

"Helena!"

Surely being burned to death had not been what Helena intended when she explained to her lover-partner that Château Mont Rose might demand "self-sacrifice" of a former student. He raced to the nearest bathroom, frantic to wash off the painful residue.

He found a spigot, turned it full blast. The water cooled. Dominick hurried.

#

Vanni brushed his hair at the vanity table in Lauren and Rachel's bedroom. The reflected image, wearing the bridal gown, smiled teasingly back at him, blew him a kiss.

"You naughty child. Aren't you supposed to be undressing?"

Vanni giggled, shook his head at his own silliness. Dark curls tickled his eyebrows. So absorbed was he in his reflection that when a loud clanging rent the air, as sharp and nasty as a prison siren, he threw his brush up so high it hit the ceiling and lodged in the hanging lamp.

"What is that horridness?" Vanni threw open the bedroom door. The hallway bell blared.

His nostrils curled up in distaste. Burned toast? Popcorn left to cook to blackened kernels in a microwave?

Vanni plunged into the corridor, tripping over the bridal gown in his high heels, landing on his knees and elbows. "Ahh!" He kicked off the shoes, impatient, then picked up his skirts to run in bare feet. By the time he got to the office from which smoke billowed, he was coughing and moist. A sparse mist of water sprayed from the intermittent functioning ceiling sprinklers.

No sprinkler worked in the office itself. Flames devoured the couch and window curtains. The couch was covered in a mound of dripping wax.

Terror seized Vanni. What had happened to Helena in her cocoon trance? He had not seen her anywhere.

Vanni lost no time, ran up the stairs, coughing, and called out "Lauren, Rachel, Paul, *Al fuoco*! Fire! Save yourselves!"

#

Spikes was walking funny.

"What's wrong with her?"

"She's made out of wax," said Rachel, hoarse.

Spikes opened her mouth. The sound that came out was tinny, like a high school announcement over an outdated speaker system: "Mademoiselle Gordon has *never* been a proper representative of Château Mont Rose."

"Do you think that hole in the stairs is too wide to jump over?" asked Lauren.

"Probably. Oh God, I don't know. Where did the stairs go?"

Lauren and Rachel were backed up against a widening hole.

"Mademoiselle Schwartz was not the only one who tried to seduce Monsieur Bonami." Spikes said, taking a step forward. The dissonance of her voice made Lauren's hair stand on end.

"Mademoiselle Gordon has kept secrets from you, Lauren. She did not arrive as an innocent. Even at fifteen, she had—how do you say in English, 'Been around the block'?" Spikes slid the other foot forward, as if Rachel and Lauren were two cats that had to be approached stealthily.

"A dirty block. She did things she never told you about. Nasty, ugly things, at Château Mont Rose."

Rachel's face took on a pinched expression.

"Rachel is a wonderful person," said Lauren.

"You don't know her as well as you think." Spikes said. She pointed an accusatory finger at Rachel.

"Are you real?" Lauren demanded.

Spikes did not answer. Across the room, Mademoiselle Villot and Mademoiselle Wertheimer put their heads together, exchanged murmurs in French.

"She is real," replied Mlle Villot in English. "Although you are correct in surmising Château Mont Rose provides a new perspective on reality. We think of it as an improvement. Anyone who resides on this estate will be served and cared for while her—"

"Sometimes there are men, Mademoiselle Villot," cut in Mlle Wertheimer. "Virginie's son, remember?"

"Oh yes. While her or *his* talents are heightened. That person will be inspired, loved, even nurtured, just like the rose the little prince loved."

"You don't need to use that analogy," cut in Mlle Wertheimer with a dismissive wave of her hand. "Danielle Schwartz overused it."

"It was the analogy of the founder of Château Mont Rose, Jeanne Bonami," replied Mlle Villot primly.

"The château takes care of its roses in spite of the thorns," intoned Mlle Wertheimer. Her voice was subdued.

"But it does not abide fungus," said Spikes, "like Mademoiselle Gordon."

"Stay where you are, you, you—" Lauren groped for a sufficient word and spat out— "*ball* of lacquered quills. And don't call my friend fungus."

"Rachel Gordon was a lurid watcher, a voyeur. She wanted to be Monsieur Bonami's secret *whore!*" countered Spikes.

Rachel's hand tightened on Lauren's.

"You didn't think, Mademoiselle Gordon," asked Mlle Wertheimer, "that you would be able to come back here without being punished?"

"You sick —" began Rachel.

"Those are lies," said Lauren. Her flesh crawled. The creatures had got something wrong and something right: Lauren had been the voyeur. "Rachel," she murmured, "on the count of three?"

"We jump over? But we might not—"

A male voice Lauren recognized and trusted, said from below, "Not over. Down. Into the gap. Immediately."

"Yes—jump into the gap," Lauren whispered into Rachel's ear, keeping a grip on her hand.

"One, two —"

At three, Lauren jumped into the gap of the staircase, pulling Rachel down with her.

Lauren heard Vanni's voice ring out above her: "*Al fuoco!* Fire!" He must have opened the door at the base of the staircase.

She fell hard on a mattress. An elbow rammed into her ribs.

"Ooof!"

The elbow was Rachel's, but the handsome, mustachioed face looking down at her was Paul's. Her eyes filled with tears.

How had he had engineered this escape route? How had he known they could jump into the darkness? She held out her arms, let him pull her up while she kissed him on the cheek. His arm held her close for a brief moment. He *did* kiss her back.

"Look!" cried Ajit. From the foot of the bed, he pointed with a swollen hand at the hole Rachel and Lauren had jumped through. Both Ajit's hands, Lauren saw, were swollen.

The gap in the ceiling was closing. Vanni's cries of "*Al fuoco*" grew muffled, then hushed.

"Was he yelling 'fire'?" asked Rachel.

Paul rushed to the bedroom door, felt it with the back of his hand. He cracked the door open, surveyed, and went out. In seconds he had returned.

"The staircase is on fire."

"Isn't there another staircase?" asked Rachel.

"Inaccessible from here," said Paul. "Open the windows."

Lauren, Paul and Rachel tried the windows. There were four overlooking the front of the estate. Paul pushed on the lever of one. It didn't budge. Lauren's hand was on another lever, but her attention was arrested by the shimmering female figure standing outside the main gate. It was Mlle Schwartz, her huge eyes gazing up at them, through the bars of the main gate.

"Lauren?" said Paul. "Does it open?"

"This one doesn't," wailed Rachel.

Lauren used all her might on the lever. She wiggled and hit it repeatedly, until the side of her palm hurt. "It won't budge."

"Use your phones," said Ajit sitting otherwise useless upon the bed, his swollen hands held up, crisscrossed, upon his chest.

"Mine is in my purse. Downstairs," said Lauren.

"Mine is here," said Rachel, pulling hers from her jacket pocket. She opened and whimpered. "Oh no. It's dead."

"So is mine," said Paul, looking at his. "Ajit?"

"I left mine in my bag," gasped Ajit, clearly in pain.

"Break the windows," said Paul, grabbing the single chair. He smashed it up against the window repeatedly until broken wood and splinters littered the floor. The glass remained intact. He took out his pistol and used up the ammunition on the panes.

Lauren took a step backward, shocked. Paul carried a gun? She remembered that all Swiss males owned guns because of compulsory military training. But semiautomatics? The group stared, aghast, at the results of Paul's pistol. The glass had a few chips, a single (small) hole, and no cracks at all.

Paul beat the empty pistol against the windows, without results. Rachel and Lauren went back to the levers, moving to each other's window as in a game of musical chairs.

"They won't open," cried Lauren. "Rachel, you were right. This place is evil. May God help us!"

#

"No!" said Virginie Duvanel. She sat up on the couch where she had crawled to lie after the attack. Jean had staggered to his bedroom, she supposed. He was not near her.

She turned on a lamp, stood up, sniffing. Her ribcage hurt. She looked out the window, then cried, "Jean! Jean!"

He emerged into the corridor, cautious, not coming near his mother.

"Smoke. Don't you smell it? There's a fire in the château."

"My creations!" exclaimed Jean, staying close to the cottage front door. "Will they be damaged? Or will they re-form, if melted, like this one did?" He pointed at the teenage girl who stood, stiff, exactly where she had emerged under the cottage door. She had a twisted nose and lacked a hand.

He looked at her face and the space where her wrist ended. "I think I can fix her."

"I don't know," said Virginie, hand on her ribs. She mustn't speculate about the power of Château Mont Rose. "A fire could be too much damage. I don't know."

"Why did you strike me, *Maman*?" Jean's voice was thick with distrust.

"Because you were undoing the château's gift to you. These figures are its servants as we are. You must not harm them."

Jean looked conflicted. "How do you know the château didn't tell me to put in the pins?"

"It wouldn't tell you that," said Virginie. "You were guessing."

"My bones hurt," said Jean.

She weakened. "I never told you how the château saved your life, as a baby."

They stood in uncomfortable silence.

Jean was first to break it. "What if the fire spreads back here to our cottage?"

"It won't."

"The sprinkler system should kick in, right?"

Jean sounded like a little boy. Virginie didn't know what to tell him. She felt bad about striking him, but the château took priority over everything. It was her—their—life.

She wrung her hands. "I hope so."

"Bells are ringing!"

"The fire department will be here soon. Get the car, Jean."

#

Detective Cloquet wrinkled his nose, sniffed, and cursed. He could smell smoke. Some part of the château had caught on fire.

He tried texting Paul, but got a "failed message" response.

He jiggled the master key in the front door of the château. It fit in but would not turn. The other key had worked an hour ago, in the side door. Cloquet had copies of every key, had verified them all. Why wasn't this one working?

He could go back to his car and retrieve his locksmith device.

He aimed his flashlight at the window. Carl Gustav Jung looked out, sweating. The wax Jung looked as if he had gone through a laborious workout at the gym.

The gusts of wind-borne rain on the outside wouldn't help the waxen psychoanalyst, trapped inside. The little wind getting in through chinks would fuel the flames. Historic buildings in Switzerland were too old to have hermetically sealed windows unless permits for upgrades had been obtained. Owners often put off such upgrades.

Cloquet went through his keys for Château Mont Rose and found one similar in size to the first one tried. Maybe some of the keys were interchangeable.

He raised his head. Jung's eyes caught his. Cloquet could have sworn Jung looked alarmed. His eyelids were melting.

A shiver spread over Cloquet and he slapped himself, hard. The action jarred him to reality.

"Whore of a building!"

He stepped away from the front door to take the path around to the side where he had earlier let out Virginie Duvanel. His attention was drawn upwards by the sounds of pounding. The rain had stopped. Water dripped from the rooftop. He tilted his head back, moving away from the building. Treading on garden plants, Cloquet thought he saw movement behind upper floor windows.

Movement might be produced by the wax statues, but Paul and the team were in that building. Cloquet saw moving lights. Statues didn't carry flashlights.

Cloquet hit in the numbers of the fire station on his phone. The first ring in his ear was punctuated by a siren's wail approaching from down the road. A fire truck ground to a halt outside the gate. He lowered his phone in amazement. Firemen jumped out to push the gates wider, and then the heavy tires crunched over the driveway.

"Roll it up!" called a fireman, descending from the vehicle. "I'll be damned. A real fire." He spotted Cloquet. "And you are?"

"Detective Inspector Cloquet, Lausanne Sûreté."

"I think we've met before." The fire chief motioned the inspector to come forward. "I'm Captain Soutter."

"Captain, I have building keys, but they are not working." Cloquet held out the keys on the chain.

"The locks could be damaged by the fire. We'll break in."

"Who called in the fire?"

The truck's ladder extended upwards. Captain Soutter raised his voice over the noise to answer: "A female teacher working here. I had no idea it was still a school."

Cloquet had expected to hear Paul's name. Or the Duvanels. "A teacher? What name did she give?"

"It's on the case sheet, but I took the call. Schwartz, I believe."

Cloquet absorbed the news without comment.

Two firemen wearing masks on their faces and tanks on their backs began climbing.

"Captain, my young partner is up there with the ghost-hunting crew. Seven people, possibly eight," said Cloquet, thinking of Mlle Wertheimer, "are inside this building."

The captain gave a signal to two more firefighters on the ground. They began assaulting the front door.

"If there hadn't been a fire now, this very minute, someone would be going to jail," said Captain Soutter cryptically. "Please remove yourself, Inspector. This is out of your jurisdiction until we judge the area safe."

The captain thrust his energy into the vortex of firefighters, and the front door at last gave way. Cloquet moved back to the garden wall and kept his gaze riveted on third-floor windows, where he believed Paul and the others were trapped.

Chapter 30

Vanni's Destiny

When Vanni stood at the bottom of the dark, narrow staircase, shouting "*Al fuoco*" and gripping the handrail with a sweaty palm, he knew he would ascend to the highest part of the château. The ultimate danger posed by the residence exceeded death by fire. Appropriation of souls was at stake.

Vanni had read enough about ancient hunting grounds of native Americans and what happened to sacrilegious violators of those places. He also knew about castles, even tiny castles, and the pride absorbed by their walls.

In the deceptive calm a mere half hour earlier, Vanni had crept down the hallway to peek into the main office. There he had seen what looked like Helena mesmerizing Dominick with anything but ghost-hunting. The Brit had looked up at Vanni with the glazed eyes of an addict.

Shocked to the core by his employers' self-indulgence, Vanni had gone out to lean against the concierge desk and wipe his forehead with a handkerchief. It was then he noticed that the real Helena—his black leather-clad, waxed employer—had been moved to the turn in the staircase landing. She lay, face upwards, under the wax figure of Madame Tussaud. Vanni tiptoed forward, holding up his long bridal skirt, to make sure she was breathing. When he looked up at Madame Tussaud, the wax retinas retracted to meet his gaze.

The creature gave a slow Mona Lisa smile.

It took a lot of backbone to ignore that smile and retreat to the bedroom. Vanni closed the door and foraged into his briefcase for the bottle of laudanum. It helped. Refreshing his makeup also assisted in the calming of the nerves. Replacing the mascara and powder brush, he snapped the box shut and bade farewell to procrastination. The château wanted a sacrifice; it was bringing its wax figures to life to make that claim. This was Vanni's destiny.

He would have preferred a destiny in Hollywood, but Vanni knew he had been prepared for something. All those castles. So much knowledge. So much love in his heart.

Perhaps a movie would be made about him?

Now Vanni looked up at the one remaining flight of stairs before him. Human sacrifices traditionally took place on highest ground. The Aztecs had done so. He swallowed hard, lifted his chin and began climbing.

#

Standing against the garden wall with clenched fists jammed in his coat pockets, Cloquet stopped counting the number of whacks the firemen attempted. He had lost track. It scared him that there were no faces clearly visible behind the windows. Behind the window panes, smoke swirled. When a third fireman took over the ax, Cloquet's heart sank like a stone into his gut. His heart formed words: "Please, dear God."

A window gave way with a crash. Smoke billowed out as it had from the front door when Captain Soutter's men forced it with crowbars and axes. The gray clouds spewed into the fire crew's lights and then reached the streetlamps. Another fire truck's wail grew louder.

The arrival of a second vehicle and its crew made it harder for Cloquet to see what was going on, but he was glad for the help. The entire neighborhood was in jeopardy.

A second ladder rolled up. Another window resisted ax blows for an unreasonable length of time. Cloquet watched in relief as a female ghost-hunting crew member was passed through the first opened window. Her sharp scream made Cloquet catch his breath. Could skin have been cut by broken window glass?

An ambulance pulled up outside the estate gate. At the same time, firemen rigged a hoist to the second opened window. Cloquet strained to identify a lanky figure, either Paul or Ajit, emerging. The fellow held both hands like stumps and bawled when they were touched. A safety swing lowered him.

The orange glow inside the château and the exiting smoke made Cloquet shift his weight nervously. Firemen fought inside with pressurized tanks. Visible flames jumped faster than the two fire trucks' crews could put them out. Two trucks! Cloquet tried not to clench and unclench his burned hand in his pocket.

He squinted at the lanky rescued male—Ajit—being detached from the hoist. Paramedics lifted him onto a stretcher.

Meanwhile, moving lights from the helmets of firemen searching for victims bobbed past windows. A limp female form was threaded out of one upstairs, handed by one fireman to another. A gas mask covered her face and her head lolled in the receiver's arms. The hoist drew near. Four people, thought Cloquet, needed evacuation. Maybe five? Six? He shifted his weight yet again, mentally counting off individuals he presumed were inside the château.

He snapped to attention when a glowing ember, the size of a piece of barbecue coal, shot out from a downstairs vent and hit the base of a tree near him. Cloquet leaped by instinct in the opposite direction, falling into a bush.

The targeted tree began burning. Another glowing missile, the size of a tennis ball, whizzed past his ear.

"*Allez vous en!* Get out!" A fireman ran to Cloquet. "Get out of this enclosure, *tout de suite.*"

The detective's coat had snagged on the brambles of the bush. The fireman tore Cloquet away, shoved him at the main gate. "Out, out!" The firemen and medics were all yelling.

Tumbleweed-size balls of fire rolled out the front door of Château Mont Rose. One hit a fire truck tire. The stench of melting rubber thickened the air. A firefighter diverted the stream of water from his hose to the vehicle.

Cloquet bumped into a paramedic as he maneuvered around the gate. "*Pardon.*"

If he couldn't see, he wouldn't know when Paul or anyone else got out. Frustrated, the detective climbed onto the hood of his car outside the enclosure's wall, and from there, onto his car roof. The estate wall was too far for him to lean against, but he could see over it. The scene was chaos.

Different parts of the garden had erupted into flames. The château's basement vents spouted fiery tennis ball comets of destruction. Some changed direction midair, like people-seeking missiles.

One sailed over the wall, missing Cloquet's head by a finger's breadth when he jerked away. He lost his balance, toppled down the car roof, and bumped his chin against the metal top. He groaned, felt his jaw. His teeth had bit his tongue. The ambulance pulled out of the open gate to park further away, out of reach of missiles. Two paramedics pulled a stretcher out of the vehicle and ran back onto the estate grounds.

Cloquet cursed his nerves. He clambered back up on the roof of his car, determined to see. The firemen were now fighting the vents as well as the fire inside the château. No matter how much the inspector strained his neck, there was no sign of Paul. Nor, in fact, of any others on the crew.

#

Daylight streamed through the windows of a patient room at Clinique Cecil. It hurt Lauren's eyes. She closed them against the glare, let her head rest against the pillow on her bed.

"It's odd how many fires take place when it's raining. You'd be surprised," said the nurse standing over her. She had introduced herself as

Marie. Lauren thought Marie watched her breathe oxygen from the tank a little too closely. Kind of like a vulture.

"Do I really need this?"

The words did not make it out of the mask. Nurse Marie held her finger to her mouth. "*Ne parlez pas*—Don't talk. Breathe."

"I'm sorry you have to go through that," said Rachel in a hoarse voice from the adjacent bed. "You shouldn't have shoved me out first. A little more smoke wouldn't kill me. Cigarettes have toughened me up."

Lauren didn't remember shoving Rachel anywhere.

"What an absurd thing to say," said Marie. "Cigarettes are as toxic as fire, they just take longer to kill you. You will have to breathe from the oxygen tank too. But later, since you are not as badly off." Marie made a dismissive wave of her hand at Rachel. "The doctor will let you go home. This lady has to stay overnight because she is coughing so much. That way we can adequately medicate her for pain."

"Everyone wants to medicate Lauren," said Rachel. "Why can't I stay too? I was in the fire. It was our hotel that burned down."

"This is a hospital, not a hotel. We need the beds for the sick."

Rachel pulled out her phone and stared at it. "A dead phone isn't much use. I had just charged it, too. How can we find out what happened . . . ?"

Lauren felt a hand squeeze her heart. She did not want to hear anyone had died, let alone been injured. Where was Paul? She could remember nothing since the last harried moments in that smoke-filled room.

Paul had found a fire extinguisher, but it couldn't do much against the greed of the flames. He had closed the doors between them and the fire, stuffing wet bedclothes—thanks to the sink in the room—under both doors to keep out toxic fumes. They wouldn't hold long.

She remembered allowing Paul to place a wet pillow cover over her head. He had kept his arm around her, but her lungs had felt increasingly raw and painful. Her head had pounded while she heard rather than saw firemen trying to break through the windows. Before she passed out, she decided the château was trying to eat them. Cooked, of course.

A man's head, wearing a fur hat, popped into the hospital bedroom doorway. The face under the hat looked familiar to Lauren. He was a big, burly sort of fellow. Where did she know him from?

The man nodded at all three females. She felt ridiculous wearing the oxygen mask. Her hands reached up to pull it off. The mask resisted as if it had a mind of its own. Lauren found Marie's fingers holding the strap in place. She looked at the nurse.

Marie pursed her mouth, shook her head. "*Pas encore!* Not yet!"

"Mademoiselle Gordon," said the man, "I am Detective Inspector Cloquet." He handed Rachel his card. "Do you remember me?"

Lauren had the odd sensation of hearing a false note.

"Of course," said Rachel, without glancing at the card. "Lauren, look who is here!"

"Mademoiselle Briant! *Comment allez-vous?*" Detective Cloquet held out a rough hand.

Lauren shook it, feeling like an alien from Mars. Then she remembered this was the inspector who had investigated Mlle Schwartz's death. He had been a very nice man.

She smiled weakly, remembering afterward he could not see her expression.

"Her lungs hurt," said Rachel.

The detective pulled a chair up and sat down between the two beds, nodding with a benign expression. "I would say you both look wonderful except, of course. . . ." he trailed off, lifting his shoulders and large hands in the air to emphasize life's vicissitudes. Sometimes one had to acknowledge oxygen masks.

"—we survived a fire."

Lauren nodded to Rachel's words. That was all she could contribute to the conversation at present.

"How did you know we were here at the hospital?" There was that false note again.

"Your names were on the list of those rescued. I was at the château last night, but I am not a firefighter. All I could do was wait. I am sorry your return to the school has turned out to be traumatic."

"Do you know how the fire started?"

That was the question Lauren would have asked if not for the mask.

"That investigation is still going forward."

Lauren realized there was a pad of notepaper near her bed. She took it and the nearby pencil, scribbled, and handed the top sheet to Marie, who handed it to Rachel.

Rachel read it. "Of course! Detective, can you tell us how the rest of the crew is? Is everyone alright?"

"Your assistants Ajit and Paul Junod are just down the hallway, receiving oxygen therapy. Ajit is suffering from multiple—how do you say—ailments or accidents, so he's worse off than Paul."

Lauren gulped in the pure oxygen with gratitude. A pang of guilt followed. Poor Ajit.

"From smoke inhalation?"

"There is that, but his arms and hands have suffered trauma. It is quite inexplicable. Ajit has a rash of infection on almost all of the skin covering his hands and arms. The symptoms tally with those resulting from the toxin of a rare wood."

"That is weird. Will he be okay?"

"The doctor hopes so."

"What about—the others?"

"The firemen had a shock when a woman appeared leaning out of the window of the highest balcony, screaming. They didn't expect someone up there."

"Helena!" said Lauren inside her oxygen mask. No one heard her, but Rachel mouthed the same name.

"Excuse me," said Cloquet, "I should not have said 'woman.' Captain Soutter of the fire brigade described what he took to be a female dressed in a bridal gown. An individual with the highest, most piercing scream imaginable, he said. The rescuer saw the bride's mustache up close, though some of his hair and the veil were torched off. It was an Italian or Swiss Italian individual wearing the costume. Do you have such a person on your crew?"

"Our makeup artist, Vanni," said Rachel. "Is he okay?"

"He is stable and in this hospital as well."

"Was anyone else saved, Detective?"

Detective Cloquet looked down at his shoes. He did not answer.

Lauren felt a distinct chill crawl over her skin. It was not caused by the oxygen in the tank.

"Before I answer that, I need to know exactly how many other human beings there were in the château last night besides Paul, Ajit, and the Italian man dressed as a bride."

Lauren felt a little light-headed from the oxygen.

"Two," said Rachel steadily. "Our employers, Helena Stamoulos and Dominick Bentley."

Lauren stared at Rachel, waiting for her to remember Mlle Wertheimer, Spikes, and Mlle Villot. Rachel met her gaze but held her tongue.

Detective Cloquet's lack of response swelled into the void, suggesting that Helena and Dominick might be dead.

The somber lull in the room was broken by a cacophony of voices in the corridor. Nurse Marie, having just unhooked Lauren from her oxygen treatment, hesitated in rolling the machine towards Rachel. Lauren gratefully removed the mask, but the nurse did not proceed to administer the same to Rachel, who was demanding,

"Who is that? Why are people yelling?"

"Surely nothing to do with you," replied Nurse Marie. "I'll go see what the problem is. We don't tolerate this kind of ruckus."

Rachel had jumped out of bed and now stood in bare feet.

"Get back in bed," said the nurse. "I will see what is going on."

"It might be our employers," croaked Lauren in a raspy voice. Rachel nodded hopefully.

"Noise makers are *always* evicted," said Nurse Marie, exiting.

"They're talking in French," whispered Lauren. Her hand went up to her throat, to the vocal cords that weren't working.

"Dominick and Helena wouldn't be speaking in French," said Rachel, wilting back upon her pillow.

Detective Cloquet had taken off his fur hat. His head was tipped to listen to the voices. The tops of his ears were red. Lauren thought his hat must have been very warm.

Nurse Marie came back in, and though she was a caramel-skinned woman, the lack of blood flow in her cheeks was obvious. The swift padding of her feet served to get her body to the only empty chair in the room, where she lowered herself.

"What is wrong?" asked Cloquet.

The nurse seemed dazed. "I heard . . . a corpse in the morgue came to life. It was in there for hours, ready for autopsy. The forensic pathologist was cutting when. . . ."

"*Pardonnez-moi*," said the detective holding up a hand for the nurse to stop. "*Attention!* That is more information than these young ladies need to hear."

"*Oh là là*, they're not babies," snapped Marie, her face going ruddy. "You asked me what happened."

"Tell us," said Lauren in her strangled voice, and Rachel seconded, "Yes, please."

"A wild man broke into the morgue and attacked our pathologist," said Marie. "The attacker abused the corpse. The pathologist is being treated for shock. The police have been called because the man who *revived* the corpse disappeared. In the meantime, our hospital staff is re-admitting the—uh—revived person to receive treatment."

"Police!" A male voice cried from the corridor.

"Forgive me, Ladies," said Detective Cloquet, standing and nodding at the women. "As long as I am already here, I must respond. *À plus tard.*"

Nurse Marie followed him.

Rachel's eyes flashed.

"Dominick?" whispered Lauren.

"I think so. It sounds like him." Rachel stood, tapped Lauren's shoulder. "Don't forget to hold the back of your gown."

Lauren nodded, closed the back of her gown with one hand. She trod behind Rachel, both of them barefoot. In the corridor, a disheveled Dominick stood between two men in blue security uniforms. Each officer had a firm grip on an arm.

He was a filthy mess. Soot covered his clothes, which were singed and torn. Unkempt hair fell into his ash-rimmed eyes. He looked like a big, ornery owl, the way his wide eyes blinked and his hair stuck out, an owl a cat had wrestled with behind a barn.

"Is this how you treat saviors, you flippin' sons of . . . my crew!" Catching sight of the Americans, calm washed over Dominick's face. Lauren covered her open mouth with a hand and grabbed the door frame with the other, completely forgetting the back of her gown. Luckily no one stood behind her. When she remembered, she caught it up and held the sides closed.

Detective Cloquet had stepped up to the nurse's desk. "I am Detective Inspector Cloquet with Lausanne Sûreté." He held out his badge.

"I am the head nurse, Inspector," said a woman in scrubs. She answered the inspector's address in English, Lauren noticed, perhaps so that Dominick would understand. The badge on her shirt was a little bigger than the other nurses' name tags. "I wish for this man to be ejected forthwith."

"He looks to be in need of treatment."

"*Quand même* . . . Admissions is downstairs."

"These hospital freaks were trying to kill my Helena!" blurted Dominick. His voice cracked. The dismay Lauren heard gave her goosebumps.

Her gaze strayed down the corridor, in search of Paul, who had been as subject to smoke as she. In the third doorway down, she saw his head. He smiled at her, his brow uncreasing.

"Thank God I knew what to do to revive her," said Dominick.

The head nurse squared her shoulders. Her voice was sharp. "Monsieur, you attacked our forensic pathologist. I have called the police."

Inspector Cloquet kept calm. "I just showed you my badge."

"Then why don't you arrest him?"

The detective conferred with the nurse. Lauren could not catch his words. Whatever they were, the head nurse slid off her high horse.

"Please let me see Helena," pleaded Dominick. "I want to see Helena Stamoulos. I need to know she's alright."

The head nurse was silent.

Running a hand through his messy hair, which didn't make it look any better, Dominick addressed all in the corridor: "I haven't broken the law. I have saved the life of an enlightened soul, a clairvoyant, Helena Stamoulos, my associate. I *knew* she was in a self-induced trance. She taught me how to revive her. I have saved her from being diced into mincemeat."

Lauren saw Dominick open his mouth again, then shut it. Not an easy accomplishment for a man like him.

"Did you come out of the château together with Mademoiselle Stamoulos?" Detective Cloquet asked. "Your names were not on the survivor list. Where have you been since last night?"

Paul had brought a chair to his doorway. His skin color around the eyes and mouth had a faint bluish tone. A nurse hurried towards him. She probably was going to harass him back into his bed. Lauren rather wished the nurse wasn't so pretty.

"I was looking for her for as long as I could in that fire," cried Dominick, "and then I got out the back when I thought there was no hope left. A man can only take so much; I believed I had lost her. The firemen arrived. . . ." He covered his face with one hand.

"This man needs attention," said Nurse Marie.

"Do you have medical insurance, Monsieur?" asked the head nurse in a chilly tone.

"Yes, I—"

"Everyone is covered," piped up Rachel in a hoarse voice. "I am the team secretary. Mr. Bentley is fully covered for medical needs under the same company policy as the rest of us."

The head nurse looked around at all the patients standing in doorways. She muttered something to another nurse seated behind the desk. That one rose to pursue a task. The head nurse clapped her hands, twice, like a first-grade teacher.

"Looks like the show's over."

Lauren nodded absently, pleased by the smile she had just received from Paul, even if it was ever so faintly blue.

Chapter 31

Chocolate Frankenstein

When Paul offered his apartment as a place for Lauren and Rachel to stay until Helena got out of the hospital, he knew the subject of Frankenstein would come up. It would surface like worms on a sidewalk after abundant rain.

They all needed to work through the recent terrors. But how would Lauren react when she discovered his role as the monster at the Château de Chillon? Paul worried she would not forgive him easily. If at all.

It would be better to address the subject before Lauren found out on her own. Paul wanted to reveal his identity as an undercover officer as well, but Uncle Julien was being stubborn. He said one of the girls knowing his identity was enough. In fact, Rachel's understanding of Paul's role was limited. She thought he was present to protect them from the menaces of a potential murderer—be it Helena or the nefarious Monsieur Bonami, theoretically living in Geneva.

Paul was doing that, but his main mission was to keep the women in Switzerland and to find out whether the curse (which he was not sure he believed in) that had brought about the demise or disappearance of Château Mont Rose alumnae was now defunct.

If he did not present a credible—and excusable—explanation for being dressed up to scare Lauren out of her wits, she might keep him so much at arm's length he would fail at both goals. Although she had kissed him during the fire, it had been a spontaneous action prompted by hysteria.

A creative, even romantic, gesture was called for if he wanted her to believe he had no complicity in abusing her. Long-stemmed roses were not good enough. He needed something that would appeal to Lauren's love of Switzerland.

Paul took his plastic statuette of Frankenstein's monster, a souvenir from a family trip, to a custom-order chocolate specialty shop in Lausanne. If he hadn't possessed the plastic figure, the chocolatier would have had to sculpt an original. Now all the crafter had to do was make a mold.

The chocolate Frankenstein cost more than roses would have. No matter. Instructions in French were inscribed on the monster in colored candy and on a sticker placed on the boutique's box: *Si on mange, il faut pardonner.*

"If one eats, one has to forgive." Swiss chocolate was both a good idea and an art form, all by itself. Making that art fit the circumstances would be unforgettable, Paul hoped, in a positive sense.

He invited Lauren on a boat ride over the lake. By the time the vessel arrived at the Château de Chillon, Lauren had heard his confession and received the chocolate Frankenstein. She looked at it for a very long time, neither eating it nor throwing it overboard.

#

Above the blue waters Lauren increasingly referred to as *"Lac Léman"* floated strings of iridescent clouds. Their reflection was mirrored upon the lake's surface like giant soft water pearls. Sunshine lit the boats and the white-capped mountains known as the *Dents du Midi*. Its light sparkled off the surface blue and the effervescent water in Lauren's glass. She leaned back in her outdoor café seat, enjoying the view of the mountains and the handsome young man with the unique mustache whose fingers had just laced through hers.

"I once met someone who claimed to be revived from the dead," Ajit said. He stuck his long spoon into strawberry sorbet. The utensil clinked against the frosty metal bowl.

"Before Helena?" asked Lauren. She offered a spoonful of pistachio ice cream to Paul. Their knees touched.

"Before Paul brought Frankenstein back to life," corrected Ajit.

"Delicious?"

"*Merveilleuse,*" said Paul.

"I need someone to spoon ice cream to me more than you do," said Ajit.

"Your hands are fine now," said Paul, his eyes not leaving Lauren's face. His tone was dismissive, befitting Ajit's role-playing of annoying little brother.

"You've got ice cream on your lip, Paul. Say, how did you miss his mouth, Lauren?"

"It was on purpose." She kissed the ice cream away.

"Oh, that is so annoying."

"Jealousy is not attractive," said Paul.

"Who said I'm jealous? Rachel might not like it." Ajit wagged his spoon at an approaching female.

Lauren waved. Paul pulled up her other hand, fingers laced in his, and kissed it.

"Rachel knows what it's like to find someone amazing," said Lauren.

"You mean each morning?" asked Ajit. "When she brushes her teeth?"

"That isn't nice, Ajit," Lauren said. She wanted to tell him he was being a creep, but noticed Rachel's purposeful stride. It signaled something, a rearrangement of affairs, perhaps. Rachel had just seen Helena. Who knew whether Helena had capitulated to second thoughts about the dangers involved in their ghost-hunting enterprise, or whether the financial costs of the fire might not have put the crew out of business?

Lauren reminded herself Rachel had taken out insurance for every eventuality—including death.

A shiver crept down her spine.

For a few days, the group had been disbanded. That was as much as Lauren wanted to think about. Rachel kept track of the details. Without a place to stay, Rachel and she had taken advantage of the offer of Paul's apartment. Paul had stayed with Ajit, who needed a pair of hands until his could function.

Much of the time, however, Paul took Lauren out and Rachel babysat Ajit. It sounded like Ajit was not as grateful to Rachel as he might have been.

For Paul and Lauren, two days had made the world a brighter place, even in the rain. He was very interested in her, and she in him. He told her he had a degree in computer programming, and confided he sometimes helped Detective Cloquet, who was his uncle, with computer issues. But that was only part time. Needing a full-time job, as she did, he hoped the ghost-hunting crew would stay on in Switzerland.

Heaven seemed to be in Switzerland. When the sun came out, it was glorious; when rain poured, it was romantic. The couple ate fondue and strolled up and down the hills of Lausanne. Paul showed Lauren places she had never known of as a teenager when she was rarely allowed out of boarding school. He took her to Montreux on the Swiss Riviera. They drove to the cheese-making village of Gruyere for an afternoon, walked through a vineyard, and went to a concert.

This was the vacation she had originally thought she was coming back to Switzerland to enjoy.

Rachel sat down and laid her iPad on the table. She pulled a couple of brochures and folded papers out of her purse, looked around at the frosty silver bowls and said, "Ice cream—the perfect celebration treat. What flavors do they have?"

Lauren let Rachel have her extra spoon to sample the strawberry sorbet and pistachio ice cream. A waiter appeared.

"I want vanilla, please," said Rachel. "And a Coca Light."

"Oui, mademoiselle."

"Are we celebrating survival? Oh no, wait, Rachel did that by mopping the floor," said Ajit. "What are we celebrating now? Not dying?"

"Your improved hands, maybe," Rachel answered, unperturbed. "I know I clean a lot. That bothers people who don't."

"I just keep wondering why every floor you see has to be clean enough to eat off of."

"Summers in Switzerland shaped me. I am surprised the country hasn't had that effect on you since you grew up here. We're celebrating the fact we haven't been disbanded."

A waiter brought the Coca Light and poured. Rachel took a sip. "I just came from Helena's suite at the Lausanne Palace Hotel. Dominick has been working on the footage and they're both excited."

"Over what? Helena passing out at Chillon?" asked Ajit. "Or the hotel burning down?"

"They wouldn't actually show me anything. I just heard about it. Anyway, we are 'on' with the next venue. Moving forward, folks! And by the way, Helena feels much better; she thanks you all for the card. I took the other card to Vanni, as you asked. He wept and claimed we are his family now."

"Thank you, Rachel," said Lauren. "Is Dominick keeping what was read of my scripts? With all the details about Mademoiselle Schwartz?"

"Mademoiselle Schwartz's story is staying in the film. Dominick likes it. There was a shot, Helena says, where Schwartz's spirit seems to have transposed to film. Not at Château Mont Rose, at the Château de Chillon."

"Oh come on." Lauren drew her sweater over her shoulders.

"Helena thinks Mademoiselle Schwartz may be your spirit guide, Lauren. She said the person who called in the fire identified herself as our dead teacher."

On the sidewalk beyond the café, a dog barked excitedly.

Paul squeezed Lauren's hand.

"So what are we doing next?" asked Ajit.

"Believe it or not, I have been in touch with the Lausanne Museum. Something to do with unexplained night activity in the Natural History section. I'll explain what Helena has in mind later."

"You mean what Dominick has in mind?" asked Lauren.

"Don't worry about them. Helena paid for a double room for us at the Gare Hotel. Right at the train station. We won't have to put these guys out anymore."

Lauren felt Paul's arm go around her shoulders. She was sure he smiled as broadly at Rachel as she did—it was impossible not to smile—and heard him say, "You're not putting us out."

"Listen to Rachel," said Ajit. "Hospitality can only go on so long."

Lauren glanced at Paul, who kissed her on the cheek.

Rachel sat across the table looking like an iceberg. Ajit was snickering.

Lauren's stomach sank. This must have been what the captain of the Titanic felt when he knew there was no steering away. It was the same stare Rachel once used on people like Helena and Mlle Wertheimer.

"Which one of you is going to quit the team?" Rachel didn't blink once.

"I told you," warbled Ajit. He ladled melting sorbet into his mouth with a slurp.

It was very unpleasant of Rachel to ruin a wonderful day. "What are you talking about, Rachel?"

Rachel blinked once. She was really good at the deadpan stare. Her ice cream glistened, untouched, in the sunlight.

"What are you talking about?" repeated Lauren, trying not to sound irritated. "No one is quitting."

"By the terms of the contract," said Rachel, "the ghost-hunting crew is not permitted to fraternize."

"We fraternize every time we talk," said Lauren. "Why are you trying to play the heavy, Rachel?"

"Forgive me if I couldn't *imagine* you of all people would leave something unread."

"What on earth are you talking about?"

'No dating. It's in the contract. Maybe it is in small print, or maybe it is at the end, but I swore as part of my job I would enforce *every word*. Helena made me hold up my right hand while swearing."

"Excuse me," said Paul. "That rule doesn't make sense."

"It was a specific point both Helena and Dominick insisted on at their first meeting with me."

"What hypocrisy! *They* are a couple," cried Lauren.

Rachel lit a cigarette and blew out smoke. "Helena explained her reasoning. She would know, wouldn't she, how hard it is to work with someone with whom one is romantically entangled? Anyway, as boss, she can make any rule she wants."

"You don't have to say anything to—" began Lauren, but Rachel was already shaking her head.

"If you two have decided to be a couple, one of you has to step off the team."

Ajit seemed to be choking with laughter over his empty ice cream bowl.

Paul withdrew his arm, but kept Lauren's hand under the table, out of Rachel's view. Nonetheless, Lauren suddenly felt alone. She looked at him and found him looking uncertain.

Surely his position as tech guy didn't mean as much to him as writing scripts did to her! He was a Swiss. They were in his country. He could do anything he wanted.

But if he wasn't on the team, how and when would she see him?

What were they going to do?

"You could break up," said Rachel. "That would be the easiest solution."

#

Detective Cloquet parked outside the locked gates of Château Mont Rose. He pulled out the key, let himself in. Jean Duvanel still lived on site, squirreled in the undamaged cottage at the back while his mother was evaluated in a psych ward. Not the slightest DNA trace of Officer Lucas Papaux had turned up.

The château had lost its highest floor, the tower. A mere three days earlier it looked like a blackened brick shell with a heavily damaged and charred wood structure.

The insurance company covering the inn/museum had reported to Lausanne Sûreté that all of the wax statues had been accounted for. Someone had carried them out and lined them up in the deepest recesses of the estate.

In this manner, Helena Stamoulos had been saved, as if she were one of the statues. Yet the paramedics who found her pronounced her dead. She arrived at the morgue with no manifestation of vital signs

"*Bordel!*" Cloquet halted in his tracks and looked around the estate in shock.

The place was healing.

Cloquet kept his sang-froid, pulled out his phone and started taking pictures. It was important to document the process. He trudged over the dry, scorched earth, peered closely at the mushrooming building. New "bricks" were the color and texture of fungus. After walking around the circumference of the château, he looked at the pictures just taken.

Then he viewed the pictures from three days earlier.

It was like a crew of laborers had been fixing the place, but no wood planks were strewn about, nor nails or bricks. It was as if the work was being done secretly and the team—like elves—was running off to hide in the forest.

He approached repaired segments of wall that did not look or smell like fresh wood. He reached out his hand to touch and swiftly withdrew it.

After putting on plastic gloves, he reached out again. His fingers pressed part of a new segment resembling wood. At first nothing happened, but then the surface gave way and his fingers left a mark, as they would when pushing against a recently used candle.

A creaking of wood and metal hinges caught his ear. From the singed floorboards, a trap door opened. The top of a head emerged. It was followed by charcoal-blackened eyes, and the gaunt, sagging face of a clown.

Cloquet reached for his pistol.

The clown was Grock, highest paid performer of Europe during his career. The real Grock had died in 1959. Cloquet had seen the clown on film as a child, and as a wax statue in Château Mont Rose.

The grinning clown extended his fist to Cloquet. He slowly opened his fingers. Something in his palm glinted.

"Look," said the fake Grock in a German accent. A pendant slipped between his fingers and dangled by a silver chain.

With a start, Cloquet recognized the Swiss blue topaz ribbon pendant. It had been a gift purchased to celebrate Michèle's attainment of the International Baccalaureate diploma.

She had worn it around her neck, and that was where it stayed, even in her casket.

"Do you see?" asked the Grock clone.

"I'm not frightened of you."

"Then you are foolish." The clown swung the pendant between his fingers. "Leave Château Mont Rose alone. It must punish its offenders."

"You have no power."

"Stupid man. What do you know? Château Mont Rose is Limbo, a place of torment or solace. Your daughter is here."

"She is not." Cloquet's throat had gone dry. He wanted to tell the clown to go to hell, then thought better of the idea. He might be standing on the very grounds of Hell.

The clown threw the pendant at Cloquet's feet. "Here is your memento." The clown's head disappeared and the trap door closed over it.

Minutes passed before Cloquet worked up the nerve to try opening the trap door himself, gloves on. It wouldn't budge. He struggled. It seemed melded shut. If he called out a squad to break through the floor and no clown was found, Cloquet might be forced into the same psychiatric ward where Virginie Duvanel dwelled at present.

He picked up the blue topaz ribbon pendant and turned it over in his hand. Good God! It had to be a replica.

Then he saw the words, "To Michèle from Papa," in the script he had chosen.

Back in his car, Cloquet fought the impulse to drive straight to a bar. He would show the locket to Paul, providing it did not turn to dust.

The case could not be shelved. Château Mont Rose was growing back. There had to be a way to fight its evil.

[The End--Sequel to Follow]

Inspiration for Château Mont Rose

Château Mont Rose was directly inspired by Château Mont Choisi, one of the first Swiss boarding schools for young women, located in La Rosiaz, on the outskirts of Lausanne.

Among Château Mont Choisi's illustrious attendees include Carla Bruni-Sarkozy and Mai Yamani, Saudi scholar and daughter of the former Saudi minister of petroleum, Zaki Yemeni. Coincidence or fate dealt another strange hand when two Saudi girls and their little brothers were co-boarders at the pensionnat Château de Vennes (also in Lausanne). I re-met them in Saudi Arabia while I lived there.

Château Mont Choisi's opening date is debated. One online entry indicates the villa was constructed in 1905 for a family. Another says the school opened in 1885. Château Mont Choisi closed in 1995.

Authors love reviews. Please consider writing one! Write to me personally at www.grassrootswritersguild.wordpress.com.

www.ingramcontent.com/pod-product-compliance
Lightning Source LLC
Chambersburg PA
CBHW071127170626
46809CB00002B/526